"Let he

The voi

no hint of excitement, just a simple command. Spanner turned to see who dared to interfere with his pleasure. He half expected to see the girl's father, but it was not. He grunted and laughed when he saw Tom standing by the front door. He made no move to release the girl.

"Let her go," Tom repeated, bringing the Winchester up waist-high, at the same time keeping a watchful eye on the three troopers still seated at the table.

"Looo . . . tenant," Spanner growled with emphatic sarcasm. "When was the last time an enlisted man told you to kiss his ass?"

"Let her go," he said for the third time.

Spanner hesitated, looking at the rifle already leveled at him. He considered for only a moment whether or not he could release his hold on the girl and draw his pistol in time. He was angry and half drunk but he had better sense than to try it. Still, he was not willing to give in so easily. "Ain't you the brave one? I thought I run you out of here once, and here you come crawling back holding a rifle on me. I wonder how big you'd talk if you didn't have the jump on me."

Tom was running out of patience. "Sergeant, you might find it difficult to ride back to your outfit with a bullet hole in your hide. . . ."

BITTERROOT

CHARLES G. WEST

A SIGNET BOOK

SIGNET
Published by New American Library, a division of
Penguin Putnam Inc., 375 Hudson Street,
New York, New York 10014, U.S.A.
Penguin Books Ltd, 27 Wrights Lane,
London W8 5TZ, England
Penguin Books Australia Ltd, Ringwood,
Victoria, Australia
Penguin Books Canada Ltd, 10 Alcorn Avenue,
Toronto, Ontario, Canada M4V 3B2
Penguin Books (N.Z.) Ltd, 182–190 Wairau Road,
Auckland 10, New Zealand

Penguin Books Ltd, Registered Offices:
Harmondsworth, Middlesex, England

First published by Signet, an imprint of New American Library,
a division of Penguin Putnam Inc.

First Printing, October 1999
10 9 8 7 6 5 4 3 2 1

 REGISTERED TRADEMARK—MARCA REGISTRADA

Printed in the United States of America

For Ronda

Chapter I

Tom Allred stood in the doorway of the small room that had served as his quarters for the past two years. The steam from the army issue cup rose upward until it met the cold, crisp morning air, where it was molded into wispy curls that swept gently across his face. He inhaled the aroma of the strong, black coffee as he gazed out across the dusty parade ground, gray now in the early morning light. Soon the first rays of the sun would touch the easternmost rank of the troopers standing down from reveille. The duty officer would soon dismiss the formation, and they would break for the mess tent. Tom knew the routine well. It had been his life for the past twelve years. But it would be his life no more. Yesterday he was Lieutenant Thomas Allred, U.S. Seventh Cavalry. Today he was simply Tom Allred, civilian, the rank and insignia having been removed from his faded blue shirt.

He allowed a sigh to escape his lips as he corralled his wandering mind, lest he permit it to linger on the sadness of this day. The army had been his life, his home, since he enlisted at the age of eighteen and marched off to offer his services, and life if need be, to the Union. Now, on this chilly autumn morning, he was to leave the only family he knew, the Seventh

Cavalry. His fellow officers, those who survived the battle at the Little Big Horn, had been his only friends and they were now lost to him. He sipped the coffee gingerly from the metal cup, taking care not to burn his lips. The black liquid was not as hot as the metal cup that held it. He couldn't help but smile when he remembered Squint Peterson's complaining that, "By the time the damn cup cooled enough to touch it to your mouth, the coffee was too cold to drink." Squint was a helluva scout, one of the two best on the western frontier, the other being Andy Coulter. Everything Tom knew about fighting Indians he learned from these two scouts. Of the two, Andy had been the closest to him. It was Andy who took him under his wing when he first arrived from Fort Riley in the summer of '65, a bright-eyed young lieutenant with thoughts of glory and a long career in the army. But Andy Coulter was gone now. His body was found no more than twenty feet or so from Custer's body on top of a desolate little hill near the banks of the Little Big Horn. He would sorely miss the scout. A friend like Andy could never be replaced.

His mind recalled a picture of the two old scouts, galloping out from the column, Andy squat and square in the saddle, Squint as big as a great bear. He wondered where Squint Peterson was now, and if he finally made it to the Oregon territory. He was always talking about going to Oregon. Maybe he was holed up somewhere, perhaps in a snug little valley, waiting for the winter that was now barely two months away. The last memory he had of Squint was the sight of his giant bulk bobbing out of sight as he and his horse struggled with the current in the muddy waters of the Yellowstone. Then the sobering thought struck him—what would Squint think about Tom's situation now?

"Morning, Tom."

"Morning, Sid," Tom returned the greeting from the stocky figure wearing the garrison uniform of an infantry officer.

"I thought I'd catch you before you left this morning." Noticing Tom's horse saddled and tied to the porch railing, he added, "I reckon you're all packed and ready to leave." He faltered a moment. "I wish I could have done more—"

Tom interrupted him. "Sid, you did the best you could. I've got no complaints over the way you presented my side of it. I appreciate what you did for me." He shrugged and threw the remains of his coffee cup into the dust below the porch. "Hell, there wasn't much you could do, anyway. I don't fault the army for it. They couldn't very well overlook what I did and just say, Don't do it again, could they?"

The lieutenant fidgeted. "Yeah, but I might have been able to save you your commission if I had been a little more experienced. I sure as hell ain't a lawyer." His glance dropped down to his boots as if inspecting them for dust. "I didn't want the damn job in the first place but somebody had to represent you, so you got stuck with me."

Tom laughed and put his hand on the lieutenant's shoulder. "Nobody could have done it better. I got no complaints. Don't worry about it. As far as the army was concerned, I did wrong and I was going to pay for it no matter who my defense counsel was."

Sid nodded, understanding. He knew Tom was right. The army had to kick him out. At least he escaped having to serve any time in prison which, under most circumstances, would have been the case. Tom's record had weighed heavily in his favor. He had served with honor at Vicksburg and Chattanooga before being transferred to the Seventh. And then, under Custer's command, he had campaigned in the raid on Black Kettle's village on the Washita, fought the Sioux and Cheyenne on the Bozeman Trail, and was in Benteen's command at the Little Big Horn. He carried two wounds, both earned in battle with the hostiles. Because of this spotless service record, it had been difficult to explain his actions that evening on the Yellowstone, actions that had precipitated his court-martial.

Lieutenant Sidney A. Pearson had less than six months service at Fort Lincoln when he was appointed defense counsel for Tom Allred. An infantry officer, he had arrived too late to participate in the campaign against the Sioux. He had been in garrison when the shocking word of Custer's annihilation was received at the fort, and he had remained on garrison duty during the three-pronged attack that finally crushed the Sioux at Wagon Box later that summer. Like Tom Allred, he had earned his commission under fire. For him it was Gettysburg but, unlike Tom, he had no experience fighting the Sioux and the Cheyenne.

Initially he had no desire to defend an officer charged with not only permitting the escape of an infamous Cheyenne war chief, but actually effecting the escape—losing not only the prisoner, but a valued army scout as well. What made it even more damnable was that the prisoner was none other than Little Wolf, a renegade so notorious that Custer himself had offered a reward of his own money for the man's capture. In the weeks before the court-martial, however, Sid came to believe the man he was to represent was an officer of obvious integrity and devotion to duty. He wanted to believe that Tom was innocent of the charges brought upon him by the three enlisted men who were assigned to escort Little Wolf back to Fort Lincoln. But the evidence seemed to point toward his guilt.

The enlisted men, a sergeant and two privates, had discussed the incident at great length among themselves before deciding they should inform the post adjutant of their misgivings about the events that led up to the prisoner's escape. It was close to dark when it was decided to take that treacherous trail beside the swollen waters of the Yellowstone. They had one of the best scouts in the army, Squint Peterson, so the men figured he knew what he was doing, although it seemed a risky trail to take at that time of day. It was almost dark and what little light there was was fading rapidly. The sergeant, a tall rawboned man named Waymon Spanner, figured it wouldn't have saved more than two hours' ride over the long way around that section of the river. Still, Spanner insisted, there would have been no problem were it not for the peculiar actions of the lieutenant and Peterson. It was plain to see that Spanner had a strong dislike for Tom Allred in the way he criticized his handling of the escape. Judging the man to be a born troublemaker, Sid wondered if Spanner knew any officers he didn't hold in contempt. Still, he was the army's chief witness, and the man who brought the charges. And it was his accounting the army accepted.

According to Spanner's testimony, they had reached a point in the narrow trail where part of it had been washed out, leaving room for only one horse at a time to pass. Lieutenant Allred had halted the detail and instructed Peterson to check the prisoner's bindings. Then he ordered the three enlisted men to pass over the wash-out first. At the time, this

seemed like a curious command to Sergeant Spanner
since they were better positioned to watch the prisoner from behind. The lieutenant had made some
remark to the effect he wanted his men safely across
the wash-out before a bloody hostile was permitted
to cross. The events that took place within the next
few seconds were not clear to him at the time, but
soon seemed overly bizarre after discussing it with
the other men.

One of the privates led. Spanner was next. Behind
him, the other private, a young trooper named
Wyatt, followed. Just as Wyatt cleared the wash-out,
several shots rang out. At first Spanner thought they
were under attack. He could hear horses screaming
and the lieutenant shouting, "Halt!" Then the sound
of the lieutenant's carbine filled the canyon. He found
out moments later that both Peterson's and the prisoner's horses had gone off the ledge into the river.
This was the strange part, as far as the sergeant was
concerned. Wyatt had managed to back his horse
around enough to see what was happening. He was
able to get his rifle out and fire a couple of shots
after the prisoner as he was washed down with the
current. But, according to Wyatt, he was lucky if he
even hit the river, what with the way the lieutenant's
horse kept bumping his own. He swore it was almost
like the lieutenant was purposely spoiling his aim. It
was all over in a matter of seconds, and they could
no longer see the two horses or riders in the half-
light. But the lieutenant assured them that he had
killed the Indian and that maybe Wyatt had shot Peterson. It didn't make sense. Wyatt doubted very seriously if he had hit anything. But Lieutenant Allred
insisted that both men were done for. Adding to the
sergeant's suspicions, they were ordered to proceed
on to Fort Lincoln without searching for the bodies.

It didn't appear to be a case of simple carelessness, and the court had little choice but to find Tom guilty of something short of treason. There was just too much evidence against him.

Sid Pearson couldn't help but like Tom Allred. He would have liked to save his commission for him, but Tom was unable to explain—or maybe he just refused to explain—why he acted as he did that night on the Yellowstone. Army records showed that the Cheyenne war chief, Little Wolf, was regarded as one of the most feared of all the hostile battle leaders. And, to make his crimes against the army even more serious, Little Wolf was not in fact an Indian but a white man raised by the Cheyennes. Lieutenant Allred himself had been wounded by Little Wolf and, had it not been for the actions of army scout Andy Coulter, he would have most likely perished in an ambush staged by the renegade. Sid had the feeling that Tom wasn't telling him the whole story behind his actions during the incident at the Yellowstone. Still, he did the best he could for him, basing his defense almost entirely on Tom's service record. Tom was found guilty, but was given a choice. He could remain in the army as a private after serving one year in prison, or he would be allowed to resign and forfeit all pay due him, which amounted to three months' pay. Tom chose the latter.

"That looks like Andy Coulter's forty-five-seventy Winchester."

Tom's comment startled him, and he realized his mind had been drifting back over the court-martial. "What?" he started. "Oh . . . yeah, it is," he answered and held the rifle out toward Tom. "I thought you might need it. From what I've heard, Andy would probably have liked for you to have it." He paused for a second while Tom took the rifle and examined it as if it were a precious thing. "I figured I'd better get it before somebody else confiscated it."

Tom was touched. "Thanks, Sid. I appreciate it." Andy had thought more of his rifle than if it had been a wife. It meant a lot to Tom to have it. Andy was seldom caught without that rifle. It was ironic that on the last day of his life, when fighting overwhelming odds, his rifle was back here at Fort Lincoln, getting a new firing pin. Tom rubbed his finger thoughtfully over the smooth surface of the stock, his mind drifting back to better days before Little Big Horn.

"Hell, I wish I could do more for you." Sid stepped over to Tom's horse and hooked the straps of a canvas satchel over the saddle horn. "Here's some cartridges for it. Rifle won't do you much good without these."

Tom smiled. "Reckon not."

"At least they let you keep Billy."

"Yeah," was all Tom answered, but he was indeed appreciative of the gift of his horse. Billy, a blue roan, had been with him for two years, and they were comfortable with each other. He was not as swift as an Indian pony. Still, Billy was not slow when it came to a full gallop, and he had staying power. Short legs and a broad chest with plenty of room for heart, Billy was a horse a man could count on.

"Well, I've got to go to work." Sid extended his hand.

"Yeah, time for me to go too, I reckon." They shook hands and Sid turned and walked briskly back toward the orderly room.

Tom watched Sid Pearson for a few moments until he disappeared around the corner of the officers' quarters. Then he went back into the small room for one last look around to make sure he wasn't leaving anything. He reached down and smoothed out a wrinkle in the blanket on the narrow cot. He didn't do it consciously. It was a reflex action from years of army routine. Had he given it any thought, he might have realized that it didn't make any difference now what condition the room was in. He didn't have to care anymore. He picked up a small shaving mirror he had forgotten to take from the washstand. As he did, he caught a glimpse of his image, and it caused him to pause and examine the face in the glass. He almost did not recognize the man he saw. The eyes looked tired, etched at the corners with tiny wrinkles from long hot days in the saddle. Already a scattering of gray was infiltrating his mustache, a little premature for a man of thirty. The reflection he saw was a hell of a lot different from the fresh-faced lieutenant who rode out on the train to Fort Riley eleven years before. Duty on the western frontier aged a man. He had to wonder how much of that aging had taken place during the last few months while awaiting court-martial.

Sid had done as much as he possibly could have in representing him. Maybe Tom should have told him the whole story, he couldn't say. It probably would not have made much difference in the outcome of the trial. On the other hand, maybe it would have. But Tom somehow felt it best to keep it to himself. There were only three men on the western frontier who knew the secret he had carried—himself, Squint Peterson, and Little Wolf—a secret he had been careful to keep from Custer, that Little Wolf's real name was Robert Allred. He was Tom's brother. Tom had only known it himself for a little over a year when Squint Peterson put two and two together and discovered the twist of fate that had placed the two brothers on opposite sides in the bloody struggle for possession of the plains. That was the reason Tom had not told Sid why he acted the way he had that evening on the Yellowstone. The army would view it as an invalid defense. Duty first, there would be no debate. In the final analysis, it was his decision alone, and renegade or not, enemy though he was, Little Wolf was his brother by birth and Tom could not let the man hang. His brother was raised from childhood as a Cheyenne warrior. Tom could not accept the fact that Little Wolf was wrong in choosing to fight for the people who took him in and raised him.

He gazed at the face in the mirror for a moment longer before turning and leaving his small quarters. Outside, he stepped up on Billy and pointed him toward the main gate. With a gentle pressure of his heels, he urged the horse into a canter and said farewell to the army and his career as a professional soldier.

Chapter II

Winter was hard that year, the hardest Tom ever remembered, and not entirely due to the weather. It was cold enough. It always was in Montana territory. It was more that he was orphaned from the military. Before, he was always assured of a warm home base where it was someone else's responsibility to provide food and housing. Now, for the first time since he joined the army, Tom was on his own, alone in the vast winter wilderness of Montana. Looking back a few months, he was not sure now why he had chosen to go north and west when he left Fort Lincoln. At the time, he felt a strong desire to lose himself completely from all civilization. He had not the slightest notion as to how he could make a living. All he knew was the army. He couldn't farm, even if he had a desire to, which he didn't. He didn't have enough money to buy stock, even if he had a notion to run cattle. There were cattle ranches in Montana. A few brave souls had even pushed herds up from Texas in search of the lush prairies, willing to take on the Indians and the cruel winters. Tom had no experience with cattle. All that was left for him were trapping and panning for gold. Of the two, he figured he knew the least about panning for gold. True, he wasn't much on trapping either, but at least he had learned a little about it from Squint Peterson during the long winter months at Fort Lincoln, when cabin fever would drive the army scout out of the fort for a few days' respite. Tom had accompanied Squint on more than one occasion, whenever the duty roster permitted. It had proven to be valuable experience, for he had learned how to build a camp in the snow and how to stay alive in the brutal winters of the plains. He would need this knowledge now because it was the wrong time of year for a man to strike out alone across the Dakota/Montana territory, what with winter just getting its second wind. But he felt the need to be on the move. Still, he disliked the idea of aimless wandering, so he told himself he was headed toward Oregon, the hoped-for destination of hundreds of other displaced souls. Once there, he could see to the business of making a new beginning for himself. But for now, it was enough to simply be on the move.

He had managed to save a little money from his army pay over the years and, although it didn't add up to a sizable stake, at least it was enough to provide a start. After buying his basic supplies and ammunition, he had enough left to purchase a dozen #4 beaver traps and a few #2 mink traps. He figured he might as well give trapping a try. He had nothing better to do. There was considerable risk for one white man alone in what was still Indian territory— the weather wasn't the only threat to a man's life. Nonetheless, he figured he should be able to survive if he kept his wits about him and was careful about where he made his camps. The main Indian threat had been squashed near the end of the summer with the defeat of the Sioux at the Tongue River and Wagon Box. The survivors, those who had not been forced to return to the reservation, were mainly scattered. Sitting Bull and Dull Knife and several others were reported to have fled to Canada. The rest, the wild ones, were most probably holed up in winter camps. Even so, he was careful to live by the rule Squint had instilled in his mind. *The key to surviving in hostile country is to make sure you see them a long time before they see you.* Twice he had caught sign of Indian hunting parties, although he did not actually see any hostiles. The only Indians he had encountered since he left Fort Lincoln were a small band of half-starved Arapahos who had decided to give it up and go to the reservation. The party consisted of one man, his wife, and his wife's two sisters. Tom traded the man his army pistol for a buffalo robe. He threw in a little beef jerky from his precious supply. Gazing at the hollow, hungry eyes of the women, he wished he could give them more, but he had none to spare as it was. The buffalo robe would go a long way in helping him survive the winter cold. He wouldn't miss the pistol. A pistol was of very little value to a man in the wild unless he was involved in close combat with an enemy. Otherwise, it was no good at any range over thirty or forty yards. He wondered how long the Arapaho brave would be able to hang on to the pistol. He was sure to be thoroughly searched for weapons when he reported to the reservation. Other than that one party of Arapahos, Tom had been virtually alone in this wilderness.

After a while, he got used to being alone. He couldn't say that he actually enjoyed it, but at least he didn't seem to mind it. For the most part, he disciplined his mind to avoid thinking about his past life and the events that led to his forced exile. He tried to always focus on only a few basic things crucial to his survival; to stay warm, to stay out of sight, and to find food for himself and his horse. The latter was the most difficult, but he found that there was food for one man if he hunted constantly. Occasionally he was lucky enough to find an elk, driven down from the high country, but mostly his diet consisted of varmints and the beaver he caught in his traps. Down in the lower basins, near the rivers, Billy could usually scratch around for forage, although it would become more and more difficult as the winter progressed. Billy's welfare was of primary concern to him. A man's horse might mean the difference between living and dying. For that reason, a good deal of his time was spent digging in the snow to find grass and roots for Billy and peeling the bark off green tree limbs and the tender willow wisps—anything he thought might give his horse nourishment. The nights were getting steadily colder, causing him to question the wisdom of moving from camp to camp. Already, he often found his breakfast water frozen solid if he allowed his campfire to die down during the night. At night he slept with Billy's bridle inside his buffalo robe to keep from placing a frozen bit in his horse's mouth the next morning.

As the winter lengthened, it became increasingly difficult to stay on the move. Soon the snows came one on top of the other, causing him to wonder if he would be able to survive if he didn't build a more permanent camp. The last several days had been spent by a winding stream that had provided him with half a dozen prime beaver plews, but the campsite was no good. The surrounding plains offered little protection from the winter blizzards he knew would be coming. He looked out across the rolling hills toward the high country and decided the best chance for him and his horse was to find a camp somewhere under the lee side of a hill. As if to remind him not to tarry in his decision, a cold breeze danced across his face, warning him to find shelter.

Billy seemed to sense the urgency in their journey as he struggled through snow up to his broad chest. At times, Tom had to hold his feet up sideways to keep the stirrups from dragging in the snow. But Billy was stout and had plenty of heart and he never faltered. Twice darkness forced them to make trail camp in open country before they reached the shelter of the foothills but, finally, they reached a steep hill covered with trees. On the far side, Tom discovered a rock formation that formed a small cliff that slanted back into the hill, creating a slight depression. He knew at once that this was the place they would wait out the winter.

The next two days were spent digging out some of the frozen ground under the rocks until he had fashioned half a cave where he and Billy could get out of the wind and weather. When he had completed his work, he had a shelter closed on three sides with a fire pit at the back. He next set about finding firewood under the snow to stockpile. He was no longer concerned about concealing his presence in the territory. His concern now was surviving the winter. He wasn't worried about roving bands of hostiles. Any Indian with a lick of sense was already holed up for the winter, and if a rare hunting party stumbled upon his camp, he would deal with it the best way he could. He decided he'd rather die with an arrow in him than freeze to death.

The days that followed were spent almost entirely at work to winter-proof his camp, his every thought centered on keeping himself and his horse alive until spring. After he had done all he could to make the dugout secure against the weather, he hunted for anything he could eat. It didn't matter what it was

as long as it had meat on it, or roots he could boil
in melted snow. The meat he was able to procure
was cut up and stored outside his camp in the snow.
More than one night was ended with a prayer of
thanks to Andy Coulter for his Winchester. It fired
as true as any rifle he had ever shot, and when cartridges were precious, accuracy was doubly important. Small game seemed plentiful in the mountains
beyond the hill he had chosen for his camp, and most
of this he managed to catch without wasting bullets.
Squint Peterson had shown him how to rig a snare
to catch rabbits, and he soon became adept at it. But
he needed more than rabbits to make it through the
winter. A stroke of luck probably contributed to his
survival more than anything else.

It was late in the afternoon and he was making his
way back down the mountain after a disappointing
day of hunting. He didn't like returning to camp
empty-handed. He needed to store all the meat he
could, feeling the urgency more and more as each
day brought colder and colder weather. Something
in his bones was telling him that storms were coming
and coming soon. The sky had a slate gray cast to it,
and there was fresh wind from the north blowing
steady all day. As nightfall approached, the wind
began to pick up in intensity. He didn't like the look
of it. He didn't have nearly enough food stored to
last him, and he was going back to his camp empty-
handed. Already the snow was deep on the mountains and it was slow going, even downhill. Coming
to a small stream that had not yet frozen solid, he
braced himself to jump across it, a feat made more
difficult because of the makeshift snowshoes he had
fashioned. He misjudged the distance by a fraction,
causing him to slip and ram his foot through the
limbs of his snowshoe, resulting in a headfirst tumble

down the mountain, ending some eighty or ninety feet later against a tree stump.

"Jesus Christ!" he exclaimed as he lay prone in the snow. "I'd be in a helluva fix if I broke my neck now, wouldn't I?" He lay there for a moment longer to make certain nothing was broken. Then he reached for his rifle and checked to make certain he hadn't plugged the barrel when he took his tumble. Satisfied that it was all right, he brushed the snow away from the lever and hammer. When he turned again to look down below him, his heart almost stopped. There, not fifty feet away, a great black bear stood watching him, evidently confused by this strange-looking animal that had just landed before him, arms and legs flailing as it tumbled wildly to a stop against the stump.

Tom was lucky that day that his chaotic descent down the mountain served to confuse the great beast, and lucky that he was able to react quicker than the bear. In a fraction of a second, Tom raised his rifle and fired from a sitting position. The bullet made a thud as it entered the animal's skull immediately below the right eye. The bear recoiled backward in surprise. Tom readied himself for the animal's charge, getting up to kneel on one knee, his rifle ready for the next shot. But, instead of charging, the beast turned to run. Tom's second and third shots were no more than two or three inches apart, right behind the bear's shoulder. The bear roared once, then tried to run, but it seemed to have lost its sense of balance and began to stagger drunkenly from side to side for about twenty feet before crumpling to the ground in a heap.

Tom could feel his heart racing from the shock of the sudden encounter. His very fingertips tingled with the rush of adrenaline that had been triggered by the expectation of mortal combat with the huge beast. When he realized the bear was dead, his panic was replaced by a great feeling of joy. The killing of the bear meant survival for him. He would now have not only the meat, but the fur and fat as well. He quickly collected himself, and after making sure the animal was indeed finished, he made his way down the mountain, wasting no time to get his horse and get back to his kill before wolves or coyotes found it. It would be impossible for him to drag the bear with him, even downhill. He would need Billy's strength for that job. As he trudged along toward his camp, his progress impeded by the one broken snowshoe, he couldn't help but wonder at his good fortune. It was almost as if providence, or whatever power, had sent the bear to him because it was way past time for the beast to be in hibernation. What, he wondered, was the bear doing wandering around after others of his kind were already sleeping, waiting for spring? It gave him a sense of faith, as if it was a sign that he was meant to survive this winter.

Darkness had settled over the hills by the time he dragged the bear's carcass down out of the mountains. The beast was huge, and it was a hard pull for the horse, but once again Billy was up to the task. He left a wide trail straight to his camp under the rocks, but Tom was not concerned. His intuition proved to be accurate, for he awoke the next morning to find a fresh blanket of snow over the land, covering any tracks left the night before under a foot of snow. It was to be two full months before he would be able to leave his little valley again.

One morning, it was finally over. Tom was awakened late in the morning by the sound of dripping water from the rocks above his camp. The snow was melting. Still, it would be several weeks before he could leave the safety of his dugout for good. These last few weeks were the worst of the severe winter months. He was almost desperate to get on the move again. He looked at his horse, rooting in the melting snow outside the dugout, searching for anything green. "Billy," he said softly, "you're looking a little peaked, but we'll be on our way before long and, if we ever find any civilized place again, I swear I'll get you a barrel of oats." He walked over to the horse and offered him a handful of green bark he had peeled from a willow switch. Billy accepted it gratefully. He watched the horse for a moment as Billy ground the bark and looked at him expectantly, wanting more. "That's all I got right now. Sorry, son." He looked back over his shoulder at the hole in the hillside that had served as his home for over three months. "Damned if I haven't had my fill of wintering alone in this wilderness. If I can help it, I'll not spend another winter like I did this one." He was fully aware that he was fortunate to be alive.

He caught sign of the settlement long before he was to see the canvas huts and rough shacks scattered along the banks of the wide stream that served as the lifeblood for the handful of souls gathered there. It was not difficult to tell he was approaching some form of civilization, for the signs he found were permanent scars upon the land. Trees had been felled, no doubt to be used for lumber, and no Indian he had ever encountered chopped down trees for any purpose other than to use them as lodge poles. The deep ruts left by a wagon were still evident, even after having been under a blanket of snow until the recent melt.

The thought of seeing another human being was

enough to lift his spirits and liven his step. He had traveled three days since bidding his winter camp farewell. At least half of the journey was on foot. Billy looked so bony he didn't have the heart to burden him with his weight. As it was, the half-starved horse had to pull a travois loaded with the plews Tom had managed to trap. This was another reason Tom was relieved to find signs of a settlement. He was more than a little concerned about the trail he was leaving, a trail that a blind Indian could follow. He would have to get himself a packhorse at the first opportunity if he was to keep his hair in this country.

Nightfall found him still making his way toward a low line of hills that he had guided on for the better part of the afternoon. It was his guess that the settlement he was near had to be in that direction. From the wagon tracks he found, it was apparent that the woodcutters had come from there. To confirm his guess, deepening darkness revealed several small flickers of light that he knew had to be cook fires. He resisted the impulse to push on through the night to reach the town. He thought it better to approach the settlement in the morning, after he had the opportunity to scout it a bit before blissfully riding in. There were all kinds of savages in this territory, not all of them Indians.

The settlement looked pretty much like a dozen others Tom had seen in the years he had spent on the frontier. An odd gathering of tents shacks, some that were half tent and half shack, were assembled along the banks of a broad rocky stream that seemed to meander drunkenly through the low line of hills, rushing first in one direction and then almost reversing its flow as it veered sharply around an outcropping of boulders and raced off in another

direction. The tents and shacks were scattered hap-
hazardly along the stream as if some giant hand had
simply rolled them like dice and they just happened
to land right-side up. It was pretty rough for a town,
but it didn't matter to Tom. It was a settlement and
there were people there and he was more than ready
to see and talk to someone after the long winter
alone.

He rode in on the north end of the stream after
having skirted the town from the south. It looked all
right to him, a typical diggings with a rickety sluice
box here and there in front of a weather-worn shack.
As he urged Billy into the icy water at a shallow
crossing that led to the main part of the settlement,
he noticed a wide board nailed to a tree that served
as a sign. The letters had been burned into the wood
and proclaimed that this settlement had a name. It
read

RUBY'S CHOICE
IF YOU DON'T GIVE NO TROUBLE—YOU WON'T GET NO
TROUBLE

Fair enough, Tom thought. He nudged Billy with
his heels, and they crossed the stream, headed
toward the largest structure in Ruby's Choice.

Looking around him, he thought at first he might
have been mistaken when he had assumed the town
was indeed settled. There was no living soul in sight.
He stepped down from the saddle onto the wagon
tracks that served as the main street and stood gazing
first north and then south. No one was in sight. Then
he reminded himself that he had seen campfires the
night before. There *had* to be people here. He turned
to look at the rough building before him. There, beside the door, was a sign that proclaimed the struc-

ture was CLAY'S STORE. Tom guessed the lettering was done by the same hand that made the sign on the tree at the edge of town. There was no hitching rail, so he dropped the reins on the ground, knowing Billy wouldn't go anywhere as long as the reins were down. He was about to step up on the small porch when he was startled by a voice behind him.

"That there top step is busted. Mind you don't break your neck on it."

He turned to face a slightly built man of perhaps middle age, standing by his travois. He was holding a kettle in his hand. The man smiled at Tom as he casually glanced over the pack of skins on the travois.

"I reckon you'll be looking to trade some of them skins for whiskey and flour and tabacky." He rubbed his bald head as he looked Tom up and down. "That's about all you mountain men want, whiskey, flour, and tabacky."

Tom smiled. "Well, I guess I like a drink about as well as the next man. But I had more in mind trading for some coffee and some beans, if you have any, and some flour and salt . . . and some grain for my horse . . . maybe some meat that ain't wild."

The little bald man looked Tom over more carefully, noticing the faded army trousers and the cavalry boots. "You ain't been trappin long, have you?" He studied Tom's face carefully. After a moment, he evidently decided that this stranger meant him no harm. "You look like you could use a good cup of coffee right now. Come on in. I was about to make some when you come up."

"Mister, that sure is to my liking," Tom said, accepting the invitation. It had been more than a month since his supply of coffee beans had run out, and the thought of a fresh brewed pot of black coffee was enough to make his mouth water. He followed the little man into the store and watched while he settled the kettle over an iron grill on one side of a huge stone fireplace. Like so many stores in the isolated settlements away from the army's forts, Clay's Store served as general store as well as a saloon. Neither man spoke until the kettle was taken care of and the little man stood back to watch it boil.

"Where's all the people?" Tom wondered aloud. "From the looks of all the tents, I figured to find some folks about."

The little man looked at him, a gleam of amusement in his eye. "Why, hellfire, they're most likely asleep in their beds, I reckon. It's just past sunup you know."

Tom considered this. "I guess it is a little early. I had no notion of the time."

The little man reached into a sack and withdrew a fistful of coffee beans and proceeded to grind them in a small, well-worn coffee mill. Then he poured them into the boiling water and pulled the kettle away from the flames to let the coffee brew. He watched it for a moment longer before turning back to Tom.

"My names's Jubal Clay. This here's my store." He extended his arm.

"Tom Allred," Tom replied, taking the outstretched hand.

"Well, Mr. Allred, what brings you to Ruby's Choice?"

Tom settled himself on a ladder-back chair on one side of the huge fireplace and held his palms out to catch the warmth of the flames. "Well, like you said, I'd like to trade some furs for some supplies. I've been up in the hills all winter and I need some things." He noticed the statement caused Jubal Clay to raise his eyebrows ever so slightly. He was quick to add, "Oh, I've got a little bit of money. The furs ain't all I've got to pay with."

"How long you been out of the army?"

"Since September," Tom replied. The question did not surprise him since he was wearing army trousers and boots.

"How'd you happen to come to Ruby's Choice? If it's for the gold, I'm afraid you're a bit too late. There's still some folks finding a little color now and then, but the big stuff is panned out." He wrapped a rag around the handle to keep from burning his hand and withdrew the kettle from the fireplace. With his free hand, he picked up a cup from the hearth and peered into it. As a precaution, he blew in the cup to make sure it wasn't full of dust. Then he filled it with the steaming hot liquid and offered it to Tom. "Most of the folks have turned to trapping, them that are still here."

Tom sipped from the cup before answering. The coffee was strong and scalding hot, but it was good. "I'm really not heading anywhere in particular. I just stumbled on your little town." He paused to sip again.

Jubal Clay studied his visitor intently. "I reckon you could use a hot meal some too, couldn't you?"

"I sure could," Tom responded immediately. Then a thought occurred to him. "First, I reckon I better find out how much this is gonna cost me." Gold mining towns were notorious for their high prices. The more remote they were, the higher the prices. And not many settlements were more remote than Ruby's Choice.

"Hell, man, I'm offering you some breakfast, one neighbor to another. I ain't looking to charge you nuthin' for that. Now later on, when we get to bargaining for them pelts you got, then you better watch your backside, 'cause trading is how I make my living."

Tom flushed, embarrassed. "I apologize, Mr. Clay, and I thank you for your hospitality."

"T'ain't nuthin'." Jubal laughed at his guest's embarrassment. "Ruby'll be down in a minute, and she'll fix us some breakfast."

This sparked Tom's interest. "Ruby? Your wife? Is she the one the town's named for?"

"Ruby's my daughter. My missus died three year ago last month—pneumonia. I drove two wagons out here five year ago. I drove one of 'em, my wife drove the other. Sold my dry goods store in Minnesota and headed west to get my share of the gold. Figured on settling in the Black Hills. Trouble was the dang Injuns was murdering every white man they could find there, so we kept north and west to Montana. I bet we tried a hundred little cricks and gullies, looking for some color before we found this place. There was a little color showing here, but I couldn't decide to stay or move on. Well, the missus was getting awful damn tired of traveling, and she wanted to set down someplace permanent. I still weren't shore this was the place to set up, couldn't make up my mind. Ruby was twelve year old then. Finally, I let her choose. "Honey," I said, "you choose. Do we go or stay?" She said, "We stay." So we did, and that's why the town is named Ruby's Choice."

"It's a silly name for a town, too."

The voice came from behind him. Tom turned to see a young girl climbing down from the loft of the building. Her skirt was pulled up almost to her waist to prevent her tripping on the steps, revealing long underwear that disappeared into the tops of her boots. Tom quickly turned his glance away to avoid embarrassment to the lady. It was wasted on the young girl. She seemed in no hurry to shake her skirt back down, standing squarely in front of Tom as she smoothed out a few of the many wrinkles in her dress. According to what her father had told him minutes earlier, she would be about seventeen years of age. She looked older, due no doubt to the hard way of life for all women in this part of the world. She studied him for a brief moment then commented, "Mister, you look like you wintered hard. I reckon you're half starved, too. Well, I reckon I can throw in a couple more eggs." There was a genuine hint of irritation in her tone.

Tom wasn't especially pleased by her attitude. He knew he looked pretty scruffy, but he didn't come looking for a handout. He couldn't help but bristle a bit. "Well, ma'am, I don't want to put you out. I can pay for my breakfast."

Jubal Clay laughed. "Ruby didn't mean to insult you, young feller."

The girl looked into Tom's face for a moment longer, her expression stern as if she was trying to make up her mind. Finally she flashed a wide smile. "I'm sorry. I'm sure you can pay for your breakfast. I didn't mean to get you all riled up." She extended her arm and said, "I'm Ruby Clay and we'd be glad to have you eat with us, no charge."

Tom, embarrassed now that he had allowed himself to rankle over a young girl's remark, took her hand and briefly shook it. "Tom Allred. Thank you for the invitation, and you were right the first time. I am about half starved."

He took a longer look at her then. She was pretty in a plain sort of way, at least for Montana territory. She wasn't exactly St. Louis pretty, maybe not even Kansas City pretty. But, on this spring morning,

north and west of the Black Hills, he could not help
but notice the depth of her cold blue eyes and the
fullness of her lips. Her hair was the color of a new
hemp rope, somewhere between the gold of grain in
the field and the bark of a cinnamon tree. It struck
him that she looked clean, freshly scrubbed almost, a
realization that reminded him of his own appearance.

"I guess I need a bath and a shave about as bad
as I need something to eat."

"We can heat you up some water. You want to eat
first or after?" She paused to hear his answer.

He rubbed his beard, feeling the growth he had
allowed to accumulate. It was tempting to eat first,
but he decided it would be better to wait. "Maybe I
better clean up first. Maybe you and your pa could
stand me a little better. First though, I reckon I ought
to feed my horse. I'd like to buy a ration of oats if
I can."

"Suit youself." She pointed to a wooden bucket in
the corner of the room. "There's the bucket. You can
start carrying water up from the crick. The tub's in
the storeroom. Show him, Pa."

He turned and followed Jubal Clay out the door.
As he walked out, he asked, "Were you teasing about
having some eggs? Have you really got some
chickens?"

Clay answered. "Shore have. And I bet you can't
find another one around here for a hundred miles."
He pointed Tom toward the creek. "You git the
water. I'll feed your horse for you."

It had been a while. Tom was accustomed to taking
baths regularly and shaving every day, a routine instilled by his many years in the military, but it was
a routine that had been abandoned over the past winter for practical reasons. He might have frozen to

death if he had tried to take a bath. Now, as he lay back and soaked in the large wooden tub, he felt as if he were losing an outer layer of skin. The water, crystal clear when he carried it up from the stream, was now a dingy gray, and his skin felt itchy from scrubbing it with the harsh lye soap. Realizing that his bathwater was rapidly cooling, he decided he had better get his razor and strap and get rid of the whiskers, else he was going to have to shave in cold water. When he was done shaving, he threw the clothes he had been wearing into the tub and scrubbed them a little as well. When he was finished and dressed in a clean pair of trousers and his other shirt, he called out to Jubal Clay to help him carry the tub out to be emptied. For the first time in three months, he felt clean.

"Well, howdy, stranger." Ruby Clay paused, a large iron skillet in her hand, taking a long look at their freshly-scrubbed guest. She made no attempt to mask her surprise at the transformation. She stood staring for a moment longer before resuming her breakfast preparations.

Tom was embarrassed, a fact that was somewhat masked by the flush already present as a result of the harsh soap. Jubal Clay was amused, a twinkle in his eye as he watched his daughter's reaction when discovering there had been a rather nice-looking young man under the dirt and whiskers and buffalo robe that first walked into the store.

It was the best breakfast Tom could remember ever having. He wasn't sure whether it was due to Ruby's skill with a frying pan or simply because he had been living off little more than thin strips of wild meat for so long. He could have eaten a couple more eggs had they been offered, but he was too polite to ask for them. There was plenty of fried corn mush and bak-

ing powder biscuits to fill in the empty spots, however, and Ruby kept the coffee coming. Jubal, who
had eaten earlier while Tom was taking his bath, sat
back and watched his guest consume the plate of
food before him. He seemed pleased by the enthusiasm shown for his daughter's cooking. When Tom
had finished, Ruby stood over him for a moment
while she inspected the empty plate.

"Well, it must not a'been too bad. The plate don't
even need washing."

Tom laughed. "It was wonderful," he said, "the
best breakfast I've ever had."

"Is that so?" she answered matter-of-factly, unimpressed by his attempt at flattery. "Well, I don't
reckon it'll kill you anyway. It ain't killed Pa yet."
She continued to stare at him as if trying to make up
her mind about him.

"I sure do appreciate it," he said. Tom was uncomfortable with the young girl's attitude. She was no
more than seventeen, yet she acted as if she was
much older than that and treated him as if *he* was
the one who was seventeen. He returned her stare,
and their eyes were locked for a few long moments
before she finally broke off and took his plate away.
Damn, he thought, *if I had a horse that looked at me like
that, I wouldn't turn my back on him for fear he might
take a chunk out of my backside.* He glanced at Jubal,
and the little man flashed a warm smile toward him.

"Don't let Ruby spook you. She's been bossing me
around since she was fourteen. Matter of fact, she
runs this whole town." His grin expanded to almost
touch his ears. " 'Sides, I figure she kinda likes you.
If she didn't, blamed if she'da scrambled up them
eggs for you. She don't do that for just anybody.
Eggs is precious."

Tom only grunted in reply. If she kinda liked him,

she sure had a funny way of showing it. Besides, he wasn't sure he cared to have her like him. She was too bossy to suit him. He'd just as soon she liked somebody else. His thoughts were interrupted by the arrival of two of the town's citizens.

"Morning, Red. Morning, Otis," Jubal greeted the two as they came in the door.

"Morning, Jubal. Morning, Ruby," they returned, almost in unison. One of them, a tall, thin man with a shaggy red beard asked, "Bar open yet? It's most 'bout eight o'clock." He looked expectantly at the storekeeper, glancing every few seconds at the stranger sitting at the kitchen table.

"Yeah, I reckon," Jubal replied. "It's close enough to eight." He got up from the table and walked over to the other end of the store, where a short bar had been built against the far wall. Taking a jar out from under the counter, he poured two glasses half full and set them in front of the two men. He started to return the jar, but paused long enough to look in Tom's direction. "You want one?"

"No thanks," Tom replied. "It's a little too early in the day for me." He glanced toward the girl working in the kitchen and caught her watching him intently. She quickly turned back to her work when she met his eye.

"This here's Red Tinsley and Otis Watson," Jubal said. "They got a little claim 'bout a hundred yards down the crick from here. They're just two more of the folks gettin rich outta that crick."

Both men snorted at Jubal's remark, a remark obviously facetious and answered immediately by the man introduced as Otis Watson. "You oughta bite your tongue off, Jubal Clay. The onliest one gettin' rich offen that crick is you, and you ain't doing no panning a'tall."

Jubal laughed good-naturedly. "Show you my heart's in the right place, I'm not even gonna charge you for that first drink."

Red joined in. "You oughtn't charge for none of it, this rotgut pizen. When you gonna get some honest-to-God drinking whiskey, anyway?"

Jubal shrugged his shoulders. "You know as well as I do. Shouldn't be long though. We ought to have wagons getting through any day now, now that the snows have pretty much gone."

Tom watched and listened, amused by what appeared to be a daily visit from the two partners. He had never been one to understand some men's need to start drinking so early in the day, but if anything was likely to cause it, he guessed wintering in a place like Ruby's Choice would do it. He almost laughed out loud as he watched Otis Watson down his whiskey. Otis made a face like it was molten lava he was forcing down, and he gasped for breath for a good thirty seconds after he turned the glass up. It must have been raw frontier whiskey. Jubal probably made it himself. Although it looked like it was killing him, Otis must have had an earnest need for the burning liquid, for as soon as he could find his voice again, he ordered up another. Once, when it seemed he had lost his voice for good, he simply motioned frantically with his hand and Jubal gave him another shot. His partner, Red, matched him shot for shot, but the poison seemed not to sear his tonsils to the same degree that it did Otis. Red simply pulled his lips back in a grimace to expose clenched teeth while he waited for the flame to die out. It took half a dozen shots before their body chemistry was evidently balanced to the point where they could carry on with their normal functions, and after the most important business of the day was taken care of, they turned their attention to the stranger just introduced to them.

"What you say your name was?" Otis asked.

"Tom Allred."

Otis nodded and paused as if to think this over. "What brings you to Ruby's Choice? You in the army?"

"I was. I'm not now. I'm just passing through."

Red spoke up. "Was you wintering east of here?" When Tom nodded that he was, Red continued, "See any sign? We ain't heard much about any Injun trouble since the fall. We been lucky up this way so far, but you never can tell, what with spring here and all."

"I didn't see sign of any kind this winter. I can tell you this, though, Sitting Bull's band of Sioux was pretty much whipped last summer at Wagon Box, and the army will be rounding up stray bands of Sioux and Cheyenne this spring and sending them back to the reservations. The last word I heard was that Sitting Bull and a few of his chiefs escaped to Canada. So any trouble you get would probably be from small raiding parties that the army hasn't been able to run down yet. I wouldn't suspect we'll see another Indian war like the one that killed Custer."

Red seemed relieved. "Well, that's good news."

Otis chimed in. "I don't reckon we better git too dang comfortable even if there ain't no Injun war. Like he said, there's still a helluva lot of savages running around that the army ain't caught." He paused to give it emphasis. "Dead is dead, whether you git scalped by one Injun or a hundred."

The discussion continued for the better part of an hour, the main issue being the probability of Ruby's Choice falling victim to a raiding party. This was actually Crow country. In fact, two of the men of

Ruby's Choice had taken Crow women as wives, and occasionally some of the Crow warriors would come in to Clay's Store to trade for blankets and trinkets. Tom didn't think the small community had a great deal to fear, but one thing he had learned since coming to this country was that Indians, especially Sioux, were unpredictable. So, who could say? Anybody who decided to live in this country was taking a risk. If Indians didn't do you in, then there was plenty to fear from the country itself. Even if you didn't freeze to death in the winter, a grizzly might kill you come spring. Still, he preferred this country, with all its dangers, to living back East. As he sat listening to Otis and Red talk to Jubal Clay, he decided he felt comfortable here and might as well stay for a few days or more. That settled, he got out of his chair and went to the fireplace for another cup of coffee. Ruby anticipated his movement and, using her skirt to grasp the handle of the kettle, poured for him. As she filled the cup, her eyes again locked on his, her face expressionless. Tom got the distinct feeling that she disapproved of him for some reason. He couldn't define the feeling—there was just something about her attitude that left him uncomfortable. His thoughts were interrupted by a question from Otis.

"You passing through right away or you staying around for a while?"

"I think I'll hang around for a few days."

"Well," Otis replied, glancing at Red for confirmation, "if you want a place to stay, me and Red's got room in our shack. You'd be more'n welcome."

"Yeah," Red agreed, "might as well bunk with us. It ain't fancy but it's outta the weather."

Tom accepted. Ruby, standing behind him, had paused to hear his answer. When he accepted, she quietly resumed her chores.

Chapter III

The few days Tom planned to spend in the little settlement on the banks of Beaver Creek stretched into weeks as he became more and more comfortable with his surroundings. He found that most of the other residents of Ruby's Choice were pretty much like Otis and Red: hard-working men, trying to find a few stray nuggets to support their existence. Having no desire to try his luck at gold mining, for he failed to see the profit in it at this particular site, he spent his time trapping and hunting. One of the first things he did was trade his old army Spencer rifle for a packhorse. His hunting provided welcome meat for Otis and Red as well as an occasional elk or mule deer for Jubal Clay. He could see no future for the town of Ruby's Choice beyond two or three years. There was nothing to support the settlement beyond the time when the last of the scant gold supply played out. Still, he was comfortable here for the time being.

He spent about as many nights out in the hills as he did in town since he often had to travel a great distance to find the game he hunted. In but a short time, he acquired a local reputation as a crack shot and a skilled hunter, a reputation that became something of a burden in that he now felt he could never return from a hunting trip empty-handed. He realized that it was a small concession to his ego, but he enjoyed a certain amount of satisfaction upon his arrival in the settlement after two or three days' hunting, with his packhorse loaded with meat. Since he always shared, he soon became rather popular with the townfolk.

Still, there was one enigma he was unable to solve, and that was Ruby Clay. It seemed she watched his every move as if she was suspicious that he might try to steal something from them. Her manner still baffled him. He had given her no cause, yet her surveillance of his movements seemed constant. He didn't even know why he let it bother him. She was just a girl, and meant nothing to him. Still, it irritated him and he couldn't explain why. The girl just got under his skin for some reason. She never spoke to him, aside from a simple answer if he happened to ask her a question.

One day her cool demeanor warmed to the point of exasperating him. He had just returned from two days' hunting and was in the process of butchering an elk down by the creek. As he laid back the hide at the animal's flank, he heard the soft breaking of a branch behind him. He turned and was surprised to find Ruby approaching him. Thinking that when she saw him, she would most likely avoid him and go farther upstream to fetch her water, he said nothing but continued his chore.

"That's a right fine-looking elk. Pretty hide."

Her words startled him, and he was not quick to reply. Finally he said, "Why, yeah, I guess it is kinda pretty."

"Mind if I watch you?" she asked. Not waiting for his answer, she turned the wooden bucket she carried upside down and sat on it.

He could not help but notice that she had removed her long underwear. Her skirt was hiked up just enough to expose her milky white calves and a glimpse of one knee. The thought breezed through his mind that this must be an official sign of spring—when Ruby took off her long handles. In reply to her question, he simply returned, "Reckon not." When he realized he was still staring at the expanse of leg she was showing, he quickly looked up, only to meet her eyes gazing at him intently. It irritated him to have her think she had caught him staring at her legs, so he turned back to his work. There was no way he could have anticipated the conversation that followed.

"I've been watching you, Tom Allred."

He kept working. "Oh?"

"You don't drink much, do you?"

"I guess not." He wondered where this was leading and, in fact, what business it was of hers.

"You don't seem to be much of a hell-raiser. Pa thinks you're an honest man, probably a hard worker. I don't know how he knows that. I ain't ever seen you do nothing but hunt." He made no reply, primarily because he knew of no proper response. She continued, "You planning on staying around here?"

He stopped what he was doing and looked at the girl, mystified by her sudden interrogation. After a long moment, he shook his head as if exasperated, then answered her. "Why, Miss Clay," he said, his voice heavy with sarcasm, "I don't rightly know. I might stay and I might leave tonight. I haven't thought much about it."

She ignored his tone. "What do you suppose you can do for a living? You can't hunt for a living . . . trapping maybe." She thought for a moment.

"Maybe you could farm. You know anything about farming?"

Totally vexed at this point, Tom threw his skinning knife so that it struck blade first in the elk's rump. He dipped his hands in the stream and rinsed them, then turned his full attention to the young girl still seated upon the wooden bucket. "Miss Clay, has the town of Ruby's Choice finally gotten a newspaper? Do I get the honor of the first interview?" He paused and, seeing that his sarcasm was lost on her, he answered her question. "No, I don't know anything about farming . . . don't want to know anything about farming. What are you asking me all these questions for?"

She seemed not to notice his irritation. "There are twenty-seven men in this town. Six of 'em are married. That don't count Robert Waits and Browny Thompson who took squaws to live with 'em. Every other man in this settlement has, at one time or another, asked me to marry him . . . except for Otis Watson, and he knows he's so dang homely it wasn't no use to ask."

Then Tom realized why she had been interviewing him. The thought almost boggled his mind. Before he could find his voice, she continued.

"I'm past marrying age, but I ain't about to jump into it with just anybody. But I've been watching you and I reckon, if you was to ask me, I might marry you." She waited for a moment, but he was too flabbergasted to answer. "Whaddaya think? You been thinking about me?"

"No!" he blurted, still astounded by the brazen proposal of matrimony. Then, realizing that he might crush the girl's feelings, he quickly added, "Not that I'm not flattered—any man would be. It's just that I'm not ready to get married now—haven't even thought about it." There was absolutely no change in the girl's expression as he attempted to smooth over his refusal. "I know you'd make a fine wife, Ruby. You're pretty . . . and you've got a fine body—"

"I ain't giving it away without I get married first," she interrupted.

"I know, I know," he was quick to agree, "and I ain't asking for it." The sudden rush of compassion he had felt for her a moment before was being pushed aside by the return of his slight irritation over her attitude. He had to remind himself that she was offering a most precious gift and he mustn't say anything that would seem to diminish the value of that gift. "Ruby, I sincerely thank you for considering me. It's a real honor and, if I was in a mood to get married, I'm sure I'd want to marry you. I'm just not. I'm sorry."

She sat looking at him for a long moment before she rose and picked up her bucket. "You think about it, all right?" She turned and walked away with no more emotion than if they had just talked about the weather.

Before the conversation by the creek, Tom and Ruby had exchanged a minimal number of words. Afterward, even fewer words passed between them. Tom was still uncomfortable around the girl, but now it was for a different reason. He was embarrassed by her proposal of marriage, although she seemed not to mind the awkwardness it afforded him. His trips into the mountains became longer and longer, and he began to think that maybe it was time to move on. He hated to admit it, but he found himself thinking about the girl much too often, even allowing his mind to fantasize on the possibility of taking Ruby as a wife. If he could have known what would come to pass in the next couple of days, he might have been tempted to move on immediately.

He was down by the creek, working some beaver pelts he had brought back from the mountains the day before, when he looked up to see Jubal Clay heading toward him. Jubal seemed to be in a hurry.

"Tom," Jubal called out, "Browny Thompson just come in the store and said there's some soldiers coming up from the south. He could see 'em from his claim, so they'll probably be here any minute."

"That right?" Tom was only mildly interested.

Jubal hesitated, studying Tom's face. "Well, I thought I'd better let you know in case there's some reason you don't want to see no soldiers."

Tom didn't understand at first. Then he realized Jubal's reasoning. He quickly reassured him. "Ah, no, Jubal. I appreciate your concern, but it's all right. There isn't any reason for me to avoid the soldiers. The army's not looking for me."

Jubal looked relieved. He didn't figure Tom for a deserter, but you could never be absolutely sure about things like that. A man could have a lot of reasons for wanting out of the army, and Tom had never talked about his military record. He left Tom, still working his pelts, and returned to tend his store.

When he had finished with his hides, Tom set them up behind the shack to dry. Red and Otis were both gone. *Up to see the soldiers*, he thought, *along with everybody else*. Visitors were infrequent in this part of the world, so when someone did happen upon the little community, it was cause for everyone to satisfy their curiosity. It had been much the same when the folks found out he was in town that first cold spring morning. He put Billy and the packhorse away and saw to their feed. Then he fed himself. After that was done, he decided he would walk up to Clay's Store and see what news the troopers brought.

There were only four horses in front of Jubal's place. They couldn't be a full patrol with just four horses. He figured they had to be part of a larger unit. Ruby's Choice was too remote from any army post for four men to be out that far alone. He stepped inside the door and stood there a few moments. Over at the bar, the four soldiers were surrounded by the citizens of Ruby's Choice who watched as the troopers sampled Jubal's rot-gut. There was a great deal of laughing and backslapping over the soldiers' reaction to the fiery liquid. The soldiers seemed to be taking it good-naturedly, each one anxious to try to gulp it down without showing the effects.

"Well, I'll be go to hell."

The voice was familiar. Tom couldn't place it at first, however. He squinted in an effort to identify the source in the dim atmosphere of Jubal's Store. One of the soldiers parted the crowd around him to create a clear path between himself and Tom.

"Damned if it ain't Lieutenant Allred." His voice laden with sarcasm, the soldier spread his arms, demanding more room. "Only it ain't lieutenant no more, is it? It's *Mister* Allred."

"Sergeant Spanner," Tom calmly acknowledged.

Spanner sneered in Jubal Clay's direction. "Mister, you don't care what crawls up and dies in your town, do you?"

Jubal didn't answer. Instead, he looked quickly at Tom. Tom did not answer the sergeant's insult, but stood calmly meeting Spanner's glare with one of his own. The atmosphere seemed to have suddenly gone deathly silent. One could almost feel sparks in the air. After a tension-filled moment, Jubal attempted to change the mood. "Come on fellers, it's too nice a day for any trouble. You soldier boys have another drink. This one's on the house."

Spanner would not be put off that easily. "I ain't drinking with that man. I don't know what's the matter with you people. Here we are, out risking our necks to round up them stray savages, and you folks are coddlin' a damn Injun-lover. This son of a bitch was throwed out of the army for helping Little Wolf get away! Little Wolf, that damn murderin' Cheyenne renegade! I bet he ain't told you that, has he?"

Every eye turned to see Tom's reaction. Still, he made no reply. He simply stood there, silent as stone. Jubal, fearful of the explosion that was sure to come, rushed to avoid any further fueling of the intense situation.

"Tom, listen, we don't want no trouble. Why don't you go on home till these fellers leave? Please, Tom, I don't want no trouble."

Tom's eyes were locked in a lethal stare that remained riveted on the sergeant's leering face. Suddenly, as if aware of him for the first time, Tom glanced down at the worried face of the little storekeeper, and the cold eyes softened a bit. After another long silent pause, he finally said, "All right, Jubal, I'll go." He turned and left the store.

Jubal Clay let out a long sigh of relief, took a moment to gather himself, then returned to his customers. "All right, boys, no need to get all riled up over nothin'. You soldier boys drink up. I bet you could use some grub too. Ruby!" He looked around to locate his daughter. "Honey, see if we can't rustle up somethin' to eat for these boys." He was intent on smoothing things over. He knew he himself was to blame for pushing the rot-gut on the four soldiers. It looked like a good opportunity to get rid of some of that stock. The residents of Ruby's Choice wouldn't drink it anymore, except Otis and Red, and he had almost a barrel of it left. This had appeared to be the perfect opportunity to sell it. Soldiers were like cowhands: they would drink anything. Now he didn't like the way things were going. He had been hoping for a happy drunk but, instead, all signs pointed toward a mean one. Happy drunks bought things and were free with their money. Mean drunks wanted to fight and break things up. The sergeant, Spanner, sure looked like a mean one. Jubal was grateful that Tom had agreed to leave. At first, he feared that Tom was going to make something out of Spanner's insults, and then his store would sure as hell have gotten torn up.

Behind him, Tom could hear the sound of loud laughter. Of the many voices, Spanner's seemed to stand out above the rest. It may have been a mistake, backing down from what might have escalated into a volatile situation, but Tom didn't want to cause trouble for Jubal. It was the wise thing to do. The soldiers would soon be on their way. Still, there was an uncomfortable feeling running along his spine. He knew the danger in showing any hint of fear in this country. Man or beast would consume you if you exhibited any trace of fear. He tried to tell himself that he did it for Jubal and to forget about it. It didn't matter. The thought again entered his mind that it might be time to push on farther west.

He must have been sitting there for over an hour, drinking coffee and staring into the fire, thinking about his life up to that moment and what path it might take from this point. The incident at Clay's Store had driven home something that he, up to this time, had not given any consideration—he had not merely been cashiered from the army. He had brought along extra baggage: a reputation as an Indian lover and a turncoat. He marveled at the irony of it, the inequity. Scouts like Andy Coulter and Squint Peterson were friendly with Indians of several different tribes, had even lived with them. Yet they were not thought of as *Injun-lovers.* He, himself, had killed many Indians from the Washita to Little Big Horn. How could anyone call him an Injun-lover? His had been an exceptional circumstance, one he could hardly be blamed for and, in good conscience, could not have avoided. He had been honor-bound to aid his own brother. Had his brother been anyone other than Little Wolf, his actions on that day by the Yellowstone might have gone unnoticed. Perhaps he should have revealed the true identity of Little Wolf. At the time of his court-martial, he chose not to. That had been his feeling then, and consequently, there was nothing he could do to change it now. So he decided to stop worrying over the matter. His thoughts were interrupted by the arrival of Red and Otis.

"We decided the party's gittin' a little too rough for our likin'," Otis offered, a look of nervous concern deeply etched in his forehead.

"Somebody's liable to get hurt before the night's over," Red added. "Me and Otis figured we'd best git on home before trouble starts. You done the right thing, leaving when you did."

Their remarks brought some concern to Tom. "What do you mean? What kind of trouble is about to start?"

Otis sat down across from Tom and poured himself a cup of coffee. "Might have to make another pot. This'n is gittin' low. You want some, Red?"

Impatient, Tom insisted, "What trouble, Otis? What are you talking about?"

"Ain't none of my business, I reckon. It's just that them soldier boys is startin' to git a little too rowdy to suit me. The other three ain't all that bad, but that there sergeant, he's working up a mean. He's already throwed a whiskey jar at Jubal's mirror, and he's got his eye on Ruby now. Jubal might have his hands full before them boys is done."

Tom was at once apprehensive. "Hell, there's only four of them. Every man in the settlement must have been there when I left. Surely they can help Jubal keep it under control."

Red answered. "Most everbody's gone. Like us, I reckon they could see there was gonna be trouble. Wasn't nobody left but Browny and Joe Sanchez when me and Otis cut out."

Tom could not believe what he was hearing. All the men of the town left because they wanted to avoid trouble, leaving Jubal to fend for himself. And what about Ruby? Was no man chivalrous enough to come to her aid? Tom suddenly had a slightly altered opinion of the little settlement of Ruby's Choice. He did not require a great deal of time to make up his mind. Saying nothing more, he got up and dumped the dregs of his coffee cup outside and tossed the cup over toward his bedroll. He picked up his rifle and checked the load. Then he headed straight for Clay's Store.

"Uh oh," Otis uttered as he and Red quickly tossed their coffee aside and scampered after him . . . at a safe interval.

Ruby Clay was not a fearful person, and never had been. She didn't fear the wild country or the Indians. Since the time she was a small girl, she had been in control of her life and the people in it. But now, for the first time in her young life, she experienced the clammy feeling of cold fear that crawled like a worm along the center of her spine. Her father had let the situation get out of hand. There had been cavalry patrols before, but on those occasions there had been someone in charge, an officer usually, who made sure his men did not get out of control. On this night, there was also someone in charge: Spanner. But he was obviously the one she had to fear the most. The other three troopers were no threat. They were just there, it seemed, to get drunk and act as foolishly grinning spectators to Sergeant Spanner's performance. Earlier in the evening, when Tom had come in, she began to feel uneasy about the way things were developing. Jubal thought things would be all right after Tom left, but Spanner just seemed to get more and more surly as the evening progressed, buoyed no doubt by his banishment of Tom with no challenge to his authority. Although she had not faced the exact situation before, there was no mistaking the leering eyes whenever he looked in her direction. She had managed to avoid his reach while she served the four of them supper, but his sneer promised that he had further plans for her. Now it seemed he was ready to make his move.

"Well, little lady, I reckon I'm ready for you and me to go up in the loft there." Spanner ogled her, a carnivorous grin pasted across his face.

"The hell you say," Ruby replied coldly, her face a mask of contempt.

The evil grin widened on Spanner's face as he got up from his chair. "Well now," he growled, "if you want it the hard way, that suits me just fine." He winked at the three troopers still seated at the table. "It's a heap more fun with a lively bitch, ain't it, boys?"

He received a couple of snickers from his comrades. Encouraged, he started toward Ruby, who was now backing away while looking around for something to protect herself with. Seeing a large skillet on the table, she grabbed it and held it up menacingly. Spanner snorted in amusement and continued to stalk the girl. At this point, Jubal stepped in between Spanner and his daughter.

"She ain't for sale. Now why don't you and your friends get on out of here."

"I ain't planning to pay for her. This is between me and her, old man, so git the hell outta my way before I bust your head open."

"She don't want no part of you. Now leave her alone!" Jubal tried to hold the larger man off with his hands on Spanner's chest.

Spanner shoved Jubal hard with one hand while he drew his large cavalry pistol with the other. Before Jubal could recover, Spanner brought the heavy pistol hard across the side of Jubal's head. He went down in a heap. Spanner barely glanced down at the stricken man before he began unbuckling his belt. "Watch him, boys," he said as he continued to approach the terrified girl.

Ruby said nothing, but the terror in her eyes seemed only to intensify his lust. She backed into a corner of the kitchen, holding the skillet in front of her. "If you know what's good for you, you'll get yourself out of here," she offered lamely, the fear all too evident in her voice. He laughed at her feeble threat.

"Come here, darlin', I know what you need, and I'm gonna give it to you right here on this table. I'm gonna show you how to do it army style."

He suddenly lunged toward her. She swung the skillet, aiming at his head, but he blocked the blow with his shoulder. She tried to swing it again, but he seized her wrist and clamped down on it until she cried out in pain and was forced to let go of the skillet. Fighting for her life, she tried to scratch his face with her free hand, but he caught her and forcing both arms behind her, he clamped both wrists in one huge hand. With her arms pinned behind her back, she still fought, trying to kick him in the groin with her knee. He slapped her hard across her face, once, twice, three times before she was finally subdued. Then he glared at her, his evil grin no more than a fraction of an inch from her face. His hot, sour breath scalded her senses as she turned her face from side to side in an effort to avoid his mouth seeking hers. Finally, he succeeded in smothering her lips with his mouth. His kiss was long and brutal. She tried to hold her breath, keeping her lips tightly closed. At last he withdrew his mouth, and his face still only inches from hers, his loathsome grin returned. She spit in his face, showing her disgust. He barely recoiled, seeming to be amused by her reaction. Her arms were aching, still locked in the viselike grip of his hand, but he made no attempt to ease her discomfort, although the pain was obvious in her face. He seemed to enjoy it. He watched her struggle for a few moments, then suddenly grabbed the front of her blouse and ripped it away, revealing soft, milky-white breasts. He was pleased. "Damn, bitch, you ain't as skinny as you look."

"Let her go, Spanner."

The voice came from the doorway. There was no hint of excitement, just a simple command. Spanner turned to see who dared to interfere with his pleasure. He half expected to see the girl's father, but it was not. He grunted and laughed when he saw Tom standing by the front door. He made no move to release the girl.

"Let her go," Tom repeated, bringing the Winchester up waist-high, at the same time keeping a watchful eye on the three troopers still seated at the table.

"Looo . . . tenant," Spanner growled with emphatic sarcasm. "When was the last time an enlisted man told you to kiss his ass?"

"Let her go," he said for the third time.

Spanner hesitated, looking at the rifle already leveled at him. He considered for only a moment whether or not he could release his hold on the girl and draw his pistol in time. He was angry and half drunk, but he had better sense than to try it. Still, he was not willing to give in so easily. "Ain't you the brave one. I thought I run you out of here once, and here you come crawling back in here holding a rifle on me. I wonder how big you'd talk if you didn't have the jump on me."

Tom was running out of patience. "Spanner," he said calmly, "if you don't let her go right now, I'm going to shoot you. Do you understand that?"

Still Spanner hesitated, but only for a second. There was something in Tom's voice that conveyed a cool resolve. He released Ruby, who immediately grabbed her torn shirt to cover her nakedness and ran toward Tom. Tom motioned for her to get behind him. Spanner stood leering at him.

"Now, you boys have done enough for one night," Tom said, turning halfway toward the three men at the table, but still keeping an eye on Spanner. "The fun's over. I'm sure you're supposed to be part of a detachment to hunt down renegade Indians. I doubt if your commanding officer would like it if he knew you were terrorizing ordinary citizens instead."

"I doubt if your commanding officer would like it . . ." Spanner parroted sarcastically. "I always have wanted to catch one of you dainty-assed officers out of uniform and go at it man to man. Why don't you lay that rifle down and we'll settle this thing right now."

Tom was not about to rise to that bait. Only a fool would give away the advantage when he already had it. "Sergeant, you might find it hard to ride back to your outfit with a bullet hole in your hide." He motioned with the rifle toward the other three. "Get moving."

They didn't look any too happy about it, but they got up from the table and shuffled toward the door. One of them, a young trooper with the imposing build of a blacksmith, spat a surly remark at Tom. "You're mighty damn big with that rifle in your hand."

Tom refused to respond. "Just move on out the door, soldier," he replied.

Spanner, after a few moments of additional defiance, finally picked up his hat and reluctantly moved toward the door. Ruby, watching the man who had attacked and humiliated her, was still bent on exacting her own measure of revenge. While every eye had been trained on Tom, she slowly moved over and picked up the iron skillet from the floor. Very slowly, she moved quietly back to a position behind Tom and waited.

Spanner was almost to the door when Ruby attacked. "You son of a bitch!" she screamed and aimed the heavy frying pan at him. Spanner saw it coming and used it to his advantage. He caught the girl's arm and, using her body as a shield, shoved her into Tom. There was no way Tom could have anticipated Ruby's sudden move. He tried to push her out of the way, but was knocked off balance and landed on his back.

Unnoticed at the far end of the room, Jubal Clay,

the side of his face covered with blood from the gash above his temple, had slowly pulled himself to a sitting position. Realizing that all attention was on Tom's rifle as he herded the four soldiers outside, Jubal took advantage of the opportunity to crawl behind the counter, where he kept a double-barreled shotgun. With Tom sprawled flat on his back, Spanner shoved Ruby out of his way and poised to spring on him. He was like a great cat sensing a kill as he drew a knife from his boot. Just as he was about to strike, he was halted in his tracks by the explosion of Jubal's shotgun blast over his head. The room, which moments before had been a roar of confused shouting and cursing, suddenly went quiet as a tomb with everyone seemingly suspended in a state of shocked paralysis, broken only by Jubal's voice.

"I wouldn't if I was you, Sergeant." He paused long enough to watch Spanner back off. "Now, by God, I'm warning all of you. This here shindig is over. You men git on your horses and get the hell outta my town."

Tom scrambled to his feet, his rifle still in his hand, and motioned Ruby over against the wall, out of the way. Spanner scowled at the little storekeeper, but took a step back. Undetected by Jubal, for he was still across the room, Spanner glanced at one of his men, the one who was built like a blacksmith, and signaled with his eyes. The subtle signal did not escape Tom.

"All right, Pop," Spanner said, returning the knife to the sheath in his boot. "You win, we're going."

He started to turn, as if he were going out the door. Instead, he lunged toward Tom, taking a wild swing at him with his fist. Tom was ready for him. He stepped aside, dodging the fist, and laid the barrel of his rifle across the bridge of Spanner's nose with all the force he could muster. There was a loud crack as the rifle barrel flattened the man's nose. Spanner stood there stunned for an instant. Then his legs seemed suddenly incapable of supporting him, and he staggered over against the door and fell outside on the steps. Jubal, distracted by the surprise attack, dropped the barrel of his shotgun. When he did, the burly soldier pulled a pistol from his belt and drew down on him. Tom reacted faster than he could consciously think. In a fraction of a wink, he whirled and fired. His bullet slammed into the side of the trooper's skull, killing him instantly, the bullet from the soldier's pistol tearing harmlessly into the ceiling over Jubal's head.

For a long moment no one moved, stunned by the explosion of sudden violence. For Tom, the moment seemed frozen in time—the image of the fallen trooper, an ugly black hole in the side of his head, his head bouncing on the wooden floor when he fell. Tom felt a choking sensation and the burning of bile rising in his throat as the realization that he had just killed a soldier, one of his former comrades, struck him like a bludgeon. This was not his first kill. He had killed at least three Confederate soldiers personally, and he had dispatched at least three times that many Sioux and Cheyenne. But this was different. This was close and personal, not like the others who had seemed little more than targets. It was a feeling he was never to forget. He didn't like it.

"All right, you men, it's over. Pick him up and get him on his horse," he heard himself saying. They showed no sign of resistance, obviously stunned by the shock of seeing the young trooper's life snuffed out so suddenly. Tom followed them as they carried the dead man outside. "Help your sergeant up on his horse." They did as they were ordered.

Spanner's face was covered with blood, and he was in no condition to put up any further resistance, but he was still able to talk. "You son of a bitch, you ain't seen the last of me." Still woozy from the blow across his face and already feeling nauseated from swallowing a great deal of blood, he had to hang on to his saddle horn to remain upright. "You signed your death warrant tonight, Injun-lover. You murdered a U.S. Army soldier. You're a dead man!"

Tom was unmoved. He turned to one of the other troopers and said, "Get on back to your unit. Tell them what happened here and don't be afraid to tell the truth. Spanner attacked the man's daughter. I had no choice but to shoot your friend. I regret that, but it couldn't be helped. I couldn't let him shoot Mr. Clay. You tell them that." He stood back and watched as they turned their mounts and headed out of town.

Jubal walked over and stood by Tom. "You think they'll be back?"

Tom sighed, "I'm afraid so. The army will have to investigate."

"You think them other two boys will tell the truth about what happened?"

"I doubt it."

Jubal looked at his friend for a moment, but decided not to put his thoughts into words. There was no need. Tom was smart enough to know that he just might have fastened a noose around his neck. A soldier had been killed. The chances of the army seeing Tom's side of it were practically nil. Jubal felt the heavy burden of regret for what had happened that night, for he knew Tom had not only saved Ruby from a savage attack, but had also saved his own life. What could he say to the man? So he remained silent as they stood there, staring off into the darkness that closed in behind the soldiers. Ruby came up beside Tom and put her arms around his waist and hugged him close to her. Tom, startled at first, put his arm around her shoulder, and they stood there for a long time before parting.

From the shadows at the end of the building, Red and Otis appeared. Like two dark specters, they moved silently over to join Tom. He had not even known of their presence, for they had watched the whole incident through a small window at the end of the store, well out of harm's way. It occurred to Tom that Jubal couldn't expect much help from that quarter if he had trouble of any kind in the future.

Otis placed his hand on Tom's shoulder and spoke with great compassion. "You can't stay around here, son. They'll hang you shore as spit for shooting that soldier."

It was unnecessary advice, so Tom didn't bother to answer. He knew he had little chance of a fair hearing if he allowed himself to be taken into custody. Spanner would see to that. He had already made up his mind to leave.

Chapter IV

Tom did not sleep well, his thoughts troubled by the events of the day. As he lay awake most of the night, he examined his actions of that evening from every angle, and he could honestly say there had been no way to avoid the outcome. Still, his conscience would not allow him to escape the guilt he harbored for taking the life of a cavalry trooper. But what choice had he been given? Spanner would have brutally raped Ruby had it not been for his intervention. And there was little doubt the young soldier he had killed meant to murder Jubal. He had to admit that the real injustice in the incident was that, if anyone had to die, it should have been Spanner and not the husky young private. Tom turned the incident over and over in his mind. There was nothing he could have done to prevent it. When it all sifted out, if you were looking for a victim, Tom Allred was a pretty good candidate himself. For now he would without a doubt be on the army's wanted list. How, he wondered, could fate play such an ironic hand? His only ambition had been to be a good soldier. Now both he and his brother were renegades. At least Little Wolf did not carry the burden of guilt for his allegiance to the Cheyenne nation. There was nothing left to Tom but to sort it out as best he could and get on with it, in hopes of finding a better life somewhere.

The next morning he said his good-byes to Red and Otis, then stopped by Jubal's store to get what provisions he could with the money and hides he had left. He had to argue with Jubal over the trade value of the skins to keep Jubal from cheating himself. Tom appreciated what he was trying to do, but some of the skins were skimpy and he didn't feel it fair to get prime money for them. His main interest was ammunition for his rifle, so he took all the cartridges Jubal had plus lead and powder to make his own. Ruby was nowhere to be seen. Jubal allowed as how she was most likely down by the creek somewhere, washing clothes. Everything packed on his two horses, he said good-bye to Jubal and stepped up on Billy.

He swung back along the creek on his way out of the settlement. He wanted to say good-bye to Ruby, although he had been dreading it all morning. He had been disappointed to find that she was not at the store when he came by.

An outcropping of rock that seemed to be the community's favorite place to wash clothes was where he found her, scrubbing some of Jubal's pants. She looked back when she heard the horses. Seeing that it was him, she stood up and came to meet him. He stepped down from the saddle.

"Well, looks like you're leaving town." She forced a thin smile.

"Yeah, I reckon so. I just wanted to say good-bye."

The sun was just now coming up over the trees on the far side of the creek, and she shielded her eyes with her hand as she looked up into his face. Noticing her discomfort, he moved to the side so she didn't have to face the sun while they talked.

"Where will you go?"

"Don't know for sure. Right now I plan to head west toward Crow country, maybe north into Shoshone country. Just away from the fort, I guess."

She made no reply. There was a long silence while both searched for words. Appropriate ones seemed to come hard. Still, they both felt there was something that needed to be said. Finally, embarrassed by the long void, he simply said, "Well, good-bye," and started to put his foot in the stirrup.

"Wait!" She put her hand on his arm to stop him. There was another brief silence while she formed her words. "I want to thank you for what you did for me." She hesitated. "And I'm sorry you're in trouble with the army. I reckon you have me and Pa to blame for that." He started to respond, but she stopped him. "Tom, if you want me to go with you, I will." Having said it, she quickly dropped her gaze to the ground, embarrassed by her own words.

He went cold inside, the frigid grip of melancholy like a frozen stone in his heart. He had never been more miserable in his entire life. He had hoped she would say it, yet he didn't want her to say it, for he knew he could not take her with him. "Ruby," he struggled, "I can't take you where I'm going. I'm sorry. I wish I could. The time was just not right for us to meet. I wish it was."

She would not beg. She had offered, he could not accept, and that was that. She started to step back, then changed her mind and suddenly put her arms around his neck and kissed him. Her mouth was warm and soft, and she pressed her body tightly against his with fierce passion. Then she released him and stepped away. "That's just so you'll remember me, Tom Allred. Now get on out of here!"

Still somewhat stunned, he replied softly, "I don't

reckon I'll ever forget you, Ruby." Then, before his emotions had a chance to change his mind, he stepped up into the saddle, turned Billy around, and rode away. He never looked back, and she was grateful for that. She didn't want him to see the tears streaming down her face.

Sunup the following morning found Tom already in the saddle. With no destination in mind, he just let Billy have his head and set his own pace. As long as the general direction was away from the little settlement of Ruby's Choice, he wasn't particular. Billy chose to leave the low mountain range behind and start out northwest across the prairie. This was Crow country and, while he wasn't especially worried about it, he was smart enough to keep a sharp eye about him in case he had to duck in behind a hill in a hurry. As far as he knew, the Crows were not causing any trouble. In fact, many of them worked for the army as scouts at the battle of the Little Big Horn. But a white man alone on the prairie might be an entirely different thing. A hunting party of Crow warriors wouldn't hesitate to leave him with a belly full of arrows and no hair while they made off with Billy and the packhorse.

The first rays of the sun finally struggled over the distant mountain range behind him, painting the tips of the rolling hills of grass before him a soft butternut gold. Stranded remnants of the night, caught in dark pools around the base of the hills, gradually began to evaporate into the spreading cloak of sunshine as the morning warmed. He pulled his buffalo robe up close around his neck against the chilly spring air. Just the sight of the sunlight warmed him, although the temperature may have dropped a few degrees since before daybreak. *It's going to be a nice day*, he thought. Off in the distance, he sighted a small herd of pronghorn antelope leisurely making their way across the prairie, too far for him to consider giving chase. If he needed the meat, he would have set out to stalk them, but for now, he had plenty of provisions. From what he had seen of the country, there was game aplenty. No need to take it if he didn't need it. That was a nice part about spring. A man knew he could get meat whenever he wanted to. The grass was already getting thick on the rolling plains, and the morning breeze seemed to set the whole prairie in constant motion. Occasionally he passed through scattered carpets of bitterroot, and he recalled the time Squint Peterson pointed out the little pink and white flowers to him. They were on a hunting trip, several days out of Fort Lincoln. Squint said a man could eat the roots of the plant in the spring of the year, but they were bitter as hell come summer. He smiled as he thought of the many such trips he had taken with the old scout. Suddenly, it felt good to be alone in the world again, as good as it had felt to find Ruby's Choice and to see people again after the long winter he had endured. His thoughts wandered briefly back to Ruby Clay and the way her soft body had melted into his, and then he decided thoughts like these could work on a man's mind. He had to put the girl out of his head for good.

Along toward midday, he sighted a flock of vultures circling in the distance. Curious, he pointed Billy in that direction. An hour's ride brought him near the base of a low butte and maybe half a mile from the umbrella of circling vultures. As Billy topped a grassy rise by the foot of the butte, Tom caught sight of the cause for the convention of the big birds. From that distance, there appeared to be a heaped pile of something at the bottom of a shallow ravine. When he had covered half the remaining distance, he realized that the pile was, in reality, a man pinned under a dead horse. Tom drew back on the reins and paused to study the situation before riding in. He scanned the horizon around him, but could see no evidence of any other living thing. Satisfied there was no threat of danger, he nudged Billy with his heels and continued toward the ravine.

He had closed to within a hundred yards, close enough to see that the man pinned beneath the horse was a white man, when the man suddenly lifted up on his elbow and brought a rifle up to bear on him.

"Hold on!" Tom shouted. "Hold on!"

The man did not fire, but the rifle remained trained on Tom. "Well, come on in a little closer then," he shouted, "so's I can get a look atcha."

Tom held Billy back to a slow walk, keeping a sharp eye on the stranger, but occasionally glancing around him to the sides and behind. He didn't like the idea of riding into an ambush. As he approached the fallen man, he could see that he was in a real bind. His leg was firmly pinned beneath the bulk of his dead horse, and by the time Tom had arrived, the buzzards were getting bold enough to swoop within range of the man's fists. In spite of the gravity of the poor man's situation, Tom couldn't help but be amused by the sight of a man trying to fight off buzzards with his fists. He pulled Billy up in front of the man, and as he sat and looked him over for a moment, the boldest of the vultures lit on the rump of the dead horse. For a long moment, bird and man stared at each other. Finally, the man pulled a pistol from his belt and shot the buzzard, causing the rest of the flock to back off for a few minutes.

"Kinda looks like I got here just in time," Tom said casually.

The man squinted one eye against the sun as he stared up at Tom. "Well, I swear, I don't know," he replied. "I reckon it depends on whether or not you're aiming to git this here horse offen me or whether you just come to watch the show."

Tom laughed and stepped down from the saddle. Then, noticing a dark stain in the shoulder of the man's jacket, he stated, "You've been shot."

"I noticed that," the man replied sarcastically, "but that ain't my immediate problem. What I'd dearly love right now is to git out from under this damn horse!"

"Don't worry, I'm gonna get him off you." Noticing a rope on the man's saddle, he took it and tied one end around the dead horse's neck. The other he looped around his saddle horn. "All right, let's give it a try."

The man watched in silence as Tom prepared to move the animal. As he stooped down, the man spoke. "Take her real slow and easy. I don't think my leg's broke, but it could be if you ain't careful. My dang foot's still in the stirrup."

Tom eased Billy forward until the rope was taut. He looked back over his shoulder and, when the stricken man nodded that he was ready, nudged Billy in the belly. The big horse paused once to test the load, then pulled the dead animal off with no apparent effort. Tom dismounted once again and stood over the man, watching as he tested his leg.

"My name's Bris Collins," he said as he carefully felt his knee and shinbone.

"Tom Allred."

Bris continued to rub his ankle and calf. "Feels like nothin's broke." He flashed a smile in Tom's direction. "Reckon I'm mighty glad you happened along. I was beginning to wonder if me and them dang buzzards was gonna have to start eating on that damn horse to git him light enough for me to lift him."

"Better take a look at that shoulder wound."

Bris looked down at his shoulder. "Don't think it amounts to much," he said as he pulled his coat and shirt away from the wound and stared at the bullet hole. "It bled pretty clean before it started to scab over."

Tom got a piece of cloth from his saddle pack, wet it down with his canteen, and handed it to Bris to clean the wound. "Who jumped you?"

Bris paused and scratched his head as he thought about the question. "Looked to me like a band of Blackfoot, six or eight of 'em."

"Blackfeet?" Tom asked. "They were a little out of their territory, weren't they?"

"Yeah, that's what I thought. I ain't exactly no expert on Injuns but, if I had to guess, I reckon I'd have to say they was Blackfoot. I know Crow and I know Flathead, and they wasn't none of them. I don't reckon it matters none, does it? Injuns is Injuns. Don't make much difference to a rifle bullet who pulls the trigger. Damn horse is just as dead. It's a shame, too. That horse was shaping up real nice. Another week or two and he'da been a right smart little cow pony."

Bris's remarks surprised Tom. Somehow he had not expected to find anyone working cattle this deep in hostile territory. Still, he thought, there was no reason to be surprised. The first big herd of cattle was driven up from Texas more than ten years before. It was simply that he had never come into contact with the hardy breed of men who were establishing cattle ranches in the Montana territory.

"Are you raising cattle near here?" Tom asked. As he said it, he looked around him as if expecting to see some of them. He saw no evidence of any cattle.

"Well, I ain't. I mean they ain't my cattle. I work for Mr. Eli Cruze. He owns a spread up on the Musselshell. Runs a right sizable herd when they ain't scattered all over hell and some. I was rounding up strays when I got jumped this morning."

"You been stuck under that horse since morning?"

"Yep. I found four head of cattle that musta spent the winter up in a little draw back yonder 'bout three miles. I was heading 'em back when them son of a bitches jumped me. I figured they was after the beef, so I let 'em have the cows and I tried to run for it. One of 'em got my horse right behind his ears. He went down so fast I couldn't git my dang foot outen the stirrup. That's when they got me, too, only I didn't even know it until I wound up under him. Damn, that horse is heavy! Well, I was lucky I could git to my rifle. Come to find out didn't but one of 'em have a rifle, so I didn't have no trouble holding 'em off. Well, they hung around for two or three hours, taking shots at me, but I kept 'em peppered so they couldn't git in range for their bows. After a while they got tired of it and went off after the cows. Then, two, three hours later, you come along."

Tom helped him up on his feet, and after a careful step or two, Bris decided there had been no damage done. He just needed to get the blood circulating again. By this time the shoulder wound, although not serious, was causing a good bit of stiffness in the muscle, so Tom fashioned a sling for his arm to take the load off the man's shoulder.

"What would you have done if I didn't happen

along? You know, if I hadn't seen those buzzards, I probably would have passed you by."

Bris scratched his beard thoughtfully. "Hell, I don't know. I hope to hell Eli Cruze woulda sent some-body out to look for me after two or three days. I reckon by then me and the vultures would have eat enough of my horse to git him offen me." He laughed at the thought of it. "But I'm right proud you come along. Them Injuns might have brought some friends back with 'em."

It took some additional help from Billy before Tom managed to free Bris's saddle from the carcass of his horse. He threw it up on top of his packhorse, and Bris climbed up behind him on Billy, and at Bris's direction, they started for the Musselshell and Eli Cruze's spread, the Broken-T. Bris was confident they could reach the ranch before dark, even with Billy carrying double. On the ride, Bris expressed his grati-tude to Tom for taking time to carry him back to the ranch and apologized for the inconvenience. Tom assured him that it was no real inconvenience since he was headed nowhere in particular anyway. This lit a spark of interest in Bris.

"You mean you was just drifting?" He didn't wait for an answer. "You ever worked cattle?"

"Nope. I was in the army until last fall."

"What you figuring on doing now?"

Tom didn't answer right away. He had spent some time trying to make that very decision. "To tell you the truth, I haven't really decided. All I've known since I was eighteen was the army. I can hunt and trap a little. I really don't know much else."

"Eli's shorthanded. Why don't you ask him for a job? The pay's good, thirty dollars a month and grub. You can't beat that."

Tom shrugged. "Like I said, I don't know anything about working cows."

"Hell, it wouldn't take you long to learn, and since you ain't goin' nowhere in particular, it wouldn't hurt to give her a try."

"How do you know Eli will even hire me?"

Bris snorted. "He'd hire you. Like I said, he's shorthanded. We ain't got but a dozen good hands now. Two of the men lit out as soon as the first snow fell. One other feller, a Mexican, come up with us from Texas, stuck it out through the whole dang winter, and then come spring, he left."

Tom mulled the notion over for a while. The idea wasn't completely far-fetched. Maybe it would give him a little time to make up his mind about what to do with the rest of his life. At any rate, it would give him a place to stay for the summer. "I don't know," he finally said. "I'll think about it."

The sun was well below the mountains on the western horizon when they forded the river and rode into Eli Cruzes's home range. It was little more than a camp. There were no permanent buildings, and although it appeared that a bunkhouse and cookhouse had been started, the walls were not chest high as yet. The men lived in two large tents on either side of a chuck wagon. A horse corral and a couple of wagons stood beside it. Between the two tents, behind the chuck wagon, was a makeshift rifle pit, the likes of which Tom had not seen since he was a young private at Vicksburg. He guessed this was for defense in the event of Indian attack. In front of the chuck wagon about ten paces, a healthy campfire blazed like a warm oasis in the approaching chill of evening. A man stood on one side of the fire, cleaning a large skillet with sand. When he spied the two men approaching, he straightened up and, rubbing an obviously stiff back, stared them into the camp.

Bris called out, "What the hell's the matter with you, Smoky? Ain't you never seen two men on a horse before?"

The man called Smoky just stood there, still staring, until Tom and Bris entered the light of the fire and he was sure who had spoken to him. "Odd damn, Bris. Where the hell you been? I thought you mighta lit out after the Mexican."

"Why, you know, that's just exactly what I did. I was all the way down to the Arkansas River and I got to thinkin about your biscuits and turned right around and hightailed it back."

"You can kiss my ass, too," Smoky responded while looking over the stranger Bris rode in with. "Who's this here?"

"Where the hell's your manners, Smoky? Can't you see we're starving? Is there any coffee left in that pot?" Bris reached over and picked up a tin cup from the edge of the fire and filled it from a large gray metal coffeepot. He offered it to Tom. "Here, Tom, I don't know who was drinking out of it, but as long as it warn't Smoky here, I don't reckon it'll kill you." After he found another cup, he poured himself some coffee and then answered Smokey's question. "This here's Tom Allred, and if it warn't for him, I wouldn't be enjoying your fine coffee on this glorious spring evening."

Smoky nodded in Tom's direction. "Tom," he acknowledged. "You boys is too late for chuck, but if you're hungry, there's some cold biscuits left."

"Thanks," Tom replied, "that would be just fine. I need to take care of my horse first though."

Bris and Smoky looked at him approvingly, knowing that a man's first responsibility was to the animal

that hauled his ass over the prairie. Bris helped him
unsaddle Billy and the packhorse and turn them out
to graze.

"You gonna hobble 'em?" Bris wanted to know.

"They won't go anywhere," Tom replied. "Let 'em
graze for a while, then I'll put 'em in the corral if
that's all right."

When they had downed a couple of biscuits each,
washed down with the bitter dregs of the coffeepot,
Bris asked, "Where's everybody at?"

"Odd damn, where you think? Where you're supposed to be—working. Everybody ain't got time to
lay around the fire, drinkin' my coffee."

Bris seemed surprised. "Everybody out on night
herd? How come?"

"Injuns. Couple of the boys spotted some of 'em
scouting around the herd this morning. They run off
when they seen 'em coming. 'Bout midday they spotted 'em again down south of the river. Reckon they
had a hankerin' for beef."

"Coulda been the same bunch that jumped me,"
Bris said. He hesitated for a moment, standing right
in front of Smoky. Finally, exasperated, he demanded, "Ain't you gonna ask me about this damn
sling?"

"What about it?" Smoky replied, his tone indicating a definite lack of interest. Then his grin widened
and he added, "I figured you broke your arm trying
to wipe your ass."

"I swear, a man would have to git shot full of
holes before he got any sympathy around here."

"You got shot? Odd damn, why didn't you say so?
Here, let's have a look at it."

Tom sat down and relaxed by the fire while the
cook looked over Bris's wound. He suddenly felt
tired. It had been a long day, and the warm fire,

combined with the biscuits in his belly, seemed to add weight to his eyelids. He didn't realize he was dozing until he was awakened by the arrival of the rest of the cowhands.

Bris was right when he said Eli needed cowhands, but Eli was a cautious man, and it wasn't the natural thing to see a man riding alone in this country with no apparent destination. Occasionally, a trapper—one of the so-called mountain men—would wander across his range. But this young fellow didn't look like a mountain man, and he wasn't carrying prospecting tools. Bris said he'd been mustered out of the army, and maybe that was the truth. Mustered out or deserted, Eli didn't care. He never had much use for soldiers anyway. He did have principles though, and he wanted to be assured he wasn't hiring on any bank robbers or murderers. He had a right fair crew. They might be a little rough around the edges, but they could turn a good day's work and there wasn't a backstabber in the bunch. He was cautious, but he also knew his manners, so he extended his hand when introduced to Tom and gave him a firm handshake.

"Bris here tells me you pulled his bacon outta the fire."

Tom smiled and shrugged, "Well, I don't know about that. All I did was pull him out from under his horse and give him a ride home."

Eli Cruze didn't look like his name, at least not what Tom expected him to look like. From Bris's comments about him, Tom expected a giant of a man with a no-nonsense nature and a disposition akin to that of a mountain lion. On first impression, Eli seemed to present just the opposite of that image. He was a smallish, wiry man whose nose seemed a size too large for a knifelike face that bore the tracks of too many hard winters on the open range. Instead of the wide-brimmed hat favored by most men in this part of the world, he wore a short-billed cap, like those Tom had seen as a boy in St. Louis when he and his friends sat on the docks and watched the riverboats unload. His choice of caps probably was the reason the men all referred to him as the Captain. While the man was relatively small, especially when standing next to the imposing bulk of Bris Collins, Tom found that the no-nonsense nature accurately applied to him. And, while his disposition may not have been quite that of a mountain lion, it was by no means fearful. His nature was more resolute, like the mountain range that stood silently on the western horizon. Tom got the impression that Eli Cruze would be here as long as the mountains, regardless of winter snows, Indians, summer storms, or whatever else came along. If the military had been his calling, Eli Cruze surely would have been a general.

Bris spoke up. "Cap'n, Tom here might be lookin' to sign on with us."

Eli turned to Tom, his expression revealing no particular interest in the news. "That right?"

"Well, maybe." Tom couldn't help but feel a little bit defensive. After all, he hadn't come begging for a job. He was really only there because he had helped Bris out of a tight spot.

"Ever worked cattle before?"

"No."

Eli stood there for a long moment, measuring Tom with his eyes. Finally, he spoke. "I'm trying to figure what good you'd be to us if you don't know anything about working cows. We already got a cook, and we don't need nobody to lead no parades."

Tom was beginning to rankle. He looked Eli in the

eye long and hard before he replied. "Well, Mr. Cruze, it's like this. I don't know if I'd be of any use to you or not. It depends. I'm a fair hand with a horse, and I reckon I can shoot as well as the next man. I didn't come here looking for a job, but I could probably use one. As far as working cattle, I figure if you can do it, then, by God, I reckon I can."

Eli didn't react right away. His expression, stern and skeptical, remained that way for a few seconds while he continued to evaluate the young visitor to his camp. Then the corners of his mouth slowly turned up to form a thin smile, and his eyes softened perceptively. "Don't get yourself all riled up, young feller. I just wanted to see if there was any sand in you." He turned back to Bris, who was grinning broadly. "Bris here can show you where you can throw your bedroll. You stick close to Bris. He'll show you what to do." He turned back to Tom and said, "Glad to have you. We're short of hands." With that, he turned on his heel and headed for his tent.

Tom stood and watched the man walk away. "Well," he sighed and said, "I guess that means I'm hired."

"I told you," Bris said, still grinning broadly. "You'll find the Cap'n is as fair a man to work for as there is."

"I don't know. I'll try this for a while, but I'm not sure how long I'll stay."

Chapter V

Spring was a busy time for the Broken-T's cow-hands. It was the time of year to round up all the scattered remnants of the close to five thousand head of beef that had managed to make it through the winter, and brand all the spring calves and strays. Spring thaws produced small bunches of cattle from obscure draws and canyons that had been inaccessible under winter snows. There was an urgency about the work, and Eli kept after his hands constantly, reminding them that their bonus was dependent upon how many head, ready for market, could be rounded up for the fall drive to the Missouri, some three hundred and fifty miles distant. The men worked from dark to dark, from can to can't, sometimes with barely a couple of hours sleep at night, sometimes with none at all.

It was a hard way to earn thirty dollars a month, but Tom found the work to be a balm, easing the despair he still harbored. His exhausted body left little room for his mind to dwell on things that had happened in his past or to speculate on what the future might hold. Bris Collins took him under his wing, and within a couple of weeks' time Tom was working like an experienced cowhand. His initial responsibility was that of a wrangler since he had no experience in roping. So, for most of the roundup, his job was to watch over the remuda, a position of decidedly lower status than that of a regular cowhand, whose task it was to cut out a calf, rope it, tie it, and brand it. It was a far cry from a lieutenant in the cavalry, but Tom didn't mind. In fact, he openly admired the skill demonstrated by the men, most of whom were much younger than he. With Bris showing him the basics of roping, he started practicing on the horses in the remuda. On Sundays, while on the home range, Eli slacked off a little on the work. He was a religious man in a somewhat free-wheeling way, enough so that he at least tried to acknowledge the Sabbath. Tom used the free hours to practice on the calves. Before long, he became a fair hand at roping. Being shorthanded, Eli decided to let him help with the branding. Bris helped him pick a string of good cow ponies. A cowhand needed six or eight horses because the work would wear down a couple of horses in no time at all. His favorite was a little buckskin named Breezy. Billy was as fine a horse as a man could ask for, but he was not inclined toward working cattle, so he was temporarily retired to the remuda. Tom made it a point to give his old companion a little attention whenever he had the time. He and Billy had been through a lot together, and it wouldn't do to have Billy feel as though he had been abandoned.

Bris had been truthful when he said the Cap'n was a fair man, and Tom found the crew of the Broken-T to be as amiable a group of men as he had ever encountered. There seemed to be no troublemakers. Of course, as Bris pointed out, as hard as they were working, nobody had any energy left to make trouble. Aside from Bris, the men Tom worked with most were Slim and Doc. Slim was called Slim for obvious reasons—he was tall and gangly, a man of perhaps twenty-five. Doc, an average-looking man, was a few years older. When asked why he was called "Doc," he had no idea at all. For as long as he could remember, he had been called Doc. Then there was Big Joe and Little Joe, two brothers from Texas who had signed on with Eli when he made the big drive up from the Canadian River range. Big Joe was the elder by two years. Little Joe's name was actually Cecil, but no one was able to remember that. They had always referred to him as Little Joe, and after a while it became his name. Tom rode with the two brothers occasionally, but most of the time he was paired with Bris and Doc, or Bris and Slim. In a short time they became real comfortable around each other, almost like family.

After roundup, most of the summer was spent riding herd. It was a lonesome job, Tom found, covering a big territory, usually by himself. For the most part he counted cattle, doctored them if they were sick, drove off occasional wolves, and talked to himself a great deal. Still, it was not a bad time. Solitude was sometimes good for the soul, so he went about his work content to be alone with his thoughts. By the time the morning came when Eli gave the order to "Move 'em out!" and they started the herd toward the east and the Missouri, Tom had all but forgotten his time as a cavalry officer. He had taken to working cattle.

Eli had been impatient to get the drive started, but once under way he was in no particular hurry to complete it. He was a practical man, and he had a set schedule for the trip to the Northern Pacific railhead at Bismarck. The drive would cover some three hundred plus miles, and he had allowed plenty of time to make it. Ten miles a day was about average for a herd this size, and that was the schedule Eli planned on. There was plenty of good grass and water between the Musselshell and the Missouri, and he planned to have well filled-out beef when he completed the trip. When Bris suggested they could easily make five miles more a day, thereby getting to the saloons that much quicker, Eli had an answer for him. "I'll get a helluva lot better price for beef than I will for soup bones." He was already aware that his Texas longhorns, while tough and resilient on the range, were second in quality to the short-horned purebreds raised by most of the Montana ranchers, and it was his plan to eventually convert his entire herd to the better strain. One of the first things he had done when he first arrived in Montana territory was to buy a couple of bulls from a rancher over near Miles City.

Most of the cattlemen, and almost all of the Texas herds, were content simply to use the open range of Montana and not own any of it outright. It seemed there was enough good open range to last forever, especially since the buffalo had been all but killed off. But Eli planned to sink roots in this new territory. He had staked claim and filed for the one hundred and sixty acres offered under the Homestead Act of 1862. The parcel he selected was on the banks of the Musselshell. It was only a hundred and sixty acres, but he had the use of an unlimited open range around his property. The way he saw it, there would come a time when all that unlimited range would suddenly become crowded, what with more railroads pushing into the land every year, and more Texas cattlemen, like himself, leaving the drought-stricken prairies of Texas to graze on the lush grass of Montana. Eli was here to stay, and when the range was no longer free, he aimed to have possession of a good bit more than a hundred and sixty acres of it.

It had been a good drive so far. They would reach Pronghorn Creek early the next afternoon. It was a wide creek that probably had another name, but they referred to it as the Pronghorn because they had seen a herd of antelope near there the year before. Remembering this, Smoky asked Eli if Tom, being somewhat of a hunter, might ride out from the herd on the chance he might run up on some wild game. Smoky, despite his gruff exterior, was not a man without compassion, and the diet on a cattle drive was not the most appetizing, consisting mainly of sourdough biscuits and sowbelly. He would sometimes dress it up a little with gravy on the biscuits, but the fare seldom varied. So if there was a chance to serve some antelope, he knew the men would appreciate it. Besides, Smoky was as bored with the diet as anybody. Eli agreed that it was a good idea, so Tom rode out early the next morning before the herd started moving. Slim asked to go along since he was a fair shot himself.

Tom turned Breezy in with the remuda and saddled Billy. It had been a while since Billy had been ridden, and he was a bit rank at first. He started kicking up his heels as soon as Tom tried to throw the saddle on him. Tom knew what was bothering him—he had been neglected while Tom worked cattle on Breezy and the rest of his string. Horses can feel jealousy the same as humans, and Billy wasn't going to let Tom forget that he had been ignored. Tom was patient with him, but had to slap him once behind the ears when Billy started to buck. It wasn't much of a bucking, just a halfhearted hump to let Tom know he was protesting. But Tom gave him a hard slap anyway. He and Billy were partners, but it was important to establish which one of them gave the orders. Billy settled down quick enough, and when he did, Tom stroked his neck and whispered a little sweet talk to him. Billy was Billy after that. Slim seemed to be enjoying the reunion.

"That there horse acts more like a wife than a horse," he said and laughed as Tom calmed Billy down. "I just kick the shit out'n mine when he acts up."

Tom shook his head and smiled back at Slim. "Billy and I have a pretty good understanding," he said. "Besides, he's got a pretty good memory, and if we get caught out on the prairie somewhere by a Sioux hunting party, we might have to make a run for it. I want to make sure Billy doesn't take off without me."

"I reckon you're right," Slim agreed. "But, if it comes to that, this plug'll play hell gittin' me off'n his back." He laughed at the thought. "And, if'n he did throw me, I'd shoot the son of a bitch before he had a chance to leave me."

Tom laughed. He knew Slim to be one of the gentlest of souls. He was just talking big. If it came down to it, he'd more than likely give up his life to save that of his horse. Tom liked Slim. He was easy to be around.

They took one packhorse with them, and as they ambled out of camp, Bris called out to them, "You boys must figure on gittin' a helluva lot of game. You sure one packhorse'll be enough?"

"We'll load this 'un up, and then herd the rest of the game back into camp so's you can watch us kill 'em," Slim called back.

"All the same, I reckon I'll git my belly ready for more sourdough and sowbelly," Bris laughingly replied. "I'm gonna be hunting strays south of here, and I don't wanna see that there horse loaded down with none of Cap'n's beef when you git back."

At a canter, they soon were out of sight of the herd, so they drew back on the horses into a more leisurely pace. The range spread out before them like a vast peaceful ocean, rolling gently toward the horizon, broken only occasionally by small stands of trees that marked the course of a wayward stream. After riding for about an hour, they paused at one such creek to give the horses a drink. Slim climbed up into a tree to take a look around.

"Hold on! There they are!"

"What is it?" Tom asked.

Slim didn't answer at once, as he strained to see. After a moment more, he said, "Looks like pronghorns to me, maybe fifteen or twenty of 'em."

By this time, Tom had climbed up in the tree beside Slim and followed the direction in which Slim was looking. "I think you're right. Looks like meat, all right, if we can get close enough to get a shot."

They circled around to get downwind and then tried to gradually close the distance between themselves and the small herd of antelope. Tom estimated that they followed the herd for about three miles, yet only managed to shorten the distance between them by about three or four hundred yards. It was almost as if the animals knew what they were up to and were careful not to let them get too close. The prairie was too flat at this point. There were no hills or draws to conceal their movements, so there was nothing to do but continue trailing them. At last they reached terrain that offered Tom the cover he needed. The antelope led them to one of the numerous streams that followed a small tree-lined ravine. While the herd drank, Tom and Slim hurried to gain a position behind a hill that formed one side of the ravine. It was their intention to use the cover of the hill to shoot from, making the antelope easy targets while they drank from the stream. But they weren't that lucky. Somehow, the herd got nervous and bolted from the stream, through the trees, and over the other side of the ravine.

"Damn!" Slim swore.

Tom jumped to his feet. "Hurry! Let's get down to that creek and get these horses out of sight. We might get our meat yet if we're quick enough."

Slim followed right behind as Tom raced down to the stream and tied the horses to a tree. Running in a crouch to keep his profile low, he quickly made his way to the top of the hill. The antelope had gone no farther than a few hundred yards before they stopped to graze again. This was what he had hoped for.

"You want to take a shot at 'em?" Slim asked. "It's a little fer but we might get lucky."

"No, wait," Tom replied. "I'll show you an old trick Squint Peterson taught me."

"Who's Squint Peterson?"

"An old friend, a scout," Tom replied as he quickly pulled his bandanna from around his neck and tied it to the barrel of his rifle. "You just sit tight right here and get ready to shoot when I do." He got up on his hands and knees and crawled over the brow of the hill. "Just make sure you shoot at a pronghorn and not at me," he called back over his shoulder.

He worked his way up to the top of a little rise in the prairie where he rolled over and lay flat on his back. He had never tried this before, but Squint swore it worked every time. He held his rifle with the bandanna tied to it straight up in the air and slowly waved it back and forth. Squint had assured him that antelope had an incurable curiosity and were unable to resist investigating this strange thing waving back and forth on the prairie. If it didn't work, he would have a hard time convincing Slim that he wasn't a lunatic.

Nothing happened for several minutes, and he was beginning to wonder if Squint had been pulling his leg, when he noticed that one of the antelope had stopped grazing and was staring in his direction. A moment more and all but a few of the animals stood dead still, their gaze transfixed on the waving rifle barrel. "Come on," he muttered under his breath. "Come on over here and get a good look." Still he waved. Finally, the boldest of the herd took a few steps in his direction, halted, then started walking slowly toward the fascinating object waving in the tall buffalo grass. Several of the others followed, their curiosity overshadowing caution. Lying on his back, Tom could not help but grin as he watched the animals approaching. *Now, if Slim doesn't get too antsy,* he thought.

Slim didn't. He stayed low, watching the performance from the brow of the hill. "Well, if that don't beat all," he whispered to himself. He checked his rifle and waited patiently for Tom to signal. The animals were getting closer and closer, stopping every few feet now to stare before inching closer. They had closed to within a couple of hundred yards, a shot Slim felt he had a fair chance of making. Still Tom made no move, just kept waving the bandanna. The antelope paused, as if considering the wisdom of continuing. Slim got ready. If they turned and ran, he would get off a shot as quickly as possible. But no, the antelope had not satisfied their curiosity as yet. Again, they edged closer to Tom. When they had advanced to a point less than one hundred yards away, they stopped once again. This was to be their last stop, for Tom suddenly rolled over and came up on one knee, bringing his rifle up as he did. Slim already had his sights fixed on the lead animal, but Tom got off two shots so rapidly that Slim hadn't even pulled the trigger when the two foremost animals fell. He was startled when the animal he was sighting on suddenly dropped, but he was quick enough to swing around and draw down on a third antelope before the whole herd bolted.

"Whoo, boy!" Slim shouted and jumped to his feet as the rest of the herd scattered over the prairie. "We got three of 'em!" He ran down the hill to join Tom, who was calmly retying his bandanna around his neck. "That was a fair piece of shootin'. You got two of 'em before I got off a shot."

Tom smiled. "Well," he offered modestly, "I had an advantage. I knew when I was going to shoot and you didn't."

"That was a fair piece of shootin," Slim insisted.

They loaded their meat on the packhorse and started back to rejoin the herd. Tom took a moment to look at the sun, then selected a line of sight across the rolling buffalo grass that figured to intercept Eli and the boys. Slim was in high spirits as he and Tom made their way back across the little stream and out across the prairie.

"Reckon ole Bris can go ahead and eat his sowbelly," he said. "The rest of us'll be eating fresh meat."

"Reckon so," Tom replied.

The sun was halfway between high noon and the horizon when they heard the first shots. It started with what sounded like an old muzzle loader and was followed after a few minutes by three shots, rapid fire from a breech-loading rifle. Tom and Slim pulled up sharply and listened. Several more shots were fired randomly. From the sound, they decided the shots were coming from northeast of their position, in a general direction of where the herd might be, although Tom figured the herd should have been farther east by then. More than likely, one of the boys hunting strays ran into some trouble. They kicked the horses into a gallop and headed in the direction of the shots.

As they got closer to the source of the sounds, they heard only an occasional shot fired, and that was from the repeating rifle. From his experience in the army, Tom could almost picture the scene before he and Slim topped the last rise between them and the fight. The picture proved to be accurate. From a distance of about half a mile, they could see the drama taking place. A lone rider was pinned down on the open prairie with no cover but that offered by his dead horse. He was holding eight hostiles at bay with his rifle. The Indians were circling out of range, obvious to Tom that the one muzzle loader he had heard was their only firearm. *Lucky for the downed rider*, he thought.

"Damn!" Slim exclaimed, "that looks like Bris's little paint."

Tom looked hard at the dead horse. It was Bris's horse, and he then remembered that Bris was working strays south of the herd. He drew his rifle from the scabbard and checked the load. Slim followed his example. "Let's separate a little. Start shooting as soon as you think you're in range. I don't expect they'll put up much of a fight." He didn't wait for Slim to respond and kicked Billy hard in the ribs and charged down the slope. Slim, right behind, fanned out to his right.

When he was within a couple hundred yards, Tom

raised his rifle and fired. When Billy was running flat out over level ground, he offered as steady a firing platform as a man could want. Tom's first shot found a home between the shoulder blades of a startled brave. Almost at the same time, he heard Slim's rifle cracking to the right of him. The seven remaining hostiles bunched at first and wheeled, pausing as if making a decision. The sight of two riders bearing down on them, filling the air with lead as they charged hellbent for leather, presented too formidable an enemy for their bows. They deemed it advisable to leave the field of battle to the superior firepower, all except one. While his companions fled toward the hills, one brave raised his lance overhead and shouted to them, his pony dancing back and forth as the rider expressed his defiance to the white men. Tom had by then reined Billy back to a canter; Slim followed his lead. Tom had learned enough of the several dialects he had come in contact with in the cavalry to recognize the Gros Ventres tongue. He couldn't understand all the insults the young brave was hurling his way, but he picked up enough to know that the Indian refused to show any fear of their guns. Slim raised his rifle.

"Let him be," Tom ordered. "He's just showing the others how brave he is."

Slim lowered his rifle, and Tom told him to go back and get the packhorse. As Slim wheeled around and galloped off, Tom sat quietly watching the young Gros Ventres, making sure he didn't make a move to fit an arrow in his bowstring. The Indian, evidently encouraged by the apparent standoff, advanced a few paces closer and continued his song of bravery. When Tom made no move toward him, he raised his coup stick and spurred his pony into a gallop. Tom hesitated. He brought his rifle up, but did not fire. He had to admire the young brave's show of courage. It was apparent that the young man now intended to count coup on him to gain the admiration of his comrades, who at this point were watching from a safe distance. *Let him have his show*, Tom thought. *The poor devils haven't got much left to live for*.

Tom remained stone still, watching the young brave as he advanced. He didn't move even when the Indian galloped right beside him and touched him on the shoulder with the coup stick. After the first pass, the Indian wheeled and offered a piercing war whoop to the heavens. He reined his prancing pony back and glared defiantly at Tom. Then he held his lance high up over his head and shook it in a sign of challenge to this confusing white man. When his enemy still showed no sign of emotion, the young buck mistook the lack of action for cowardice, a mistake that cost him his life. He drew a long skinning knife from his belt and, raising it high over his head, issued a challenge to the white man. Tom knew enough Gros Ventres to know he had been challenged to mortal hand to hand combat. He looked at the young man for a long time, his own face expressionless. Then he put a bullet between his eyes. The Indian rolled over backward and landed on his back in the dust. Tom looked at the crumpled form that had but moments earlier been a fierce young warrior. "Take me for a damn fool?" he muttered to the still form, then turned to retrieve Bris Collins.

Slim was already helping Bris collect his gear from the carcass of his horse when Tom rode up. Both men had watched in amazement the confrontation between Tom and the Indian brave. It did not surprise them that Tom shot the Indian. Instead, they wondered why he had hesitated in the first place.

"Damned if it isn't getting to be a habit pulling

you out from under a dead horse," Tom called out as he pulled Billy up and dismounted.

Bris laughed, able now to enjoy the humor in the situation since the danger was over. "I'll tell you one thing—I'm mighty glad you come when you did 'cause them red bastards would've figured out pretty quick I done fired my last bullet."

Tom stood looking at the dead horse for a moment. "You sure are hard on horses."

Bris chuckled again. "It warn't my idea to use him for cover. I was flat trying my best to outrun them buggers, but ole Pokey here warn't no match for them Injun ponies. I reckon I'm lucky they wasn't better shots than they was. They'da hit me instead of my horse."

Slim spoke up. "What the hell was you doin' with that Injun back there? I went after the packhorse, and, when I looked back, you looked like you was having a little chat with him. How come you didn't shoot him when he rode up to you like that? I was afraid you'd lost your nerve or something."

Tom merely shrugged indifferently. When Bris paused in his efforts to free his saddle and waited to hear the explanation, Tom answered. "He was a young buck, wanted to show his friends how brave he was. I've killed enough of his people in the last five years. I didn't think it would do any harm to let him count coup."

"That don't make no sense to me," Slim said, "ridin' up and tappin' somebody with a blame stick."

"It's big medicine to them. An Indian figures it's a lot braver thing to get up close and touch an enemy than it is to shoot him from a distance."

"What made you shoot him?" Bris wondered.

"He wasn't satisfied. I reckon he thought he had

me buffaloed. After he counted coup, he wanted to fight me with knives and really make a name for himself."

Bris laughed. "Well, hell, Tom, why didn't you knife-fight him?"

Tom looked serious for a flicker of a moment before he smiled and replied, "Because he might've won, and nobody but a damn fool fights with a knife when he's got a gun."

"I reckon," Slim agreed emphatically.

Bris climbed up behind Slim and they started off after the herd. The six remaining Indians rode back to retrieve their two dead companions after the three white men were well out of range. Tom was thankful they were armed with nothing more than bows or it might have been a different story. They were lucky that day.

Serious thoughts filled Tom's head as he rode in silence behind Bris and Slim. It was getting easier and easier to kill a man, and this troubled him. When he and Slim charged down the slope and he shot the first Indian at a distance he estimated at one hundred yards, it was no different to him than when he shot the antelope earlier that morning. With the second Indian, it was not the same. He had sought to spare the young man's life. It seemed like such a waste. He could still see the expression of disbelief on the Indian's face. What troubled him was that at the instant it happened he felt no remorse at all, no compassion, no regret . . . nothing. He hoped he wouldn't have to face the situation again.

The nights were already getting chilly by the time the herd reached the Little Missouri, although the days were still hot, and, since there had been no rain for most of the drive, the trail was dusty. They were making good time, so Eli decided to rest the herd for a day after they had forded the river. It turned out that he ended up resting them before they even crossed it. Cattle aren't too fond of crossing any river, and it was always a difficult job to push the ornery beasts into water. They had not expected the Little Missouri to be high enough to spook the cattle because there had been so little rain. What had been anticipated to be an easy crossing turned into a standoff between the drovers and the cattle. After spending the better part of an afternoon trying to push the lead steers into the water, only to have them panic and go plunging off in all directions causing the rest of the herd to balk at the river's edge, Eli finally admitted defeat. "We'll cross 'em in the morning," he decided. "Might as well take advantage of the good grass by the river and let 'em feed for the rest of the day. It ain't no more'n fifteen days to the railhead now anyway."

The cattle weren't the only ones ready for a rest. Everyone was bone tired, and those who were so inclined thought it a good opportunity to take a bath and wash some of the trail dust from their clothes. Most of the men peeled down to their bare skin and ran splashing into the cool waters of the river. Big Joe and Little Joe preferred to jump in, clothes and all. Tom begged a bar of lye soap from Smoky and moved downstream a few feet from the frolicking cowhands to give his clothes a serious scrubbing. He was soon joined by Bris and Doc. Bris waded into the shallow water and sat down up to his neck. Doc sat down under a tree on the bank.

"Better come on in and set down, Doc," Bris said. "This feels mighty good on a sore ass."

"No thanks," Doc replied. "I reckon I can still

stand myself. It ain't good for you to soak in water too long."

"Don't know what you're missing." Bris looked over at Tom, who was busily scrubbing his shirt with the bar of soap. He studied the man's bare back for a long minute before his curiosity got the best of him. "Tom, what in the hell tore up your back like that?"

At once self-conscious, Tom turned away in an effort to hide his scars. "Cheyenne," he stated simply and resumed his laundry.

"Cheyenne?" Bris pressed. "Arrow?"

"No, a bullet. That mess was made by the surgeon when he tried to get it out."

There was a long silent pause while they waited to hear the details of the story. It was soon evident to his two friends that the story was not forthcoming, and it seemed the prudent thing to let it lie since that was obviously his intention. While he said nothing more about it, the memory of it was still vivid in Tom's mind. It had been on a river much like this one, only now it seemed like a century ago. Still, he remembered every detail up to the point when the bullet slammed into his back. The memory was not pleasant. He was still green on the frontier, a young lieutenant with very little exposure to Indian warfare, when he had led a detachment of cavalry into that river, straight into an ambush. He was never blamed for it. It was a clever tactic and no one even suggested he was at fault for not seeing it as such. Andy Coulter was there. He rode into it blindly, too, and he was as sharp a scout as there was on the frontier. In fact, it was Andy who pulled him out of the river and hid the two of them, the only survivors, up under a riverbank while Little Wolf's Dog Soldiers combed the river for them.

"What?" He realized that Doc had said something

to him, but he had been so engrossed in his thoughts that it just then registered. He looked back at Doc, sitting under the tree. "What?"

"I said Smoky is a'ringing the supper bell. Ain't you gon' eat?"

His mind relaxed and a smile crossed his face. "Hell yes, I'm going to eat. Soon as I put on my pants."

Tom filled a plate with Smoky's concoction of antelope stew, seasoned with sowbelly, helped himself to a couple of biscuits, and poured himself a cup of pitch-black coffee. He found a place to lean up against a tree between Bris Collins and Slim. Balancing the plate in one hand and his coffee in the other, he sat down cross-legged. The brothers, Big Joe and Little Joe, found a tree close by them. They ate in silence for a while until Slim cleaned his plate and set it aside to roll a smoke. Slim always finished eating before anyone else. Smoky accused him of being part wolf, never chewing, just gulping it down.

Slim was eyeballing Little Joe while he rolled his smoke. After he lit up, he remarked casually, "I swear, Little Joe, when did you start wearing that pistol crossways like that?"

Big Joe, his mouth full of biscuit, answered for his younger brother. "Ever since he seen that bounty hunter in Oklahoma City wearing his'n like that."

"That ain't the reason," Little Joe answered quickly. "Maybe he did wear his'n like this, but that ain't the reason. It's quicker on this side."

Slim found the answer amusing and couldn't resist a little good-natured ribbing. "Quicker? Quicker than what?"

"Quicker than you can pull that damn horse pistol of your'n outta your belt."

"How you figure that?" Slim winked at Tom, pleased with the young boy's reaction to his teasing.

Little Joe was dead serious, unaware that Slim was simply having a little fun with him. He drew his pistol from the half holster he had fashioned from cowhide. "Quicker than your'n because my holster is pointing the handle right where my right hand wants to naturally reach." He held the pistol up for Slim to see. "I filed the sight offen the barrel so there ain't nothing to snag when I reach for it." He looked admiringly at the pistol, a Colt forty-five Frontier six-shooter, and cocked the hammer back, then carefully released it so that it didn't fire. "And she's got a hair trigger. When I need my gun, I want it right now." He returned the weapon to its holster on his left hip.

Slim laughed. "Well, you may git your'n out a couple of seconds before I do, but when I git mine out, I hit what I'm aiming at. That's the most important thing. A couple of seconds ain't that important when you're shooting at a rattlesnake."

Little Joe looked hard at Slim, not sure whether he was being joshed or not. It was plain to Tom that Little Joe didn't consider it a joking matter. "I'll tell you this, Slim, I ain't worrying 'bout no rattlesnakes but, if you and me was to have it out, a couple of seconds would be the reason I got you instead of the other way around. And I wouldn't miss."

Suddenly there was a silence over the little group of men, and it became apparent that the subject of conversation might be getting somewhat touchy. Tom was immediately aware of the potential for a good-natured ribbing to escalate into something beyond a joke. It was obvious that Little Joe did not find anything humorous about it. Tom recognized a somewhat immature but hotheaded young buck in Little Joe, a young rooster who was eager to test his spurs. And Slim was too easy-going, and too down-right dense, to realize Little Joe would take him seriously. It was time to diffuse the situation. He placed his hand on Slim's arm and said in a soft voice, "Let it lay, Slim, it ain't funny anymore."

"Aw, hell, Tom, I didn't mean nuthin' by it. Little Joe knows that. Don't you, Little Joe?"

Tom didn't like what he saw in Little Joe's face. The boy wasn't sure whether his manhood was being tested or not. The intensity in the boy's expression looked as though he was already working himself up to a face-off against Slim. This was the first sign of friction Tom had seen in the entire Broken-T crew, and he didn't want to see it go further, especially when Slim was too dumb to see his teasing wasn't taken lightly by Little Joe. "Sure, Little Joe knows that," he said. "He knows you don't mean anything by it." Turning to Little Joe, he added, "If you're lucky, you won't ever need to shoot anything but rattlesnakes with that pistol."

"Maybe so, Tom, but I ain't a'feared to use it on a man if I have to."

Big Joe spoke up at that point. "No, little brother, you ain't a'feared to use it on a man." His tone was laden with the impatience of one who had heard the discussion before and grown weary of the talk. "Ever since he seen two half-drunk cowhands face each other in Oklahoma City to see which one could shoot the other one first, he's been practicing and practicing with that damn gun."

Little Joe pulled his pistol again and looked at it thoughtfully. He wiped a drop of oil from the handle and replaced it in his holster before he answered. "You don't never know when you're liable to be called out by somebody, and I aim to be faster than anybody else in the territory."

Big Joe threw up his hands in despair and turned to Tom for support. "I swear, I give up. You talk to him, Tom. He's gonna git his ass shot off one day, talking like that."

Tom looked long and hard at Little Joe. He knew there was nothing he could say to influence the boy. "Little Joe's man enough to make his own way. All I can say is I wouldn't waste my time or risk my neck in a showdown with somebody who might be faster getting his gun out than I was. If I know a man's set on killing me, I'm not likely to give him any edge. Most likely I'd shoot him on sight. I expect most men would do the same." His face softened into a smile. "But that ain't got nothing to do with anybody on the Broken-T, has it, Little Joe?"

"I reckon not." Little Joe got up and carried his empty plate back to the chuck wagon.

Tom looked at Slim. "You better mind how you tease that boy."

Chapter VI

According to Eli Cruze's calendar, they left the Little Missouri on a Thursday. He was no doubt the only one of them who knew the day of the week, or cared, for that matter. For the crew of the Broken-T, one day melted into the next and was no different from the day preceding it. When they were on the home range, the weeks were delineated by Sundays, for Eli didn't expect his men to work a full day on Sunday, aside from the necessary chores that had to be done even if Christ Himself came again. But on the trail, there were no Sundays, so they started the herd out on the last leg of the drive. Tom and Bris rode point. Behind them, Slim and Doc were the swing men, Big Joe and Little Joe rode the flanks, and two young boys from Texas, Henry Cousins and Johnny Crabb rode drag. Smoky rattled along behind in the chuck wagon with the remuda bringing up the rear. The weather was good, and there was plenty of grass and water for the herd. Tom felt at peace with himself and with his past.

"How's it going, Tom?"

He looked over his shoulder to see Eli riding up behind him. When he caught up to him, he reined back and let his horse pace Breezy. Tom didn't answer, and just nodded to his boss. He knew Eli could see how things were going, and he obviously was in a mood to talk.

"No more sign of Injuns," Eli offered. "I don't expect none between here and Fort Lincoln."

"I expect not," Tom replied.

They rode along in silence for a few minutes before Eli spoke again. "Well, how do you like punching cows for a living?"

Tom smiled, "Better than pulling teeth, I reckon."

"I'll say this—you sure caught on to it quick enough." When Tom didn't answer, he continued, "I won't beat around the bush, Tom, I've been watching you pretty close for the last few weeks, and I admire the way you handle yourself. You ain't like the rest of these boys. I mean they're all good boys, but they're just young and wild. You appear to be a lot more responsible. Don't think I ain't noticed how most of the boys already look up to you. Well, what I'm gittin' at is I could use a good man to help me run the Broken-T." He hesitated, looking for the right words. "Like a foreman, I reckon."

Tom was completely taken by surprise. When he had signed on in the spring, he didn't expect to stay for the fall roundup. Now, Eli's offer was so sudden and unexpected that he was almost at a loss as to how he felt about it. "Damn, Cap'n, I don't know. I appreciate the kind words. I guess I'll have to think about it."

Eli pressed the issue. "You know, you ain't exactly no kid no more. You can't just drift around the country all your life. And the cattle business is solid. People have to eat, and they're always gonna want beef, unless somebody invents some new kind of animal, and I don't reckon that'll happen."

"I have to admit you're right there. I just never gave it any thought before. Hell, at one time I thought I was going to retire from the army. I don't have any idea what I'm good at, that is, good enough to make a living."

"You're good at cattle, that's what you're good at. Not only that, but you can handle the men, and you're a helluva shot with a rifle, and you ain't afraid to use it, according to what Slim and Bris tell me."

"Damn, Eli . . ." Tom started. It was obvious to his boss that Tom was trying hard to decide what to do.

" 'Course I don't expect you to stay on at thirty dollars a month. We'd have to adjust that some. If things work out, why, hell, I might be able to cut you in for a share. There's gonna be plenty for two men. Whaddaya say, Tom? You wanna help me build the Broken-T into the biggest spread in Montana?"

Tom hesitated for a moment more, looking for a reason not to. Finally, he shrugged and smiled. "Hell, why not?"

Eli's face broke out in a wide grin. "Good! By God, we'll be a team to reckon with." He stuck out his hand and Tom shook it. "Now, let's git these critters to market." He wheeled and rode off toward the far side of the herd.

"I guess I'm in the cattle business," Tom said to himself. The more he thought about it, the more it pleased him. It was a solid feeling. He was going to put down roots.

Four more days found them skirting the fringes of Bismarck, its buildings now visible on the horizon. To Tom, it was a very familiar sight. He had seen it countless times before when returning to Fort Lincoln from the many patrols into hostile country, only this time he would be avoiding the army post and going to the cattle pens by the railroad instead. There was a noticeable sense of anxious anticipation floating over the entire Broken-T outfit. The men were chomping at the bit to complete the drive. They were in sight of the saloons and bawdy houses that were to them the rewards for the hardships of the trail. Even the cattle seemed to exhibit an air of urgency, unaware of the fate awaiting their arrival at market. Tom attributed their behavior more to the fact they could smell the Missouri than a celebration of the end of their long walk across Montana. They would be riding the train from here on but they weren't going to be too happy when they made their final destination.

Eli directed his men to move the herd south of the pens to be held there while he rode into town to negotiate the sale of his beef. There was good grass there, and he figured that maybe they could add on a pound or two while awaiting sale. Understandably, there was a rush of volunteers to go into town with Eli. Since there was no threat of trouble this close to the fort, Eli conceded that a skeleton crew should be all that was necessary to watch over the cattle, but he questioned their eagerness to see the town before he sold the cattle and could pay them. It didn't seem to matter to the men, starved as they were for the pleasures a town could offer. A few of them had saved a little money. The others would be content to borrow or just look until payday. The thought of merely seeing a female was enough to excite most of them, so the problem was who to appoint to stay behind and watch the herd.

Unlike the other men, Tom was not especially anxious to see the town. He had seen it before, although he had never been to the small collection of stores and saloons that bordered the stock pens. Consequently, he volunteered to stay with the herd. Smoky volunteered to stay with him, and Eli had to appoint two others to help them. If things went as they usually did, Eli assured them, the cattle would be sold almost immediately and they would soon get their turn at the saloons. There was a little good-natured grumbling from the two unlucky drovers as they watched the rest of the Broken-T crew gallop off toward the collection of rustic wooden buildings.

Following Eli's instructions, Tom assigned one of the younger boys to the remuda while the rest of them watched over the herd. It was late afternoon, almost dark, and the rest of the crew had been gone for several hours when Tom pulled up by the chuck wagon. Smoky had just put on a new pot of coffee, so Tom stepped down to have a cup before making another circuit of the herd. The quality of the coffee had improved tremendously over the last several days of the drive since Smoky was no longer concerned with running out of beans. He would be taking on new supplies in a day or two, so it was unnecessary to reuse the old grounds over and over.

"I swear, Smoky, this coffee almost tastes like the real thing," Tom teased. "You must not have used as many buffalo chips in this pot."

"Odd damn, you better be glad you got any a'tall."

Tom laughed. "How come you stayed behind? I figured you'd be roaring to get into town to visit the ladies."

"Shit," Smoky snorted. "They ain't nuthin in that there town potent enough to excite these old bones. Cows are better company."

Tom grinned at the old man. "You may be right," he replied. He stood silently for a long time, sipping the black, hot liquid, listening to the low murmuring of the peaceful herd. A hint of breeze stirred the buffalo grass in the shallow basin, making the prairie appear to be gently bobbing in the growing dusk. He realized a feeling of peace within him, and he was glad his days of Indian fighting and military life were behind him. The cattle business was the future, and he was glad now that fate had directed him to the Broken-T. He would help Eli build a cattle empire on the rich grasslands of Montana.

"Somebody's wearing out a horse," Smoky observed casually, breaking Tom's reverie.

Tom turned to follow Smoky's gaze. In the gray light of early evening, he could make out a rider coming from town at a full gallop, a small cloud of white dust leaving a phosphorescent trail behind him as his horse weaved his way around the small gullies and rises. They continued to watch the progress of the rider as he approached the herd. When he was within about fifty yards of the chuck wagon, they recognized the rider as Slim, riding as if the devil himself were after him. Within seconds, he burst into the circle of firelight and, leaping from his horse, called out frantically, "Tom!" He gulped a couple of swallows of air before he could form his words.

"Odd damn, Slim . . ." Smoky marveled.

"Tom!" Slim exclaimed and thrust out a piece of paper he had folded up inside his shirt.

Puzzled, Tom took the paper and unfolded it, holding it up to the firelight. He was at once struck by the bold headline on what proved to be a Wanted poster. Beneath the Wanted was a five-hundred-dollar reward offered for information leading to the capture of one Thomas R. Allred, for the murder of an army private. For a moment, he seemed to black out, his mind reeling from the shock of seeing his name in bold print. At first, he couldn't understand, and then, almost immediately, it was obvious to him—Spanner! That lying son of a bitch had undoubtedly coerced the men who were witnesses to the incident at Jubal

Clay's store. At once he admonished himself for being fool enough to think the other two men would hesitate to tell the authorities anything other than what Spanner told them to.

"What the hell?" Smoky wanted to know. Tom didn't answer him, just handed him the poster. "Odd damn, Tom, what's it say? I cain't read." Tom still did not answer, his mind racing wildly.

"It says Tom's wanted for murdering a soldier," Slim blurted. "And that ain't the worst of it, Tom. I hightailed it out here to warn you. They know you're riding for the Broken-T."

Tom recoiled visibly, and jerked his head around to look Slim in the eye. "How do they know that?"

"Doc told 'em."

"Doc!" He couldn't believe it. "Doc told them? Told who?"

Slim held his hands up in an effort to calm Tom down. "Wait a minute, Tom. He didn't go to do it. We started to walk in the saloon, and Big Joe saw this here poster on the wall beside the door. There was a deputy sheriff standing right out front, and Big Joe was just joshing, said he could use five hundred dollars. Before he thought what he was saying, Doc blabbered out, 'Thomas Allred! Why that's Tom!' and that there deputy had him by the collar before he could say spit." Slim put his hand on Tom's arm, pleading, "Honest to God, Tom, ole Doc never meant to spill it. It just come out."

"I know, I know," Tom assured him. He was trying to think. His first impulse was to saddle Billy and run. What should he do? He couldn't decide whether he should ride in and try to clear his name, or head for the high country. It was all happening too fast.

"Tom," Slim pressed, "you got to git goin'. There'll

be a posse making up in town. You need to put some ground between you and them and I mean right now!"

"He's right, Tom," Smoky said. "I'll git you up some grub to take with you."

Tom still did not move. He was fighting with his sense of justice and, at the same time, listening to his soul's natural instinct to survive. He realized that the decision he made at this moment could have a monstrous impact on the rest of his life. He didn't want to make the wrong move. Quickly, he tried to play the events out in his mind, based on probability and his experience with army trials. He knew that once he was handed over to the army, there was the distinct possibility that he could languish in an army stockade indefinitely, waiting for a court-martial. And, even though he was now a civilian, he was sure he would be bound over to the military for trial since civilian law in the territory was still in a fledgling stage at best. Still, if Jubal and Ruby could testify, they would certainly attest to his innocence. But no, he told himself, the court would place more emphasis on the testimony of the three soldiers over that of the civilians. They always did. He could imagine the scene in the courtroom: him, a former officer who had been cashiered from the service, already hated by many of his fellow officers for letting a hostile prisoner escape. He didn't like the odds.

"Tom," Slim pleaded, "you better git goin'."

His back stiffened suddenly. His head jerked up like a wild mustang when it senses danger on the wind. "I'm going," he stated. "Slim, thanks for warning me. Do one more favor for me, will you? Cut Billy out of the remuda while I load my packhorse."

"Yessir!" Slim replied and started for the remuda on the run.

In less than fifteen minutes he was ready to go. As he prepared to step up in the saddle, Smoky came running from the chuck wagon with a large sack of provisions.

"There's enough possibles in here to carry you for a while," Smoky said as he tied the sack on Tom's packhorse.

"Thanks, Smoky." Tom climbed into the saddle and looked down at his two friends. A sudden wave of sadness swept over him as he realized he was giving up a way of life that had seemed to be right for him. The impact of it hit him hard. His partnership with Eli was not to be. Once again, he was adrift. He reached down and took Smoky's extended hand, shook it, then grasped Slim's waiting hand. "Just to set things straight. I did what any man would have done. That soldier was fixing to shoot Jubal Clay."

"Odd damn, Tom, you didn't have to tell me that. I know you ain't the murderin' kind."

"Maybe I'll see you again someday." He turned Billy west, back toward Montana territory. "Tell Eli I didn't feel I had any choice. I'm sorry to have to run out on him like this."

"You take care of yourself, boy," Smoky called after him. "If I don't see you again, I'll save a place in hell for you." He and Slim stood and watched the two horses until they faded into the darkness, now falling in earnest as the final rays of the sun were clipped off at the horizon. When they could no longer see him, Smoky said, "I'm gonna miss that boy." He nudged Slim on the arm. "Might not be a bad idea if you was to get on your horse and ride out toward the south a mile or two and circle back to the herd."

*　　*　　*

When Eli Cruze heard the news about Tom, it was the same as if someone had told him there was alkali in the water hole. "Damn!" was all he said at first. "Damn!" He had been looking for someone like Tom to come along for two years, and now this. The sheriff and two deputies rode out to the herd just after sunup that morning, hoping to find Tom, but he was long gone by then. Eli found it hard to believe what they said about Tom. He didn't think he could be so wrong about a man. A murderer they said. If Tom did murder the man, maybe he needed killing. "Well, I reckon I got along before he showed up. I reckon I'll get along just as fine when he's gone."

Of all the Broken-T crew, Bris Collins was the hardest hit by the turn of events. He was close to Tom, and counted him as good a friend as he had. He was genuinely disappointed at not having had a chance to say good-bye. He and the rest of the boys who were in town the night before got back to the herd barely ahead of the sheriff and his deputies. Bris had borrowed enough money to buy himself a bad head in the Cowtail Saloon, and he was in no mood to receive the news as it was. He got even more riled when, in answer to the sheriff's questions, Smoky said he thought Tom might have ridden out toward the south last night. But he calmed down when Slim confided that it was him, not Tom, who had ridden south. Bris watched, a thin smile on his face, as the three lawmen scouted around until they picked up Slim's trail and disappeared over a rise south of the camp.

"Now who's gonna pull me out from under my horse next time Injuns get after me?"

Chapter VII

A thin frosting of snow lay along the top edge of the crude sign nailed to a lone tree standing guard over the road into town. Tom paused to study the sign for a moment. It proclaimed the odd assortment of wooden buildings and tents to be Miles City. Tom was cold. His fingers were numb, and his feet felt as if there were a thousand tiny needles pricking them, and real winter had not even arrived yet. A steady wind had beaten the back of his neck all day as he rode south, causing him to wish he had taken his buffalo robe from the bottom of his pack before he broke camp early that morning. Although late in the fall, the days had been pleasant enough for the past several weeks, so he had no clue that this day would turn so cold. But it seemed apparent that old man winter was at last giving notice. A strong wind came in from the north around midmorning, bringing dark clouds with it. By noontime, the temperature must have dropped twenty degrees, and with it a light dusting of snow powdered the prairie. It encouraged Tom all the more to press on to Miles City before nightfall.

When he stopped to think about it, he had to admit he was pretty lucky to be there on the outskirts of the small settlement. He had spent the last month on

the upper Missouri, trapping. It was a dangerous
place to hunt beaver because the Blackfeet didn't permit any trappers in their territory. They were a warlike people, even more feared than the Sioux or
Crow, and he knew he was gambling with his scalp
every day he remained there. When Tom left Bismarck that night over a month ago, just ahead of the
sheriff, he needed to find a place to hide for a while.
He also needed some money since he had been forced
to leave before he could collect his wages from Eli. The
upper Missouri territory was the logical place, provided he could keep his scalp. Nobody would be too
anxious to search for him in the heart of Blackfoot
country. Add to that the fact that the upper Missouri
offered the richest beaver trapping around—better
than the Yellowstone country, better than the Milk
or Judith rivers. The big fur companies had been trying for years to trap the upper Missouri, but their
efforts were met with such fierce resistance from the
Blackfeet that their expeditions almost always ended
in failure, costly in horses, supplies, and the bloody
loss of lives. Tom knew it to be a huge risk, but he
reckoned that a man alone could stay out of sight of
the treacherous Blackfeet where a party of trappers
could not. This was a philosophy he had picked up
from Squint Peterson, who had spent most of his life
alone in the mountains in the midst of hostile
territory.

So he trapped the small streams and rivers of the
upper Missouri country, at least until the winter
started to set in and he was forced to quit. It was a
lonely, dangerous existence, up to his waist in icy
water for much of the time, constantly looking over
his shoulder for the sudden Indian attack that might
be imminent, always careful to hide his horses and
his campfire. He was especially cautious when check-

ing his traps, for if his bait sticks with their castor-scented tips were not concealed, a sharp-eyed Blackfoot might find them and lay in wait for him.

The weeks passed slowly, the danger weighing down the passage of time. Occasionally he felt sure he would be discovered before he could pack out with his furs, and it tested his courage to remain day after day alone in that hostile land. *Well,* he thought now, *I've done it, trapped the Blackfoot country and lived to tell about it, and have a fair load of pelts to buy the supplies I need.*

There was still some risk involved in going to Miles City. It was near Fort Keogh for one thing. But he had never been there before, so he didn't expect to meet anyone who might have known him. The fort hadn't been there long. It was built after the mop-up operations of the Sioux war when the warriors of Sitting Bull had been defeated and the great chief himself had escaped to Canada. The garrison at this fort would not very likely know about Tom Allred. Besides, he had been cold long enough. He yearned for a warm place to spend the night so he decided to chance it. Cold and loneliness could do funny things to a man, even to the extent where he would take sizable risks just to find a warm place to lie down. The Wanted poster he had seen at Bismarck had no picture of him, just his name, so he didn't think there was much real danger of his being recognized.

As a town, Miles City didn't appear to be much more than a few buildings, but he could see signs of potential. There were more buildings under construction, and there was already a two-story structure that looked to be a saloon and trading post combined. He pulled his coat collar up around his face, pulled his hat down low on his forehead, and nudged Billy forward.

He rode the length of the main street, keeping Billy at a slow walk so he could look the place over thoroughly. It looked peaceful enough. Down at the far end of the street, he found a livery stable and pulled Billy up in front. "Well, boy, looks like you're going to stay in a hotel tonight. I still got enough money left to do that. Maybe buy you a little supper, too." He dismounted and, pulling the wide door open, led his two horses inside.

The stable was dark. Tom stood in the open doorway for a moment, looking for someone to take the horses. No one was in sight. "Hello," he called out. "Anybody here?" There was no answer. *Well,* he thought, *there are plenty of empty stalls.* He led Billy to a stall on the end of the row and unsaddled him. He put the packhorse in the stall next to Billy, then threw his gear in with Billy. He planned to sleep in the stall with the horses. That pack was all he owned in the world, and those pelts were the only things he had to trade for supplies. He didn't want to be separated from them.

"Howdy."

He turned to discover a squat bowlegged barrel of a man watching his movements with seemingly casual interest, a double-barreled shotgun cradled in one arm, a lantern in his other hand.

"Evening," Tom replied. He finished arranging his saddle pack into a bed and then came out of the stall. Nodding toward the shotgun, he said, "I hope that doesn't mean you aren't going to rent me a stall."

The man acted surprised. "What, this? Ah nah, mister. This here shotgun always rides on my arm. I'd be glad to see to your animals. Long as you can pay fer it."

"Well, I've got enough for tonight, not counting a little that I hope to find some supper with. If it's all right with you, I'll leave the horses till I can change my plews into cash."

"Fine with me." It was obvious this was not out of the routine for him. Not many travelers came in with money. At least this one had some furs. Even if he tried to get out without paying, the stable keeper had his horses and the customer had to get by him and his shotgun to get them. "My name's Dan Turley. Folks around here call me Pop. Me and my two boys own this here stable. As far as something to eat, you can get you a good supper up the street at the Cattleman's. I'll watch your stuff for you."

"I appreciate it, Pop. I've been eating wild meat for a month, and I could sure use a change." He looked around to see if there was anything that needed his attention before leaving his possessions in the care of this squat little man. He must have appeared hesitant.

"Don't worry 'bout your possibles. Anybody in Miles City'll tell you Pop Turley is as honest as he is ugly." He held the lantern up to study Tom's face more closely. "And I'm most always here. If I ain't, one of my boys is. I sleep up there." He pointed toward the hayloft. "If you're short of money, you can sleep with your horses for ten cents more a day."

"Fair enough," Tom said. "I'll be going then." He pulled his rifle from the saddle boot and walked toward the stable door.

"Where'd you ride in from?" Pop called out after him.

Tom kept on walking, answering over his shoulder, "Dakota."

"I won't ask you where you're headed. You'd more'n likely say it was none of my business."

Tom laughed. "Maybe."

"What's your name, young feller?"

"Does it matter?"

"I reckon not." He hesitated a moment, then added, "I'll just call you Dakota."

Tom stood inside the door for a few moments until he took in the entire room. There were maybe a dozen customers in the Cattleman's at that hour. Most of them were seated at tables eating supper, although it was obvious that most of the supper crowd had already gone. Many of the tables still had dirty dishes on them. Over against one wall, three men—drovers by the looks of them—were standing at the end of a long bar. Behind the bar, and talking with the three drovers, stood a heavyset man with a bald head and a long handlebar mustache. He paused in the middle of his conversation to study the stranger standing in the doorway, rifle in hand.

"Howdy," the barkeep called out. "Come on in and make yourself to home."

Tom nodded in reply and walked across the room to the bar. All conversation in the saloon ceased while everyone stopped to consider what manner of man had joined them. There was no hostility apparent, merely curiosity. After a short pause, the general hum of conversation resumed.

"What's your pleasure?" the bartender asked, flashing a manufactured smile for Tom. "Beer? Hard likker?"

"No thanks. Is it too late to get some supper?"

"No, sir. It's not too late. I'm sure there's some stew left back in the kitchen. My wife'll fix you up something." He came around the end of the bar and pushed some dirty dishes aside on one of the tables, clearing a place for him. "Set yourself down and I'll fetch Marthy." He watched Tom seat himself and then he yelled toward the kitchen, "Marthy!"

After a moment, a bony little woman in a dirty apron appeared in the doorway from the kitchen. Her face looked tired and drawn as she reached up to brush a thin wisp of gray hair from her face. She did not change her expression as she stared at the stranger seated at the table. "You want supper?" she asked without enthusiasm.

"Yes, ma'am, if it isn't too much trouble."

"Stew and biscuit, all that's left."

"That'll do fine."

She turned and retreated to the kitchen. While he waited, Tom unbuttoned his coat and made himself a little more comfortable. He laid his rifle across the arms of the chair beside him and casually glanced around the room. Here and there he met a curious eye, occasionally followed by a polite nod. In a country where it wasn't wise to ask too many questions, especially from a stranger, the atmosphere in the Cattleman's seemed cordial enough. In a few minutes, the woman came back with a plate heaped with a thick stew, with three biscuits riding on top.

"Pay Kirby," was all she said when she placed it in front of him.

He assumed Kirby was the barkeep. "Yes, ma'am," he replied and immediately dove into the plate of food. He hadn't realized how hungry he really was until the beefy aroma filled his nostrils. He was half-way finished when the door opened and Pop Turley came in, quickly shutting the door behind him in an effort to keep the chill night air outside. He nodded to Kirby and the others in the room, looking around until he spotted Tom.

"Kirby," Pop called out, "how 'bout a drink of that there kerosene you call likker. I need somethin' to warm my blood." He walked over and pulled a chair up across from Tom. "I see Marthy fixed you up with something to eat."

"She did," Tom replied, "and it's pretty good eating, too."

When Kirby brought his glass of whiskey to the table, Pop gestured toward Tom. "Kirby, this here's Dakota. Just rode in tonight." He looked back at Tom. "Watch out for this cuss. This stuff he sells for likker'll take the hide offen your teeth." Both men laughed. "But his wife can sure cook."

"Pleased to meet you, Dakota. You plannin' to be in Miles City for a spell or just passin' through?"

"I'm not sure. To tell you the truth, I'm just looking for a place to stay warm till winter's over. I've got some pelts I'd like to sell. Know where I could unload them?"

Pop answered. "Jacob Branch buys some skins. He's got a store over near the fort. 'Course it ain't like it was ten, fifteen years ago when the American Fur Company had a fort near here. A man could make some money on skins then. I reckon it's near petered out now, but, like I said, Jacob Branch still buys some to ship back East."

Tom nodded, "I'll go see him in the morning."

The trip to Jacob Branch's store was disappointing. As Pop had lamented the night before, furs were not bringing much money anymore. Branch seemed a fair man, but he burdened Tom with the long sad story about the demise of the beaver hat back East. Everything was silk now. Tom understood, but was still disappointed to have to settle for the price he got. It wasn't much of a grub stake—most of it was traded for the possibles he needed. There was but a small amount of cash money left over, enough to acquire a well-used Sharps Forty-five, One-twenty, and some cartridges. His Winchester was all he needed in most cases, but he felt the need for a good buffalo gun. His Winchester would fill the buffalo's hide full of holes before it finally stopped the animal. The Sharps would knock the beast down with a forty-five bullet with a hundred and twenty grains of powder behind it. Although it had been used a good bit, the weapon was well taken care of, and Mr. Branch gave him a fair deal on the price.

Low on money now, Tom could still last for a while, anyway. He badly needed his pay from the Broken-T, and he resolved to make the trip over to the Musselshell to collect it. He had earned it, and he was certain Eli Cruze would hold it for him. He was probably taking too much risk by remaining in this part of the country, but with winter coming on he felt it was all right to chance it. He could not really accept being a wanted man. In his mind, he had done nothing wrong. What he did, any man would have done. Perhaps if he had stopped to give serious thought to the danger he was in, he might have realized the need to leave the territory. Still, he rationalized, no one in this part of the territory knew what he looked like. As for the garrison at Fort Keogh, he didn't know where soldiers were sent from to man the new fort, but he was certain it was not a detachment from Lincoln. *Hell,* he thought, *nobody pays attention to every drifter who rides into Miles City. If I keep my nose clean, there won't be any reason to call attention to me.* He was right for the most part, at least for three more days.

"Damn, Sarge," the young trooper complained, "my behind is about froze off." They had been in the saddle all day, and there was only an hour or so of daylight left. "Why don't we ride on in to the fort and find us a place to get warm?" His was the only complaining voice, but he knew he spoke for the other six men.

Sergeant Waymon Spanner did not answer at once. He was thinking about other things. The cold air made his nose ache. Since he had the cartilage smashed by a rifle barrel across the bridge of his nose, he had difficulty breathing, and the cold weather made his nose sore, as if he had rheumatism. It didn't do much for his disposition as he was reminded of the man who had changed his profile so drastically. In fact, since that day, he had lived with one thought in his mind—to track down Tom Allred and kill him. He had volunteered to lead the search detail, and he had been charged with the responsibility of bringing the fugitive back to Fort Lincoln for court-martial. Those were his orders—to capture him if at all possible. But Spanner had no notion of bringing Tom Allred back alive. And now time was running short. Winter was about to set in, and if he didn't find Allred before the first heavy snows fell, he had little hope of finding him at all. His superiors would call it off with the bad weather. They had already been combing the towns in the territory for over a month. He was beginning to think Allred had left the plains and headed for the mountains. He rode on for a while in silence, then finally answered the young trooper.

"Wilson, you whine like a damn woman. But I'll tell you what we're gonna do. We're gonna ride into Miles City before we go to the fort, and you boys can have a little drink while I look around. That oughta warm up your backside some, hadn't it?"

Wilson grinned. The thought of a visit to the saloon before reporting in was appealing. "You're giving the orders, Sarge. I reckon if we had to, we could stand a little drink."

"I thought you could. If you got any money, you might want to get something to eat, too. It'll beat anything you're likely to get at the fort."

The light of day was beginning to fade away when they rode down the main street of Miles City. Those who weren't patronizing the Cattleman's had gone home to supper. At Spanner's instructions, the men tied up in front of the saloon while he continued on to the sheriff's office. There was no one in the small wooden building but a boy of perhaps fifteen or sixteen.

"Sheriff's gone home to supper," the lad replied to Spanner's question.

"Damn. When will he be back?"

"He won't, 'lessen somebody sends for him."

Spanner looked irritated. "Are you a deputy?"

"No, sir."

"What do you do?"

"What I'm doing right now. I tell people the sheriff's gone to supper."

Spanner was rapidly losing patience. "Boy, I need to see the sheriff. This is official army business."

The boy was unmoved. "Well, sir, I reckon you could go out to the sheriff's house. I can tell you how to get there."

"I reckon *you* better do that." Before the boy could begin, Spanner continued, "You had any strangers through town in the last few weeks? I'm looking for a man, a man name of Tom Allred."

The lad thought on it for a moment. "Well, there's always strangers coming through town. I ain't seen nobody by that name. Why are you looking for him?"

"He's wanted by the army for murder. You ain't seen anybody? A man traveling alone?"

"No, sir, 'cept maybe a feller named Dakota. But he don't sound like the feller you're looking fer."

"Is that so? How long has he been in town?"

The boy scratched his head. "Two or three days, I guess, but he don't seem like the kind of feller'd murder somebody."

"Yeah? Well, this feller I'm lookin' for might not seem like that either. Where can I find this feller, what was his name, Dakota?"

"Most anywhere around town, I reckon. He eats at the Cattleman's, been staying at Pop Turley's stable down at the end of the street."

"I reckon I'll go down to the stable and have a look before I go to see your sheriff."

"How you doin' boy? You getting tired of standing around in here?" Tom held the bag of oats and stroked Billy between his ears while the horse munched eagerly. "You know, you've been getting kind of spoiled, sleeping in a warm barn, eating oats. You'll be so spoiled you won't be worth a nickel come springtime." Suddenly, Tom was alert. He couldn't say he heard something: it was a sixth sense maybe. He couldn't explain it, but for some reason he sensed danger. Billy's ears flicked up. The horse sensed it, too, or sensed Tom's reaction. Tom wasn't sure which, but it was enough to spook him. He slowly lowered the feed bag to the floor and eased over to the front of the stall where his rifle was leaning up against the wall. Moving very slowly and deliberately, he placed one foot down carefully after the other in the straw, making as little sound as possible. Outside the stall, in the center of the stable, he stopped to listen. Had he heard something? If it was Pop or one of his boys, they would have made a great deal more noise. Maybe he was just jumpy. It was probably a rat in the hayloft, or one of the horses rustling the straw. He listened—nothing. He decided he was just overly edgy.

"Just throw that rifle down right on the ground there, and put your hands up real high," a voice said from behind him.

For an instant Tom froze.

"I said drop it," the voice commanded. It was followed by the metallic click of a hammer cocking. Tom let the rifle fall to the floor. "Now, Loootenant, turn around real slow."

Spanner! Even in the half-light of the stable, there was no mistaking the tall, rawboned figure of Sergeant Waymon Spanner. Tom felt every muscle in his body tense.

"Now you just stand right there and keep your hands high where I can see 'em."

Tom stood motionless while Spanner struck a match and lit a lantern that Pop kept hanging on a post. The flame glowed bright and illuminated a ragged circle of light in the darkened barn, throwing long shadows across the floor. Spanner set the lantern on top of a feed bin, keeping his long cavalry pistol leveled at Tom while he did so. As Tom watched the sergeant, a feeling like a cold round ball invaded the pit of his stomach. He could not be sure what Spanner might do, but Tom knew he would not be long in enlightening him.

"Well, now, if it ain't my favorite officer. You know, I've been covering a helluva lot of territory looking for your sorry ass. And here we are, just you and me." The flickering light from the lantern caused the shadows to dance an eerie pattern across his face, a face that appeared broken and scarred, the result of Tom's rifle barrel across his nose. Seeing the focus of Tom's gaze, his lips parted in a sneer and he smiled wickedly. "Admiring your handiwork? How do you like my nose, you son of a bitch?"

"You brought it on yourself, Spanner," was Tom's sober reply.

"Is that so?" Spanner spit back at him. "Well, that's what I'm gonna tell the provost marshal when I get back to Lincoln—he brought it on hisself. You might be thinkin' I'm taking you back for trial, but I ain't 'cause you're gonna try to escape. Too bad the rest of the detail is in the Cattleman's having a drink, ain't it? Nobody but me and you, and you gittin' ready to try to escape." He raised the pistol and took aim at Tom's chest. "You know something, Looote-nant? I'm gonna really enjoy this."

Tom didn't wait for the bullet to come. He dove into the stall, rolling over and over, grabbing his rifle as he did. The roar of the revolver split the silence of the stable at almost the same time. Tom heard the splintering of wood as a bullet ripped into the side of the stall. It was followed almost immediately by a second shot that buried itself in the post where Tom's head had been a split second earlier. In the confusion that followed, he was not clear on the chain of events. He was aware of the horses screaming and stamping, and he remembered rolling over and over until he crashed up against the back of the stall. He did not remember cocking his rifle or even pulling the trigger. In the blur of the moment, he remembered seeing Spanner's image standing in the open end of the stall and the look of shock on his face when he was almost cut in half by three shots from Tom's rifle. The shots were fired in such rapid succession that he didn't recall cocking the lever between each shot. The most vivid image he retained of the incident was the last brass cartridge shell as it flew, end over end, up against the side wall of the stall, and the surprise on Spanner's face as he seemed to be staring at its flight.

Tom didn't move from his position, sitting with his back against the hard boards of the stall, for what seemed like a long time. It was as if he were paralyzed, oblivious to the screaming of the stamping horses around him. He wanted to get up, but his legs felt drained of strength, so he simply sat and stared at the lifeless body of Sergeant Spanner. He might have sat there until the sheriff or the rest of the soldiers came had he not glanced toward the hayloft and encountered a pair of terrified eyes peering over the edge of the loft. He had forgotten that Pop's youngest boy, Jimmy, was still around the stable. The sight of him served to shake Tom from his trance, and he scrambled to his feet and attempted to calm Billy down. His sense of reasoning having returned, he knew what he must do.

"Jimmy!" he yelled. "Get down here and help me with these horses!"

While the boy slid down the ladder from the hayloft and went from stall to stall, quieting the nervous horses, Tom saddled Billy and rolled up everything he owned in his buffalo robe. He strapped on his saddle pack and led Billy out of his stall. Before mounting, he reloaded his rifle and shoved it into the boot. Pausing for a moment, he said, "Tell Pop I'm leaving ten dollars to pay for what I owe him. I'm taking this sack of oats to boot."

Jimmy just stood there, staring wide-eyed at the body lying at his feet, the straw underneath it darkening with blood.

"You hear me?" He thrust the money into the boy's hand.

"Yessir," the boy choked out, "I'll tell him."

Chapter VIII

Tom pointed Billy's nose across the Yellowstone until the lantern glow of Miles City faded away. Then he crossed the river again and headed northwest. About midnight, a light snow began to fall. *Good*, he thought, *they'll play hell trying to pick up my trail now.* Still he pushed on, wanting the security of knowing there was plenty of distance between him and whoever might be following. The snow stopped before daylight, and he was pleased to note that a blanket of at least a couple of inches had settled over the prairie. At sunup, he pulled up in a stand of trees that offered some protection from the wind and made camp. Knowing there was little danger of someone spotting his smoke in the early morning sunshine, he built a fire and spread out his buffalo robe for a few hours' sleep.

Rested, he started out again in bright sunlight that promised a better day than the one before. The snow had not amounted to much, being no more than a squall and merely a rehearsal for what would soon be coming. It crossed his mind that he had sworn not to spend another winter holed up by himself under a mountain. But here he was, on the run and as alone as a man can get. Maybe he could winter with the crew at the Broken-T. He considered the possibility for a while. Eli Cruze was a man of principles, and Tom was a wanted man. How would he feel about having a fugitive from the law on his crew? The more Tom thought about it, the more he discounted the likelihood of being welcome at the Broken-T. Other ranchers might not be so concerned, but Eli *was* a man of principles. He dismissed thoughts of wintering with his former companions. Still, he could pick up his money and push on until he found a town far enough away to be out of Fort Lincoln's or Fort Keogh's jurisdiction. There were dozens of little mining towns buried back in the hills where civilization was but a glimmer on hope's horizon. Maybe his brother, Little Wolf, and Squint Peterson were somewhere far off to the west. He was as much an outlaw as his brother, maybe even more so. If he could find them, he might be welcome there . . . or he might not.

He let Billy choose an easy pace as he rode over the rolling hills of buffalo grass. If he had estimated his location accurately, and he was pretty sure he had, he should be able to make the Broken-T by early the next day. His mind was occupied with thoughts of the friends he had left behind at the Broken-T when Billy suddenly stopped and threw his nose up in the air, snorting the wind. Tom's first thought was *Horses! There must be another horse nearby.* Then he glanced down and noticed the obvious trail left by a travois and two horses crossing his own trail. His mind had been so preoccupied that he would have missed the tracks if Billy had not stopped. "A good way to lose your hair," he scolded. After a quick look around him, to make sure he was not about to be attacked, he studied the trail. It led off across a hill toward a deep draw. The trail was still fresh. They could not be far away, and they were Indians for sure. The ponies were unshod, and, after examining the tracks more closely, he figured there were maybe three or four of them, one pulling a travois. It seemed an odd time of year for a small party to be traveling the plains. They should be on a reservation or in winter camp by now. He decided it might be a good idea to have a look for himself.

The trail was easy enough to follow through the small patches of snow left by the previous night's storm. There seemed to be no attempt to disguise the tracks. He decided to circle and pick up the trail on the far side of the draw. There was no use taking a chance on riding into an ambush since he wasn't sure the Indians hadn't spotted him. He pressed Billy into a gallop and rode to the east for a half mile or so before cutting back north to pick up the trail at the far end of the draw. When he got there, however, there was no trail to pick up. He scouted back and forth for a while before deciding the Indians he followed were still in the draw. He considered forgetting about them and pushing on toward the Broken-T as he looked at the lined sides of the ravine where the Indians must surely be. The best thing he could do might be to leave well enough alone. But his curiosity was too greatly aroused at this point, and he decided he would at least take a look from the hill on the downwind side of the draw, if for no other reason than to eliminate his worry about them.

There were three of them, two women and what appeared to be either a sick or wounded man. Tom could not be sure from that distance. Though early in the day, the women appeared to be making camp. Their horses were tethered among a stand of cottonwoods. Tom assumed that meant the man's condition was too critical to travel farther. It was obvious the three Indians posed no threat to him, but still, he was curious enough to want a closer look. He hesitated for a long time, deciding. Finally, he crawled over the crest of the hill and worked his way down behind a dead tree from which he had a better vantage point. He lay there for perhaps a quarter of an hour, watching the activities of the three Indians. He could not see the man but he was sure that the women were Cheyenne. Tom found it odd that they should be traveling alone, and almost in Blackfoot territory at that. As he watched, he struggled with another decision. These miserable-looking hostiles meant nothing to him. They had once been his enemies. He had fought them, along with the Sioux. They were supposed to be on a reservation anyway. The government had declared that any Cheyennes or Sioux not on the reservation were considered to be hostile. But, he reminded himself, he was not in the army now. It was no longer his job to kill Indians. These three human beings were obviously in need of help, and he found it difficult to turn his back on them. "Ah, what the hell," he muttered and rose to his feet.

He was almost upon them before his presence was detected, which he found strange in itself. In fact, when he thought about it, it was damn unusual he had even been able to watch them from back there on the hill without their knowing it. The horses discovered him first, causing the women to look up from their task of building a fire. When they saw him, their first impulse was to take flight and both women started to run but they were held by the wounded man on the travois. Not knowing what to do, and obviously unwilling to abandon the man, they stood helpless, shifting from one foot to the other as if in a resolute death chant. Their eyes were wide with fright as they stared at the menacing form of the white man.

Tom held up his hand in a sign of peace and advanced slowly toward them. The women's unblinking gaze fixed on him, their pitiful swaying now accompanied by a soft guttural moaning. They were preparing to die. Tom made sign language to tell them he came in friendship. It served to halt their death chant, but still the women stared at him in obvious fear. When he was close enough to talk, he attempted to tell them in sign language and the few words he knew in Cheyenne, that he was there to help and meant them no harm. Both women relaxed somewhat. At least they seemed to accept the obvious: they had little choice but to trust the white man's words. They were in no position to resist. He looked at the two young women. These people were obviously starving. Their weary unblinking eyes, peering at him from the deep hollows of their gaunt faces, told him why they had been unaware of his presence—they were too weak to care. He turned his attention to the man on the travois.

He was a Cheyenne Dog Soldier by the look of his weapons—a bow and lance, now lying impotent beside him on the travois. He was wounded, a thick mud-and-leaf poultice covering an area the size of Tom's hand on the warrior's chest. He was not fully conscious, yet Tom could see a faint spark of life in his eyes as he removed the poultice to get a look at the wound. When he removed it, he almost gagged. It was a bullet wound apparently, and it had festered, the scarlet rays of spreading infection radiating out from the center of it.

"Damn!" he muttered. Then in Cheyenne he asked one of the women, "How long?"

She answered in sign, "Nine days."

He had seen wounds like this in battle when they didn't receive medical treatment right away. Sometimes, the most insignificant of wounds were mortal when they became infected. It depended on the constitution of the man. Tom had to cut the bullet out and cauterize the wound in hopes that would stop the spreading infection. That was the only thing he knew to do, and there was a definite risk he might kill his patient with the treatment, but he was damn sure going to die without it. But first, he told himself, he had to get them something to eat or he was going to have three dead Indians on his hands.

Something in his manner must have conveyed his intent to the two women, for they seemed to accept his instructions eagerly. He was sure they had been at their wits' end as the man got progressively worse and they went longer and longer without food. First he helped them gather up more wood to liven up their small campfire. They watched in amazement as he put his two little fingers in his mouth and whistled two shrill blasts. In a moment, Billy came trotting over the crest of the hill, his reins dragging along the ground. From his saddlebag, he got two strips of jerky and gave them to the women. They took them eagerly and immediately started chewing the tough meat. From the looks of the wounded man, Tom figured it was useless to try to feed him jerky. He needed some strong broth, and the only way he was going to get it was if Tom could find some game. So, once the women were warm and their hunger temporarily satisfied, he told them he was leaving, but he would be back as soon as he found some meat. They nodded, but he could see in their eyes that they never expected to see this white man again. After trying his best to reassure them, Tom climbed up on Billy and rode out of the draw toward the open prairie.

It was late in the year for hunting on the prairie. It would be pure luck if he found anything other than a rabbit or some small game scurrying from a hole. His best bet, he figured, was to ride toward a line of small hills he could see on the horizon. They were partially covered with trees, which indicated there might be a stream there. If there was any game around, it would most likely be there. If he had minded his own business, he thought, he knew he would be no more than a day's ride from the Broken-T. He immediately reprimanded himself for his selfishness and returned his attention to the business at hand, to find some food for three starving people.

It took the better part of two hours to reach the hills. When he reached the shelter of the trees, he encouraged Billy with a slight pressure of his heels and the horse labored momentarily to scale a steep slope that guarded a small, shallow stream. He reined Billy up to an abrupt stop. Something, some slight movement, caught Tom's eye and he froze. Below him, on the other side of the stream in a patch of scrub, a branch wiggled. The scrub was too thick to see what had caused the movement. He glanced quickly from side to side before riveting his gaze on the branch. As he watched, he slowly drew his rifle from the saddle boot. The bush shook. Whatever it was was moving now. He raised the rifle and took aim on the scrub, following the shaking branches as they progressed toward an open space. *Come on out of there*, he thought. *Let's see if you're man or meat.* He waited. The shaking stopped, and he thought for a moment that whatever it was had turned and gone the other way. Then it appeared. He started to squeeze the trigger then stopped. It was a calf! He

hesitated for only a moment more before pro-
nouncing, "You're meat."

He would never forget the look of gratitude he
received from the two Cheyenne women when he
rode back that night with the yearling. If there had
been any remaining distrust between them before he
rode out earlier that day, it was gone now. One of
the women skinned the calf and proudly held the
hide up for him to admire. He nodded his approval,
unable to avoid a wry smile at the prominence of the
Broken-T brand. There was plenty to eat that night.

The next order of business was the surgery on the
wound. Tom didn't look forward to it, but knew it
had to be done. He explained as best he could what
he was going to do, and the women seemed to understand. He explained that it would be very painful
for the man. They nodded understanding. One of the
women spoke then.

"This man is my husband. If you do not cut the
evil from his chest, he will die."

Tom nodded. He wanted to make doubly sure they
understood what he was trying to do. He didn't want
to take a chance on digging out the man's infection
and getting a knife in his own back because of a
misunderstanding. He drew his knife from his belt
and got the sharpening stone from his saddle pack.
While he worked on the blade, he studied the man
he was about to operate on. He was still feverish.
His wife had tried to feed him some soup she made
from the calf's heart, but he was unable to get any
of it down before sliding off into a half stupor. Tom
tested the knife's edge and decided it was as sharp
as he was going to get it.

"You might have to hold him down when I start
cutting. I don't know how weak he is, but I reckon
you two can hold him." The women took a hand

each and sat on it. When they were ready, Tom straddled his patient and got ready to cut. After pulling the poultice aside and cleaning the wound with hot water, he sat poised, the knife ready to strike. He glanced at his two assistants. "Ready?" They nodded. He looked back at the young man. "Boy, I hope you're ready, 'cause this is gonna hurt like hell."

He pressed hard on the skinning knife, cutting deeply into the festering wound. The wounded man's whole body stiffened and his back arched like a horse about to buck. There was one long low grunt, like what a man would make if he had been hit with a large rock, and then his body went limp and his breath emptied from his lungs. Tom glanced up to see the alarm in his wife's eyes. She thought her husband was dead. Tom himself wasn't sure he hadn't killed him. He felt for his pulse with his finger, then reassured the woman that her husband was still breathing. She responded with a weak smile. He decided he'd better get on with it while the man was totally unconscious. He made a long incision across the length of the wound and immediately had to sit back for a moment to catch his breath when a quantity of bloody pus oozed from the wound. He shook his head and snorted in an effort to rid his nostrils of the acrid odor of rotted flesh. He glanced again at the women. Neither had moved or even reacted. "Damn!" he swore and returned to his task.

It seemed to him that he cut and probed for hours. In fact, it was probably no more than ten or fifteen minutes. In spite of the coolness of the early winter evening, he was sweating heavily by the time he triumphantly held up the ugly little ball of lead for them to see. They smiled their grateful approval. He had removed quite a lot of rotted flesh from around the wound and there would be a noticeable hole in the poor man's chest but he knew, if he didn't get it all, the infection would simply continue to eat away at him. When he had done about as much as he thought he should, he wiped off the knife, then buried the blade in the coals of the fire. He noted the puzzled expressions on the faces of both women.

"You do not sew the wound together? Do you want me to do it?" one of the women asked.

"Yes," Tom replied. "It must be sewn up but first it must be sealed off or he might keep on bleeding inside. Can you sew it?"

"Yes," she answered solemnly. "I did it for my father but he died anyway."

Well, I'd just as soon have you do it, he thought to himself. *This one will probably die, too. He doesn't look any too perky right now.* To the woman, he said, "I'll burn the wound now and then you can sew it up."

He withdrew the knife from the glowing coals, the point of the blade heated to a red glow, and, before it had a chance to cool, he thrust it into the open wound. Both women recoiled in shock as foul smoke rose from the burning flesh. Tom held his head to one side to avoid the smell as he pressed the knife firmly against the exposed wound. Satisfied that his work was done, he turned the patient over to the women. They stripped some sinew from the slaughtered calf and used it to sew up the wound as neatly as any army surgeon he had ever seen. Then he convinced them to leave the dirt and buffalo dung poultice off and let the wound breathe. He took a long look at the man before covering him with his buffalo robe. As he gazed at the still body of the Cheyenne warrior, he thought, *Well, we'll see if God wants to perform one of his many miracles, because I wouldn't bet on you making it till morning.* The irony of the situation did not escape him. He had spent years trying to kill these people. Now he was trying to keep one from dying.

The man was strong. Morning came and he was still alive, much to Tom's amazement. He had troubled thoughts about his predicament all during the night. If he had kept his nose in his own business and kept on riding, instead of stopping to help the Indians, he would be at the Broken-T that morning. As it was, he felt somewhat trapped. Since he had undertaken to play the Samaritan, he felt obligated to stay with them until they could travel again on their own. He wasn't sure how long that would be, and he wasn't sure what he should do if the man didn't make it and he was left with two Cheyenne women. So he was greatly relieved to see his patient regain consciousness during the afternoon. Tom was further amazed to see that the man's fever was gone and his wife was able to get some of the broth in him. After another night's rest, the man was lucid, and there was little doubt that he was going to recover.

The young warrior was totally confused as to the events of the past several days and what had taken place to cause him to come out of his great sickness. He was further astonished to find a white man in their company. He was alarmed at first sight of Tom, but his wife soon calmed his fears and explained that, were it not for this white man, he would most likely be among the spirits. When he understood what had happened, he was anxious to express his gratitude.

"My name is Sleeps Standing," he told Tom. "My wife, Lark, has told me of your kindness to her and her sister. I am in your debt."

Tom smiled and shrugged. "You owe me nothing. I'm just happy to see you recovering."

During the days that followed, Tom became more acquainted with his three new friends. It seemed a strange friendship, more akin to a truce. Although the two men were not enemies at this point, still Tom learned that they had fought on opposite sides at the Little Big Horn when Tom had fought his way in to Major Reno's relief with Captain Benteen's regiment. Who could say how many times before this meeting they might have actually fired at each other? Tom had led many patrols against the Cheyenne and Sioux. For Sleeps Standing's part, he had never met any white man on peaceful terms before. He came to trust Tom, and they would talk in the evening by the campfire when Tom returned from his daily hunting trips. Sleeps Standing explained to Tom that he and the two women were running from the soldiers. They had hoped to join some of their people in the mountains to the north. He refused to report to the reservation after the big battle at Wagon Box, saying he would not live as a white man's dog in a pen. He and several other warriors started on a journey to the land of the Nez Perces with their women and old people. They had been on the trail for little more than a week when the soldiers found them and attacked. This was when he received the wound in his chest. He managed to escape with his wife and her sister, whose husband was killed. All the others were slaughtered. No prisoners were taken.

Tom stayed with them for three more days until Sleeps Standing regained enough strength to travel. Both men knew they could not stay camped there on the prairie for much longer. Already, the days were getting colder. The small grove of trees would not offer enough protection against the frigid weather that was soon to blanket the prairie. Also, there would be no game to hunt. So, as soon as he was strong enough, Sleeps Standing instructed the women to pack up the camp and prepare to leave. On the morning the white man and the three Cheyennes parted, Lark and her sister both hugged Tom and thanked him again. He and Sleeps Standing clasped hands, and the Cheyenne warrior pledged his undying friendship to his white friend.

"Here," Tom said, "let me take a look at that wound before you go." He waited while Sleeps Standing pulled his robe aside exposing the still hideous wound. "I think it's healing right along. I'm sorry I had to make such a mess of it. I had to get all the rotten part. Left a helluva hole."

Sleeps Standing laughed. "It does not matter." He turned to his wife and remarked, "Now I have a hole in my chest like Little Wolf. He would laugh to see it."

The mention of the name brought Tom up short. "Little Wolf? Did you say Little Wolf?"

"Yes, Little Wolf." He seemed amused by Tom's reaction. It was a name that brought fear to the hearts of many white men. "You have heard of him?"

Tom found it hard to believe the coincidence. "Yes, I have heard of him," he replied softly. He realized there was more than one Indian with the name of Little Wolf, so he added, "At least I know one Cheyenne warrior named Little Wolf."

Sleeps Standing smiled proudly and stated, "Little Wolf is my brother-in-law. His wife is Rain Song, my wife's other sister. He and I have fought many battles side by side."

Tom was speechless for the moment as he considered this strange twist of fate. He had thought a great deal on the probable fate of his brother, even though other more pressing needs had occupied most of his thoughts. Finally he looked at Sleeps Standing and stated calmly, "Little Wolf is my brother."

They did not understand at first, thinking that Tom was saying all Cheyennes were his brothers, a statement of friendship. Sleeps Standing smiled broadly and nodded his approval. Tom realized he did not understand the significance of his statement.

"Little Wolf," he repeated steadily, "Little Wolf is my brother."

Sleeps Standing did not answer. Tom could see the confusion in the man's eyes as he looked first to his wife and then to her sister. Seeing the same confusion in their eyes, he turned back to Tom. "Little Wolf, the son of Spotted Pony, is a Cheyenne war chief," he tried to explain.

"I know this," Tom responded. "He is a mighty war chief now, but he is my brother. We have the same mother, same father." Still met with a look of disbelief, he asked, "Is his skin white, like mine?"

Sleeps Standing did not answer at once, as if having to pause and think about it. Then he conceded, "Yes, his skin is white, but his heart is Cheyenne." It was plain to Tom that even though Sleeps Standing now counted him as a friend, he was reluctant to believe Little Wolf could be related to any other white man, Tom included. Such was the lofty status his brother held among the Cheyenne.

"Do you know where he is?"

"No," Sleeps Standing answered. "He has gone away into the far hills, beyond the land of the Nez Perces. It is my hope that I will find him someday."

The Cheyenne's answer was sincere—Tom decided he was not being evasive. "Did he go alone? Was there another white man with him? A big man?" He held his arms wide at his shoulders, emphasizing Squint Peterson's massive bulk.

Sleeps Standing nodded excitedly. "Yes, a big white man," he answered.

Tom stood thinking about the coincidence of this meeting with Little Wolf's brother-in-law. He could not decide what to do about this information. In truth, he wasn't sure he wanted to find his brother at all. Maybe Little Wolf had no desire to be reunited with him. After all, they hardly knew each other. Their only common interest was Squint Peterson, who was friend to them both. It was little more than speculation anyway, he decided. Sleeps Standing had no idea where to find Little Wolf, and only knew that he was in the high mountains. That covered a hell of a lot of territory. He decided it best to forget it for the time being. His immediate concern was to find a place to pass the winter. He had already lost almost a week's time with the three Indians.

They wished each other well and parted company, the Indians headed to the north toward Canada, the white man to the west. Before they said their final good-byes, Tom said, "If you find Little Wolf, tell him you met Tom Allred." Sleeps Standing nodded and smiled, then rode out of the wooded draw.

Chapter IX

Eli Cruze looked up from the bridle he was mending. He paused in his work to watch the lone rider approaching from across the river. He was leading a packhorse, and, since he was coming on at a leisurely pace, Eli was only mildly curious. He was still too far out to identify, yet there was something familiar about the way he sat his horse, and Eli strained a little harder to make the figure out. As the rider came up from out of the shallow crossing, Eli still couldn't identify him. The man was wrapped in a heavy buffalo robe. It wasn't until there was barely two hundred yards between them that he recognized the man's horse.

"Well, I'll be . . ." he muttered aloud. "That there's Billy." He put the bridle down and stood up. A crooked smile broke the usual stoic expression on his face as he now recognized Tom Allred. "Tom!" he called out as he walked out of the rough harness shed to meet him. "Goddam, Tom! What are you doing here?"

"Howdy, Cap'n," Tom replied, smiling. "Figured you'd seen the last of me, I reckon."

"Hell, no. I knowed you'd show up sometime to collect your pay. Step down and let's see if Smoky's got some coffee."

"I ain't wasting good coffee beans on ever' saddle tramp that stumbles in here!" a voice boomed from behind them, and Tom and Eli turned to see Smoky, grinning from ear to ear, coming out to greet their visitor. He grabbed Tom by the hand and shook it vigorously. "Odd damn, Tom, I thought you'd done be in Canada by now . . . or gone under."

"How you doing, Smoky?" Tom could not help being touched by the warm welcome he received. It was like coming home. "I've been in the upper Missouri. I didn't get to Canada, but I wasn't far from it."

Eli's grin faded, and his face took on a serious look for a second. "I reckon you know the army's still looking for you. Ain't it a bit risky hangin' around these parts?"

"I reckon, but I figured there wouldn't be much going on after this long and it being close to the middle of winter. I plan to keep on moving, but I need to pick up the money I got coming."

"Well, I got it for you," Eli stated. "It belongs to you, and I was gonna hold it till you showed up, no matter if it was next year."

"I knew you would, Cap'n, and I'm grateful. God knows I need it."

Smoky poured up three steaming cups of black coffee, and the three men sat down under the lean-to by the harness shed. Tom inquired about his friends on the Broken-T; Bris and Slim, Doc, and the others.

"The whole crew's out working for a change," Eli answered, "trying to keep the cattle from wandering too far from our range and freezing to death. I swear, I don't know how many we'll still have after this winter. It's gonna be a rough one."

Tom held the hot coffee cup in both hands and

gazed thoughtfully into the fire. "I notice you been doing a little work around here. Finished the bunkhouse, I see." He looked around to see what other changes had been made. "Got a harness shed, too."

"Yeah." Eli grinned. "We'll have us a ranch here one of these days."

After a moment's silence, Tom asked, "Seen any army patrols?"

"No, not for 'bout a month. Like you said, cold weather must of slowed 'em down some." Eli paused before adding, "But there was a fellow come through here a week ago. Said he was a special deputy. Looked more like a bounty hunter to me. Said he was lookin fer a feller called Dakota. Said he killed a soldier over in Miles City." Watching Tom's eyes, he saw the slight glint that told him what he already suspected. "He described this Dakota feller's horse. Sounded like Billy."

Tom's eyes shifted to the ground, then back to meet Eli's gaze. "Yeah, it was Billy. I should have known better than to think I could get by without anybody knowing who I was." His eyes went cold as steel. "But I'll tell you this, Cap'n, I had no choice. He was bound to kill me if I didn't get him first. He said he had no intention of taking me back to Lincoln alive."

Eli placed his hand on Tom's arm to reassure him. "Hell, I know it, boy. But the fact of the matter is, now it ain't only the army looking for you. Now there's bounty hunters too. What are you gonna do? Keep on running?"

"I don't know. Hell, I reckon. Would you turn yourself in if you were me? I don't see any way I can convince a court-martial I didn't have any choice but to shoot two men."

Eli looked as if he was about to argue the point,

but he just shook his head and said, "I reckon not."
He was silent for a long moment while he thought
about it. "But I'll say this, if you're gonna run, then
you better get on with it because this here bounty
hunter looked pretty damn woolly. Didn't he,
Smoky?" He looked at the cook and got an enthusias-
tic nod of agreement. "He looked like the kind that
won't stop for winter or nuthin' else."

Smoky chimed in, "Cap'n's right, Tom. That there
feller looked like bad luck, a back shooter if I ever
saw one."

Tom paused to consider this latest development.
The thought of the bounty hunter didn't scare him
as much as it brought a feeling of frustration and
dismay. The whole series of incidents had been one
misunderstanding after another. It seemed ridiculous
that anyone should be hunting him for any reason.
He had done nothing more than defend himself.
There was a long silence while Smoky and Eli waited
for him to speak. Finally, he sighed in resignation,
stood up, and threw the dregs of his coffee cup out.
"I guess I have no choice but to move on." Then he
looked back at Eli and asked, "I wonder how he
knew to come here looking for me, if he didn't know
my real name."

He was met with blank expressions from both
men. "Why, I don't rightly know," Eli said. "I think
he was just working a circle of ranches out from
Miles City, hoping to strike pay dirt."

Tom thought it over. "Yeah, you might be right.
He was probably just working the whole territory,
looking for somebody named Dakota." He hesitated
again, trying to work out the best course of action
for him to take. He was reluctant to leave. This ranch
had been the closest thing to a home he had found
for a while. He would have at least liked to stay and

see Bris and the other boys before pushing on. But the more thought he gave it, the more Tom was convinced that the smartest thing for him to do was to leave this part of the country, and the quicker, the better. "I reckon I'll start out first thing in the morning."

"It's probably the best thing to do," Eli replied. "I'll get your pay for you."

"Well, you better take out enough to pay for one yearling, 'cause I butchered one of your cows to feed a starving Indian family back on the prairie." He went on to tell them about his chance meeting with Sleeps Standing and the two women. While Smoky found it hard to imagine why he had gone to so much trouble to keep three Indians alive, Eli was a compassionate man and declined to take settlement for the cow.

"Hell," he allowed, "I wish I knew how many I lose every year to them thieving savages. One more won't matter much." Eli constantly strived to hide his generous nature behind a gruff facade, but Tom knew better—he had known Eli to purposely cut out a few head and leave them for the Indians when game was scarce.

The three friends sat in front of the campfire until well after dark. The talk was light, and the lean-to reflected enough heat to keep them warm even though the temperature dropped, turning the night air to a brittle cold. When the conversation finally played out, they moved inside the log-and-mud bunkhouse to sleep. Tom was grateful to get at least one warm night's rest, having no notion that morning would change his plans entirely.

It was the first sound night's sleep Tom could remember in quite some time, without the worry of who or what might be sneaking up on him. He didn't bother to analyze his feeling of security. Maybe it was the sense of permanency afforded by the solid walls of the bunkhouse, or being reunited with friends. Whatever the reason, he slept like an exhausted man and awoke the next morning to a world covered with a blanket of snow. It must have started soon after he had fallen asleep and continued all night, for it took the efforts of both himself and Smoky to shove the door open the next morning.

"Odd dam!" Smoky exclaimed as he carefully stepped through snow up to his stubby knees, trying unsuccessfully to keep the snow from spilling over the top of his unlaced boots and onto his faded red long handles. He didn't even get to the corner of the building before stopping to empty his bladder, shivering as he stared at the yellow pattern he was etching in the snow, and pleading with that part of his anatomy to make haste before he froze to death.

Tom laughed at Smoky's discomfort as he relieved himself on the opposite side of the building. It was damn cold. The storm had moved in overnight, and none of them saw it coming. As quickly as he could, Tom finished and struggled through the snow to get back inside, where he found Eli, standing in his underwear, stoking the woodstove in the middle of the room.

Eli looked up as Tom came in. "I don't reckon you'll be starting out in this mess. It's still coming down, and that sky don't look too promising. You'd best wait it out."

"I think you're right. I'll wait and see how bad it's gonna get. At least I don't think I'll have to worry about anybody coming to look for me in this weather."

"Odd damn," Smoky fretted as he scrambled

around with the coffeepot. "I wonder if the boys got caught out in the open." He pushed the door open again and reached out to scoop up a coffeepot full of snow to boil.

Eli paused and watched Smoky as he placed the pot on the little stove, which was glowing a cherry-red by then. "I hope you didn't scoop up any of that yellow snow," he joked, then added, "It won't be the first time those men woke up under snow. Bris and Doc oughta be close to the line shack. They probably holed up there last night." His tone turned serious for a moment. "We probably got cattle scattered all over."

There wasn't much they could do that day except make sure their horses were protected from the weather as much as possible. Around midmorning, the snow tapered off and there was a little break in the overcast skies so that for a portion of the after-noon, the sun broke through. After seeing to the stock, the three men concentrated mainly on staying warm. Tom helped Eli patch a couple of places in the roof of the bunkhouse where some melted snow found its way inside. After that, he spent the remain-der of the day working on his personal gear, cleaning his rifle, and seeing to the condition of his saddle and bridle. It appeared likely he would be working in snow for quite a while, and he didn't want to have to mend any worn gear out in the open when his fingers would be so cold he could hardly bend them.

While they worked on the roof, he and Eli talked about his staying on at the Broken-T till spring. After some discussion, they both came to the conclusion that the army would, in all likelihood, wait until the winter let up to send a detail out to search for Tom. And, they reasoned, the bounty hunter had already been there looking for him. He would most likely

not return. The prospect suited Tom. He was happy
to hole up with his friends for the winter. The Broken-T felt more like home to him than any other
place he could think of.

They awoke the following morning to clear skies.
The storm hadn't lasted as long as they had expected.
Tom rode out to the south to check on any strays
that might have gotten themselves in trouble in the
snow. Eli headed north, leaving Smoky to take care
of the ranch by himself. Most of the men would be
working the main herd back toward the Broken-T
to a sheltered draw near the river. The tough, trail-
hardened Texas Longhorns did not provide the
prime beef that the purebred strains did, but when
it came to surviving the elements, they were by far
the best. Eli was confident they would scratch
enough grass out from under the snow to survive.

Tom found one cow frozen to death beside a small
stream, no more than a half mile from a tree-lined
pocket where a half dozen cattle had huddled together to ride out the storm. It seemed as good a
place as any to leave them, so he rode on, looking
for any other strays he could find. He took a wide arc
to the east before turning back toward the Broken-T
without sighting any more of Eli's cattle. He got back
to the ranch about an hour before dark.

A few of the men were back at the ranch when he
got there. He recognized Doc's speckled gray from a
distance. The other horses were not as easily identified as Doc's, his gray holding the distinction of
being the mangiest critter in the Montana territory.
When he turned Billy into the corral, he turned to
find Doc walking to meet him.

"Well, look what the cat drug in," Doc called out,
his grin creating a wide gash in his beard. "Smoky
said you was back."

"How you doing, Doc?" Tom said, returning the grin. "Yeah, you know what they say, a bad penny . . ."

"Me, and Big Joe, and Little Joe come in a little while ago. 'Bout froze our asses off last night. Reckon most of the other boys'll be in tomorrow or the next day." He grabbed Tom's saddle and threw it on his shoulder and the two of them started toward the bunkhouse. "Smoky said you might stay on till spring."

"Yeah," Tom replied, "I was considering it."

Big Joe and Little Joe were inside talking to Eli and Smoky when Tom and Doc entered the bunkhouse. Big Joe got up from his chair by the stove and greeted Tom warmly, but Tom couldn't help but sense a coolness from his younger brother. He nodded hello to Tom, but it was devoid of any warmth. At the time, Tom didn't give it much thought. Afterward, it occurred to him that Little Joe had very little to say during the entire evening. In contrast, Big Joe was in a jovial mood, obviously cheered by being in the warm bunkhouse after spending several nights out in the cold. Little Joe barely grunted in response when spoken to, sitting away from the others, his chair tilted back against the wall. Finally, when the conversation found a lull, he startled the group of men with a question.

"Tom, I reckon you still got a price on your head, ain't you?"

A ponderous silence fell on the room. Tom hesitated before answering him. It was obvious the subject had been carefully avoided up until that moment. "Yeah, I guess I still have, Little Joe."

Little Joe pressed the issue. "I reckon the bounty's more than it was, now that you killed that other soldier in Miles City."

"I reckon." He glanced quickly at Eli, wondering who had told Little Joe about the incident.

Eli was quick to jump in and change the subject. "Hellfire! Everybody knows Tom Allred ain't no dang murderer. The sooner we drop that subject, the better. Smoky! Ain't there some cold biscuits or something left to help soak up this coffee? I swear, it's about to eat a hole through the bottom of my belly."

The other men seconded Eli's request, and the subject was successfully avoided during the balance of the evening. But there seemed to remain a slight pall over the conversation. It served to make Tom feel a mite uneasy, knowing the thought was on their minds, no matter how deeply buried. One thing for sure, Little Joe appeared to be troubled by it. Tom glanced at him several times during the evening to find the boy staring at him, only to look away quickly when their eyes met. Finally, Smoky declared that he was ready to call it a day, and shortly after, one by one, the men took to their blankets until only Tom was left to reflect on the strange manner in which Little Joe had greeted him. The boy's attitude troubled him. It reminded him of what he had become, and he didn't care much for the picture.

Morning brought another clear day, and as he rose, Tom caught the unmistakable aroma of sizzling steaks from the cookhouse. The weather was evidently good enough for Smoky to cook breakfast in the open lean-to they referred to as the cookhouse. Tom dressed as quickly as he could and hurried around the corner of the bunkhouse to tend to his bladder's insistent nagging. Finished, he started straight to the cookhouse to get his morning coffee. Rounding the corner of the bunkhouse, he was startled to find Little Joe waiting for him.

It was immediately apparent that something was wrong. It was the way Little Joe stood, his feet spread wide, with no heavy coat in spite of the freezing morning air. Tom could not help but notice the pistol on his left hip, the handle angled across his stomach, his right hand hanging loose and relaxed at his side. Tom remembered Little Joe's questions about the reward in the previous night's conversation. He did not want to believe what his common sense was telling him at that moment. Little Joe was supposed to be his friend. He had ridden with him all summer. And he was still little more than a boy. Surely he must be reading this wrong. He cautioned himself to be very careful how he handled this.

"Morning, Little Joe." His words were delivered evenly with a calmness in his voice that was almost soothing, the way a man would talk when approaching a wild horse. "Aren't you a little chilly out here without your coat?"

Little Joe's expression did not change, his eyes unblinking, and they narrowed when he spoke. "Tom, I reckon I'm taking you in for murdering them soldiers."

Tom did not reply at once, his gaze meeting Little Joe's and holding it. When he did speak, it was still in a soft, calm voice. "Little Joe, I don't think you've thought this through. You don't want to do this."

Little Joe took one step backward as if to give himself more room. "It ain't gonna do you no good to talk about it. You're wanted by the law, and I'm the one's gonna take you in."

Doc and Big Joe happened around the corner of the building and stopped cold in their tracks when they realized what was happening. At first, neither man could think of anything to do but stand and watch, their mouths agape in disbelief.

Tom made no move. It was not hard to figure why Little Joe was facing him off. Five hundred dollars was a lot of money and, as Little Joe had pointed out the night before, maybe it was more than that by now. Yes, he figured, the money was part of it, but he knew the main reason. It wasn't really about money at all. Little Joe was set to face him down in a gunfight if Tom took the bait. It was an instant way to gain a name for himself, killing the man who was wanted for two killings himself. This was what was eating at Little Joe last night. Tom berated himself for not recalling the discussion about gunfighters on the cattle drive last fall, and how dead set Little Joe was on becoming the fastest gun in the territory.

"I'm afraid I can't let you take me in, Little Joe. Now, why don't we just forget this ever happened and go get some breakfast? You're too good a friend to come to this."

Tom's words seemed to break Big Joe's silence and he blurted out, "Cecil," calling his brother by his given name, "what the hell's the matter with you?" He started toward Little Joe. "Have you gone plumb loco? Tom's our friend."

Little Joe quickly held up his hand, warning his brother back. "Hold it right there, Joe, unless you want to be the first one gets shot." There was no mistaking the tone of his warning. He was deadly serious. Turning his attention back to Tom, he said, "I'm willing to give you a chance. You got a pistol. Go git it on and we'll settle this man to man."

Big Joe was mesmerized. He could not believe what he was hearing from his younger brother. Barely able to find his voice, he fumbled for words, "Cecil . . . damn . . ."

"Stay out of this, Joe," Little Joe warned. His hand

moved slightly away from his side. "I'm waitin, Tom."

Tom was beginning to lose patience with the young fool. He did not want to kill Little Joe. He had no desire to rid Big Joe of his little brother, even if he was a hothead.

"Little Joe, you got no call to act like this." It was Doc who had suddenly found his voice. "We don't turn on one another at the Broken-T. Tom ain't no damn outlaw and you know it."

"I'm done talking," Little Joe said evenly. "Now, you go git that pistol, or I'm gonna cut you down where you stand."

"No you ain't. Not on my spread you ain't." Eli's warning was punctuated by the metallic slap of a rifle being cocked. "Now unbuckle that gunbelt and let it drop to the ground."

Little Joe hesitated, unwilling to give up the advantage he held over Tom. When he saw the determination on Eli's face, he thought better of the situation and did as he was told.

Tom relaxed a little, but he knew he was not done with this business. "Little Joe, you might as well forget it. I'm not going to have a damn-fool contest with you to see who can get his pistol out the quickest. Killing a man isn't some kind of game."

Big Joe, his face a confusion of shame and disbelief, looked first at his younger brother then back at Tom. "Damn, Tom! I don't know what's got into him. I'm sorry . . ." he sputtered, unable to account for Little Joe's behavior. Looking back at his brother, he scolded, "Cecil, you damn fool. A man don't turn on his friends."

Little Joe was not to be shamed or dissuaded, and he fairly snarled in reply. "When did he git to be such a damn big friend of our'n? Hell, Joe, he's a wanted man. Five hundred dollars, Joe. That's more than we can make in a year chasing these damn cows around. Some damn bounty hunter is gonna collect that money anyway. We might as well have it.''

Big Joe was appalled. "That there's blood money! I don't want no part of it and you ought not either.'' His expression was creased by a deep frown, and he pointed his finger at Little Joe accusingly. "It ain't really the money anyway, is it? You been hellbent on gittin' yourself a reputation with that gun, ain't you?'' He took a step closer, his hand raised as if to strike his brother. "Why you young jackass, I ought to . . .''

"Uh-uh, Joe,'' Little Joe warned. Something in his tone conveyed a sinister warning that stopped his older brother in his tracks.

"What would Pa think if he was alive to see this?'' was all Big Joe offered. He knew he should do something to control his younger brother, but it was also obvious that he had never seen this side of Little Joe before.

Tom had moved back a few steps, giving the brothers a little more room. At first he thought Big Joe was going to take charge of the situation and subdue his little brother. Now he wasn't so sure he could. Little Joe had revealed a sinister side that none had suspected, even his own brother. He glanced at Eli, who was still holding the rifle on Little Joe. It was plain to him that Eli wasn't sure what he should do about this unexpected turn of events. After a long moment of uneasy silence, Eli finally spoke.

"Little Joe, you been a good hand for me. I got no complaints with your work. But I can't have this on my ranch. I'm gonna have to ask you to move on.'' His voice was soft, almost apologetic. He glanced at Big Joe and added, " 'Course, Big Joe, you're wel-

ome to stay. It's just that I can't have this on the
Broken-T."

Big Joe did not answer right away. His eyes locked
on his brother's, watching for his response. He was
considering the position his brother had placed him
in, having to choose between family and friends. He
was also thinking of the time of year. Winter was not
a good time for a cowhand to be out of work with
no place to call home. Tom could not deny the compassion he felt for the man.

When it appeared that neither of them was going
to speak, Eli said, "Big Joe, pick up the gunbelt. I'll
trust you to hold on to it for a while till your brother
cools down enough to see right from wrong."

"All right, Cap'n," he replied and did as he was
told, wrapping the belt around the holstered pistol.

During the confrontation, Tom had been doing
some serious thinking. Right or wrong, he was the
cause of the trouble, and he knew now that it was
little more than wishful thinking that he could stay
on at the Broken-T and hide from the past.

"Cap'n," he said, "I think it best for everybody if
I'm the one who moves on." Eli started to object, but
Tom stopped him. "I appreciate what you're trying
to do for me, but it won't work. If it ain't Little Joe,
it'll be the bounty hunter coming back, or the army,
come spring. It ain't your problem to have to deal
with. It's mine, and I'll be moving on."

Eli said nothing. The look in his eyes told Tom
that he understood and thanked him for it. Big Joe,
looking helpless, offered, "Damn, Tom, I feel real bad
about this."

Tom smiled at him. "Don't, Big Joe. There's no
hard feelings." He then looked at Little Joe, his eyes
still cold and hard. "There aren't any hard feelings
your way either if you let this be the end of it. But

get this straight. I'm not going to start you out on the road to being a gunfighter. You can forget about that. I've got better sense than to play at killing."

"Maybe you ain't got the guts to stand up to me in a fair fight," Little Joe hissed.

Tom just stared at him for a moment with a look of total exasperation. "Well, I prefer to think I've got better sense. Make a name for yourself with somebody else." He turned back to Big Joe. "Can I depend on you to hold this young killer down long enough for me to saddle my horse and get my things together?"

"If he can't, I will." Smoky spoke up.

"Yeah, Tom," Eli said. "You go ahead and git your stuff. I'm mighty sorry to see you go like this, but I reckon, like you said, it's the best thing to do."

It didn't take Tom long to get his scant belongings together and load his packhorse. Smoky made sure he didn't start out without plenty of food. The only thing he needed was some coffee beans, as he had everything else he needed. Still, Smoky insisted that he should take some sowbelly and dried beans, so Tom accepted the offering graciously. Billy seemed ready to leave. He didn't even bother trying to blow up his belly when Tom pulled up on the girth strap. Tom suspected his horse was never comfortable around cattle in the first place. Maybe it was his long cavalry background. Maybe it was a sense of jealousy whenever Tom saddled up Breezy to work cattle. Whatever the reason, Billy fairly pranced and pulled at the reins, eager to get started when Tom climbed into the saddle. He held the horse back for a few moments while he said his good-byes to Eli and his friends. Smoky and Doc reached up to shake his hand, followed by Big Joe, who still showed some signs of the shame and frustration that had all but overcome him only minutes before. Tom glanced in Little Joe's direction. His gaze was met with a defiant stare, indicating the boy felt no remorse for his actions. Tom felt compelled to warn him.

"Let this be the end of it, Little Joe. Don't get it in your mind to come after me. Once I leave Broken-T and get out in the open country, any man who stalks me is a dead man."

Little Joe made no reply. Tom looked the boy in the eye for a moment longer before turning Billy west, releasing the pressure on the reins. Billy responded immediately, breaking into an easy gait toward the snowy prairie.

Big Joe was not alert enough to prevent the events in the next few seconds. He stood watching Tom ride past the bunkhouse, his brother's gunbelt in his hand. Eli, who had been keeping an eye on Little Joe, his rifle hanging loosely in his hand, relaxed his vigilance for an instant to glance at Tom. In that moment, Little Joe suddenly lunged into his brother, knocking him off balance. At the same time, he grabbed his pistol from the holster and yelled out, "Tom! Go for your gun!" That was the only warning he gave before opening fire on the unsuspecting man.

Tom's back was turned to the little group of men, so he barely heard Little Joe yell before he felt a bullet slash through the shoulder of his heavy coat, followed immediately by the sharp crack of the pistol. At first he thought he had been hit. He was to discover later that the bullet ripped through his coat, but at that moment, he had no time to think about it. It was the same as it had been when Sergeant Spanner cut down on him in Pop Turley's stable. He didn't consciously think about what he was doing, he just did it. Within a fraction of a second after he felt the impact of the bullet against his shoulder, he rolled out of the saddle, his right hand grasping the stock of his rifle so that he drew it out of the scabbard as he fell to the ground. He landed on his side and in one continuous motion rolled over in the snow and pulled the trigger, cocked the lever and fired again. Both shots found Little Joe's chest, dead center. Tom would never forget the look of complete disbelief on the boy's face as he took two steps backward and sat down heavily in the snow. Tom cocked his rifle in case another shot was necessary, but it was obvious the boy was finished.

For a moment it was as if time had stopped. The other men stood frozen by the sheer horror of what had just taken place before them. Then Big Joe was jolted from his paralysis by the sight of his younger brother's crimson blood spreading brightly on the snow. He ran to him and cradled him in his arms, sobbing. Little Joe could not hear his brother's mournful cries—he was already dead. Big Joe moaned as tears streamed down his face, continuing to rock his brother back and forth in his arms.

Tom rose slowly to his feet, his rifle ready, for he was not sure what Big Joe's reaction might be. "I'm sorry," he said softly. "He didn't give me any choice."

Big Joe had no thought of revenge. He continued to cry, still holding his dead brother. "I know it, Tom. I know it. You couldn't help it. Just get on out of here. Please, just get on your horse and go and let me bury my brother."

Tom wanted to say more to console him, but there was nothing to say. He slid his rifle back in the saddle sling and stood there for a moment longer, looking at the two brothers. Then he stepped up in the saddle and rode out.

Chapter X

He was a wiry little man, rough in his ways, with the conscience of a weasel. Bent over his camp-fire, his heavy skin robe draped over bony sloping shoulders, he looked like a coyote hunkered down over a kill. So intent was he on the small snow hare he was turning over the flames, he was unaware he had a visitor until the man spoke.

"Evening."

Startled, the little man almost fell into his own campfire as he tried to get to his feet. He tripped over the tail of his robe and landed on his backside in the snow.

"God damn! You could git yourself kilt, sneaking up on a man like that!"

His warning rang a bit hollow when he realized the situation he found himself in. His rifle was on the opposite side of the fire now, and he was seated in the snow while his visitor stood on the edge of the camp, his hand resting casually on the handle of a heavy Frontier forty-four, six-shooter. With the sharpened sense of a weasel that had been cornered, he found himself at a distinct disadvantage. There was nothing for him to do but sit there and await whatever fate had caught him by surprise.

The visitor stood there for a long while, watching

the little man. He seemed as large as a grizzly from the weasel's perspective, his heavy coat made of animal skins opened and pushed back from his hips so as to leave his pistol free. He seemed to take no notice of the little man's fright or his discomfort at having his backside in the snow.

"Smelled your rabbit cooking," he stated simply and moved in close to the fire. He sat down beside the weasel's rifle, seeming not to notice it, and held his hands out to warm at the fire. "Name's Cobb. What's your'n?"

Weasel hesitated a moment while he struggled to his feet. "Smith," he said, brushing the snow from his pants. He eyed the stranger suspiciously, wondering how a man that size was able to slip up on him without his being able to hear him. His horse didn't even give him any warning. "What the hell you doing, walking around out here? Ain't you got no horse?"

Cobb looked at him, unblinking, his eyes dark and deep as night. Then he grinned, not a warm smile, but sinister, a leer that gave weasel a chill down his spine.

"Yeah, I got a horse. I left him back there a piece." Without waiting for an invitation, he reached over and pulled the rabbit from the spit and tore off a leg. "I didn't wanna just come riding right in. You might not a'been friendly. You know what I mean, Mr. Smith?" His malevolent smile stayed in place while he tore the flesh from the hare's leg with his teeth.

The outright brass of the huge man made the hackles rise on the smaller man's backbone, but there was nothing he could do about it. The stranger was sitting right beside his rifle. He had the feeling he was being toyed with, the way a cat plays with a mouse. He could do nothing but sit and watch Cobb eat the supper he had cooked for himself. He wasn't sure what manner of man had taken over his camp. Maybe he would eat and be on his way. All he could do was wait and hope for a chance to get his rifle.

Cobb paused in his chewing and seemed to be studying his reluctant host. With one long, dirty fingernail, he worked at a piece of rabbit's flesh that had stuck between his teeth, until it loosened enough so he could suck it out. That done, he cocked an eye at the weasel and winked. "You know what I think, Mr. Smith? I think you don't want me eatin' your rabbit. I don't call that very neighborly. Ain't you ashamed of yourself?" He paused, still grinning at the hapless little man. When there was no response, he continued. "You know what else I think? I think your name ain't Smith. If I had to guess, I'd say your name was Rupert Slater. Now what do you think about that?"

There was a definite reaction to Cobb's statement. "I told you," the little man blurted, "my name's Smith." He began to fidget in an effort to move closer around the fire toward the rifle. "I don't know no Rupert Slater."

"That so?" Cobb answered casually, seeming to be unconcerned as he pulled another leg from the rapidly disappearing rabbit. "Too bad. I got a Wanted Poster in my saddlebag that says this here Rupert Slater's worth a hundred dollars for a little piece of work he done back in Kansas. I don't 'spose you've run into him, have you?" He paused while he licked some grease from his fingers. The weasel did not answer, so Cobb continued, obviously enjoying the discomfort the little man displayed. " 'Course I ain't got no picture of him to show you, but I can tell you what to look for in case you run across him. He's about your size, rides a horse just like that bay over there, and he's got a long knife scar from his ear, down across his face, just like that one on your face."

Slater knew his situation was hopeless. He could sense his life running out as he sat there staring at the uninvited guest who had just devoured most of his supper. He had to make a move. He couldn't sit there and wait for the slaughter. And he had the distinct feeling this damn bounty hunter would just as soon shoot him as not. He leaned slightly toward his rifle, but Cobb quickly reached over and picked it up.

"Now this here's a mighty fine rifle. Mind if I look at it? You warn't about to reach for it, was you?"

Slater tired of the cat-and-mouse game that was providing so much entertainment for Cobb. He was caught, and he knew it. Finally he gave in. "All right, you got the jump on me. I'm Slater. Maybe we can talk this thing over. You say the reward's a hundred dollars? I got some money hid in a cabin over near Virginia City. What if I give you two hundred to let me go?"

Cobb rubbed his chin thoughtfully, as if he was giving the offer deep consideration. "Well, the problem is, Rupert, I ain't really shore you got that two hundred dollars. And I'm pretty shore I can git the wanted money from the sheriff over in Bozeman. You know, two hundred dollars is a lot of money, but I ain't got time to go to Virginia City. I got bigger fish to fry than you."

Slater was doing his best to keep his nerves from showing, but it was impossible. The expression burned into Cobb's dark features bordered on being gleeful. "Hell, man, it's a lot of trouble to take me all the way back to Bozeman, 'specially in this kind of weather," Slater tried.

Cobb shook his head thoughtfully. "No, it ain't

really that much trouble. See, the poster says dead or alive."

That was all the warning Slater needed. In a panic, he scrambled to his feet. His intention was to run, but in the process he stumbled and fell, sliding a few feet, face first in the snow. Cobb calmly waited for the terrified man to struggle to his feet again and start running before he carefully raised the man's rifle and cut him down. That done, he sat where he was and finished the last of the rabbit. He picked up a battered copper kettle that had been resting on some stones beside the fire and swished the contents around while he peered at them. Pleased to find that it was coffee, he poured himself some in the dead man's cup. Satisfied with his day's work, he sat back and enjoyed his coffee.

After a short respite, Cobb sighed and told himself he had to pack up and get ready to leave at morning light. If he waited much longer to load Slater's body on his horse, it would be too stiff to bend. He picked the dead man up with very little effort. "You're a scrawny little rat," he said as he threw him over the saddle and tied his hands and feet. "If it was me, I wouldn't give no hundred dollars fer ya." He smiled to himself when he noted the two bullet holes in the man's back. Most of the men he brought in had bullet holes in their backs. It was sort of his signature. As he always insisted to the law, if they hadn't been trying to escape, the holes would be somewhere else.

Slater wasn't a big payday for Cobb, but a hundred dollars was a hundred dollars. It would sure as hell carry his expenses while he was hunting a bigger payoff: an ex-army officer named Tom Allred, and some other fellow named Dakota. Cobb had his suspicions they were one and the same. There was a thousand dollars offered on Allred and five hundred on Dakota. If he could convince the law that they were the same man, he still might collect both rewards.

He slapped the dead man on his backside and stated, "Rupert, you're just expenses. That's all you amount to, just expense money."

First light found Cobb already in the saddle, winding his way out of the narrow valley that had been Rupert Slater's hideout. Slater's horse, bearing the body of the unfortunate little fugitive from the law, trailed along behind. There was some disappointment for Cobb when he found that Slater had very little property of value to salvage. He had hoped the man at least had a packhorse. It always helped to have another horse to sell, a kind of bonus on the deal. As it turned out, there was little to offer in the form of bonus goods—a pretty good rifle, some supplies and ammunition, but nothing else. He would have to be satisfied with the hundred dollars. He could get enough for the one horse to take care of his expenses in Bozeman while waiting for the reward money to come.

It was a two-day ride to Bozeman, two cold days. But Cobb didn't seem to mind the cold weather. He never paid much attention to it. He was cloaked in layers of skins that never came off during the winter months. The top layer was a buffalo cape with a hood that could be pulled up if needed. He was padded with so many layers of hides that he appeared to be a foot wider at the shoulders than he actually was, which was bigger than most men west of the Missouri. With his greasy, shoulder-length hair and dark furry beard, he presented a frightening vision to men like the late Rupert Slater, often terrorizing his quarry upon encounter. Cobb was smart enough to realize this advantage. It gave him an edge. He

was not fast with a handgun, nor did he find it necessary to be, preferring to kill his prey at long range if
he was unable to take them by surprise at short
range.

Emerging from the valley out onto a long, flat
stretch of prairie, he stopped and climbed down to
urinate. While he stood there relieving himself, he
studied the horizon all around to spot any sign of
other human activity. Satisfied there was none, he
walked back and checked the body to make sure it
was riding all right. The thought flashed through his
mind that, if that was Tom Allred or Dakota, he
would be worth a lot more money. This started him
to thinking about the man. He was convinced it was
one man he was searching for. After talking to witnesses and hearing their descriptions of the killings,
it was too much coincidence for two men to be as
fast with a rifle as that. No, his instincts told him
that Tom Allred and Dakota were the same man, a
man too dangerous to get careless around. For now,
it was no more than a general search effort, for he
had no trail to follow. His man had disappeared. But
Cobb was confident he would resurface and, when
he did, Cobb would pick up his trail. Once that happened, he was as good as dead, for Cobb had over
ten years' experience tracking outlaws. Once he
picked up the trail, he would follow it to hell if necessary, and dare the devil to get in his way.

Sheriff Aaron Crutchfield took his fork and punc-
tured the soft yolks of the three eggs resting on top
of his fried potatoes, then paused a moment while
he watched the runny, yellow ooze seep into the
crevices. Then, with his knife, he cut the brick-hard
salt-cured ham into small chunks. When it was all
sliced down to pieces he could handle, he mixed the

ham, eggs, and potatoes together and covered the entire mixture with a layer of salt and pepper. Then, with a fork in one hand and a slice of bread to help load the fork in the other, he set upon his breakfast in the earnest fashion of a man who knows no higher priority in life. On this morning though, his breakfast would be interrupted, an occurrence he always met with a scowl.

His young deputy, Will Proctor, stuck his head in the door of the saloon and announced, "Sheriff, they's a feller wants you over to the jail."

Crutchfield took another huge mouthful and without looking up from his plate, asked, "Who is it?"

"I don't know, bounty hunter, I reckon. He's got a dead man. Sez he's wantin' the reward money on him."

"Shit!" Crutchfield grunted. He didn't like bounty hunters, and he didn't like to have to bother with their prisoners, or corpses as was usually the case, and have them hanging around town while he sent for the money. He washed the mouthful down with coffee and loaded up another forkful. "Dammit, I'm eating!"

"Want me to tell him to come up here?"

"Shit, no. Tell him I'll be there when I'm done." He continued to eat.

"Yessir, but don't be too long. He's a mean-lookin' son of a bitch and big as a house. Looks like a cross between a buffalo and a grizzly bear."

Crutchfield was unimpressed. "Tell him I'll be there when I'm done."

When he had consumed the last bite, he took the last small piece of bread crust and wiped the plate dry with it, then ate it. After draining his coffee cup, he pushed back from the table and sat there a moment, waiting for the satisfying belch he knew would come. Contented, he got up and left the saloon.

He picked his way carefully across the muddy street. Although it was referred to as a street, it was in reality a dark, sticky river, churned by the hooves of horses and the wheels of mule skinners' wagons. Crutchfield swore repeatedly as he tried to avoid the worst spots, punctuated by a loud "Goddammit!" whenever he misjudged a step and splashed mud on his twenty-five dollar Justin boots.

The bounty hunter was waiting for him outside the jail. He stood by his horse, seemingly oblivious to the mud he was standing in. Will Proctor was right. He looked like a cross between a buffalo and a grizzly bear. A meaner looking man Crutchfield had never seen, and, though he had never seen this man before, he needed no introduction.

"You're Cobb, ain't you?"

Cobb smiled, pleased that his reputation was so widespread. "I'm Cobb," he answered, "and this here gentleman is Rupert Slater. I got paper on him." He produced a wanted poster from his saddlebag and handed it to Crutchfield.

Crutchfield took the piece of paper, unfolding it while he eyed the huge bounty hunter. Glancing down at the written description on the paper, he looked for references to identifying marks. Then he walked around to the dead man's horse, and with the poster in one hand he grabbed the corpse by the hair and attempted to pull his head up in order to get a better look at him. The corpse was frozen stiff, however, and his neck wouldn't bend. He had to stoop down on one knee to look him over. It was near impossible to tell for sure that the man was, in fact, Rupert Slater. There was the long scar from his ear down across his face, and the body was about the right size. It could be Slater, Crutchfield didn't really concern himself that much. It was never easy to identify a man from a wanted poster anyway.

"You're pretty sure you got the right man here, I reckon," he finally said.

"It's Slater," Cobb stated matter-of-factly.

"Didn't feel like surrendering, I suppose," Crutchfield said, a hint of sarcasm in his voice.

"Reckon not."

"I notice he got it in the back."

"He run."

"Yeah, I reckon," Crutchfield replied. "From what I hear, most all the fugitives you bring in come in draped across their saddles instead of settin' in 'em." He made no effort to disguise the disgust he held for bounty hunters in general, and this one in particular. It irritated the sheriff further to see that his words had no effect on the bear of a man standing before him.

"One hundred dollars," Cobb calmly stated. "The poster says he's worth one hundred dollars. When do I git it? I got other business to attend to."

Crutchfield eyed the man for a long moment before answering. He truly had no use for this manner of man, and yet there was little he could do about their existence. "Well, it won't be anytime soon—I can tell you that. He's wanted in Kansas. That's where the money will have to come from, Kansas City."

Cobb eyed the sheriff coldly. "I reckon they can wire it, can't they?"

Crutchfield did not try to hide his impatience. It was cold, standing outside, and he didn't have a mountain of hides draped over him as Cobb did. "Yeah," he answered gruffly, "they can wire it, but you didn't notice any dang telegraph lines coming into town, did you? You'll get your damn blood

money, but first I'll have to send the papers on the
stage to Corinne, in Utah territory. That's the closest
railroad. Then they'll go by mail train to Kansas City.
Then you'll have to wait for them to send the money
back the same way."

Cobb's eyes narrowed. He was not pleased by the
conversation. "How long?" he asked.

"Hell, I don't know, four, six weeks, if they feel
like gittin' on it right away in Kansas City. That is,
if the weather don't turn bad and close up the passes
between here and Corinne so the stage can't git
through. Then, it might take two months." Crutchfield
took a certain amount of satisfaction in the reaction
caused by his prognosis and the bounty hunter's obvious distaste for the news. " 'Course, if that ain't
fast enough to suit you, you can haul him on down
to Utah. Maybe they'll telegraph for the money for
you."

Cobb stared hard into the eyes of the sheriff. He
was not pleased with the turn of events. He wanted
his money, but he wanted to rid himself of the dead
man more. After thinking it over for a moment, he
said, "No, I'll pick it up when it gits here."

Crutchfield was disappointed. He hoped Cobb
would take his dead man and ride out of town. "All
right," he said sighing. Turning to his deputy, he
directed, "Will, untie him and see if you can unbend
him enough to get him off his horse." He watched
the deputy struggle with the frozen corpse for a few
minutes. "Hell, we might have to bury the horse
with him."

Cobb was quick to interject, "That there's my
horse. His'n got shot."

Crutchfield looked hard at the bounty hunter for
a moment before a slow grin formed on his face.

"Yeah? It sure was lucky you had another one, wasn't it?"

"Warn't no luck to it, Sheriff." Cobb's eyes narrowed. Crutchfield was getting on his nerves. "I always have what I need to git the job done." He was thinking to himself that it would be a great pleasure to come across this self-satisfied, potbellied sheriff alone somewhere out on the prairie. He didn't like the idea of any man looking down his nose at him, especially a lawman.

The paperwork didn't take long to complete, in spite of the sheriff's complaining. Cobb had done it dozens of times before. All that was required of him was to make his mark on an affidavit claiming the reward. Crutchfield sent Will for the undertaker to certify the death, then he confirmed Slater's identity and that was it. Promising to return to Bozeman in three or four weeks to get his money, Cobb got on his horse and rode down to the livery stable to sell Slater's horse and saddle. With some of the money, he bought supplies and ammunition. Then, after a hot meal at the saloon, he rode out of town, back toward the Musselshell. Cobb had very little use for towns of any size. He preferred the frozen mountains and prairies. Besides, he had a notion that it wouldn't hurt to visit the Broken-T again. Allred had worked there before, and might have decided to return. It was a four-day ride back to the Broken-T if the weather held, maybe twice that if a winter storm hit. Cobb didn't concern himself with it. Good weather, or bad weather, it was all the same to him. He had camped out in the open in weather most men wouldn't leave the hearth in. There was a meanness about him that defied even the elements.

Chapter XI

While Cobb loaded a packhorse and set out east from Bozeman to strike the Yellowstone, the man he hunted was making camp after one day's ride from the Broken-T. It had been a long frigid day, although the snow that had fallen the night before was not deep enough to impede Billy's progress. Tom could have made a few miles more before daylight faded, but he felt a strong desire to make a camp and warm his bones. His spirits could stand a little lifting after the episode with Little Joe, and he figured a warm fire and a hot cup of coffee might go a long way toward perking him up. He had sworn that he would never spend another winter alone in the wilderness after he nearly froze to death in his dugout cave the previous year. But it looked like he was about to do it again. It seemed that every place he tried to light, people spawned another unpleasant encounter for him. And this time it had resulted in the useless killing of a young boy, one he had counted as a friend. Maybe he was better off being alone after all.

When he said farewell to Eli and Smoky that morning, he decided to follow the Musselshell west. There was a court-martial waiting for him back East, so there were very few choices left for him. He considered Canada but he was unsure of that territory, that and reports of trouble with the Gros Ventres and the Assiniboines as well as the Blackfeet. Maybe he could find himself a little valley somewhere away from the army and the bounty hunters, a valley where the streams were still loaded with beaver, as it used to be in the Musselshell country before the American Fur Company trapped it out. Tom recalled the disappointing price he had received for the plews he had trapped that fall; three dollars for prime. It was discouraging but, at present, he could think of no other way to earn a living.

Sighting a clump of cottonwoods and willows that promised to offer some protection for a campsite, he decided he had ridden far enough that day. Upon riding up under the trees, he discovered that he was not the first to camp there. Someone else, probably Indians, had camped there before. From the signs, it wasn't recent. There were large patches of grass where the snow had melted during the day, so he tethered Billy where he could graze. He turned the packhorse loose to forage for himself. He wouldn't wander far and, if he did, Tom had Billy to go after him. He ground up a handful of coffee beans, and before long he sat before the fire, bundled up in his buffalo robe, eating his supper. As darkness approached, he roused himself from his warm cocoon and took his rifle for a quick scout around his camp just to make sure he was alone. Everything seemed to his satisfaction. His packhorse was down by the water, grazing on some shoots and weeds along the river's edge. Billy seemed quiet enough. As a precaution, he took some extra blankets and made up three dummy beds around the fire. This was a trick he had learned from Squint Peterson. Squint figured it at least increased his odds in the event he was caught napping, which Tom doubted ever happened, and gave him a one-in-four chance of getting the first bullet. Tom had taken to using the dummy beds when he learned about the bounty hunter, even though he was not overly concerned. He figured he was probably the only fool out in this kind of weather. Anybody with any sense, Injun, white, or breed, would be sitting by a warm fire. Tom wanted to remain alert, however, sleeping with one eye open that night, just in case someone from the Broken-T might be tracking him. Big Joe allowed as how the death of his brother was no fault of Tom's and couldn't have been helped. Still, Tom figured there was the possibility that after it worked on his mind for a while, Joe might see things in a different light and decide he was honor-bound to avenge Little Joe's death. It wouldn't pay to discount trouble from that direction. Despite all of his intentions, fatigue overtook him and he was soon sound asleep.

The morning broke clear and bright, sending the first rays of light snaking through the cottonwoods that ringed his campsite. He was at once alarmed by the lateness of the hour, having daylight catch him still in his blankets. He was about to deliver a good scolding to himself for his laziness when he discovered a more serious predicament—Billy was gone!

He rolled out of his blankets, clutching his Winchester. Scrambling to his feet, he quickly scanned the trees that surrounded him. He suspected the worst. Billy would not likely have broken his tether. A moment was all that was necessary to confirm his fears. The sign was not hard to read. Someone, Indian by the look of the tracks, had run off with his horse while he slept. He felt hot with anger and disgust for his carelessness.

As he ran down toward the river, hoping to find

his packhorse, a flood of questions troubled him. Why didn't Billy make a sound? How had the thief— the tracks indicated only one man—been able to approach within that distance without his having heard? Another thought, more puzzling than these, was why the thief had not killed him? Any Indian, even those who were considered friendly, would not hesitate to kill and scalp a lone white man out on the prairie. It didn't make sense. But he would have to think about it later. Now he had more urgent things on his mind.

At the river's edge, he took cover behind a large boulder while he scanned the horizon for signs. It appeared that he was the only man within miles, alone and on foot. It was plain to him, from the tracks in the hard frozen sand and the snow patches, that the Indian forded the river on foot. Probably tied his horse on the other side near a sprinkling of willows, Tom figured, led the packhorse a few yards downstream and tied it to a tree while he went around the other side of Tom's campfire and got Billy. From the way the moccasin was made, he figured the thief to be a Blackfoot. The more Tom read the sign, the madder he got, though not as much at the Blackfoot, for stealing horses was an honorable pursuit. No, he was disgusted with his own stupidity for being taken like a rank greenhorn.

"Well, greenhorn, now what the hell are you gonna do?" He stood there a moment longer before deciding to return to his campfire and get something to eat. He was going to have to leave this place right away. Whoever had stolen the horses was not likely to ride off and leave a man on foot with his saddle pack and harness, not to mention guns and ammunition. He could only wonder why he had not been attacked when the thief took his horses. He puzzled over it while he stirred up the coals and ate a piece of dried jerky. It was only one man. That much Tom was sure of. And since he was alone and not with a hunting party, he must be a renegade or someone in disfavor with his tribe. Otherwise, he most likely would not be by himself in this winter wilderness. *Kinda like me*, Tom thought. The man must have been poorly armed, or he would have simply shot Tom where he lay. Possibly the dummy beds made him hesitate. If he thought there were actually four men, he might have figured it was not worth the risk. *But, hell*, Tom reminded himself, *there weren't but two horses. Did he think four men were riding two horses?* The more he thought about it, the more it began to make sense. One Indian, probably armed with nothing more than a bow and a lance, didn't have to take a chance on getting shot once he stole the horses. He was probably sitting back right now, behind one of those hills, watching to see how many white men came out of the trees. He had to figure if it was only one, he could not carry the saddle and pack with him. He would have to leave everything but his weapons if he had any notion of walking. Then it would be a simple matter to ride into the camp and load the white man's belongings on the stolen horses. Then, with the natural patience of the Plains Indian, he would track the man until he became exhausted from trying to cross the snowy hills on foot, or until a blizzard struck and the man froze to death. If Tom elected to hole up in the cottonwoods where his Winchester could keep the Indian at bay, then the Indian would no doubt decide to share his plunder with his brothers and go back to his village for additional warriors. That is, unless he was the renegade that Tom suspected he was. Everything considered, Tom decided he'd rather be on the move than sitting still.

So he figured he had little choice but to start walking and hope that his enemy would make the mistake of coming within rifle range of the Sharps.

As quickly as he possibly could, Tom rigged a backpack using half of his saddle pack. In it, he carried enough jerky to last him a week, a blanket and as much ammunition as he thought he could carry. He cached his saddle, along with everything else he had left under a deadfall near the bank of the river. That done, he propped his Winchester over one shoulder and his Sharps buffalo gun on the other. Keeping low behind the willows, he set out along the riverbank and left the camp behind. If he was being watched, he hoped he could keep out of sight long enough to get a head start. Before leaving the cover of the cottonwoods, he forded the icy river and headed south. He was not absolutely certain how far he had ridden the previous day, but he figured if he struck out straight south, he would have to reach the Yellowstone in about three days' time. Then he would follow the Yellowstone west until he found a settlement or, if he had to, until he walked all the way to Bozeman. His original plan to stay away from any towns was now overridden by the necessity to get another horse. At present, aside from the obvious threat of attack, his biggest concern was the weather. If he got caught out in the open by a blizzard, he was as good as dead. As far as the Indian tracking him, he didn't worry that much. He had his rifles and he was confident he would come out on top should the two of them meet. In fact, he sincerely hoped the lowdown thief would track him. He'd let him get within about five hundred yards and then introduce him to Mr. Sharps.

As much as he possibly could, Tom kept to the coulees and draws, but inasmuch as his desperate situation required him to maintain a more or less true course to the south, he was occasionally forced to take the high ground. From habit, he took some pains to cover his trail whenever he could, but he was on foot, and the snow patches were too frequent and broad. At best, his efforts might gain him a few minutes' time. Whenever he topped a rise, he paused momentarily to scan his backtrail. For a good hour or so, there was no sign of anyone behind him. He guessed the Indian was no doubt scouting his camp-site, searching for the goods that had to be left behind. He only hoped he had hidden his cache well enough. Tom's driving thoughts now were simply to make haste. There was always the possibility the Indian would decide not to trail him. An Indian would sometimes change his mind for no other reason than he was an Indian.

Tom was moving at a good pace, a rifle in each hand, as he alternated between a slow trot and a fast walk. He was not accustomed to traveling on foot, and his breath became heavy after only a short while, necessitating longer periods of walking. Coming to a slightly higher rise, he kept below the crest as he topped it, keeping his profile below the hilltop. As he started down, his foot slipped on an icy rock, and he sprawled in the snow. He lay there for a few moments to let his breathing calm down, then crawled back to the crest of the hill to check his backtrail.

"Damn!" he uttered under his breath. The Indian was on his trail all right, perhaps a mile behind him. He would close that distance in no time at all. He quickly looked around him from side to side, and decided this was as good a place as any to wait for him. He had the high ground and, as long as he had the rifles, the open prairie was to his advantage. So he made ready for his adversary. He brushed the snow from a flat rock at the top of the rise and laid the Sharps down. Then he checked the load in both rifles. Satisfied that his weapons were ready, he settled back to wait for his target to approach. He didn't have long to wait.

"Thieving son of a bitch," he muttered when the hostile closed to a point of flat prairie, close enough now for Tom to confirm that it was indeed an Indian who stalked him. He was riding a scruffy-looking pony. Behind him Billy and the packhorse trailed along on a tether. It made Tom's blood boil to see Billy being led by the thieving savage. One of the few ways a warrior could gain status within the tribe, outside of bravery in battle, was stealing horses. Tom understood this and accepted it, but it was different when it came to his own horse. Stealing Billy was more akin to kidnapping a family member. His anger may have caused him to act a little prematurely, for he cocked the Sharps and sighted on the Indian, allowing him to get to within only about four hundred yards before he squeezed the trigger and felt the solid kick of the weapon against his shoulder. He easily could have waited until the man closed another two hundred yards, a distance from which he could have placed his shot right between the eyes. But, he told himself, there was a slight rise between them, about one hundred yards out, and he might lose sight of his target if he allowed him to approach it. As soon as he pulled the trigger, he knew he was too rash and cursed himself for being a damn fool. As it was, the shot caught the Indian high on the shoulder and knocked him off his horse. Tom hurried to load another cartridge in the Sharps, but the Indian's reactions upon finding himself shot were too quick for Tom to get another clear shot. The wounded man rolled when he hit the ground and, quick as a fox, grabbed his lead rope and led the horses down into a gulch and out of sight.

"That was another damn greenhorn thing to do," he berated himself. "Now I don't know which direction he'll be coming from." He made haste to strap on his pack again and scramble down from the hilltop. As he hurried to find a better position to wait for the Indian, he tried to evaluate the damage done by his shot. The man, though knocked off his horse, seemed spry enough when he pulled the three horses down in that gulch. Tom could only guess that he had barely nicked him. A forty-five bullet, with one hundred and twenty grains of DuPont's finest black powder behind it, would have knocked a hole as big as a fist in the man's shoulder, if it hit solid meat. He could have kicked himself for firing so soon. If he had waited another couple of minutes, he'd probably be riding Billy now instead of puffing along on foot.

There was no way he could hide himself for very long before the Indian would discover his hiding place. The country was too open with only occasional trees. The good news was that the Indian would not likely be able to sneak up on him as long as it was daylight. Tom's guess was the man would most likely hobble the horses in the gulch and stalk him on foot, making an effort to circle around behind him. His plan of defense was to find another spot on high ground where he could watch the area around him. Then, when night came, he would get on the move again, and it would remain to be seen who was the better hunter, Tom or the Indian. So, when he came to a rise that appeared to stand a bit higher than the surrounding terrain, he dug out a shallow

trench with his knife and settled in to wait. His wait
was a long one.

The sun was almost directly overhead when he
dug in on the rise. Now it was sinking ever closer to
the tops of the peaks in the western sky. Tom, lying
in the cold earth of the trench, shifted his position
constantly in an effort to keep a watch on the area
around him. As the hours passed with no sound nor
sign, his body became stiff with inactivity as the cold
began to creep into his bones. *Maybe he's hurt worse
than I figured*, Tom speculated. It was a possibility,
but he knew it was more likely the Indian was watching him from some point, patiently waiting for darkness, for why should he risk Tom's firepower when
it would be far less risky to steal upon him under
cover of a deep prairie night? He had no choice but
to match the Indian for patience, so he made himself
as comfortable as possible while keeping his eyes
peeled. He got some jerky from his pack and ate. *Too
bad*, he thought, *there's no wood to make a small fire.
Coffee would be good*. Then he remembered that he
had no means to boil coffee anyway. All his gear was
cached by the riverbank, if the Indian had not found
it that morning. Maybe the Indian was enjoying a
cup of hot coffee. There were fewer than two hours
of daylight left when he heard a shot.

He scrambled to one knee, scanning the prairie
around him. There had been only one shot, but peering out across the rolling hills, he could see no sign
of man nor beast. The shot had not been aimed at
him, of that he was certain. Or, if it was, whoever
fired it missed the whole damn hill. No, it seemed
to have come from the gulch where he had last seen
the Indian, but he could detect no puff of gunsmoke
over that way. He wondered if the Indian had been
armed with a rifle after all. From the sound of it,

Tom guessed it to be a repeating rifle and not one of the needle guns that many of the Indians had traded for. The mystery was not explained for fully another hour, during which time Tom watched the prairie anxiously, but saw nothing. Long shadows from the hills had begun to form dark pools in the draws and low places, when a man suddenly appeared, coming out of the gulch, leading four horses.

"Hallo up thar! Hold your fire, I'm comin' up."

Tom was amazed. It was no Indian. That much he was sure of, for this was a fair-sized hulk of a man. From that distance, he looked to be the size of Squint Peterson, who was the biggest man Tom had ever met. He was cloaked in skins, and the fur of his cap seemed to be a mere extension of the heavy growth of his beard. Tom figured him to be a mountain man, a prospector or trapper. He came on toward Tom, holding up a dark flag-like object about the size of a bandanna. He was calling out something to Tom as he advanced, but Tom couldn't make out the words. Billy whinnied as he recognized Tom, and Tom stood up to receive his guest.

"Blackfoot!" the huge man called out and Tom realized the dark bandanna was in reality a scalp. The man waved it over his head a few times more before carefully folding it and stuffing it in his buffalo coat. "Reckon he was figurin' on gittin' your'n 'stead of losing his'n." He dismounted, looking Tom over with a curious eye. "Reckon you was in a fix till I come along."

"I reckon I was."

"I'm thinkin' this here rig belongs to you," he said, indicating Billy and the packhorse.

Tom smiled. "That's a fact." He was wary of the grim-looking stranger, no matter how cheerful his talk, so he was relieved to hear he was willing to acknowledge the horses as his.

"How'd you come to be in a fix like this?" the stranger asked, whereupon Tom proceeded to relate how the Blackfoot had stolen the horses during the night, leaving him on foot, but holding all the cards as far as weaponry. Tom, in turn, wondered how this giant of a man managed to get the jump on the Blackfoot.

"Hell, he war so interested in you, he didn't pay me no mind. What with that and him tryin' to fix up that hole you put in his shoulder, it war easy. I just left my horses back in them willows and tippy-toed up behind him and blowed a winder in the back of his head."

At any rate, Tom felt it to be his good fortune that this man happened along. They talked a while longer about the incident, and then, since darkness was not long in coming, they decided to find a more hospitable place to make camp. "I reckon I owe you a better feed than I can offer," Tom said, "but you're welcome to share the jerky I brought with me. Maybe sunup we can find some game."

The stranger smiled, or attempted to. It seemed to Tom that the man had precious little practice in that exercise, the finished product resembling a scowling exhibit of his upper teeth. Tom formed the distinct opinion that the man was generally uncomfortable with pleasantries, but was making something of an effort to appear cordial.

"Why, tain't no call to eat jerky when I got a rabbit hangin' on my saddle pack," he replied. He watched Tom fashion a rawhide halter and slip it over Billy's nose. "Name's Cobb. What's your'n?"

Tom started to reply, then paused while he swung up on Billy's back. This trapper probably hadn't the slightest care whether he was a wanted man or not. Still, there was no sense in being careless. "Johnson," he replied, "Tom Johnson."

They made camp near the banks of a small stream that divided a stand of cottonwoods. The ground was devoid of grass for the horses, but the bark of the cottonwoods offered some nourishment. After Tom had peeled a quantity of small limbs to feed his animals, he went about helping Cobb with a fire. The two men went about their business of making camp, neither man speaking for a long period of time, evidence that both men were accustomed to camping alone. Tom noticed that Cobb saw to his own needs before looking after his stock, a practice Tom disapproved of. Every man had to do according to his own beliefs, so he would never criticize. But Tom had always been taught that a man took care of his animals first, and when the going got hot and heavy, the animals would take care of him. It was more than that, however. There was something else about the huge grimy man that told him he had better sleep with his rifle handy. Cobb seemed to be friendly enough, but it seemed a mite less than sincere, and after they had settled in and cooked the rabbit, he had a tendency to ask an awful lot of questions.

"Tom Wilson, you say your name was?"

"Johnson," Tom corrected him. He suspected Cobb knew he hadn't said Wilson.

"Oh, that's right, Johnson—you did say Johnson at that." He appeared to mull this over for a while then he asked in a manner meant to be casual, "Where you headed for, Mr. Johnson?"

"Bozeman," Tom answered.

"Bozeman—I just come from Bozeman. What you aiming to do in Bozeman?"

"Find a place to get warm. I hadn't thought about it much further than that."

"Well now, ain't that strange? I'm headin' back to Bozeman myself," Cobb lied. "We might as well travel together. Be a lot safer in case we run into any of that there Blackfoot's friends." He had been studying Tom as he moved about making camp and Cobb's naturally suspicious mind began to work over several small details in Tom's behavior.

"Maybe," Tom replied with little enthusiasm. "You might not want to wait for me though. I've got to double back and get my possibles I left cached back there a'ways." He was beginning to get a feeling about his camp partner, a feeling that didn't sit well with him. He might be better off alone than with this sinister-looking wild man.

"I see you got you one of them repeating rifles. Winchester, ain't it?" Tom nodded. "I seen you plugged that Blackfoot with that there Sharps, but that Winchester there, now that's a dandy rifle." He stretched his massive arms and resituated himself against the tree trunk he was leaning against. "I knowed about a feller over to Miles City had a Winchester like that. Folks over there said he was a helluva shot with it, too. Cut a soldier boy damn near in half with it." He paused, watching Tom closely.

"That so?" Tom answering, feigning boredom.

When the response was not forthcoming, Cobb continued, " 'Course, myself, it don't make a tinker's damn to me if he kilt that there soldier, or a hundert more. It ain't none of my affair. But I would like to see a man shoot like that."

Tom didn't answer, but he was immediately alert. He didn't like the direction of the man's conversation. It was a hell of a coincidence for this stranger to bring up the subject. Now, as he looked more closely at his chance companion, he remembered Eli and Smoky's warning about a bounty hunter. *A mean-looking son of a bitch* they called him, *a big fellow.* Well, this fellow Cobb surely fit that description. If it was him, Tom figured he wasn't sure of Tom's identity, but he was mighty suspicious. The sooner he got clear of this fellow, the better. Although his every nerve ending was alert, Tom maintained a calm, disinterested expression. It wouldn't do to let Cobb see that his talk made him nervous. "Well," he said as casually as he could effect, "I think I'll turn in. It's starting to get a mite chilly." He made a show of arranging his blanket. He had no intention of closing his eyes that night, and if all went well, he figured to pull out before Cobb woke up the next morning.

Cobb continued to talk as he took a few steps to the edge of the firelight and untied his buckskin britches to relieve himself. "I don't mind the cold myself. Matter of fact, I'd just as soon make a cold camp." Finished with his toilet, he laced up again. "Think I'll take a look-see around, make shore they ain't no Blackfeet sneakin' around the horses."

Tom watched him walk out of the firelight toward the tethered horses. When he was sure Cobb was not looking back at him, he quickly ejected the cartridges from his Winchester. Taking a quick glance to make sure the Sharps was loaded, he slid it inside his blanket so that it lay across the inside of his right boot. Then he propped the empty Winchester up beside a tree and backed up against it himself, as if he were ready to sleep. From the darkness, where the horses were tied, he heard Cobb call to him.

"Say, Johnson, this here horse of your'n looks like he's limpin' some. I'll take a look at 'em. Does he kick? What's his name? I don't want to git kicked in the head."

"Billy. But you better watch him. He don't take up with strangers," he answered. He thought, *Unless you're a damn thieving Blackfoot and then he'll let you run off with him.* Billy would hardly kick but he didn't like the idea of Cobb fooling around with his horse.

A few short moments of silence passed before Cobb stepped back into the circle of firelight. He wore an expression like that of a coyote with a prairie dog pinned under his paw. "I reckon there warn't nuthin' wrong with your horse after all. Billy, you say his name is?" He moved over to Tom's side of the fire, making a show of warming his hands over the flame. "You never asked me what my line is, Mr. Johnson." When it became apparent that Tom was still not going to ask him, he continued with obvious relish in his discourse. "I'm a trapper, kind of like you say you are. Only I don't waste my time on beaver. I trap skunks and polecats, the two-legged kind." He paused for a moment, but was still met with no response from Tom. Suddenly, in one swift move, he reached down and grabbed the Winchester. When there was no reaction from Tom, he stepped back a few feet and grinned, the same twisted grimace that Tom had seen earlier. "Like I said before, this here is shore a fine lookin' rifle. The polecat I'm trackin' now uses one just like this one. He cut a soldier plum nye in half with it over to Miles City. They said it was a feller called hisself Dakota, rode a horse named Billy. That's what the stable man said." He stood over Tom then, waiting for his reaction, the smile slowly fading into a scowl. "Now there's just one thing I want to know before I cut you in half with this fine-lookin' Winchester. They ain't no doubt you're the one they call Dakota. The description fits you right enough. But you can satisfy my curiosity about something. Your name's Tom Allred, ain't it? You might as well tell me. You're a dead man anyway, and they ain't no sense dying with a lie on your lips." He brought the Winchester down to level at Tom.

"What if you don't have the right man?" Tom asked, his voice calm and deliberate.

"I reckon that'd be too bad for you, wouldn't it? Besides, if you ain't Dakota, then I reckon it'll just be my mistake. Either way, your bones bleach out here come summer, and I'll just keep on lookin' till I find the real Dakota."

"That rifle's not loaded," Tom stated coolly.

Cobb grinned. "The hell it ain't," he sneered, firm in the knowledge that a man who lived in this part of the world never went to sleep with an empty rifle beside him. He paused but a moment, the grin implanted on his grisly features. Then he cocked the hammer back and pulled the trigger. A look of astonishment replaced the grin, and he quickly cocked the rifle again and pulled the trigger. Once more there was no sound save that of the dull metallic click of the firing pin on an empty chamber. With an angry snarl, he threw the rifle away and pulled his heavy buffalo coat aside to uncover his pistol. The grin returned to his face when Tom slowly raised his right leg up off the ground. *A feeble effort*, Cobb thought, *to ward off a bullet*. Cobb's hand had not quite touched the handle of his pistol when he was knocked backward, landing squarely in the campfire.

Tom did not move for a moment, the roar of the heavy Sharps almost startled him, it was so loud. He stared at the smoking hole in his blanket where the bullet went through. In the next instant he scrambled out of his blanket, pistol in hand. Cobb roared like a wounded grizzly and managed to roll out of the fire, which he had almost smothered with his bulk. His buffalo coat was smoldering from the countless sparks that had lit up on his back and shoulders. Tom was quick to make sure Cobb didn't draw his pistol. He stood with his own pistol aimed at Cobb's head, ready to finish him. But Cobb was in too much shock to pull his weapon. Tom's bullet had torn a sizable hole right through Cobb's side, and the bounty hunter was trying to hold his insides in with both hands. Tom stood over him.

"Damn you," Cobb spat. "Damn you to hell. You gut shot me."

"It was you or me," Tom replied, his voice emotionless as he watched the writhing agony of the man who, moments before, sought to kill him. Cobb, trying desperately to keep his intestines from spilling, snarled like a wounded animal. He tried to pull his pistol but blood gushed from the wound in such profusion that he quickly jerked his hand back over his side.

"Damn you! Damn you!" he continued to spit at Tom, his eyes beginning to glaze over in pain. Tom watched him for a moment, then slowly pulled the hammer back on his pistol. The move did not escape Cobb's notice, and at once there appeared a calmness in the doomed man's face. "Tell me, you son of a bitch, are you Tom Allred?"

"Ask the devil when you see him," Tom replied coolly and pulled the trigger. The huge man jerked once when the bullet tore through the top of his thick fur cap, then he settled heavily on the ground and was still.

Tom felt very little emotion for the deed he had done. The thought that he had killed a man never entered his mind. It was more like killing a buffalo or a steer for slaughter. Suddenly he felt tired. Not wanting to look at Cobb's body any longer, he took him by the heels and dragged him over to the edge of a deep ravine. It was at least fifty feet down. There were mature lodgepole pines growing up from the bottom, and their tops barely cleared the top of the ledge. He rolled the body to the edge of the ravine and then, with his boot, sent it crashing down into the pines and rocks below. That done, he returned to the campfire, rolled up in his blanket, and went to sleep. If there were any Blackfeet waiting for a chance to take his scalp, they were welcome to it. Right then he didn't give a damn.

He awoke the next morning shivering with the cold. Cobb had smothered most of the fire when he fell in it the night before, and Tom had been too tired to bank what remained of it. Now he was paying for his negligence as he scurried about gathering up something to use as tinder. He gave not a thought to the body at the bottom of the ravine while he loaded the horses with what possessions of the late bounty hunter he deemed useful. He had two pack-horses now in addition to Cobb's big bay with the white stockings on three of his feet. He cut the Blackfoot's scrubby pony loose and let him go. Then he climbed up on Billy and, pausing to tip his hat toward the ravine and the late Mr. Cobb, doubled back on his trail to get his saddle and belongings from the cache.

Chapter XII

Once his cache was recovered, Tom rode south to strike the Yellowstone. A light snow had covered the ground before petering out sometime before the sun rose to midday. He let Billy set an easy pace, leading the string of three extra horses with his belongings. Even though it was the middle of winter, he was in no particular hurry. The weather was none too severe and, upon studying the sky to the north and west, he didn't expect it to change much within the next few days. There was a concern, as there always was, that he might be caught out in the open by a band of Blackfeet or Crows. But Tom felt he could give a sizable raiding party more than they wanted when it came to firepower. He had his Sharps plus two repeating rifles, and as long as there weren't too many hostiles, or he wasn't surprised by them, he could hold his own. Even against a large band, he could make the cost of his scalp too dear. With the demise of the late Mr. Cobb, his main worry that a bounty hunter might be stalking him, was erased, bringing instead a feeling almost approaching cheerfulness.

He had not made up his mind where he was heading, beyond striking the Yellowstone and following it west. He still had no love for wintering in the wilderness alone. Maybe Bozeman would be far enough away from Fort Lincoln and the army. He could wait out the cold weather there, perhaps. He could afford to pay for lodging, thanks to the generosity of the late Mr. Cobb. When he searched Cobb's pack that morning, he had found a pouch of gold dollars inside the lining of a huge buffalo coat. Seeing that Cobb would have no further use for the money, he decided he could put it to good use. In all likelihood, Cobb had probably come by the money by tracking down unfortunate fugitives like Tom. This thought caused him to consider another potential problem. Cobb had identified him by his horse. He wondered if it was general knowledge now that he rode a blue roan named Billy. He might be wise to swap Billy for another horse, although he just couldn't bring himself to do it. He and Billy had been together for a long time. They were partners, and they were comfortable with each other. Tom even forgave him for letting the Blackfoot run off with him. "But, if you let it happen again," he lectured the horse, "I'll let him keep you. See how you'd like being an Indian's pony. He'd ride you till you dropped, then he'd eat you."

Early the next afternoon, he struck the Yellowstone and almost rode right into a raiding party of about twenty Blackfeet. They were camped on the banks of the river and were grazing a large number of horses, so he figured they were returning from a raiding party on the Nez Perces or Flatheads. He was lucky he spotted them before they were aware of his presence but he was forced to lay low behind a low ridge and wait them out. The country was too open to circle around them without being discovered. He would have to take a wide detour to avoid them. He elected to wait until darkness when he felt it safe to continue. It struck him as being a little far south to run into a party of Blackfeet this time of year. If it had been summer, he would not have been surprised. But times were hard for all Indians these days, what with the army punishing all those not on reservations, and the buffalo damn near killed off. Maybe it was not so surprising that raiding parties were traveling a good way out of their usual territories.

Under the cover of darkness, he was able to continue west. His foremost intention was to leave the raiding party as far behind as possible, so he rode on through the night, not stopping until the first rays of light began to fill the valleys. It was unlikely the raiding party would be on the same trail he was riding, but he had learned from Squint Peterson that you never figure an Indian to do what he's supposed to do, because that's when he doesn't. He continued on until he crossed a high ridge that afforded a sweeping view of the country around him. Looking back the way he had come, he could see no sign of anything moving. *Good*, he thought, *I'm alone, the only man left on earth it seems.* All around him for as far as he could see, the land was empty. There was no game in sight, not even sign to indicate game had ever been there. For a fleeting moment, he could not suppress a feeling of melancholy, as if he and his horses were the only living things left on earth. High overhead, thin clouds began to form high up in the morning sky, and the sun, after a brief appearance, disappeared behind a dark bank of heavier clouds that were now rolling in from the northwest. The temperature had dropped at least ten degrees since he first saw sunlight that morning, and it looked likely to drop further. He had to admit to himself that he had guessed wrong on the weather. The turn in the weather added to his sense of loneliness, and

he urged Billy to get moving again. It seemed that
all other living things had sensed the spell of bad
weather coming, and that was the reason the land
was devoid of any signs of life. The animals and the
birds were holed up somewhere out of the oncoming
storm. Only the foolish man and his horses were out
in the open. Something told him he had better find
some cover for himself and his horses.

Even though it was not yet noon, the sky darkened
steadily until it might as well have been evening. The
wind picked up slightly, as the temperature continued to drop. He urged Billy on, scouting the river
banks for a likely spot, under a bluff possibly, to take
shelter from the storm that he now knew was coming. The first scattered snow flakes began to drift
down, acknowledged by a snort from Billy, as if he
meant to call it to Tom's attention. As he pressed on,
the snowfall increased in strength until it became
more difficult to see in front of him, making the hills
vague and misty, hidden behind a filmy curtain of
white. He rode on for another hour. By then, snow
was accumulating on the ground. He had no idea
how far he was from Bozeman, and he could only
hope that the storm would not last long. This much
he did know—he had to make a camp, and soon, for
with the wind increasing steadily now, it showed
signs of turning into a blizzard. Off to his right, away
from the river, Tom spied a wide gulch, lined with
trees. It appeared to narrow as it deepened toward
the far end. This was where he decided to make
his camp.

He followed the gulch until it came to a point with
evergreens forming a buffer around the sides and
end. It would have been difficult to find a better
choice of campsites if he had all day to look. The
trees offered protection for his horses, and it would

be a simple matter to fashion a makeshift shelter for himself. The snowfall was heavy by then and accumulating rapidly, so he wasted little time in preparing his camp. With his hand axe, he chopped four of the taller pines high up on their trunks so the stumps would be tall enough to provide him a high roof support. He took care to fell the trees inward toward each other so that, when they laid across each other, their tops supported by the narrow walls of the gulch, they provided a sturdy structure for his roof. Next he cut small trees and laid them across the larger ones. Cobb's huge buffalo coat provided the insulation necessary to keep melting snow from dripping on his head. He spread it over the large trees before covering his roof with the smaller branches.

His shelter ready, he gathered deadwood to get a fire started. He had no way of knowing how long he would be forced to use his shelter. It might stop snowing and clear up in an hour, but on the other hand, he might be snowed in for days. If that turned out to be the case, he wanted to make a solid shelter while he still had time to work on it. He had jerky and fire and plenty of snow for water. The only thing that worried him was the lack of food for the horses. There was nothing he could do about that now. He would just have to wait it out and do what he could to keep himself alive. At least they were out of the wind, and the trees should help keep them from freezing to death. About a half a foot of snow had accumulated on the floor of the gulch by the time he had a good fire started and settled himself in for the night.

He was awakened once in the middle of the night by a sharp cracking sound when a pine limb broke under the shifting of his roof. He went outside to check on it. There were probably six or seven addi-

tional inches of snow piled on top of his shelter, but
the structure seemed to be holding up. The air outside his camp was bitter cold, and it stung his skin
wherever it was exposed. The frigid air hurt his
lungs, causing him to hold the side of his buffalo
hood over his mouth in an effort to breathe. He
checked on the horses, huddled together in the small
stand of evergreens, their breath falling like smoke
from their nostrils. He hoped the storm didn't last
too long—they wouldn't make it if he couldn't find
food for them in a day or so.

Morning broke gray and cold with the snow still
falling, although not as heavily as the night before.
Tom stirred his fire and soon had it blazing again.
The sap snapping in the green branches gave off an
angry protest against the freezing air. His firewood
would soon be depleted. He would have to gather
more. He estimated the snowfall to be approximately
a foot and a half to two feet, and, while it was still
coming down, it had definitely slackened. If it didn't
last too much longer, he might still continue his journey, and, from the looks of the western sky at that
moment, it looked promising that it might stop.
While that thought gave him encouragement, he discovered that all had not gone well through the night.
Upon checking the horses, he found that Cobb's
packhorse had frozen to death during the night. Billy
and his packhorse, along with Cobb's saddle horse
with the three white stockings, had survived the cold.
White Stockings stamped impatiently when Tom approached them. Billy knickered softly, and his eyes
seemed to question his master. Tom looked at the
horse, then looked up to study the gray morning sky,
straining to find some encouraging sign.

Luck was with him. The snow stopped about midmorning, and the sky, although still overcast, bright-

ened perceptibly. Tom studied the sky and tried to make a decision. He desperately needed to get the horses moving, but he did not want to get caught out in the open if more snow was on the way. He estimated a total of about two to two and a half feet of snow. That much snow didn't worry him. Travel would be slow but not impossible. Still, he worried over his decision. After another hour, patches of pale blue began to break through the cloud coverage. When, after an additional half hour, a single beam of sunlight bored a hole through the gray overhead and focused on the snow in front of his shelter, Tom took that as a sign and his decision was made.

The horses were anxious to move. He picked over the supplies and the few plews that the dead horse had carried, loaded them on White Stockings, and left the rest. By the time he led the horses back to the mouth of the gulch, the sun had broken through in a few more spots. He was relieved to find that the snow in his gulch had drifted a little higher than that in the open, and the going was even better than he anticipated. Still, it was bitterly cold and his horses needed feed. Once again he made his way back to the river and followed it west. It was close to midday when he crossed a wide coulee with a narrow stream that was frozen over. Where the stream emptied into the river there was a heavy stand of willows and cottonwoods, so he stopped and stripped enough bark to feed his three hungry horses.

For the next two days the weather held, and he was able to make reasonable progress. He occasionally crossed ravines where the snow had drifted to a depth that almost reached Billy's belly, and the horses had to struggle to keep from foundering. But for most of the way, the going was not as tough as he had feared it might be. Cobb's horse, Buster, as Tom had officially dubbed him now, proved to be a strong animal, and Tom shifted some of the load from his own packhorse over to him when the smaller horse showed signs of struggling.

On the afternoon of the second day, Tom crossed the trail of a large party of hostiles. By the tracks of their unshod ponies, he knew they were Indians, and from the look of it there were no women or children with them. That meant only one of two possibilities: a raiding party or a hunting party. Whichever it was, he wanted to avoid them. They had crossed the river and turned west, the direction in which he was traveling. It was his guess they had crossed early that morning, so he decided to follow their trail for a while. They were going in the same direction, and it wouldn't hurt to mix his hoofprints in with theirs. He cautioned himself to keep a sharp eye out. He was pretty sure they were half a day ahead of him, but it wouldn't do for him to accidentally ride up on a party of what he estimated to be about twenty braves.

He followed the Indians' trail for about seven or eight miles before it abruptly left the river and turned north, an occurrence that greatly relieved his mind. His relief did not last long, however, for he had not ridden more than a mile farther when he heard shots.

He pulled Billy up sharply and stopped to listen, trying to locate the direction they had come from. His first thought was to see if he was in danger. Quickly scanning the horizon on all sides, and expecting to see a horde of savages charging down on him, he saw nothing but the white empty land. He did not have to wait long before hearing more shots, three in rapid succession. They were then followed by sounds of a volley, and then sporadic firing. There

could be little doubt that someone was in a pitched
battle. Evidently, the raiding party he had been following had found what they were looking for. He
hesitated for only a split second, then turned Billy in
the direction of the shooting.

Finally, only one hill separated Tom from the battle. As he came closer to the fight, he looked around
for a place to leave Billy and the packhorse. He also
didn't want to top the rise and find himself silhouet-
ted against the sky. From the sound of the gunfire,
the fight had to be just beyond the hill. Off to his
left, a gully cut into the hillside, deep enough to
picket the horses out of sight. That taken care of, he
rode up the rise, stopping to leave Billy just below
the crest. He crawled to the top and lay on his belly,
his Winchester ready.

Below him, a brisk battle was in progress. He
watched for a few minutes to get a full picture of the
situation before deciding what he should do, or even
if he should do anything at all. As he suspected, it
was the band of hostiles whose trail he had followed.
From his position, maybe a quarter of a mile or less
from the action, he could see that his original estimate proved to be correct—they appeared to be
about twenty strong. A steeply banked streambed
ran through the center of the small valley, and the
Indians were using it for cover to fire on a party of
whites—traders or trappers, he couldn't tell. There
were no wagons, only mules and horses, and they
were corralled in the center of a makeshift fort. Tom
tried to count the smoke from the guns as they returned fire from behind a flimsy breastwork of willows. It appeared that the numbers were fairly even
with about as many rifles on one side as the other.
Tom studied the terrain and picked his spot. If he
could make his way down along the edge of the hill,

he could pick up the cover of a line of trees on the creek's bank. From there, he could work his way up to within about a hundred yards behind the hostiles. From that position, he figured he could raise a lot of hell with his Winchester, as their backs would be exposed to his fire.

It took about fifteen minutes to work his way down to the position he sought. On foot, he led Billy along the back slope of the ridge until he reached the safety of the cottonwoods. From there he followed the frozen creek to a point where he picketed his horse well out of sight of the battle. He was close enough to identify the raiding party as Blackfeet. They were well armed, and from the cover of the steep bank, they controlled the battle. On his belly, Tom inched his way up to a log that lay along the creek. He situated himself there with his rifle and Cobb's repeating rifle. From his position behind the log, he had a clear field of fire out across the flat streambed where the smaller creek flowed into the stream the Blackfeet were using for cover. *A real turkey shoot*, he thought, as he cocked his Winchester and sighted down on the rearmost hostile.

In rapid succession, he went down the line of Blackfeet. Each time he squeezed the trigger, an Indian crumpled and slid down the creekbank. He took out four of the raiders before they figured out what was happening. When they finally realized that their brothers were not getting hit by rifle fire from the breastwork before them, they scurried around trying to find cover, not yet aware of the origin of the attack. Tom dropped two more of their number before they pinpointed his fire and scrambled to find protection behind the opposite creekbank. No longer with a clear shot, Tom continued to keep the Blackfeet pinned down behind the bank until he emptied his rifle. At that point, all firing ceased and a deathly silence fell over the little valley. While watching the creek, Tom calmly reloaded his Winchester, waiting for the attack that he figured would come. He didn't have to wait but a few seconds. The Blackfeet were sure now that there was just one man behind them. Figuring that he was reloading, they decided to rush him, and suddenly, with a blood-chilling war cry, three warriors leaped to their feet and charged him. Tom lifted Cobb's rifle and took careful aim. If he was of a mind to discourage their attack, he would have sighted on the warrior in front, so that the other two would see him fall and possibly turn back. But his intention was to reduce the number of the enemy by killing as many as he could. Consequently, he drew down on the rearmost man and squeezed the trigger. He missed, the bullet clipping a branch to the right of the man. Without hesitating, he resighted, allowing for the pull to the right, and watched the rear Blackfoot tumble as he pulled the trigger. With little loss of motion, he drew down on the second warrior and fired, hitting him square in the middle of the chest. The third warrior, unaware that he was now the lone survivor of the three, was within twenty yards of the log. Running full out, he fired his rifle at the gun barrel he could now plainly see. Tom took his time, ignoring the splinters that flew up when the warrior's bullet thumped into the log, sighted carefully, and placed his shot between the Indian's eyes. Though he was killed instantly, the Blackfoot continued to charge forward until he fell in a heap over the log Tom was lying behind.

The result of Tom's assault was general confusion among the rest of the Blackfeet. In less than a quarter of an hour, they had lost nine warriors and found themselves caught in a crossfire. Encouraged by the confusion of their attackers, a couple of the men came out from behind the flimsy breastworks and were now firing at the Blackfeet from above them on the creek's bank. Totally demoralized, the Indians withdrew, carrying as many of their dead as they could manage to recover. Satisfied that there would be no more trouble from this band, Tom held his fire while a Blackfoot brave risked his life to pick up a fallen comrade and made his way back to their ponies. He stood silently watching as the band of raiders mounted in haste and rode out of the valley.

"God's bones!" Scarborough swore. He stood on the bank of the stream, cold and still now where moments earlier it had crackled hot with flying lead. "Look at 'em run!" He turned to the man at his side, who was busily reloading his rifle. "I swear, John, they was dead Injuns all over this here crick. I ain't never seed sich shooting." Both men were straining to get a look at their rescuer. As they stood staring out toward the point on the creek where the rifle fire came from, they were soon joined by several others, now that the danger appeared to be over.

One of the party said, "Yonder he is," as Tom stood up from behind the log he had used for cover.

John asked, "You know him, Scarborough? I cain't make him out."

"I don't 'low as how I've ever seed him before, but I'll tell you this, he's shore as hell a dear friend of mine now." Noticing that Tom was now raising his arm in greeting, he called out, "Welcome, friend. Come on in!"

The men watched as Tom acknowledged their welcome with a wave of his arm, then turned away and disappeared into the trees. "Hell," Scarborough exclaimed, "he ain't coming in." But then Tom reappeared on horseback, starting across the stream.

"He just had to get his horse," John voiced the obvious. They stood in silence, watching the stranger ford the stream and climb up the bank. "He shore looks familiar somehow," he said, his voice trailing off as he studied the approaching rider. There was a moment of silence, and then he remembered. "Damn a mule, Scarborough! You know who that is?" He didn't wait for his friend's response. "That's that Dakota feller . . . kilt that soldier in Miles City!"

"You shore?" Scarborough replied, his voice low now that the rider was almost in hearing distance.

"Shore as boars got nuts and sows ain't. Look at 'em! We seen him in the saloon the night before he done it. You remember. You warn't that drunk. It's him, I tell ya. Ain't no surprise he's mighty handy with that rifle."

"Danged if I don't believe you're right. It's him all right." Scarborough quickly thought this revelation over, wondering if the identity of the man posed any threat to his pack train. There was very little he could do about it at that point, so he decided that it was not for him to question. It wasn't any of his affair, the thing that happened between Dakota and the soldier. Maybe Dakota had little choice in the matter—only Dakota could answer that one. But one thing Scarborough knew for a fact—the man had saved their bacon on this day and for that he was obliged. "Mister," he called out, "you shore come along at a proper time!"

Tom reined up and dismounted. "Looked like they had you pinned down. Just lucky I heard the shooting, I guess."

"I'm James Scarborough. This here is John Butcher. We're leading this party of folks to Bozeman." He gestured toward the small group of men gathering to see the man who had driven off the savages.

John Butcher stepped forward and extended his hand. "Dakota, ain't it? You shore tied a knot in them Injuns' string."

Tom was startled, surprised that the man knew who he was. He had not expected it, and in fact, had not even considered it. Tom managed to conceal his concern for having been recognized. He took John Butcher's outstretched hand and shook it briefly, a nod of his head the only reply to the greeting.

Scarborough stepped forward and offered his own hand, which Tom accepted. "Well, Mr. Dakota, come on over to the fire and we'll see if one of the women-folk can rustle you up somethin' to eat. You done a day's work out there. You could most likely use somethin', couldn't you?" He led the way toward the willow fort.

"I would appreciate a cup of coffee, if you have any to spare," Tom replied, following him.

The group of men parted to make way for him. A small, slightly built man standing to one side of the group had been studying the stranger very carefully. As he watched the tall young man in the buckskins and buffalo coat pass within a few feet of him, he suddenly asked, "Tom? Tom Allred?"

Tom halted in his tracks. He turned to face the man. At once he recognized the little man. "Jubal!" he exclaimed. His reaction brought a broad smile to the little man's face. "What in the world are you doing out here?" He hurried to grab Jubal's out-stretched hand, and the two men pounded each other vigorously on the back. The unexpected reunion left the rest of the men staring in wonder, waiting for the two of them to finish their greeting and get on with the explanation.

Jubal Clay took Tom by the arm and quickly told him how he happened to be in a mule pack train headed to Bozeman instead of running his store back in Ruby's Choice. "The town petered out," he explained. "We might'a stayed anyway, but we was visited one night by a band of Sioux, and they decided it would be a good idea to burn the store down. We saved what we could. Then Scarborough and this bunch come by, and we figured, hell, we might as well go with 'em."

"This is a helluva time of year for a train to be traveling through this country, even if you don't have wagons. How come you're camped over here anyway? You're a'ways off the trail to Bozeman, aren't you?"

Jubal shrugged. "It was Scarborough's idea. After that storm hit a couple days back, we was afraid we was in for it, and he knew about this place. Said it was a better place to hole up if we were gonna be snowed in for any time. But, hell, the storm let up and quit after a day. We're fixin' to get started again in the mornin'." He paused to give Tom a huge grin. "I know somebody's gonna be surprised to see you."

Tom felt a tingling sensation run down the length of his spine. He tried not to reveal the excitement he felt at the thought of seeing her again. As casually as he could manage, he asked, "You mean nobody's married Ruby yet?"

"Nope. It ain't like she ain't had plenty of chances."

Suddenly Tom went all numb inside, a feeling that was hard for him to understand. His heart had nearly skipped a beat with the mention of her name. He could now feel his pulse quicken in anticipation of seeing Jubal's daughter again, but he sought to delay the encounter, at least until he could prepare his emotions. It had been almost a year since he last saw her, though it seemed longer. Still, he had made a considerable effort to banish her from his thoughts, and now the mere mention of her name proved that he had been unsuccessful.

"Wait," he said, "I've got to fetch my packhorses. I left them back on the other side of the hill." He stepped up in the saddle and turned Billy back toward the stream.

Jubal stepped out of his way. "You need some help fetchin' 'em?"

"No, no thanks. I'll be right back."

"Hurry up then. I'll have Ruby make us some coffee."

From inside the makeshift fort, she had watched with more than a casual interest as the men talked to the stranger who had come to their aid. He had come at an opportune time, for it had appeared that the savages would be able to pin them down indefinitely. From this distance she could not see the man very well, but there was a feeling deep inside her that she could not explain, an urgency mixed with a feeling of coming home, as if everything would now be all right. When he mounted his horse and turned away, she felt a sinking in her bosom, feeling despair that he was leaving. She continued to stare at the point in the trees where she last saw him as she absentmindedly reached up and pulled the fur cap from her head making an effort to straighten her tousled hair. She glanced down at her hands, soiled with grease from loading and reloading rifles for her father during the attack. Walking away from the fire, she picked up some snow and cleaned her hands. It was obvious that her father knew the man—she could tell that by the way they greeted each other.

So she went about making the coffee before Jubal returned to their campfire. She only paused to watch her father when he came striding back, a grin covering his face.

"Ruby!" he called out cheerfully. "Looks like we got some company for supper."

"That so?" A feeling of excitement was building up inside her, but she would never show it. Instead, she appeared to be disinterested as she busied herself with preparing their meal. Finally she paused and looked at her father, who was still grinning as if he held a powerful secret. "Well, are you gonna tell me who it is?"

"I reckon you'll know him when you see him."

It was obvious her father was enjoying the surprise, so much so that she was now certain why she had felt this excitement. Although she had never voiced it, Jubal was smart enough to know there was a marked change in his daughter when Tom Allred rode out of Ruby's Choice a year ago this spring. *It was him!* She was sure of it now. She knew he would come back. He had to because she had known for some time now that Tom Allred was the only man she could marry.

When the coffee was on and a pot of boiled venison was set on the coals to warm, she brushed her hair and pinched her cheeks lightly in an effort to bring some color to them. *It'll have to do*, she thought. In this rough camp, there was little opportunity for primping.

Outside again, she glanced briefly at the pot, then stood by the fire and watched Tom approach the camp, leading two horses. He had taken off his heavy buffalo coat and laid it across the saddle. Clad in buckskins and high-laced moccasins, he looked more like a mountain man than when she had last seen him. When they said good-bye at the stream that day, he was still wearing army issue trousers and boots. He looked thinner than she remembered, and his face was covered with what looked to be a week's growth of whiskers. Still, the sight of his tall figure striding through the camp was enough to quicken her heartbeat. She felt a strong desire to run to greet him, but she restrained herself. She had her pride, even though she had once cast it aside to offer herself to him. But having done it once, she would not permit her feelings to be openly displayed again. He knew how she felt. It was his place to make the next move, if there was to be a next move for them. She stood silently, her face expressionless, waiting for him to speak.

"Hello, Ruby," was all he said—a simple greeting, nothing more. He hoped she could not read the confusion in his eyes, for he couldn't explain the emotions she caused. He truly did not know what his real feelings were for this girl. He felt clumsy in her presence, and while he was around her, he seemed always aware of how he stood and what his hands and feet were doing. No other human being had affected him this way. Did this mean he was in love with the girl? He honestly did not know. One thing for certain, she sure as hell bothered his mind.

"Tom," she returned simply.

They stood looking at each other, both feeling the awkwardness of the moment, not knowing what to say. All at once, they both blushed and laughed nervously like two children caught in some mischief. Ruby was first to see the humor in the situation and regain her composure. "Well," she said, "it seems like every time you show up, you're about starved to death and I have to feed you."

He laughed. "I reckon that's right. I seem to recollect I was pretty hungry when I showed up in Ruby's Choice that first time." He looked directly into her eyes. "It's good to see you, Ruby."

She returned his gaze, unblinking. "It's good to see you, too, Tom."

Just then, Jubal appeared from behind the tent. "I see you got your horses. If you want to, you can hobble 'em by the tent or you can turn 'em out with the rest of the horses."

"I reckon I'll turn 'em out with the rest of the horses," Tom replied. He added, "I wondered where you disappeared to."

Jubal grinned. "I thought I'd let you say hello to Ruby. I had to attend to some business out in the bushes. I was about to do it when them damn Injuns jumped us. My bowels was tied up in knots by the time you come along."

Ruby blushed. "I swear, Pa, everybody don't want to hear about your business."

Tom laughed. "I'll go take care of my horses."

After they had eaten the meat and some panbread Ruby had mixed up, they sat in front of the fire and talked. Jubal wanted to know why Scarborough and Butcher had called him Dakota, so Tom explained the series of events that had brought about the alias. He had not purposely taken on the name, he explained. He had simply refrained from giving his real name. The owner of the stable in Miles City, Pop Turley, had christened him Dakota, so Tom let it go at that. Jubal told him the army had sent a special detail of soldiers to look for him in Ruby's Choice, just as Tom had anticipated. He had been right to run, because the story the army had of the shooting in Jubal's store was a long sight from the truth. And, Jubal added, the lieutenant in charge of the detail had no interest in hearing the real story either.

"That sergeant was with 'em, too," Jubal continued, glancing at his daughter when he said it.

"Spanner?" Tom asked.

"Yeah, Spanner. You shoulda seen that son of a bitch lying his no-good self outta assaultin' Ruby. You'da thought it was the other way around, to hear him tell it. I started to get my shotgun and dust his sorry ass right there." He snorted and wiped his nose on his sleeve. "I would've, too, if he hadn't had so many soldiers with him."

There was a swollen moment of silence before Tom spoke again. He picked up a half-burned stick and poked around in the ashes with it for a few moments before tossing it back in the flames. "I guess Dakota dusted Spanner for you. That's the reason I had to leave Miles City."

"I know," Jubal replied. "John Butcher told me you done him in."

"I didn't have a whole lot of choice. He was aiming to kill me. If I'd had a choice, I would have run, but he jumped me in the stable, and there was no way out but through him."

"John told me about it when you went to fetch your horses. Him and Scarborough was in Miles City at the time. The way they told it, you damn near cut him in two with your rifle. Anyway, I reckon you know the army's put a price on your head."

"I know." He glanced quickly in Ruby's direction, but she was staring into the fire, listening intently to their conversation. Tom wished he could know what she was thinking.

Jubal studied his young friend's face for a long moment, then said, "Tom, I don't know if it's bothering your mind any, but you don't have to worry about any of these men trying to collect any rewards." He paused a moment longer. "Fact is, don't nobody but Scarborough and Butcher know you're that Dakota feller, and they ain't gonna say nuthin' about it. These people we're traveling with were heading west in a wagon train when a bunch of Sioux jumped 'em—burned their wagons and most of their belongings. They're already scared half to death. It wouldn't help none for them to know they got a wanted gunman campin' with 'em." He snorted and wiped his nose on his shirtsleeve once more. "Matter of fact, after the way you run them Injuns off today, they might want to make you captain of the train."

Tom didn't say anything for a while. He sat there staring into the glowing coals, the realization of what had become his life having just been hammered home in the simple, innocent words of his friend. "Wanted gunman" was what Jubal called him. Of course he knew he was wanted. But "gunman"? Was that what he was? A gunman? When he thought about it, he could find no reason folks would think any differently. It was just that he had never thought of himself as anything but a man defending himself. *No need to fret about it now,* he thought. "I appreciate it, Jubal. I guess most folks wouldn't welcome a wanted man at their campfire."

"Hellfire, Tom. I know you ain't no outlaw. I was there when you shot that there soldier in my store. I know you didn't have no choice. 'Course I warn't there when you got Spanner, but I know you done what you had to. Besides, that was one man that needed killin'."

They talked on until long after dark. Tom told them about his summer and fall running cattle and how he had almost become a partner with Eli Cruze.

Ruby listened to the two men talk, only adding a word here and there, not really participating in the conversation, just listening. More than once during the course of the evening, Tom and Ruby's glances found each other. He still did not know what to make of his feelings toward her. Her presence made him nervous, yet he did not want her to leave. Ruby, for her part, had made a decision. She loved him, of that she was certain, but she decided it was up to him to take the next step. Finally, Jubal announced that it was time to turn in.

"We can make room for you if you want to sleep in the tent," he offered.

"Thanks, Jubal, but I think I'll just roll up by the fire." He got up and stretched his back. Taking his rifle, he said, "I think I'll go take a look around before I turn in."

"Mind you don't git shot at by the lookouts."

"I'll watch out," Tom assured him. He knew Scarborough had sentries posted to guard against any surprise visits from the Blackfeet, but he preferred to have his own look-see. *No use taking chances.* Scarborough's men might be dependable, and Scarborough might know what he was doing, but the man had camped his party in a coulee where the Indians could just line up along a creekbank and take potshots at them. And that didn't indicate a man who knew what he was doing, as far as Tom was concerned. He turned to glance at Ruby and found the girl gazing intently at him. Their eyes held for a brief moment before Tom mumbled good night, then turned to disappear into the growing darkness.

Chapter XIII

At sunup the next morning, they packed up and broke camp, Tom with them. He was assured by Scarborough that he was a welcome addition to the party. Tom was soon to discover that Scarborough and his partner Butcher meant well, but had very little experience leading a group of travelers through the mountains. Of course that was evident from the beginning, otherwise they would not have even started the journey until spring. When Tom expressed his surprise to Jubal that a man of his experience had agreed to go along on the trip, Jubal's only explanation was that he had little choice. He had been burned out at Ruby's Choice. Besides, the weather had been mild for early December, and he just figured it was worth the risk of getting through before the winter storms. To Tom, it was not worth the risk, and he figured they had been greenhorn-lucky to get as far as they did. Jubal told him that the attack by the Blackfeet the day before had been the first trouble they had encountered, other than the weather and slow travel.

Scarborough may have been naive but he was quick to recognize the mettle of the young man called Dakota. He wasted no time persuading Tom to act as scout and guide. Since there was very little need for a guide now that the party had made it to the mountains, and they were no more than three days from Bozeman simply by following the river, Tom accepted but decided his services would best be utilized as a scout. With a little luck, he could at least save the party from a surprise attack by any more hostiles.

Tom didn't see very much of Ruby during the day's travel. At night, when he finished scouting the country around their campsite, he came back to Jubal's campfire to eat and sleep. Even then there was very little conversation between them. For one thing, Jubal was always present, and then he normally did most of the talking, leaving Tom and Ruby with little opportunity for more than stolen glances. Still, it was enough for Tom. He was almost grateful that the two of them were unable to spend time alone, for he was afraid he would be hard-pressed to control his emotions. He only wished he could keep his mind off her during his lonely scouts.

Listening to Jubal talk as they sat by the fire, Tom learned that he had a brother in Bozeman, Carlton, who had a small store in town. Jubal planned to add what money and merchandise he had saved to that of his brother. They felt that, together, they could make a handsome living selling supplies to the miners and the settlers. There was still a good deal of tracer mining in that area, and the Indian problem had been curtailed to a great extent, especially since Chief Joseph's Nez Perces had finally been captured. Bozeman already had several trade businesses in addition to the half-dozen saloons. It also boasted a sheriff and a couple of deputies. All in all, Jubal calculated, it looked like a promising start to a permanent town.

Tom had to revise his estimate of getting to Bozeman in three days. He had not figured on the slow travel of the greenhorn party he had joined. It was going to be more like four days if they kept a steady pace. It turned out to be five days in the end—the extra day was to celebrate Christmas. When the train left Miles City, after contracting with Scarborough and Butcher to guide them, they had planned to celebrate Christmas in Bozeman. But Christmas Day found them still two days' hard travel from the town. Being a somewhat religious group, with one ordained minister in the party, they voted to stop for one day to observe Christmas on the trail. Tom thought they were pushing their luck, but still something—possibly God—had watched over them this far: they might as well stop and take a holiday.

Tom, with John Butcher's help, selected a place to camp on a hillside covered with tall pines. Early the next morning, Christmas Day, he scouted around the camp for any sign of unwelcome visitors. Seeing none, he rode off up in the mountains, for he had seen sign of elk on the lower slopes and the thought of roasted elk was his idea of a real Christmas feast. Tracking an elk in the snow was a fairly simple thing to do. Getting close enough to shoot one was another. The tall pines made that part of the job easier though, and he soon spotted one of the animals pawing in the snow, looking for grass in a small clearing. When he returned to camp, he was met with a genuine hero's welcome, and everyone turned out to help prepare the feast.

The camp was certainly infused with the Christmas spirit in a hurry. There were some seven women in camp, and they all scurried around, searching through their supplies in an effort to find something to contribute to the dinner. Tom could not help but feel sorry for them. It had no doubt been a hard journey for them. Off and on, they had been on the trail since last spring. They had endured the parched prairie in the summer, starting up the Bozeman Trail only to be turned back by angry Sioux. They had used up precious money and supplies waiting for another wagon train from the Platte, only to be turned back again, this time losing their wagons and many of their belongings to another Indian attack. With the season nearing an end and getting desperate in their situation, they converted what resources they had left into a pack train and joined a party traveling north to Fort Lincoln. By the time they left Fort Lincoln and made their way to Miles City, it was already winter. When Tom joined them, the women looked tired and haggard, but still they started out determined every morning on the trail. They were a hardy lot, and Tom guessed they deserved a holiday.

Of immediate concern to him, however, was the same festivity that pervaded the minds of the men-folk. All thoughts of safety seemed to have evaporated as the men were caught up in the spirit of the season. He stressed the need to maintain the usual sentries to Scarborough, and Scarborough had assured him that the guards were posted. Still, Tom was not comfortable with that assurance. He decided he had better take it upon himself to patrol the perimeter of the camp, so he left the preparation of the festivities to the cheerful men and women and rode up into the hills behind the camp. After making a couple of circuits around the camp, his apprehensions were confirmed. The sentries all seemed more interested in the activities going on in camp than watching for a Blackfoot war party. One of them, a young boy of perhaps eighteen years of age, was even facing the camp instead of looking out for Indians. So intent was he on the dinner preparations that he did not know of Tom's presence until startled by the voice in his ear.

"If I was a Blackfoot, I'd start my scalp knife right about here and work right around your hairline." For emphasis, he pricked the shocked young man on the forehead with his skinning knife.

Mortified, the young man could do little more than stammer a lame excuse for his laxity. Tom scolded him, though not too severely. After all, it was Christmas. But the incident convinced him that he had better stay on watch while the celebrating went on. Since he had picked a campsite in some tall pines that stood above a sizable clearing, he knew that any attack had to come from above the camp. Anyone would be too easily seen if they tried to move across the clearing below them. So he decided to keep a watch in the trees above the camp, moving from time to time so he could keep an eye on the men on guard.

He complimented himself on his selection of campsites. The trees provided a buffer for the noise of the celebration going on below him, and the smoke from the fires would hardly be visible beyond a half mile or so. He knew there was very little risk of another attack this close to Bozeman, at least for a party this size. But there was also little wisdom in taking foolish chances. True, he missed out on the feast, but, other than that, he felt at peace with himself. Then thoughts of Ruby entered his mind, and he recalled the image of her that he had last seen when he rode out of camp. She was helping butcher the elk he had killed, and, when he climbed into the saddle to leave, she paused, stood up, and watched him go. Her eyes seemed to question him, although she said not a word. He met her gaze but, like her, said nothing. Now, as he sat beside a small boulder, gazing out over a miniature valley, the picture of her face returned to him and he could see every line clearly as if he had memorized it. He thought of the people below him, happily celebrating Christmas. *Some Christmas*, he thought, *half froze, half starved*. Still, they had survived an extremely tough ordeal in making it this far. And although they had lost most of what they started out with, they would soon be in Bozeman with most of their dreams still intact. There was land to be claimed. Some of them would find the gold so many sought. Most would farm or raise cattle. They would survive because they were families. A moment before, he had pitied them their lot. Now he wondered if he shouldn't envy them instead. He thought of the young girl again. He had sought to clear his mind of Ruby Clay, because he was afraid he wanted to make a commitment to her, and he knew he could not. How could he? He was a wanted man, an outlaw, and there was no way he could go back and change the road his life had taken. He could not outrun his past. He knew this, and it would always linger in the recesses of his mind even though he would still search for the new start he prayed was waiting for him somewhere beyond the mountains.

His thoughts were suddenly jolted back to the present by the sharp snap of a branch. Without thinking, he brought his rifle up, his eyes now searching the thicket before him, every nerve in his body alert. A moment later he relaxed.

"How did you know I was up here?" Tom asked, leaning the rifle back against the boulder.

"Pa said you were up here." She made her way around the heaviest part of the thicket and climbed up beside him at the foot of the boulder. Then she unfolded the cloth she carried. "I brought you something to eat. It didn't seem fair for you to get left out on the elk when you were the one who killed it."

"Why, thanks. That was right thoughtful of you." He had to admit he was beginning to regret missing out on the only fresh meat they had seen in days. "Damn, that smells good. Why don't you help me eat it?" He offered her a piece of the roasted meat.

"I've already ate," she replied. "I would've brought you some coffee but it'da been cold by the time I climbed all the way up here."

"That's all right," he said and laughed, "I'm just glad to get the meat."

She sat quietly watching him eat. When he had finished, he got up and went over to a patch of snow and washed his hands. Then he came back and sat down beside her. She smiled at him, and then, taking a corner of the cloth she had brought his food in, she very gently wiped a spot of grease from his cheek. The mere touch of her hand sent a ripple up his spine, and he knew at once that he was in serious trouble. He could not trust his emotions alone with this girl.

He got to his feet. "Well, I guess I'd better get you back down to camp."

She ignored his nervous fidgeting and remained seated on the buffalo coat he had spread out for her. "Sit down, Tom. I'm not gonna bite you. I'm not ready to go back yet." She spread the coat out, making a place for him to sit beside her.

Her remark had caused him to blush. "Well, I didn't think you would," he offered feebly. He paused to take a quick look around before settling himself beside her. "I guess it wouldn't hurt for a few minutes. Then I reckon it would be best for you to be in camp. No sense in taking chances."

She arched one eyebrow as she looked him straight

in the eye. "Tell me the truth. Do you think we're in danger of Indian attack?"

"The truth?" He paused. "I doubt there's an Indian within twenty miles of here."

Her expression quizzical now, she asked, "You mean you're just roaming around up here in the woods to avoid talking to me?"

"No!" he quickly stammered "I mean . . . that's a crazy thing to say. Why would I avoid talking to you? I talk to you every day, don't I?"

"Yeah, you talk to me," she said, smiling, "as long as Pa's around." She brushed a wayward strand of hair from her forehead. "You act like you got candy or something and you're afraid I'm gonna try to steal it. Well, I just want you to know, Tom Allred, I ain't gonna try to steal your candy. And I ain't been settin' around waitin' for the likes of you to come sweep me off my feet either." He started to stammer a reply, but she cut him off. "Just because I said some silly things and let you kiss me don't mean I care a fig about you. Besides, I was just a girl then. I was just playing anyway."

He was taken completely by surprise by her broadside verbal attack. He was so flustered by her statements that he wasn't sure whether he owed her an apology, or if he should be indignant himself. He didn't remember until later that it was she who did the kissing. As for the part about being only a girl then, she was seventeen at the time and all of eighteen now. But those thoughts did not occur to him while she sat so close to him that he could feel her body shiver with the chill of approaching evening. He could do nothing but stare at her, unsure of just where he stood in her emotions. In his confusion, he said nothing.

After a long moment of silence, she finally shook

her head, exasperated. "I swear, you do beat all. Well, I guess I better get back. I got chores." She gathered up the cloth she had used to carry his supper, and got up to leave.

He scrambled to his feet. "Ruby," he started, "I don't know what to say . . ." His voice trailed off as she stood waiting for him to do something, say anything, give some indication that his brain was even working. Finally, he blurted, "I really appreciate the supper."

"I swear!" she uttered, her tone heavy with sarcasm. "You're welcome." With that she turned on her heel and started down the hill toward the camp.

"Ruby, wait!" he called after her, but she continued walking, not even turning her head. He ran to catch her. Grabbing her arm, he whirled her around to face him. "Ruby, I'm sorry. I'm not very good with words. I don't know what to tell you except that I think about you a lot." He released her arm and stood gazing at her face.

"Is that it, then? Is that what you wanted to tell me? You think about me a lot?" When it became apparent that he was not going to elaborate, she shook her head in amazement, and turning again, left him standing there drowning in his confusion.

He stood there a long time, staring at the empty forest where he had last seen her as she made her way down the hill. "Tom Allred," he muttered, "you are the stupidest jackass God ever put on this green earth." His head was in complete chaos. He was at once forlorn and miserable over his bumbling of what could have been the most wonderful thing to happen to him. Yet, at the same time, he was more that a little angry with himself to think this slip of a girl could befuddle him so. He did not know what he wanted. He had been truthful when he said he thought about her a lot. He thought about little else since he had joined the train. Now, when he had the opportunity to tell her how much he did think about her, his brain went to sleep and his mouth froze up. *Maybe,* he thought, *I should go down there and tell her I'm sorry.* He rejected the idea as soon as he thought it. It was plain that he had been given his opportunity and failed to pass muster. "Best forget it," he whispered softly to Billy. He did not return to camp that night, preferring to roll up in his big buffalo coat and sleep under the stars.

The party broke camp and got under way the next morning. The weather continued to favor them, and on the afternoon of the second day they reached Bozeman. Tom and Ruby exchanged no more than a few words during the entire two days. He felt very self-conscious around her. She, on the other hand, simply seemed not to notice him. He could not understand the misery that had suddenly descended upon him. As recently as three days before, he was trying to avoid the girl because he did not want to become involved in any permanent relationship. Now, he couldn't stand to be around her, yet he was even more miserable when away from her. It was a relief to see the buildings of Bozeman on the horizon. Maybe now he could start trying to get her out of his mind.

As Bozeman was the final destination of the mule train, the party broke up and went their separate ways. Most of the travelers found temporary quarters hard to come by in the fledgling town of saloons and supply stores. Some were forced to weather out the season in makeshift tents and huts. Tom shook his head in amazement that anyone would attempt to come to this country in the dead of winter. But he had long since learned not to be surprised by the actions of the emigrants from the East. Little wonder the Indians looked upon all whites as lunatics.

Jubal and Ruby were met by Jubal's brother. They at least had a home to go to. As was his custom, after saying good-bye to Jubal and Ruby, Tom rode down to the livery stable. He wanted to see to his horses, but aside from that he knew there was usually some space a man could bed down in for a small sum. His needs were simple enough, and, since he had no hut to go to, the stable was the next best thing. Besides, a man wanted by the law, even if from another territory, would be wise to sleep close to his horse.

Broadus Sims, Tom discovered, kept a clean stable and his rates were reasonable. He welcomed Tom's animals, and after thinking the proposition over for barely more than a few seconds, agreed to rent Tom the back part of the tack room for temporary living quarters. Tom assured him that it would only be for a short period, at least until he decided to find a permanent place in Bozeman or to move on in the spring. After he got himself settled, his horses taken care of, and his belongings put away, he left the stable and went in search of some supper and maybe a drink of whiskey to warm his bones. Mr. Sims had recommended the Miner's Saloon for supper, simply because it was the only one that served food. So Tom walked up the muddy street to the Miner's.

After one stiff shot of whiskey that seared his gullet all the way down to his groin, he moved over to a table in the corner of the room and waited for his supper. In a few minutes, an old Oriental man shuffled out of the kitchen with a plate of beef stew and beans. Without a word, he placed the plate down in front of Tom and turned to leave.

"Coffee?" Tom called after the man.

The Oriental stopped and nodded his head vigorously up and down, then disappeared through the kitchen door.

"He don't understand much English. You'll be waiting for that coffee till hell freezes over." Tom was startled by the voice beside him. He had been so engrossed in his supper that he hadn't even noticed the huge man when he moved silently up beside him. "Pete!" the man called out to the barkeep, "feller here wants some coffee." He pulled a chair back and sat down. "And tell that little squint-eye of your'n to bring me a cup, too."

"Much obliged," Tom said, eyeing his guest curiously.

"My name's Crutchfield," the man said as he settled heavily into the chair. The chair creaked in protest from the bulk of the man. He flashed a wide smile that seemed to be friendly, but Tom could feel the man's eyes searching his face. Almost casually, as if he wasn't even aware he was doing it, he unbuttoned his coat and let it fall open enough to show a badge. "I'm the law around these parts," he said, in case Tom didn't notice the badge.

Tom's muscles tensed. He didn't think he was wanted in this territory, and the sheriff didn't seem to recognize him. He admonished himself to remain calm. After all, the man was friendly enough. Maybe he was just being neighborly. He probably didn't know Tom from Adam. Tom returned the smile and continued to eat.

"I reckon you're just passing through our little town."

It was a statement, but Tom recognized the question in it. He finished chewing a tough mouthful of stew meat before answering. "Well, I hadn't decided yet, to tell you the truth."

Crutchfield paused and waited while the Oriental set two cups of coffee on the table. "Well, let me see if I can help you make up your mind." He turned his head and yelled over his shoulder, "Pete! Give me some of that sugar you keep hid behind the bar." He turned back to Tom, his smile again in place. "Makes out like he ain't got no sugar, like it was too damn scarce to give away." He looked at Tom for a long moment with a twinkle in his eye. It was almost as if he was about to share a wonderful secret. "You come in with that mule train, didn't you?" When Tom nodded that he did, he continued, "I was talking to another feller come in with that train, feller by the name of Scarborough. And he was telling about a young feller that joined up with 'em just a few days back, went by the name of Dakota." Crutchfield could see he was hitting close to home by the sudden steeling of Tom's eyes, though he gave no other sign of concern. Crutchfield continued, "This Dakota feller's supposed to be a real mean character, gunned down some people over in Miles City. Now, you seem to be the only stranger in town that fits that description. I figure you've gotta be Dakota."

"Maybe," Tom replied coolly. He didn't care for the way the conversation was shaping up. He glanced quickly at his rifle, propped against the wall beside his chair.

Crutchfield followed his glance. "Now don't get excited. You ain't in no trouble with me . . . yet." He paused to stir some more sugar in his coffee. "There's just a few things we need to get settled right from the start, that's all. The main thing is, I don't intend to have no trouble in my town. Now, I reckon if I go over to the office and start looking through the handbills, I might find some paper on somebody named Dakota, or maybe somebody under another name. I ain't concerned about that. As far as I know, you ain't wanted for nothing around here. Being a lawman, I can't collect no reward anyhow. Tell you the truth, I'm damned if I don't just about have less use for bounty hunters than I do for the outlaws they're huntin'. All the same to me. Don't see no difference." His smile faded into a deep frown. "What I'm concerned about is this town, and I ain't gonna stand for no trouble here. That's why I'm giving you some friendly advice right now that it might be better if you make your visit here a brief one."

Tom took his time in responding. He gave the sheriff's words a few moments' thought, then answered quietly, "Sheriff, you have my word, I'm not looking for anything but a place to get warm and fill my belly. If there's any trouble here, somebody else will have to start it. I just want to mind my own business."

The smile returned to Crutchfield's face. "Well now, I hoped you'd say that. You look like a sensible enough young feller. But I think your visit here still ought to be brief. I got a feeling you might attract bounty hunters and I've done told you what I think of them. They'd be most likely shooting at you, and you'd most likely be shooting back at them. And me and my deputies would most likely be shooting at both of you. And, with all that shooting going on, some of the town's law-abiding citizens might git hit with a stray bullet." He paused to let his words sink in, enjoying his own wry way with words. "And I can't have that in my town."

The sheriff's condescending air was not lost on Tom. Crutchfield obviously endeavored to run the town completely, and, despite his cavalier attitude,

Tom harbored no doubts that the man could get pretty nasty if the occasion called for it. After a moment, Tom sighed. "All right, but give me a couple of weeks to rest up some and get my backside warm. Then I'll move on. Whaddaya say? Is that asking too much?"

Crutchfield laughed. "Fair enough." He seemed to mellow a little toward the young stranger. He sat back in his chair and sipped his coffee. He thought for a minute, then said, "You know, there was already one bounty hunter through here a while back, and he went looking for somebody back toward Miles City." He looked quickly at Tom. "He went lookin' for you, didn't he? Big ole ugly feller, name of Cobb." He searched Tom's face for confirmation.

"I don't know. Maybe."

Crutchfield's eyes fairly sparkled. "That feller's a mean one. He'll be back any day now lookin' for some reward money from Kansas City."

Tom shrugged, unconcerned. "I don't think so."

"You don't? Why not?"

"I think he lost interest."

"Is that so?" Crutchfield's smile broadened to an open grin. "Is that so?" he repeated. He seemed to be highly amused by Tom's remark. "You know, Dakota, I kinda like your style. Too bad you're only gonna be in town for a couple of weeks." He got up to leave.

"Thanks, Sheriff. I appreciate it."

Chapter XIV

During the next couple of days, Tom found that the sheriff was one of the few people to show any measure of hospitality toward him. Evidently, Scarborough had managed to spread the word throughout the whole town that the recently arrived stranger bunking in the stable was none other than a wanted gunman named Dakota. Not that anyone gave Tom any trouble. To the contrary, he was politely avoided everywhere he went. He found it difficult to believe, in a town that small, the entire population could manage to avoid even casual contact with him. He might as well have had the plague. Even some of the recently arrived pilgrims, people who had so welcomed his help when they were struggling through the snowy foothills with Scarborough and Butcher, walked around him. *Queer,* he thought, *they weren't so particular when I saved their bacon from the Blackfoot raiding party.* It wouldn't have mattered then if I was Satan himself. He didn't like the notoriety he had suddenly found. His intention all along was to lose his identity in hopes of starting over, far away from the army and the bounty hunters. Occasionally thoughts of moving on farther west crossed his mind, maybe striking out to find his brother Little Wolf and Squint Peterson, if they were

still alive. He could see few choices and little time to
make them. Crutchfield was friendly enough, but
Tom had no doubts that the sheriff meant what he
said. Two weeks and the lawman would likely turn
his mean side.

The one person who still remained friendly, of
course, was Jubal Clay. But Tom did not push this
relationship because of his feelings for the man's
daughter. Still, he saw Jubal occasionally, usually in
the saloon, where Tom spent most of his daylight
hours. Jubal was busy in his brother's store, getting
ready for the spring when they planned to add on
to the original structure and bring in new stores of
drygoods from Kansas City. Tom had more or less
made his temporary headquarters at the corner table,
where he took his meals from the old Oriental, sometimes sitting in on a small-stakes poker game with
Doc Brewster, the town physician and veterinarian,
and Crutchfield's two deputies. The fact that the deputies were sociable did not surprise Tom. He was
sure they were there by design to keep an eye on
"the gunfighter."

The game was friendly enough and helped to pass
the time during the cold winter days. Nobody won
or lost very much, and none of the three players
seemed to think anything about Tom being a wanted
man. A man was taken pretty much at face value as
far as Doc Brewster was concerned, at least in this
part of the world. Times were too hard and the land
was too harsh to worry about what a man had done
in his past. If rumors could be believed, Doc himself
was hardly one to criticize another man's past life.
Carlton Clay said Doc had left a practice, along with
a wife and children, back East. And, as Carlton
pointed out, folks figured it was Doc's business and
none of theirs. He was the only doctor around, and

folks hereabouts were glad to have him, even if he was half drunk most of the time. In fact, more than a few people felt he was better at doctoring when he was drunk—his hands shook too much when he was sober. The long cold winters of Montana had turned more than one man to drink. Doc was fond of talking about any subject and, drunk or sober, Tom found the man an entertaining companion.

As for Crutchfield's two deputies, there could not be two more directly opposite men. One was an older man of perhaps fifty. His name was Breezy Martin. He sported a full beard of gray whiskers that spread in all directions like a bramble bush, and dirty gray wads of hair hung limply around his neck. He always wore a wide-brimmed hat with a pointed crown, the kind most folks called a "Montana Peak." The hat never left his head, and, during the whole time Tom was in Bozeman, Breezy never changed his woolsey shirt or the dingy gray underwear underneath. When it came to talking, he could converse on as many subjects as Doc could, leading Tom to suspect why he was called Breezy. Tom found it a humorous coincidence that he shared a name with his old horse, Breezy, the main difference being that the horse was somewhat windy on the other end.

Will Proctor, the other deputy, was a much younger man. He didn't talk a great deal. Perhaps, Tom speculated, this was because there was very little opportunity to get a word in edgewise with Doc and Breezy around. But he seemed friendly enough, and he did provide a fourth for poker.

Tom had not seen Ruby since the first day he arrived in town. According to Jubal, she was settling in just fine with his brother's wife, helping her around the little farm Carlton owned outside of town. He thought about her a lot more than he

wanted to. He just couldn't help it. She would creep
into his thoughts at odd times of the day and night,
and he would find himself wondering what she was
doing at that moment, and if she ever thought about
him. Then he would have to remind himself to rid
his mind of the girl. He could offer her no future, so
he had no choice but to forget her. But he soon realized that it was going to take more than whiskey and
poker to shut her out of his thoughts, thoughts that
were beginning to make his life miserable. He knew
it was time to move on.

Young Will Proctor had never had a great deal of
ambition to do anything, especially if it entailed hard
work. At age twenty-two, he had already tried his
hand at working cattle and sheep, as well as spending a short time as a farmhand. He didn't care for
any of it, and he was always looking for a softer
deal. For that reason, he jumped at the job of deputy
when Aaron Crutchfield offered it. And he was
pretty much satisfied with life for two years. But
now, with another new year beginning and still no
increase to his thirty-dollars-a-month salary, he
started looking around for an even softer deal that
offered more money. Bozeman offered few prospects
for a man with the particular ambitions of Will Proctor, that is, until an outlaw called Dakota came to
town. Crutchfield had no use for bounty hunters and
no interest in collecting a reward himself, saying it
was unlawful as long as he wore a badge. But Will
didn't always agree with Crutchfield's philosophy.
Wanted handbills on dozens of outlaws came in from
all over every month, when the stage could get
through. It didn't take a long search through the
stacks of papers before Will found what he was looking for. His eyes grew as big as saucers when he saw

that the reward for a man named Tom Allred, alias
Dakota, was twenty-five hundred dollars. Dead or
alive! He was dumbfounded. This man with whom
he played cards almost every night for the past week
seemed like a sqare enough fellow, yet he was worth
twenty-five hundred dollars to the U.S. Army!

Will figured his prayers had been answered. His
own gold strike was sitting right there at the corner
table of The Miner's. He needed little time or thought
to make up his mind. He would resign his job as
deputy. The thought of having that much money in
one lump sum was enough to overshadow any notions of wearing a badge until he was as old and
fat as Aaron Crutchfield. His decision made, and the
course of his future laid out for him, Will became
even more diligent in keeping an eye on Dakota,
going so far as to befriend the man he planned to
collect on. And so it happened that Tom found himself with an almost constant companion during the
final week of his stay in Bozeman. In fact, Tom began
to realize that it was near impossible to turn around
without finding Will Proctor standing there. Tom did
not suspect anything, however. He just assumed Will
was a bored young man with little else to do during
the slow months of winter. Will Proctor may have
figured he already had a claim on the reward, but
he found that he had competition when it came to
the pursuit of blood money.

It happened one evening at suppertime. Tom was
seated in his customary corner chair eating, when the
two strangers walked into The Miner's. He paid little
attention to the pair as they walked slowly over to
the bar and called for whiskey. The warm sanctuary
offered by Sheriff Crutchfield, along with the conge-
nial company of his poker companions, had effec-
tively blunted the edge of Tom's alertness. He

assumed he was safe as long as he was in town with the sheriff's blessings. This assumption was a mistake on his part. He soon learned that a wanted man could never relax his guard. Given the same situation two weeks before, he would have noticed every detail about the two men the moment they entered the room. Now, he didn't even bother to glance up as they stood at the bar drinking, talking in hushed mumbles while they stared at the solitary man eating in the corner.

Pete, the bartender, was not as unconcerned as Tom, for there was something about the pair that made him want to keep his eye on the cash drawer. They had a look of uncut meanness like that of half-starved coyotes, both as thin as knife blades with heavy whiskers spilling over their stained hide coats. Both men wore two pistols, a fact made obvious by the twin bulges under their coats. Pete moved down to the end of the bar where his shotgun was hidden, then made a show of polishing his shot glasses while he watched the two out of the corner of his eye. When one of the men reached inside his coat and pulled out a folded piece of paper, studying it intently while whispering to his companion, Pete motioned for his son. "Boy," he said, "run on down to the sheriff's office and tell Aaron it might be best if he was to come up here. Hurry now." The boy nodded and disappeared out the back door.

Tom, still intent on finishing the boiled beans on his plate, was unaware of the two men until they were suddenly standing right in front of him. In that instant, he became fully alert to the danger facing him. He was familiar with the sensation now, a cold dead feeling that penetrated his bowels and seemed to set his spine tingling. The first time it happened, and maybe the second, he thought it to be cold fear.

But he had learned to identify it as a signal to his nervous system to ready his mind and body to fight for his life.

With no outward sign of concern, he slowly placed the knife and fork on his plate and slid it a few inches away from him. He said not a word, but his eyes never blinked as he measured the two men confronting him. He slowly withdrew his hands from the table and placed them in his lap. His rifle, propped against the wall, had not escaped the notice of the pair. Both men had unbuttoned their coats and pushed them aside to reveal holstered six-shooters. Their reluctance to draw their weapons in the crowded saloon before making sure they had the right man was about the only advantage in Tom's favor. Judging from their glances at the rifle against the wall then back again at him, Tom figured they were pretty sure they could draw their pistols before he could reach for his rifle and cock it. He had to agree. His options were bleak. He just sat and waited.

"What you callin' yourself these days? Dakota or Allred?" one of them asked. He appeared to be older than his partner. Tom figured them to be brothers, and the one who spoke looked like he was accustomed to doing the talking. He was rawboned and grizzled and sure of himself. The younger one, though apparently carved from the same pine knot as his brother, seemed nervous and edgy, glancing from side to side at the other patrons of the saloon.

"Mister, what I call myself is my business." He met the man's glare with a steady gaze. "What's on your mind?"

"Ha!" he snorted. "I'll tell you what's on my mind. I got a wanted poster on you right here in my pocket, and I reckon I'm hoping you make a try at that there rifle so's I can put a bullet right between your eyes.

That's what's on my mind. What you say to that?"
He glanced briefly in his brother's direction, a smirk
painted on his face.

Tom's expression remained the same, showing no
sign of being overly concerned. He studied the man
before him and then the younger one behind him for
a moment before answering. "I say that would be a
damn fool thing to try with a pistol aimed right at
your balls."

This sobered the expression on the man's face momentarily as he considered Tom's reply. Then the
smirk returned to his face. "Is that so? You 'spect me
to believe you got a gun under the table?" The smirk
spread into a wide smile. Without taking his eyes off
Tom, his hand resting on the handle of his holstered
pistol, he commented to his brother, "Says he's holding a gun on me under the table. What you think,
Quincy? Think he's got a gun under there? Or maybe
he might be thinkin' he can buffalo us."

Quincy scoffed, "He's lyin'. He ain't got no gun."
With that, he pulled one of his pistols from the holster and leveled it at Tom. With the appearance of
the drawn pistol, the other customers in the saloon
immediately backed away, giving them plenty of
room. A couple of the less stouthearted patrons
bolted for the door. Pete edged over toward the shotgun under the bar.

The older brother grinned openly now. "You know
what, Mr. Dakota? I think Quincy's right. I think you
ain't got no gun under there." He slowly drew his
pistol from the holster. "Watch him, Quincy."

"This is all the warning I'm going to give you,"
Tom stated with a fatal calmness in his voice. "You
and your brother put those weapons away and get
out of here."

"Ain't he the feisty one, Quincy?" His smile

stretched even wider. "You're bluffing. If you got a gun under there, then let's see it." When Tom did not respond to his challenge, he said, "I thought so." He slowly bent down to look under the table, his eyes locked on Tom's until his face was level with the table. "Watch him, Quincy," he warned before letting his gaze drop beneath the tabletop.

The explosion of the pistol sounded as loud as a cannon in the crowded confines of the saloon, startling everyone there as if the whole room had blown up. The bounty hunter's face could not have been more than a foot from the muzzle when the bullet knocked a hole right through his forehead. It was followed a split second later by another shot from the doorway that dropped Quincy where he stood, his gun still leveled at Tom.

Tom, expecting a shot from Quincy as soon as he pulled the trigger, kicked the table over and rolled on the floor behind it. He thought at first that Quincy had fired the second shot, and he stared in amazement as the younger of the bounty hunters slumped to the floor, dead. Tom whirled around, ready to return the fire, only to find himself aiming at Will Proctor standing in the doorway. They froze, their pistols aimed at each other. Then Will suddenly grinned and let his gun hand drop to his side.

"I reckon it's a dang good thing I was in the office when Jimmy here come running in," Will said, replacing his gun in his holster. "Aaron's out to his ranch, be there all week. Looks like I got here just in time."

Tom relaxed. "Looks like you did." He stuck his pistol in his belt and slowly got to his feet. "I'm damn glad you did, too. I wasn't real sure I could get the other one before he got me." He instinctively reached for his rifle, feeling more comfortable with it in his hand.

Will walked over to look at the two bodies sprawled on the floor in grotesque fashion. He rolled the younger one over with his foot, revealing the pool of blood that had gathered under the man's chest. Satisfied that no spark of life remained, he then looked at the older brother. The bounty hunter wore a look of horrified surprise, an expression no doubt affixed no more than an instant before his death. His face was covered with a gray powder burn spreading from the ugly black hole in his forehead. "I reckon you broke him from peeping under tables," Will said.

By this time, the customers who had fled when the shooting started were crowding back into the saloon, along with a few other curious spectators. Will was about to send Jimmy for Doc Brewster, who was also the town's undertaker, but Doc walked in at that moment, having heard the gunfire. Doc paused to scratch his scraggly chin whiskers thoughtfully as he glanced from one corpse to the other, which was the extent of his examination of the bodies. "Well, gentlemen, I suppose this will delay the poker game for a bit." He asked a couple of the spectators to help carry the bodies out.

Will turned to Tom. "Come on, I'll buy you a drink."

As they stood at the bar, Tom tossed his whiskey down quickly and watched for a moment while Jimmy went to work on the bloodstained floor with a scrub brush and a pan of water. After a moment, he turned back to Will Proctor and asked, "Are you gonna be in any trouble over this?"

"With Aaron? Naw. Hell, everybody saw it. I couldn't just stand there and let him shoot you. Besides, Aaron don't care much for bounty hunters coming in town here and taking the law in their own hands." He gave Tom a pat on the shoulder. "Anybody here would say you shore as hell didn't start it."

"I guess you're right. I appreciate what you did. I just wouldn't want you to get in any trouble for saving my bacon." Now that it was over, Tom began to reflect on the circumstances that had resulted in yet another notch on his kill stick. This, he supposed, would further complicate his life, adding more to his already too-infamous reputation, no doubt sending more bounty hunters his way. When he glanced around him at the curious patrons of The Miner's, he noticed that the respectable distance they had always maintained was now even wider. They stared openly at him as if gawking at an animal in a zoo, looking away the moment his gaze met theirs. He didn't like the portrait they had painted of him. Once again it was time to move on.

It was a gray, cheerless morning. The sun seemed to have abandoned the town entirely, having not shown its face for more than a week. Tom had thought to wait for good weather, but he decided it would never come and besides, he felt he had worn out his welcome in Bozeman. Though Will was friendly enough, Aaron Crutchfield made it plain that Tom's presence there was not exactly comforting to the townfolk, and this was before the shooting. He wasn't likely to be overjoyed when he heard the latest news. Tom figured it best to leave right away, before Aaron came back. So, on this cold and cloudy morning, he tied Billy and his two packhorses up in front of Clay's Store and went in to say good-bye to Jubal.

Jubal truly hated to see him go, but he understood

why he felt he had to leave. Tom expressed his desire to say farewell to Ruby, and Jubal encouraged him to do so. Tom said he would swing by Carlton Clay's farm on his way. Not wanting to prolong the departure, he quickly shook Jubal's hand and wished him well. Jubal watched from the door as Tom wheeled Billy and rode out of town.

It was about an hour's ride to the farm, but it was still the middle of the morning when he turned into the narrow path that led to the house. Carlton Clay had built himself a cozy little log house atop a grassy knoll. There were no trees around the house, making it easier to defend in case of attack by hostiles, a feature that Tom figured to be of prime importance a couple of years back. Now, the threat of Indian trouble had diminished to the point where it had become a rarity this close to town. He could already feel a chill down in his bones from the short time he had spent in the saddle, and the sight of the stone chimney, with its thin ribbon of smoke cheerfully reaching up toward the gray clouds, was a mighty welcome sight. He admonished himself for getting soft, sitting around in a saloon in town. He would have to get used to the bitter cold again.

The door of the log house opened as he crossed the yard, and Ruby Clay stood in the doorway. She watched him as he pulled Billy up and dismounted stiffly. Not until he tied his horses did she speak.

"Well, good morning." She glanced toward the pack animals, then back at him. "Looks like you're getting ready to light out for somewhere."

"Morning, Ruby. Yeah, I guess it's time for me to move on."

"It's kind of a bad time of year to go traveling, ain't it?"

He laughed. "Yeah, I guess it is. Believe me, if I thought I had a choice, I'd wait till spring."

He was beginning to wonder if she was going to keep him standing out in the cold when Charlotte Clay, Ruby's aunt, looked over Ruby's shoulder and greeted him. "I bet you could use a good hot cup of coffee. Ruby, are you gonna ask him in or make him stand out there all day?"

Ruby blushed. "I'm sorry, Tom. Come on in." She stood aside to let him pass. "You want a biscuit? There's some left from breakfast." The sight of his horses all packed up and obviously ready to travel had caused her to forget her manners for a moment. She had been here at her uncle's house for almost two weeks, and she wondered when, if ever, Tom Allred was going to show up for a visit. Now when he did, it was apparent it was just to say good-bye.

Charlotte poured coffee from a large gray pot that sat on the back corner of the stove and placed the cup on the table next to a plate of biscuits. It had been a long time since he had had the opportunity to eat a biscuit baked by a woman who knew how to bake biscuits, and even longer since he had been served coffee in a china cup. Charlotte, pleased by the obvious enthusiasm he showed for this simple fare, stood watching him eat, her hands on her hips, ready to fill his cup again if necessary. Ruby poured herself a cup and sat down opposite him at the table.

When Tom had finished the second of the two biscuits he had taken from the plate, Ruby broke the silence. "So, you're moving on again. Where are you heading to?" She attempted to make her voice as casual as possible.

"I don't know for sure, west I guess, Flathead country maybe." She made no comment, but the look in her eyes searched for an explanation. "I reckon Jubal told you about the trouble last night."

"He said you shot a man."

Although it was a simple statement with no apparent condemnation, he felt the need to defend his actions. "I didn't have any choice. He was gonna kill me as sure as I'm sitting here now." He searched her eyes for understanding.

"I know. Pa told me. He said Will Proctor shot the other man, so I don't see how anybody'd blame you for it."

"He didn't give me any choice," he repeated.

"Then what are you running for?" she asked.

He had to think for a moment before answering. "I don't know, to avoid more trouble, I reckon. It seems like it has a way of finding me."

"Tom," she implored, impatient with him now, "it wasn't your fault, no more than it was with that soldier in Pa's store."

"Huh," he responded, the irony of her remark etched in his tone. "That's true. It wasn't my fault. But it sure landed my name on a wanted poster." He shook his head when Charlotte Clay started toward him with the coffeepot. "No thank you, ma'am, I've had plenty." Turning back to Ruby, the fire still in his eyes, he continued, "That fellow last night won't be the last one. There'll be another one, and another one. I don't know how much I'm worth now, but you can be sure the ante'll keep going up every time something like last night happens."

She shook her head, exasperated with him. "You've got to stop running sometime. Maybe, if you settle down around here, Aaron Crutchfield might help you get your good name back."

"Ruby," he replied impatiently, "Crutchfield already gave me two weeks to get out of town and that was before last night! He'll probably want to put me in jail now!" He threw up his hands in exasperation. "I've got to find someplace where I can get a new start, where nobody knows me. Hell, I'm probably putting a noose around my neck now for sitting here when I ought to be riding." He looked into her eyes, searching for understanding, wanting her to see what he could not yet bring himself to say. "I just didn't want to leave without saying goodbye to you."

Charlotte Clay was still standing at the corner of the table, listening to the conversation between the two young people. It took but a moment more, as they sat in silence, gazing into each other's eyes, for Charlotte to realize there was something stronger than mere friendship smoldering between the two, and she at once felt her intrusion there. "Well, I've got chores I'm getting behind on." Pulling a heavy coat down from a peg by the door, she said, "I'm going out to the barn to see to the chickens."

They sat for what seemed a long time after the door closed behind Charlotte, still looking deeply into each other's eyes. Finally, Tom broke the silence. "Ruby, I don't know what to say. I just wanted to see you again before I left."

"I know," she whispered. Her eyes softened. Then, as if she realized she had shown a weakness, she laughed and added, "You better know you couldn't leave without saying good-bye."

Her attempt to lighten the situation was lost on him. He already felt the pain of having to ride out of her life again, especially now, when he had all but admitted to himself that his feelings for her ran a lot deeper than he thought sensible. He got up from his chair. "I guess I better get going." He paused. It was hard for him to say it. "I mean to tell you what I wanted to say Christmas when you brought my supper up on the hill. What I mean to say, I guess, is that I think about you a lot. Hell, I guess I think about you all the time." She started to reply, but he stopped her, holding up his hand. "Wait. For God's sake, let me finish. It took me long enough to get up the courage to say it. What I want to say is, if I wasn't in the trouble I'm in, I'd be asking you to marry me." Again, before she could respond, he quickly added, "You'd probably say no, but at least you know how I feel about you."

She stood up and faced him. "Maybe not," she said, her eyes softening again. She took both his hands in hers. "Tom Allred, you know damn well I've loved you since you first set foot in Ruby's Choice, half-froze to death." That said, she reached up to put her arms around his neck and pulled his head down to meet her lips.

Her kiss was like fire to him, not hot and burning, but warm and soft like the flames on a warm hearth, and he could feel the loving gentleness of her passion. The sensation caused his brain to whirl. He drew her up tightly against him, feeling the softness of her body on his. In that instant, all impressions he had had about the girl, her flippant and cocky manner, her bold and callous attitude, all of it was swept away. At this moment, she was everything he could ever want. He had never known a moment like this, and his only thought was that he never wanted it to end. He kissed her hard and long. She eagerly returned his passion, pressing her body even more tightly against his until suddenly she broke away from his embrace.

"We better not go too far," she whispered breathlessly. "Aunt Charlotte may be back any minute."

He felt desperate. "Dammit, Ruby, I don't know

what to say to you. You know I love you and I want to marry you, but I don't have the right to ask you to go with me. I can't stay here. You see that, don't you?"

She took his hands in hers. There was a sadness in her eyes as she spoke. "I know that. I know you have to run. And I love you, Tom, but I can't go running off into the wilderness with you. I just can't. I'm not some squaw that can follow you everywhere, from camp to camp." She dropped her gaze from his and looked down at her feet. "I reckon the Good Lord has His reasons for things happening the way they do. I know you're a good man, but you're an outlaw, and, even though it ain't your fault, they'll still be coming after you until you've found a place to hide . . . or you're dead. And I don't want to be around when that happens. I couldn't stand it. I won't stand it. I'd rather not know about it." She hesitated a moment, then reached up quickly and kissed him once more before she broke away from him. "Go on now, run, before I start crying."

His helplessness was paralyzing. "Ruby—" he started, but she placed her fingers over his mouth, silencing him.

"Don't say anything, Tom. Just go. It won't work for us. For God's sake, go!" She opened the door and pushed him toward it.

His heart felt like a lead weight as he slowly placed his foot in the stirrup and stepped up into the saddle. Billy immediately backed away from the hitching post. Tom could only gaze forlornly at her. "I'm sorry," he murmured softly. She could not look at him and, closing the door, left him alone in his despair. He turned Billy and rode out of the farmyard. Out of the corner of his eye, he saw Charlotte Clay standing in the doorway of the barn, watching him as he rode away. He pretended not to notice her, ashamed for her to see the tears in his eyes.

Charlotte put down the bucket of chicken feed she had been carrying and closed the barn door. If she knew anything about young girls, she was sure Ruby needed someone to talk to right about then. Ruby was a cheerful and hard-working girl. There wasn't much that could serve to dampen her mood. But Charlotte had sized up the situation as soon as Tom Allred walked into the house. Ruby was not the type to share her intimate thoughts with her aunt, but Charlotte would have to be blind not to see the fire burning between Ruby and Tom. Judging from the look on Tom's face when he left, she decided she had better give Ruby a few minutes more alone, in case she needed time to regain her composure.

When she felt enough time had elapsed, she started back across the yard toward the house. She had almost reached the door when she heard hoofbeats on the road up to the house. Thinking that Tom had decided to come back, she waited, looking down the road until she caught sight of the rider approaching. As soon as he came into view, she could see that it wasn't Tom after all. It was a single horse. Curious as to who might be their second caller in a single day, she waited outside the house, watching the rider. When he was close enough, she recognized Will Proctor.

"Well, Will, what brings you out this way?"

"Morning, Miz Clay," he called out cheerfully.

"There might be a little bit of coffee left in the pot," she offered.

"Oh, no, ma'am, thank you, ma'am. I'm kinda in a hurry."

"Oh? Well, what can I do for you?"

"I'm looking for Dakota—I mean Tom Allred. Mr. Clay said he might be headin' this way. I borrowed ten dollars off him, and I'm afraid he might be leavin' before I pay him back. Did he pass this way?"

"Why, yes, he did. You just missed him as a matter of fact. Couldn't be gone more than a half hour or so."

"He didn't happen to mention which way he was headin', did he?"

"Well, no, he didn't say. I was in the barn when he left, but I noticed he headed west, toward the pass I would guess."

"Much obliged, Miz Clay." He wheeled his horse and galloped out of the yard.

Tom let the horses drink from the tiny stream that made its way around the rocks and down the slope toward the valley. While they drank, he dismounted and walked to the top of the hill. He stood there for a while, studying his backtrail. Maybe it was just a routine precaution, or maybe something just told him to watch his back. Whatever prompted him, it turned out to be justified, for on the horizon some three or four miles back, a lone rider was coming on at a fast pace. Could be he was tracking him. Or it could be that he was just in a hurry to get where he was going, and just happened to be going the same direction Tom was. There was nothing so unusual about that. If a man was heading west, as Tom was, the easiest route was to cut through the pass and then traverse this low ridge to the valley on the other side. *Still*, he thought, *that rider is pushing his horse pretty hard, like he was trying to catch up with someone.* Since he was the only rider on the trail, Tom decided it might be a good idea to find out if he was being trailed.

He went back to the horses, mounted, and rode out across the ridge. Once he had traversed the low ridge and reached the valley, he changed his direction, heading on a more southerly course. He rode on for another mile or so, climbing up into the low hills again, until he came to a good place to stop and again watch his backtrail. From the cover of the trees growing on the small knoll, he could see almost back to the stream where he had changed directions. It wasn't long before his suspicions were confirmed. The rider stopped, studied his tracks, then turned south and followed Tom's trail.

He quickly tied the horses off in a deep gully and, pulling his rifle from the saddle boot, ran back up the trail to a large rock outcropping that gave him a good defensive position to check out his pursuer. He lay on his belly and waited. His wait was not long. The rider soon came into view. They saw each other at the same time. Tom rose to one knee, his rifle leveled at the rider. The rider abruptly reined to a stop, his horse's hooves plowing up snow and dirt.

"Tom! Hold it!" he called out, fighting to control his horse, which had been spooked by the sudden appearance of the man before him. "It's me! Will Proctor!"

Tom released the hammer on his rifle and stood up. "Will, what the hell are you doing out here?"

Now that his horse was quieted some and under control, Will smiled and dismounted. "Trying to catch up with you," he said.

Tom was still cautious. "Sheriff's business?"

Will flashed his smile again. "Naw, hell no," he was quick to reassure. "You don't see no badge, do you? I quit this morning."

"Quit? What for?"

"Well, to tell you the truth, I'm sick of being a lawman. Time I was moving on."

Tom made no attempt to hide his opinion on the matter. "Damn, Will, I don't know if that was a smart thing to do or not. Looked to me like you had it pretty nice there, working for Aaron. What the hell else are you going to do that's any better?" He slid down from the rock he had been lying on. "It might have been a better idea to at least wait until spring."

"Maybe, but I figured to catch up with you. I didn't know you was plannin' on leavin' town today."

Tom was puzzled. "Why did you want to catch up with me?"

Will shrugged. "Hell, I thought maybe you and me could be partners, do some trapping, pan for gold . . . something."

Tom found it difficult to believe what he was hearing. Will Proctor was too lazy to root hard for anything, and here he was talking like a schoolboy about panning for gold and trapping. Will was young, but this talk was too naive, even for him. He didn't want to tell him how dumb he sounded. After all, the man had saved his life. If Will hadn't been there, who knows whether Tom would have been fast enough to get both bounty hunters. It was probably a fifty-fifty proposition at best. Also, Will had made it a point to befriend him while most of the townspeople avoided him. He couldn't forget that. Will's proposal to join up with him seemed even more naive when Tom noticed that all he brought with him was his horse and a saddle roll. If he was planning to start out on a new life, he sure as hell didn't come very well outfitted.

"Will, I appreciate that you want to go with me, but take my advice—go on back to town. Tell Aaron you made a mistake. He'll understand. You don't want to team up with me. Hell, I don't know myself how I'm going to get by. Nobody's found any gold around here in a year and trapping's dead—has been for a long time. Believe me, if I had a situation like yours, I'd sure as hell stick with it. Take my word for it, it gets mighty miserable making camp in the snow."

Will stood there looking at him for a long time before answering. He seemed uncertain about what he wanted to say. "Maybe you're right. Maybe I oughtn't to go with you." He smiled and shrugged. "Well, anyway, have you got any coffee? Maybe we could make a little coffee before I go back. I didn't have no breakfast this morning, and it's a long ride back."

Tom hesitated. "Coffee? Well, yeah. I guess we could build a fire and make some coffee. I hadn't planned to stop to eat till I made camp tonight, but I guess I could." He was somewhat taken aback by the request. It seemed like a rather strange thing for Will to ask. A germ of suspicion began to grow in Tom's mind. Will was acting mighty peculiar. A moment ago he was hellbent to set out with him to God knows where. Then one word from Tom, and he was ready to change his mind completely. Suddenly the whole scene didn't sit well with Tom.

"Where's your horses?"

"Back down in that gully," Tom answered.

"Well, lead the way to that coffee. My bones are cold." His tone was a mite too cheerful.

Tom didn't say anything and started down through the trees. He carried his rifle casually, but something inside warned him to be on his toes. There was already a round in the chamber, and as he made his way down the slope toward the gully, he quietly cocked the hammer back. Will followed behind him, leading his horse, keeping up a steady stream of idle chatter.

They had scarcely covered twenty yards when Tom heard the distinct click of the hammer behind him. He didn't wait for the next sound. He suddenly dropped to the ground, whirling as he did so. The roar of the rifle startled him, it happened so fast. Tom had pulled the trigger without even knowing he was doing it. Will was already doubled over from the first slug that caught him in the gut before Tom could remember clearly seeing the drawn pistol in his hand. From simple reflex, Will fired two shots into the ground beside him, his gun hand hanging harmlessly at his side. In less than a second, Tom pumped two more slugs into Will, who was already mortally wounded and sliding to the ground. His horse, panicked by the explosion of gunfire, bolted, dragging Will a few feet before the dying man released his hold on the reins.

Tom lay on the ground for a few moments. He was stunned. Will Proctor was lying a few yards from him. His initial thought, beyond disbelief that it had actually happened, was that he was thankful there was a gun in Will's hand when he turned. Otherwise, it would have been murder, pure and simple, for Tom had reacted so fast to the sound of the hammer cocking that he actually shot Will before he had time to make sure he was holding a gun. For a moment he was overcome with remorse for having killed the young deputy. This was quickly replaced by anger. Suddenly he was aware of Will's groaning, and he crawled over to the dying man.

Will's eyes were open, though it appeared they were not focusing. They rolled from side to side as if searching for something. Then they stopped moving and he squinted in obvious pain. "Oh, God, it burns!" He clutched Tom's arm, his grip like a vise, as he fought against the pain. Then he relaxed a bit, his eyes now clear. "Damn, Dakota, you're as fast with that damn rifle as they said you was."

"Jesus, Will, why did you try it?" He knew the answer, but he still found it hard to believe.

Will forced a smile, although it was obvious it required great effort. "I'm sorry, Tom. Honest to God, I wish I hadn't done it." His speech was becoming more and more difficult, his breath coming now in short gasps. Tom tried to hold his head up when it seemed his lungs were filling with blood. A large patch of blood spread across the front of his coat. "The money," he gasped. "The money, I wanted the money. Nuthin' against you, Tom. I swear . . ."

Tom tried to move him to ease the pain, to get him in a position that might make his breathing easier. "Dammit, Will, I didn't want to do this to you. You gave me no choice. I had to do it!"

"I know, I know!" he whispered, his eyes closed tightly against the pain. "I ought'na tried it." He clutched Tom's arm tighter, almost squeezing off the blood flow. "Tom, don't leave me out here for the wolves. Please Tom . . ."

"I won't, I won't," Tom tried to reassure him.

Will relaxed. "It don't hurt so much now," he whispered. "I think I might make it." Tom held him while the life drained from his body. A moment later he was gone.

Chapter XV

Tom just sat there for what must have been the better part of an hour, staring at the body that was once young Will Proctor, weighing the decision he had to make. The man was dead through no fault of his. *It was a shame*, Tom thought. Will had not seemed like a bad sort, but his decision to come after Tom was a bad one, and it was Will's decision that caused him to end his young life, not Tom's. Yet Tom could not explain his feelings of guilt, the same feelings he had when he killed Little Joe back at the Broken-T. Could he have avoided either killing? Searching his soul, he could not honestly say that either one was avoidable. The thing that still haunted him, however, was that he had fired at Will before he even saw the gun in his hand. He had been right this time, but what if he hadn't? What if Will had no gun? He had to shake such thoughts out of his head. It happened the way it happened, he told himself. If he had not been quick enough, he would be lying there instead of Will.

Will's horse stood looking at him about one hundred yards away. It had bolted when the shots were fired, but made no move to back away when Tom approached it. He took Will's slicker from the saddle roll and wrapped it around the body. Will's corpse was heavy, and Tom struggled a bit before he managed to hoist it up and across the saddle. He had been turning the question over in his mind whether he should bury him there or take him back to town and explain his death to Aaron Crutchfield. There was always the chance he wouldn't be believed when he told Crutchfield what happened. But, one thing for sure, if Will's body was found out there, there would be little doubt in anyone's mind that it had been foul play. In the end, he knew he had to take the body back to Bozeman. He had promised Will he wouldn't leave him out there.

It was late afternoon when he passed the southernmost buildings of the town and rode slowly down the middle of the muddy street. Breezy Martin was just coming out of the sheriff's office. When he looked up the street and saw Tom leading the horses, one with a body draped across the saddle, he quickly ducked back inside. Moments later, he reappeared, this time with Aaron Crutchfield right behind him. The two men stood on the narrow board walkway in front of the building and watched silently as Tom approached.

"Tom," Aaron stated simply as Tom dismounted and tied the horses to the rail.

"I brought Will in. Figured you'd want to know what happened."

Aaron said nothing for a moment, but only glanced at the body wrapped in the slicker before looking back at Tom, his gaze steady. "Suppose you tell me what happened," he suggested, his voice low, his manner patient.

"I didn't have much choice, Sheriff. Will caught up with me and said he wanted to ride with me. Before I knew what he was up to, he tried to shoot me in the back. I got him first." He studied the sheriff for his reaction to this before adding, "I was on my way to Flathead country. I wasn't looking for any trouble."

"You don't seem to have much luck avoiding trouble, do you, Tom?" His tone was noncommittal. Tom wasn't sure if Crutchfield's reaction was sympathetic or merely sarcastic. He glanced at Breezy. "Git him down from there and let's take a look at him." Breezy did as he was told. Tom stepped up to give him a hand lifting the body off the saddle, and together they laid Will down on the walkway.

Tom stepped back as Aaron and Breezy uncovered Will and knelt over him. Will had bled quite a bit, soaking the slicker. There were three bullet holes in his gut, no more than a hand span apart. He watched the two lawmen examine the body. After a few minutes had passed with no spoken word, he offered his regrets. "I'm really sorry I had to do it, Sheriff. I didn't have anything against Will. Hell, he saved my bacon in the saloon last night. Like I said, he really gave me no choice."

Aaron stood up. "You damn shore made shore he was dead," he said, indicating the three bullet holes.

"It happened so fast . . ." Tom began.

"You must have been at pretty close range."

Tom shrugged. "I don't know, maybe fifteen, twenty feet."

"You say he tried to shoot you in the back?" Crutchfield pushed his hat back on his head and scratched his forehead as if trying to get the picture straight in his mind. "How come he didn't hit you, if you was that close?"

Tom was beginning to wish he had simply gone on his way instead of bringing Will back to Bozeman. He didn't like the way Aaron Crutchfield was looking at him. "I heard him cock his pistol, and turned around just in time. I was quicker than he was. He got off a couple of shots into the ground." His patience was wearing thin. "Look, Sheriff, I didn't have to come back here, but I thought it was the right thing to do. Your boy tried to shoot me down, but I was quicker than he was. That's the whole story right there."

"You must be pretty damn fast with that rifle," Breezy said. "Will was pretty good with a handgun. He shore warn't slow. Fact is, he was about as fast with a pistol as anybody I've ever seen."

"Well, he wasn't fast enough this time," Tom replied calmly, looking at the deputy with a steely glare. He took another step back toward his horse and casually rested his hand on the stock of his rifle. He realized then that his version of the incident might not be believed.

Aaron Crutchfield did not fail to notice Tom's hand resting on the rifle stock. He moved slowly and deliberately as he pulled Will's pistol from the holster and opened the cylinder. He looked at it for a long time, then glanced back up at Tom. "Well, two shots was fired all right." He replaced the pistol in the holster, Tom's eyes following his every move. " 'Course they could have been fired any time. Could have been fired by you, as far as that goes."

"I don't guess I particularly care for the sound of your thinking," Tom said. "Are you saying I shot him down in cold blood?" His hand tightened on the rifle stock. "Because, if you are . . ."

"Now hold on, son! Don't go gittin' riled up. I'm just askin' questions is all. I ain't sayin' you shot him down. I ain't sayin' you didn't either. I don't know what happened between you two boys out there in the hills. Will did turn in his badge this morning. And I noticed he'd been goin' through the wanted posters. So I reckon I can add two and two and git four as good as anybody. Will might of been aiming to collect the reward money on you. I don't know and I don't care. But I'll tell you what I am sayin'. I'm sayin' you attract trouble, and I don't need no trouble in my town. I told you that the first day you set foot in Bozeman. You been here two weeks and already two bounty hunters come lookin' for you. They're both dead, and now my deputy is dead. Maybe you killed Will in self-defense and maybe you didn't. All I got is your word on it, and that don't comfort me a whole bunch. So what I'm sayin' to you, Tom, or Dakota, whatever the hell your name is, I want you out of my town. That's all. Just clear out."

That was good news to Tom. "Well, I can certainly accommodate you there, Sheriff. That's just what I was aiming to do in the first place." He relaxed his caution in relief, a mistake he discovered too late. Had he not been so incensed by Crutchfield's attitude and rankled by the insinuations, he might have been more watchful and noticed the shifting of the sheriff's eyes and the slight nod of his head. As it was, he noticed Breezy was missing just a split second before the deputy's rifle barrel came crashing down across the back of his head and everything went dark.

"God damn, Breezy! You damn near killed him!" Doc Brewster worked to stop the bleeding from the nasty wound in the back of Tom's head. The blood had run down his neck and soaked the back of his shirt and coat. Tom only groaned as Doc tried to clean him enough to shave the hair away so he could stitch up the gash. He talked as he worked, never glancing up. "Don't you know you can kill a man, knocking him in the head like that, up under the back of his skull?"

Breezy shrugged indifferently as he watched Doc cut away a large patch of Tom's hair. "I had to catch him up under his hat."

"Yeah, but did you have to poleaxe him like that? You might have scrambled his brains for good."

"Aaron said put him out. I put him out. Besides, I wasn't about to take a chance on lettin' him git his hand on that rifle of his'n."

"Well, you damn sure put him out." Doc finished shaving the back of Tom's head and started stitching the wound.

The furry images in his brain slowly cleared to the point where Tom was aware of intense pain in the back of his head. When he finally regained consciousness, his first sensation was that of Doc Brewster's thread pulling through his scalp. He jerked in an attempt to get to his feet.

"Hold still!" Doc scolded.

"What the hell . . ." he started, but could not finish. Gradually his eyes focused, and he realized he was lying on his stomach on a cot as he recognized the voice of Doc Brewster. His first thought was that he had been shot. "What happened?" he finally managed.

"Hold still," Doc repeated. "Your friend, Breezy here, tried to see if he could bust your skull open. He damn near succeeded. Sorta his way of saying you're under arrest, I suppose."

Tom heard a grunt from behind him that he took to be Breezy's. He couldn't see him from his position facedown on the cot. He started to turn his head to the side, but thought better of it when a stab of pain seared his temples. "Under arrest? For what?"

"I don't know," Doc replied. "For killing Will Proctor, I reckon."

The picture cleared some in Tom's mind then, and he remembered the conversation leading up to his blackout. The last words he remembered Aaron saying was that all he wanted was for Tom to get out of town. He knew now that Aaron was just setting him up to relax his guard. *Well,* he thought, *it damn sure worked.* It had never really occurred to Tom that Breezy was a threat to him. "Dammit, Doc, there's no cause to arrest me. I didn't tell Will to come after me. It was him or me, self-defense, pure and simple."

"I believe you, but it ain't up to me. All I'm interested in is sewing your head back together. You'll have to talk to Aaron about the other." He finished up the stitches and tied a bandage around Tom's head. When he stood up, Doc paused a second to admire his handiwork, then said, "You're probably going to have one helluva headache for a while."

"I got one now," Tom replied. Very slowly, for his head was pounding, he rolled over on the cot and tried to sit up. He didn't make it the first time. The room started spinning around, and he had to lie back to let everything settle down. He tried again in a few moments. This time he managed to sit up on the side of the cot, and after a little pause his head stopped spinning enough to enable him to take inventory of his situation.

"Better come on out now, Doc." This was Breezy's voice. "I got to lock him up."

Doc took his time putting his instruments away. He stood in the small cell for a moment longer, watching his patient. When he was satisfied that Tom was going to be all right, he stepped outside, and Breezy closed the heavy wooden door. Tom lay back on the cot again, fighting a wave of nausea.

* * *

"Here's you some grub."

Tom sat up as Breezy shoved a tray of breakfast inside the door, then quickly slammed it shut. Tom was more than ready to eat, since he had had nothing since the morning before when he had coffee and biscuits with Ruby. His brain was a good deal more clear now, and the dizziness had gone when he woke up that morning. The only discomfort that remained was a dull headache that increased to a sharp throbbing whenever he moved his head too fast. The coffee was strong and rapidly cooling as a result of its journey from The Miner's Saloon, but it tasted wonderful to Tom. He drank almost half of it before tackling the eggs and sowbelly. Breezy stood outside the door, watching him through the small window.

"Way you looked last night, I warn't shore you'd still be kickin' this morning."

Tom paused to glance up at the deputy. "Damn considerate of you to be concerned," he grumbled. "I wasn't sure I'd make it myself. I'm still trying to figure out why you cold-cocked me like that."

Breezy grunted in response, a snide grin creasing his whiskers. "Hell, I just give you a little love tap. Wanted to make shore you didn't run off and leave us."

"Dammit, Breezy, there was no call to do that. What am I in here for, anyway? Aaron said to get out of town, and that's what I was trying to do."

Breezy's grin broadened. "Now, Dakota, you know Aaron ain't gon' let nobody drift in here and kill one of his deputies and then let him just drift right back out, 'specially somebody with a reputation like your'n. Why, outlaws all over would think they could come in here and do as they pleased."

Tom stopped eating. "You know damn well Will

came after me. I had no choice but to defend myself. You've got no reason to lock me up."

"Will was a pretty good ole boy. He was a mite lazy when it come to doing his share of the work, but folks around here liked him. We don't like to see hotshot gunmen come into our town killin our citizens . . . and him a lawman at that."

Tom could not understand the change in Breezy's attitude. They had played poker for two weeks, him and Doc and Will. Breezy had seemed easygoing, almost friendly. Now his tone was definitely antagonistic and downright hostile. Could he and Will have been such close friends that Will's death had produced this change? There had been no evidence that Breezy cared a drop for Will. Why then this sneering countenance he now displayed? Tom didn't have long to wait before the reason surfaced.

"Maybe you figure some of your Injun friends will come rescue you," Breezy suddenly blurted.

"What?" Tom didn't understand. "What Injun friends?"

Breezy grunted, the sneer still pasted on his face. "I know all about you, boy. Aaron read me the papers come in on you, Mister Injun-lover."

"What the hell are you talking about, Breezy?" Tom was losing his patience.

"I'm talkin' about you lettin' that damn devil Little Wolf git away. I'm talkin' about you gittin' kicked outta the army for givin' aid to the enemy." Breezy was obviously enjoying his wealth of information and the opportunity to display it. "I'll tell you somethin' else, Lieutenant Allred. I was there when you done it. By God, I was there at Little Big Horn with Major Reno! 'Course I warn't no officer like you, but I was there. Got mustered out two months after that campaign." Breezy glared at Tom as if he had exposed the devil himself. "I thought somethin' about you looked familiar the first day you showed up in town. Took me a while to place you, but I by God know you now."

Chapter XVI

With some reluctance, the sun finally broke through the shrouds of steaming mist that cloaked the western slopes of the Bitterroots, causing the still-frozen spires of countless waterfalls to fairly sparkle as they cascaded down to the basin below. Spring had come. There was no doubt that winter's grip had at last weakened and the snow would be gone in a matter of weeks. It was a joyous sign to Squint Peterson. He had never been overly fond of the cold weather, and now that he was getting a little long in the tooth, it seemed to affect him even more. He pulled his buffalo coat up around his ears and drew in a deep lungful of the icy air. The first signs of spring had inspired a lightness in his heart. Soon this valley would transform itself into a paradise of thousands of many different colors as wildflowers covered the lower slopes. And the high peaks that surrounded his valley would cast off their heavy winter coats, sending crystal-clear water leaping over the rocks in a frantic effort to reach the grassy floor of the basin. Squint and Robert, or Little Wolf as he still insisted on being called, were expecting at least a dozen new foals this season. Squint had always been interested in raising horses, and he was especially partial to breeding Appaloosas, a skill they had been taught by an old Nez Perce that helped around the ranch. Once this whole valley, and the one on the eastern side of the pass, was the home of the Nez Perces. But most of them were gone now. The soldiers had driven Chief Joseph and his people out and, after a helluva fight, finally run them to ground September just past. The army had not been successful in driving out all of the resistant Nez Perces, however. There were still a few renegade bands back in the small pockets of the Bitterroots. Squint and Little Wolf lived in peace with the surviving bands, mainly due to Little Wolf's reputation as a Cheyenne war chief. Their situation was one of mutual trust. He didn't tell the white men in the little town of Medicine Creek about the presence of the few remaining Nez Perces and they didn't spread the word around that the Cheyenne renegade, Little Wolf, was holed up just thirty miles from their little town.

The past year and a half had been pleasant for Squint, away from the fighting and the army. Little Wolf had taken to ranching just fine. He was still a mite high-strung, but most of the venom had boiled out of his heart. It was mostly the country, Squint decided. The high peace of the mountains mellowed a man's heart, if he had any heart at all. Even so, Little Wolf still thought like an Indian. When he gave it serious consideration, it was little wonder because Squint was the foreigner in this wilderness. Little Wolf and Rain Song belonged here.

Yes, he thought, these were peaceful times and all that a man like Squint could hope for in the twilight of his years. Still, he could not help but permit worrisome little thoughts to creep into his mind. They had been isolated from the white man's warring with Chief Joseph's band. No soldiers had found their way into this secluded valley. How long, he wondered,

would that be true? He dreaded the thought of a
cavalry patrol stumbling onto the valley. He could
not predict how Little Wolf would react. But, if he
had to bet on it, he would put his money on his
friend reverting back to his warlike upbringing. He
shook his head as if to dispel such worries from his
mind. Why worry about something that hasn't happened yet?

His reverie finished, Squint stepped up in the saddle and turned Joe back toward the cabin. The horse
headed back down the slope at an easy pace. Like
his master, Joe was in no particular hurry to get anywhere. Sore Hand, the old Nez Perce, walked out
to greet him as Joe plodded slowly up to the barn
and stopped.

"Little Wolf say he go hunt with Sleeps Standing.
Him be back tomorrow maybe."

Squint nodded. He knew that meant Little Wolf
wanted him to stay close and keep an eye on Rain
Song. He hadn't planned to go anywhere anyway.
Sleeps Standing was another Cheyenne renegade
who had found his way into this valley, along with
his wife and her sister. He had fought the soldiers at
Wagon Box, the battle that signaled the end of the
great Sioux and Cheyenne wars. Like many of his
brothers, he had no belly for reservation life, and
while he was trying to run from the soldiers, he got
himself shot. As a result of that wound, Squint and
Little Wolf received the amazing news that Tom Allred had been cashiered out of the army. Far back in
the mountains as they were, they had very little news
of the outside world, and that was the way they
wanted it. When Sleeps Standing found them this
past winter, Squint was amazed to learn that Tom
was no longer in the army. Sleeps Standing told them
of his wound and the desperate situation he was in

when Tom stumbled upon him and the two women. Without Tom's help and the food he brought them, all three of them might have gone under. According to Sleeps Standing, Tom was on the run from the army. If he got the story straight, Tom had killed a soldier, maybe more than one. It left Squint more than a little baffled. It didn't sound like something Tom would be mixed up in. He would have to hear more of the story before he made judgment. At first, he wondered if Tom was trying to make his way to this part of the country, maybe hoping to find him and Little Wolf. But Sleeps Standing said he was headed toward the Musselshell country. Little Wolf had naturally shown great interest in Sleeps Standing's news. After all, Tom was responsible for his escape from the soldiers. And, although he had never accepted being brothers by blood, he felt he owed a debt to the young cavalry officer in spite of fighting on opposite sides at Little Big Horn. Squint had to remind Little Wolf that he, too, fought on the side of the army in that battle. But that was water under the bridge. Little Wolf retorted that it made no difference anyway. He had gone his way and Tom had gone his. So, why discuss it?

The citizens of Medicine Creek didn't concern themselves with what went on in the small, isolated valley where Squint Peterson and his partner raised horses and a few head of cattle. They kept to themselves and that was all right with the townspeople. Various rumors floated around, but folks figured that as long as they weren't threatened in any way, why concern themselves? Squint was the only person from the valley who ever came into town, and he seemed square enough. It had been confirmed that his partner was also a white man, though no one had ever seen him in town. It wouldn't have surprised most folks if there were a few Nez Perces hiding out in the valley, but they didn't expect any trouble from that quarter. So, from Squint's way of thinking, things were working out just fine. Life was peaceful and a little bit dull—just the way he liked it. It would not remain that way for long, however.

In two weeks' time, spring was evident in earnest. The mountain passes had opened up, and the streams were over their banks with the melting snow from the mountains. Confined for months by the heavy snows, Little Wolf and Sleeps Standing were at last able to range far from the valley on their hunting trips, staying out for several days at a time. This time they had been out only one night, working their way along the eastern slope of a high range of mountains that bordered a long valley the Nez Perces called Sweet Grass.

Sleeps Standing saw them first. "There," he said, pointing toward three small figures making their way across the valley below them.

As the figures approached the foot of the mountain, they could see that there were two men and three horses, one a packhorse. Little Wolf and Sleeps Standing watched for a while in silence, then Little Wolf spoke. "They are not hunting. What are they doing in this land?" It was difficult to tell at that distance whether they were white or Indian. Both figures were wrapped in heavy hide robes. It was apparent that they were trying to follow a trail through the mountains by the way the lead man scouted through the patches of snow that remained in the lower draws and gullies.

"One of the horses is lame," Sleeps Standing commented. Little Wolf only grunted in reply as they continued to watch the progress of the strangers. The

horse carrying the second rider seemed to be hob-
bling badly and appeared close to faltering. The distance between the first rider leading the packhorse,
and the lame horse gradually increased, until the second rider was several hundred yards behind by the
time the lead man reached the pines at the foot of
the mountain. He dismounted and appeared to be
making a fire.

"They camp early," Sleeps Standing remarked.

Little Wolf said nothing, but continued to watch.
It was obvious now that one of them might be Indian
but the other was definitely a white man. When the
second rider caught up, he dismounted and the two
seemed to have a lengthy discussion. After a few
minutes of talk, the Indian mounted again and, leading the packhorse, started out alone, leaving his companion standing by the fire.

"Let us see where this one goes," Little Wolf said,
and started off across the ridge. Sleeps Standing followed. From a position halfway down the opposite
slope, they could follow the man's progress until
he was out of sight. He skirted the mountain until he
came to the river. Once there, he paused for a moment, then turned south along the riverbank, and
finally disappeared from their view. Little Wolf was
curious enough by then to return to scout the second rider.

They crossed back over the ridge and made their
way down almost to the valley floor, where they
stopped in the tall trees to observe the man by the
fire. He seemed intent only on keeping the large fire
burning. No effort was spent in making camp or in
taking care of his lame horse.

"What is he doing?" Sleeps Standing finally uttered.

After a long time, during which the man appeared
to do nothing more than shuffle aimlessly around the

fire, Little Wolf tired of the game. "White men!" he said in disgust. "Who knows what they think? Come, let us take our meat back to the valley." With that, he leaped upon his horse and prepared to leave. When Sleeps Standing mounted his horse, Little Wolf held up his hand. "Wait," he said. Something had caught his attention back at the campfire.

"What is it?" Sleeps Standing asked.

"Look," Little Wolf replied, pointing toward the fire.

When Sleeps Standing's eyes followed Little Wolf's outstretched arm, he smiled at what he saw. The stranger had walked over to the edge of the brush and was now squatting to urinate. The rider was a woman. Now, in spite of his impatience, he was really curious. Why had the man ridden off and left his woman? He had taken the packhorse with him. It was obvious the man did not leave to hunt for food, for he made straight for the river and took the south pass out of the valley. *It is not my concern,* Little Wolf told himself. *If the man wants to leave his woman by herself with a lame horse, why should I care?*

"Are we going to find out?" Sleeps Standing interrupted his thoughts.

He looked at his friend for a moment, then glanced back at the woman, then back at Sleeps Standing. Finally he shrugged and wheeled his horse back toward the campfire. Sleeps Standing followed.

She dried herself with a small piece of cloth, quickly pulled the buckskin trousers up and tied them, then strapped the heavy cavalry pistol back around her hips. Her backside was still chilled by the exposure to the raw spring air, and she was anxious to get back to the fire. She was not aware of the two figures approaching until they were almost within fifty yards of the fire. At one moment they were not there and then the next moment they were right behind her. She was startled, an involuntary cry of surprise caught in her throat. *Indians!* She glanced frantically from side to side, fearful that there may be more even now surrounding her. But there were only the two. Her hand fumbled for the handle of her pistol.

"Wait!" one of them called out in English. "We mean you no harm."

She hesitated, her hand still on the revolver. She had a natural distrust of Indians, and while she allowed them to approach her fire, she kept a wary eye on the two of them, still glancing behind her from time to time just to make sure. "I'm sorry. I don't have any food to give you," she blurted, figuring Indians always wanted to be fed.

They sat on their horses for a few moments, looking at her, their faces as devoid of expression as stone. Finally, they dismounted, and stood across the fire from her. She backed away a few steps, terrified but trying desperately not to show it. After what seemed an interminable pause, the tall one spoke.

"We don't want any food. We have food." He gestured toward their packhorse. His voice was deep and his words carefully measured as if he deliberately thought about each word before he spoke. A presence about him bespoke a quiet power that made her feel her pistol would be of no use to her, even had she drawn it. "Where is your man?"

"He'll be right back," she answered, quickly adding, "He ain't my man. He's a guide."

The two Indians exchanged brief glances, and the shorter, stocky one said something to the tall one in an Indian dialect. The tall one shook his head, then turned back to her. "Where did he go? Is he looking for food?"

"No," she sputtered. "No, he went to town."

"Town?"

"Yes. He rode ahead to get some help. My horse is lame, and his was too wore out to carry double. So he rode in to get a couple of fresh horses." She was puzzled by their baffled expressions. "There's a town just on the other side of that mountain."

He didn't answer her at once. Instead, he looked unblinking into her eyes, uncertain as to whether or not he should believe her story. After a long moment, during which the lady seemed to become more and more concerned for her welfare at the hands of this tall savage, he decided she was telling the truth. That is, she was telling the truth as she believed it to be.

"Lady," he said, "there ain't no town on the other side of that mountain." He watched the reaction in her eyes. She was obviously confused and becoming alarmed. "Add to that, your guide didn't go that way. He took the south pass down the river. Looks to me like he ain't planning on coming back."

She didn't answer right away, just staring at them in disbelief. When she spoke, it was with a certain amount of resignation that surprised them both. "Well, that figures. He's been trying to get me to turn back for the last two days. I shoulda known he was fixing to bolt when he talked me into letting him take the packhorse with him."

"Where are you heading?"

"Some town called Medicine Creek. Sam—that's the half-breed you just seen hightailing it down the valley—he said he knew where it was. I paid him to guide me there. Only he promised me we'd be there two days ago."

Little Wolf thought the woman wasn't any too

careful about who she set out across the mountains with. But from the looks of the big pistol slung on her hip, he could pretty much guess why she wasn't afraid. "Well," he sighed, "I reckon we can see you to Medicine Creek. You can ride up behind me."

They unsaddled her horse and threw the saddle up on their packhorse. She climbed up behind the tall warrior because she figured she had little choice in the matter. She chose to believe they would be as good as their word and deliver her to Medicine Creek. She didn't doubt for a minute that they were correct in their assessment of her guide. When it was all sifted out, she guessed she was lucky to have made it this far without that sneaky half-breed killing her in her blankets. They rode for the better part of the afternoon, and when the shadows began to fill in the valleys, she asked, "How far is this town?"

"Two days. We'll make camp pretty soon. Then we'll make my place in the afternoon. That's as far as I'll take you. Somebody else will take you into town."

It was somewhat unsettling to her to discover that they would be spending the night together. They had shown no interest in her beyond offering to help, but these Indians were so stoic, she could not be certain what was going on in their heads. What if they had whiskey? She had heard countless tales of how crazy Indians get with whiskey. This silent pair could have great plans for their entertainment that night, with her being the main event. *Well*, she promised herself, *if that was their plan, it was going to cost them dearly*. She was not at all shy about using her frontier revolver, and she would find Medicine Creek by herself if she had to. Her worries were wasted, she found, because the two Indians made no threatening advances. In fact, there was hardly a word spoken to her when they finally stopped to make camp.

"Can you cook?" Little Wolf asked.

"Yeah, I can cook," was her reply.

He drew a long skinning knife from his belt and tossed it toward her. "Good. Slice off some strips from that elk rump on the horse. That'll be the price of your passage."

"Fair enough," she answered, and did as she was told. After they had taken care of the horses, they ate the meat. Then the two men rolled up in fur robes and went to sleep, apparently unconcerned about the woman.

They were packed and on their way by sunup the next morning, the woman behind Little Wolf, Sleeps Standing following behind, leading the packhorse and the woman's mount. The tall Indian spoke not a word to her during the entire morning. It was as if she were not there. Following his example, she deemed it advisable to likewise hold her tongue.

A short time after midday, they rode down into a wooded draw that dead-ended against a tree-covered ridge. Upon climbing the ridge and crossing over, they made their way down into a narrow valley that was bisected by a deep rushing stream. On the far side of the stream, she saw a corral and a couple of crude log buildings. This was their destination. As they crossed the stream, she saw a large white man and an Indian driving a small band of horses into the corral. Upon seeing them, the Indian called out, "*Ki yi.*" He was answered by Sleeps Standing, riding behind her.

They rode up to the cabin. Three Indian women came out to greet her traveling companions. They eyed her openly, making no attempt to mask their curiosity. She stood waiting while the two men exchanged greetings with the women. Hearing a voice behind her, she turned to see the white man, a mountain of a man, striding toward them, his face lit up by a wide grin.

"Well, boys, I see you had a good huntin' trip. I ain't shore the women know how to cook this one though." When he saw the uncertain look in her eyes, he quickly sought to put her at ease. "Howdy, ma'am. How'd you come to get tangled up with the likes of these two bucks?"

"She wants to go to Medicine Creek," Little Wolf answered for her.

"Medicine Creek?" Squint exclaimed. "What in the world is a little gal like you traveling all by yourself for? You got folks in Medicine Creek?"

"No, but I got to get there as fast as I can. Can you take me?" The urgency in her eyes told him she meant it.

"Why, yessum, I reckon I can, if it's that important." He turned to one of the Indian women and said, "Rain Song, reckon we could make the lady some coffee and somethin' to eat?" Turning back to their guest, he said, "My name's Squint Peterson, ma'am. Come on in by the fire."

She didn't move to follow his outstretched hand. Instead, she appeared stunned by his words, unable at first to believe what she had just heard. When she spoke, she could not hide the excitement in her voice. "Squint Peterson? Did you say Squint Peterson?"

Squint was taken aback by her reaction. "Why, yes, ma'am, Squint Peterson."

She could barely believe her luck. "Squint Peterson! You're the man I come looking for!"

"I am?" Squint was at a loss for words. "Well, you found me. Are we kin or somethin'?"

"No," she fairly screamed, "but they told me to

find you and you would know where to find Little
Wolf!"

"They did? Who did?" The woman's startling an-
nouncement had the effect of rendering the others
into shocked silence. They listened in amazement.

"Sam Running Fox, the guide that brought me
here, his people are Flatheads. They said you were
living in this part of the territory. And they said,
if anybody knew where Little Wolf is, it would
be you." Her eyes were wide with excitement, her
face transformed into a mask of apprehension that
she might have been misled. "Do you know?" she
pressed, "do you know where I can find Little
Wolf?"

Squint glanced briefly at the tall Indian behind her.
"Yeah, I reckon I might be able to track him down
if I had a little time. It depends. What do you wanna
find him for?"

"My name's Ruby Clay. I need his help. I don't
know who else to turn to. It's his brother. He's in
jail in Bozeman, and they're gonna hang him."

Squint rocked back a step. "Tom?" he exclaimed.
"They're gonna hang Tom? What in hell fer?"

Ruby went on to explain how Tom came to be in
trouble with the law as well as the army. The sheriff
in Bozeman had attempted to collect the reward on
him and was told that, as a lawman, he was obligated
to apprehend criminals as a part of his job. The army
wanted him sent back to Fort Lincoln, but the sheriff
responded that he didn't have the time or manpower
to do that and, if the army didn't want him bad
enough to come get him, he would hang him himself.
Ruby feared that it would be impossible for Tom to
get a fair trial even if the sheriff was of a mind to
try him before the hanging. Even now she was pray-
ing they didn't hang him before she found someone

to help him. Not knowing where else she could go, she figured a man's own brother ought to try to help him, even if he was an Indian.

"And maybe there ain't nothing he can do. But I had to do something," she pleaded. "Do you know where he is?"

Squint glanced at Little Wolf and received a nod of approval before answering. "Yessum, I know where Little Wolf is. You rode in behind him."

Rain Song worked feverishly at the cornmeal she would fashion into cakes. She had never made bread in this fashion before she met Squint, who had taught her to make it. It was his favorite. She would bake it in the stone oven Squint had built behind the cabin for the sole purpose of baking the corn bread. She and Little Wolf liked it, too, so she was always happy to make it when Squint requested. She worked silently, but her mind was racing with thoughts, discomforting notions spawned by the sudden appearance of the white woman who came pleading for help. Rain Song was worried. Their life had been so perfect during the two years past, and now this. She wished the woman had gotten lost in the mountains and never found Little Wolf. He was safe here in the mountains. She feared the soldiers would find him if he went with this woman now. Burdened with these heavy thoughts, she worked away at the meal until Squint went outside and she and Little Wolf were alone.

"Why must you go?"

He continued to inspect his weapons while he answered her. "Because he is my brother, I suppose."

She stopped her work and sat back on her heels. "He is not your brother. He is a white man. You are Little Wolf of the Cheyenne! He is the enemy of your people. You have fought him and his soldiers all your life, and now he comes whimpering to you because his kind have turned against him, like wild dogs turn on their own."

He listened patiently to her lecturing. Then he laid his rifle down carefully and talked to her in soft but firm tones. "I owe this man my life. If it were not for him, Squint, you, me, none of us would be here in this valley. I would be dead or rotting away in the army's stockade." He paused a moment. "There is another reason. This man is Squint's friend. If I don't go, Squint will go alone."

She knew there would be no more discussion on the matter. Little Wolf's word was final. Still, she worried. "Then take Sleeps Standing and Sore Hand with you."

"No," he answered. "Squint and I will go. Sleeps Standing and Sore Hand must stay here to look after you and the other women."

The decision was made. She knew she could not change his mind. Resigned to this, she came to him and put her arms around his neck. "Then promise me you will come back safely," she whispered, her voice a soft murmur in his ear, "and make love to me tonight so you will remember to return soon." She giggled as he reached down and playfully spanked her bottom.

The morning was clouded over with a high blanket of misty gray. A chilly wind swept through the valley, promising a change in the weather soon. Squint Peterson stood facing west and squinted at the clouds as if he was straining to see the weather coming. It was not too late in the season for snow, not by a long shot, and he was not anxious to get caught in the mountain passes by a late spring storm. Sore Hand watched him for a few minutes, guessed his concern, and spoke.

"Not snow, rain maybe, not snow."

Squint cocked an eye at the old Nez Perce. "You seem awful damn shore about that," he said. He felt better about it though, for if the old Indian said it wasn't going to snow, chances are it wasn't. Hearing a noise behind him, he turned to see Sleeps Standing come from the corral, leading Little Wolf's horse. When he turned back, he was startled to find Little Wolf standing beside him. He had not heard his friend approach. "Dammit!" he scolded, "I wish to hell you wouldn't do that!" It embarrassed him to be surprised like that, even by Little Wolf.

"Your ears grow old, old man," Little Wolf teased.

"Huh!" Squint snorted, "this old man can still kick your rump for you."

Little Wolf laughed. "Well, old man, see if you can get your rump up on your horse. We are wasting time." He dodged a playful swing of Squint's arm. "Maybe Rain Song and Lark can help you up in the saddle."

Although the mood was light, they both knew the danger they were about to ride into. When they were mounted and ready to leave, Rain Song ran up to Little Wolf's stirrup to say good-bye. He leaned down and squeezed her hand affectionately.

"Do not worry, little one. I will be back before the new moon. Sleeps Standing and Sore Hand will watch over you." He smiled and nodded toward Squint. "I have to bring this old man back to sit on the front porch and eat your corn cakes."

"Huh!" Squint snorted. "Your tongue will be dragging, trying to keep up with *this* old man."

Sore Hand had been correct in his forecast. Before they had made their way out of the pass and into the valley beyond, a light rain started to fall. But there was no snow. Squint was thankful for that. Since Little Wolf's eyes were a good bit sharper than Squint's, he led. Both men kept their senses keen, a practice that had preserved their scalps thus far, even though they expected no real danger as long as they were deep in the mountains. As they threaded their way through the mountain passes and along the ridges, Squint considered the girl, Ruby Clay, whose arrival had instigated the mission they were now undertaking. She had some spunk. He had to give her that. She must think a helluva lot of Tom to risk her neck riding through the mountains with a no-account Injun guide. If she was to ask him, he'd have to say it was a damn fool thing to do. It was pure greenhorn luck that she stumbled onto Little Wolf and Sleeps Standing. She was a little put out when she found out she was not going back with them. She argued long and strong for her cause, trying to convince Little Wolf that she needed to go with them to show them where they had Tom locked up. Little Wolf had simply grunted no, but Squint had advised her that if they couldn't find the jailhouse in a place no bigger than Bozeman, they probably couldn't find their way out of their own valley. Little Wolf wanted to travel fast, and he didn't want a woman along to slow them up.

"I reckon I can travel as good as any man," she advised them in no uncertain terms.

Squint told her she might think so, but she had never tried to keep up with a Cheyenne Dog Soldier when he was in a hurry to get someplace. He smiled to himself. "She's got spunk, though. I give her that."

"What are you mumbling, old man?"

Squint laughed. "I said it looks like you got yourself a spunky little sister-in-law."

Little Wolf did not smile. He looked at his friend

for a moment before turning his attention back to the trail. "Maybe so," he said. His mind was turning over more serious thoughts, and some of his conversation with Rain Song troubled him. Although he had squashed all discussion about riding to help Tom Allred and insisted there was no decision to be made, in his private thoughts there were still doubts. After all, he did not know this man, this brother of his, Tom Allred. But, he argued, the man did go against the army and effect Little Wolf's escape. But, he reasoned, did not the man owe him his life? After all, Little Wolf could have killed him when he caught the young lieutenant by surprise on the banks of the Little Missouri. *Waugh*, he thought, *this thinking is hurting my head.* He knew he was going to help his blood brother, even though he was a white man and an ex-soldier. He would do it for Squint. Squint held a fondness for the man.

Squint did indeed hold a fondness for Tom Allred. Tom had been as fine a young officer as he had ever met during his years scouting for the army. More than that, Tom was a decent man and a close friend. He was glad to try to help him. And, while he felt a strong urgency to get to Bozeman without delay, he had no earthly idea exactly how he was going to effect Tom's rescue. He didn't cotton to the idea of the two of them just riding in, guns blazing, to free Tom. They'd have the army and every lawman west of the Missouri looking for them. He knew Little Wolf didn't have a notion of a plan either. "Well," he sighed to himself, "we got four days of hard riding ahead of us. We'll think of somethin'."

Chapter XVII

Sam Running Fox was pleased with himself. A cunning man, he had done quite well in his business dealings with Ruby Clay. True, he only got half the money she promised him to guide her into the Bitterroot country. The other half he was to have received when he found Medicine Creek. But, because of his cleverness, he was now in possession of another horse and a full pack of various goods that would see him quite comfortably on his way to Canada. Now, as he bent over his campfire, tending his supper of salt pork and dried beans courtesy of Miss Clay, he couldn't help but smile to himself over his good fortune. The woman was stupid to try to find Little Wolf. They could have searched for a month in those mountains and never found a trace of him. She might as well have searched for the wind. No one could say for sure that Little Wolf was not dead anyway. There were many rumors that circulated among his people. No one knew for sure.

He had harbored thoughts of killing the girl and leaving her to the wolves, but decided it was not worth the risk of getting himself shot. The woman was never without the huge forty-four pistol she kept strapped to her side. And she never slept, as far as he could tell. On two separate nights on the trail, he crawled silently from his bedroll only to find her staring at him wide-eyed, causing him to mumble that he needed to relieve himself, after which he would make a show of going off into the woods. After those attempts, he gave up the notion of killing her and was content to simply run off and leave her when the opportunity came. She would probably wander around in the mountains for days before she starved to death, or a grizzly or mountain lion got her. Perhaps he should double back and trail her till she got herself in trouble. Then it would be a simple matter to surprise her and take the rest of her money. He paused to consider the wisdom of it, then shook his head. *No need to be greedy,* he thought. *I'm free and clear of it. Still, it would be nice to have the pistol.* He rolled that thought around in his mind for a moment before turning his attention back to his supper.

Suddenly he tensed. The unmistakable sound of a soft hoofbeat below his camp caused him to become instantly alert. He grabbed his rifle and rolled out of the circle of light created by his campfire. *How the hell did that bitch find me?* was his first thought, as he strained to catch sight of his visitor. Then logic told him it was highly unlikely. There was no way she could have trailed him. So he waited, watching the trail below his camp intently, his rifle ready.

"I'm coming in," a husky voice announced, followed immediately by the appearance of a rider.

Sam could not help but feel a shiver of alarm. This was no ordinary rider. The dark form seemed monstrous as it came into the light. He was not sure what he was seeing was not an apparition, a mountain of fur mounted upon a scrawny Indian pony, until the form spoke again.

"Hold your fire."

Sam rose to his feet and walked back into the fire

light, his rifle still ready. "Damn, you ain't gonna live a long time out here, riding up on folks like that."

The huge stranger did not reply. He walked the pony right up to the fire and sat there without dismounting. The firelight caught enough of the man's face to cause Sam to inhale sharply. "Damn! You look like you tangled with a grizzly."

Still, the stranger did not reply. He sat on the pony and continued to stare at Sam. Breaking his gaze away from the nervous half-breed, he glanced at the two horses tethered beneath the trees, then scanned the campsite as if taking inventory of Sam's wealth. Satisfied, he returned his relentless gaze to lock on the half-breed. Sam was about to ask him what he wanted when he detected a slight movement of the heavy skin robe as it opened barely enough to allow the barrel of a pistol to peek through. Sam saw the pistol a fraction of a second before it exploded into his face, sending a bullet into his brain.

Cobb dismounted. Taking his time, he walked over and stood looking down at the lifeless body at his feet. He rolled him over with the toe of his boot and watched him for a few moments more to make sure he was dead. He felt no need to waste ammunition. Satisfied, he holstered his pistol and searched the corpse for anything that he might find useful. The man meant nothing to him, a damn Injun who happened to be in the wrong place at the wrong time. It was just his misfortune to get in Cobb's path. Cobb needed a horse, a rifle and some ammunition, and some food and supplies, and he didn't have time to talk about it.

For two long months Cobb had stayed alive on little more than pure hatred. Any other man would have been dead long ago, long before he scratched and clawed his way out of the ravine with one thought burning his brain: *Dakota!* He would find Tom Allred and kill him. Left for dead with a hole in his side and a crease across his skull, his face slashed and torn by the pine limbs as he crashed down to the bottom of the ravine, he had lain there for two days. But he was too mean to die. He simply refused to before he settled this score.

On the third day, he cut some thin strings from his hide shirt and sewed up the hole in his side. It was two weeks of hell before his wounds healed sufficiently to permit even a few painful steps at one time. All the while Cobb kept Tom's face foremost in his mind, nursing himself with thoughts of the revenge he would take, and nourished by the pure bile of his hatred. At times he almost welcomed the pain, thinking that he would repay Dakota in kind for every gut-wrenching stab of pain that punctuated his every step. He would find Tom and kill him, and all the demons in hell would not stop him.

When he could walk, he started out of the wilderness on foot, every step in agony. Another day had passed when he stumbled upon the Blackfoot's emaciated pony. By the time he happened upon Sam Running Fox's campfire, the Indian pony was near death, ridden into the ground by the vengeful giant on his back.

Little Wolf rode easy, his body becoming as one with the untiring gait of the Appaloosa. Though seemingly relaxed, as his body rolled gently with each movement of the horse, Little Wolf's eyes and brain were constantly working, searching the trail ahead for any threat of danger. He was still a wanted man, though many believed him dead, and he did not like the idea of leaving the security of his valley. Behind him, Squint Peterson rode silently. There was not a word spoken between them for hours on end as they stayed doggedly to the trail. A few years before, they might have taken turns at the lead. But time was beginning to chip away at Squint—Little Wolf saw more and more evidence of that lately. His eyesight was failing. There was never anything said about it by either man, but Squint never offered to take the lead when they were on the trail. He needed eyeglasses, but they were too far from any city large enough to boast an eye doctor. Squint would probably have been too vain to wear them anyway. He never mentioned it, but Little Wolf knew Squint was troubled by the first signs of approaching age. For that reason, he was careful to avoid any comments that might call serious attention to it. He would playfully tease Squint and call him "old man," but there was a clear line drawn between the banter that the two had always indulged in and serious criticism.

On the fifth day, they sighted the outskirts of Bozeman. After considerable discussion, Squint convinced Little Wolf that it would be best for him to go in alone and try to find Tom. Squint would try to talk to him if possible, and look over the setup. Then the two of them could decide on the best way to break him out.

"You know," Squint remarked, "it would be a helluva lot easier if you would dress like a white man. Then we could both ride into town." He felt he had to say it, knowing full well what Little Wolf's reaction would be.

"I am not a white man. I am Little Wolf of the Cheyenne nation. My father was Arapaho and my mother was Cheyenne. Why should I try to be a white man?"

"Because your dang hide's white, same as mine, that's why," Squint returned, more than a hint of irritation in his tone. They had held this discussion at regular intervals over the years. Squint could not convince his friend of the wisdom of losing his identity as the renegade Cheyenne war chief sought after by the army. Little Wolf was stubborn in his pride and refused to abandon his adopted people.

He simply smiled at his old friend. "In the dark, it won't matter anyway. That's when I'll strike."

Squint rode leisurely into Bozeman, making note of the layout of the assortment of rough structures that made up the town. His mind was searching for the best possible escape route, provided he and Little Wolf were successful in freeing Tom. He would have to look over the jail itself before even attempting to come up with a plan. He had done a lot of things during his lifetime on the western frontier, sometimes on one side of the law, sometimes on the other. But this would be his first try at a jailbreak. He wasn't quite sure he liked the idea of gaining this experience, but he had no doubt that freeing Tom Allred was the right thing to do. At the moment, though, he had not the faintest spark of a plan. But the two of them were going to get Tom out of jail if they had to fight the whole town to do it.

The jail and the sheriff's office turned out to be one and the same, a couple of cells having been built onto the back of the structure. Squint rode around behind the building and paused momentarily to take a quick look at the barred windows. He made a mental note that it would more than likely take both Joe and Little Wolf's Appaloosa to pull the bars out. If they didn't come up with any better plan, that might be the way they had to go. Trying not to be too conspicuous, he circled around the drygoods store next to the jail before riding up to the front of the building.

"Danged if that boy ain't got popular of a sudden," Sheriff Aaron Crutchfield remarked. He leaned back in his chair to get a better look at the huge stranger who was blocking the sunlight through the open door. "You're the second one come lookin' for him this morning." Crutchfield wore a smirk on his wide face. "You're near 'bout the same size as that other feller. You boys is just too late for this one. I reckon the law beat you to him."

It seemed to Squint that Crutchfield got a great deal of satisfaction from his remarks, words that lost their significance on Squint. When the sheriff noticed Squint's confusion, he asked, "Ain't you a bounty hunter, too?"

"Hell, no," Squint was quick to reply. "I'm a friend of his'n. I just want to see him."

"Oh, I thought you was another bounty hunter."

"Can I see him?"

"Well, I reckon you could. Only he ain't here. I expect he's halfway to Corinne by now." He watched the big man puzzle over that one for a moment. "What do you want with Tom Allred, anyway?"

"Just wanted to see him. Like I said, I'm a friend of his'n." Squint was still puzzling over what he had just been told. The only Corinne he knew about was a week's ride, down in Utah territory.

Crutchfield stretched and shifted his bulk in his chair. The conversation seemed to bore him. "A friend of his, huh? 'Bout like that damn Cobb is a friend of his'n. I'll tell you the same thing I told him this morning. I don't cotton much to bounty hunters in my town, and you shore look like another bounty hunter to me."

"Well, I ain't."

Crutchfield leaned forward, his eyes suddenly serious. "Well, if you was, I'd tell you that you're wasting your time on that one. He's in the hands of a federal marshal now. Him and my deputy are taking him down to Corinne to get on a train back to Kansas. Left yesterday, so I reckon this just ain't your day."

Squint stood there for a few moments, mulling over this latest development. He hadn't counted on this. After a long silence, during which the sheriff studied his face intently, Squint simply muttered, "Much obliged," and turned to leave.

"All that reward money . . . gone," Crutchfield called after him. Squint could hear the sheriff chuckling to himself as he stepped up in the saddle.

Upon hearing Squint's report on the status of his brother, Little Wolf immediately packed up his few camp items and prepared to mount his horse. Squint, unsure of his friend's resolve to ride farther from his base in the Bitterroots, watched with interest. When Little Wolf was mounted, Squint asked, "North or south?"

Little Wolf looked surprised. "Unless they moved it, Corinne lies to the south, don't it?"

Squint grinned. "I reckon. And we better git a move on because that there bounty hunter might be having a notion to spring Tom hisself."

The trail to Corinne was rough, and one that neither man had traveled before, so there was no thought of shortcuts. The stage road was barely more than a trail and had evidently deteriorated a great deal from winter's fury. But at least it was a trail They had little choice but to follow it and hope to make up the head start the U.S. Marshal had on them. They kept the eastern ridges of the southern end of the Bitterroots on their right, while off to the left the lofty spires of the Tetons could be seen whenever they crossed the high ground. Squint was glad that Little Wolf could not see into his thoughts because, as each day passed, he became more and more convinced that theirs was a useless mission. They spent two long days in the saddle, pushing the horses as hard as they dared, never stopping to camp until there was no light left. Squint was beginning to think the two lawmen escorting Tom were pushing just as hard to complete the trip as he and Little Wolf were. Still, in vain or not, he felt they had to make the effort to overtake them. He was not certain what was going to happen when they did catch them. He could not guess what Little Wolf's reaction might be. He was still ninety percent Cheyenne as far as Squint could tell. His idea of a rescue might simply be to murder the two lawmen by picking them off with a rifle. Squint wasn't sure how he felt about that. When the time came, if it came at all, he wasn't sure he could let Little Wolf do it. These thoughts weighed heavily as Squint followed behind his Cheyenne friend through the mountain passes. He hadn't a clue what Little Wolf was thinking—Little Wolf's expression never changed from the stoic concentration upon the trail ahead.

Chapter XVIII

The past couple of months had not been especially pleasant for Tom Allred. Almost a week had passed since Breezy Martin had laid him out with his rifle barrel before the ringing headache disappeared. The force of the blow had split the skin and raised a lump that was tender to the touch for several days. Doc Brewster had bandaged him up, and now, two months later, he was still a little unsteady as he rocked back and forth to Billy's steady gait, his hands tied to the saddle horn. Up ahead, Breezy rode along on a scruffy-looking paint that appeared as unkempt as his master. Behind him, rode the U.S. Marshal, Alvin Pickens. A straightlaced, no-nonsense lawman, Pickens was intent on doing the job he was paid to do. Tom felt that the man had no emotions about anything. As far as he was concerned, his prisoner could just as well have been a keg of molasses or a barrel of flour he was consigned to deliver.

Breezy Martin was another matter. He seemed intent on tormenting Tom at every opportunity, both verbally and with a kick now and then. Tom was certain Breezy's attitude could not be totally due to Tom's having shot two soldiers, both of whom attacked him. It had to be more than that. Tom had played cards with the man for the better part of two weeks. And a man's character showed itself pretty quick at a poker table. Breezy Martin would not give a damn when one soldier shot another. Tom was sure of that. No, it had to be something more. He claimed he had been with the Seventh at Little Big Horn and wanted to see Tom punished for letting Little Wolf escape. *Maybe so*, Tom thought, *but it still didn't figure that Breezy gave a damn about that either, as long as he wasn't one of the men in Custer's battalion.* He decided that Breezy was just one of those bullies who had a wide mean streak and delighted in tormenting anybody when he had the upper hand. *Well*, Tom thought, *it's a long way to Utah territory, and anything could happen.* Tom could only hope the opportunity might come to repay Breezy for his attentions.

"Be damn keerful how you handle my horse there, Injun-lover," Breezy taunted as he pulled back to let Tom catch up to him.

Tom didn't answer. Breezy chided him all the way from Bozeman about his horse, telling him he was claiming Billy as soon as they got Tom on a train to Kansas. Tom was careful to show no emotion in response, but he galled at the thought of Breezy Martin on Billy's back. *I'd rather that damn Blackfoot back on the Yellowstone had him,* he thought.

"I might just use him for a packhorse," Breezy said, pretending to give the matter deep thought. "I don't reckon he could hold a candle to ole Sparky here," he added, referring to the scrubby paint he rode. " 'Course I know you don't mind. You ain't got no need for a horse where you're going." He scratched his chin whiskers as if in serious thought. "I don't know though." He called back over his shoulder, "What do you think, Mr. Pickens? You reckon they ride horses in hell?" He paused a moment, leering at Tom, his obstinate grin painted across his whiskered face. When Pickens did not bother to reply, Breezy started up again. "Let's see now. What else you got that I might can use? Crutchfield's got your rifles. That there Forty-five-seventy Winchester's a dandy, too. That the one you're 'sposed to be so damn good with?" He stared at Tom, hoping to provoke some response. He was not discouraged when Tom continued to ignore him. "Hell, I know somethin' I could use. Warn't you kind of sweet on that little Clay gal? She come to see you, you know. Only Aaron wouldn't let her. Too bad, ain't it?" He let his hand drop down to his crotch and made a point of rubbing himself there. "Yeah, I reckon I might go callin' on that little gal when I git back to Bozeman. She looks like she needs a man that can ride her hard, and I'm just that kind of man. Yeah, if I recollect, she's got a right fine lookin' behind on her. Just my style. Tell me, Mr. Dakota, is that ass of her'n as good as—"

"Shut up, deputy." Pickens spoke without emotion, but with a generous helping of authority. "Git on back out front and watch the trail. I didn't bring you along to irritate the prisoner."

Breezy laughed, but did as he was told. Before pushing the paint up to the lead, he tossed one more barb at Tom. "I'm gonna git me some of that little gal."

Breezy Martin's harassing did not bother Tom. His thoughts were hundreds of miles away. But the deputy's rantings did serve to bring him to focus on Ruby. He had been in the Bozeman jail for over two months. *Why*, he wondered, *did she not bother to come to see me?* There were things he wanted to say to her before he was taken away. He was unable to understand why she stayed away. Now, thanks to Breezy's constant harassing, he learned that Ruby *had* tried to see him. The realization provided a tiny feeling of warmth. This would explain Jubal's reaction to his inquiries about Ruby. Of course, Jubal thought that Ruby had been to visit him and, consequently, acted surprised that Tom asked about her. Tom, for his part, thought that Jubal was simply reluctant to discuss his daughter with a man headed for the hangman's noose. Tom really couldn't blame Jubal for feeling that way, so he didn't push the issue. And now he found that Ruby had been there to see him. It didn't matter as much that Crutchfield wouldn't permit the visit. Just the thought that she wanted to see him gave him a small ray of sunshine.

They rode until just before dark, when Pickens spotted a stand of lodgepole pines that still bore evidence of a long-past lightning strike. Many of the trees were still stunted from the fire that had ensued. They were separated from their more stately cousins by a wide stream that the fire hadn't jumped. This was where they made camp.

"Untie him," Pickens ordered.

Breezy ambled over and began to work on the knots binding Tom's hands to the saddle horn. A rope under Billy's girth held Tom's feet together in the stirrups. Tom was ready for him this time. The night before, Breezy untied his hands before untying his feet. When Tom kicked his feet out of the stirrups to make it easier for Breezy to get to the knot there, Breezy gave his hands a hard jerk, causing Tom to spin sideways and land on his head under his horse, much to Breezy's entertainment. This night, Tom anticipated Breezy's little game and kept his feet in the stirrups. When Breezy freed his hands from the saddle horn, Tom braced himself, keeping Billy's reins firm. As expected, Breezy made a sudden move to jerk Tom out of the saddle. But Tom timed the move with one of his own, hauling back hard on Billy's reins. It was a surprised Breezy who was suddenly yanked off his feet from the powerful surge of the horse. He landed on his belly in the gravel and pine needles.

"Gawdam you!" he screamed and scrambled to his feet.

Tom backed Billy away a few feet, waiting for the irate man to charge him. His gaze was stone hard as he fixed on the stout little deputy he had come to despise over the last few weeks. Both men were stopped cold, as if suddenly suspended in time, brought back to reality by the distinct sound of a lever action rifle cocking.

"I reckon that'll be enough," Pickens's cool monotone advised. There was no mistaking the authority behind it. "Deputy, go fetch some wood and git a fire going." He turned to Tom, the rifle cocked and looking in his direction, leaving no question as to his command of the situation. "Your hands are free. You can untie your feet yourself."

With Pickens standing guard, Tom dismounted and took care of all three horses. When that was done, Pickens cuffed his hands around a lodgepole pine about a foot in diameter. He would stay that way until the marshal released him to eat.

Tom had decided that Alvin Pickens was a fair man after the first day on the trail, and he was thankful he was. If his fate had been left with Breezy Martin alone, there was no doubt that he would be dead by now. "Shot while trying to escape," he would say. Breezy was a bully. But Pickens gave the impression he could handle three or four like Breezy Martin. He was as lean as an axe blade, with dark eyes deep-set under heavy eyebrows—a seriousness approaching melancholia. Words were never wasted by Pickens and were not employed at all if a nod or a gesture would suffice. Under different circumstances, Tom might have liked the man.

Tom was awake long before Pickens freshened the campfire and roused Breezy out of his blankets. He slept fitfully, catching short periods of sleep before his arms would become so uncomfortable he would wake up and have to shift his body in an effort to relieve them. Finally, he gave up trying to sleep and waited for his captors to awaken.

Pickens didn't allow any time wasted on breakfast. Jerky was enough to sustain them on the trail as far as he was concerned. His one concession in the morning was coffee. He would allow that, fixing it himself to his own satisfaction, which was black and strong as a rattlesnake's bite. He let Tom remain shackled to the tree until he had started the coffee. Meanwhile, Breezy crawled out of his blankets, scratching and complaining.

"Gawdamn, Mr. Pickens, it wouldn't hurt to take a few minutes to stir up some pan bread or fry some salt pork before climbing in the saddle."

Pickens did not look up from his coffeepot. "We're burning daylight. Let's git moving. We got a piece to go yet."

"Burning daylight?" Breezy whined, "Hell, the sun ain't even up yet."

"Coffee's boiling. If you want some, you better git moving. I ain't gonna wait around all day for you."

Breezy stared at the back of the marshal's head for a prolonged moment. Pickens did not bother to turn around, choosing to ignore him. After a few moments, Breezy grumbled something about being put under unnecessary hardship. Pickens continued to ignore him. Getting no satisfaction from the marshal, Breezy turned his attention to the prisoner.

"Well, good mornin', sweetheart," he cooed sarcastically. "Did you have a good sleep huggin' that there tree all night?" He shuffled over to stand at Tom's feet, leering down at him. "I bet it warn't the same as huggin' that little Clay gal's fanny, was it?"

When Tom refused to rise to the bait, Breezy undid his trousers and proceeded to empty his bladder. Tom was forced to jerk his feet away quickly to avoid having them urinated on. Breezy laughed and stepped toward him in an effort to splash his boots. Tom pulled both feet up to him and then kicked at his tormentor. He landed both boots directly on Breezy's kneecaps, causing them to buckle, dumping the squat little man on his backside, spraying himself with his own urine in the process. Breezy howled as if his legs were broken and scrambled to his feet in an effort to redirect the flow of his bladder before his trousers were soaked.

"Gawdamn you, you son of a bitch! I'll kill you for that!" He reached in his bedroll and pulled out his pistol.

"Put it away." The command was soft but stern.

Breezy turned to Pickens. "Gawdammit, Marshal, I ain't gonna let a man do that to me! 'Specially a damn no-good Injun-lover like him!"

"Put it away," Pickens calmly repeated.

Breezy knew by the marshal's tone that he meant business. Still he complained. "What the hell is so all fired important about taking this son of a bitch to Kansas anyway? If you hadn't showed up in Bozeman, we'da done hung him by now. This is just a damn waste of time and effort, nursemaiding this coyote all over the territory. Why don't we just string him up right here and now and be done with it

They gonna hang him in Kansas anyway. I say do it now and save the trouble."

If Pickens was the least bit concerned about Breezy's rantings, he gave no indication. He moved over beside Tom and unlocked the handcuffs. "If you're gonna take a leak, better git to it. You can git yourself a cup of coffee before saddling up." That said, he turned to Breezy, who was still standing there glaring at him. "I've had about enough of your foolishness. If you can't leave this prisoner be and keep your mouth shut, you can git on that damn horse and head on back to Bozeman." He paused to fix the deputy with a cold stare. "Or, if you're thinking about using that pistol of yours, you can try that, too. But I wouldn't advise it."

Breezy hesitated to consider the rifle hanging casually in the marshal's right hand. When it got right down to anteing up, Breezy wisely decided he didn't hold a strong enough hand to call out Marshal Pickens. "Ah, hell, Marshal, I was just having a little fun." He stuck the pistol back in his holster and turned to fetch his horse.

There was a knifelike chill in the wind that sauntered through the passes, even though the sun was high over the treetops. It seemed that old man winter was reluctant to release his hold on the mountains, coveting little pockets of snow in the shaded draws and ravines. They made no conversation as they steadily plodded along, the only sound the creaking of saddle leather and the soft bumping of the horses' hooves, punctuated occasionally by some incoherent mumbling from Breezy.

Having had fitful nights with very little sleep, a result of having his arms locked around a tree trunk, Tom was almost asleep in the saddle. Billy's easy motion served to rock him to sleep. He was awakened by Breezy calling back something to Pickens.

"I don't know," Breezy was saying. "Looks like a bear . . . or a pile of furs stacked up by the trail. From here, I cain't say fer shore."

Pickens rode up to take a look. "Keep your eye on him," he said to Breezy and the deputy fell back alongside Tom.

Tom looked up the trail to see what Breezy and Pickens were peering at, and he could see the object of their attention. Something up ahead beside the trail looked like a small haystack. None of the three could decide what they were approaching, but there was no doubt it was something that didn't ordinarily belong there. The object, whatever it was, prompted no caution from Pickens, merely curiosity. They advanced to within one hundred yards of the mound before they were able to tell what they had been staring at. It turned out to be a huge buffalo robe, draped over the head and shoulders of a man, a large man by the look of it. He was simply sitting by the trail, his back partially turned toward them. If he was aware of the horses approaching, he gave no sign.

When they were within fifty yards of the man and he had still not moved, Tom began to wonder if he was dead. It was too far into spring for a man to sit down and freeze to death. A snort from a clump of aspens off to the side caught his attention, and Tom spotted two horses tied up almost out of sight. He glanced at Pickens and saw that the marshal had also seen the horses. Tom watched Pickens closely to see his reaction to this unusual encounter.

Pickens, though not overly concerned, was no careless in his approach to the buffalo mound by the side of the trail. Tom noticed that he opened hi heavy coat so as to clear his holstered pistol whil silently motioning for Breezy to stay behind him with the prisoner. More than a few old mountain men were wandering around half-crazy from the long lonesome winters and the rocky mountain winds whistling through their ears. This was more than likely one such mountain man. They were almost in front of the man now.

"How do?" the marshal called out.

When there was no immediate response, Tom thought that they were indeed addressing a dead man. Then, finally, the mound moved. It turned to face them, and Tom gasped in surprise. *It was Cobb!* No mistake, it was Cobb . . . or Cobb's ghost. Tom wasn't sure which, because he had left the man for dead when he kicked his body over the edge of the ravine. When Cobb slowly rose to his feet and stepped out in front of Pickens's horse, he looked real enough. His huge body seemed to block the trail, leaving them no room to go around. Pickens pulled up.

"Somethin' I can do for you, mister?" Pickens asked calmly. He was not a man to get overly excited no matter how fearsome the obstacle. His hand fell naturally to rest on the butt of his pistol.

"I'll take my prisoner," Cobb said, pointing at Tom. "He belongs to me, and I've come to git him." He either did not notice Pickens's hand resting on his gun handle, or didn't care. His eyes were locked on the marshal's.

Breezy, recognizing the bear of a man who had brought the body of Rupert Slater in for the reward, pulled up beside Pickens. "It's that damn bounty hunter."

"That right?" Pickens asked, returning Cobb's stare, steel for steel. "You a bounty hunter?"

Cobb ignored the question. "That man belongs to me, and I aim to git him," he stated.

Pickens had had about enough of this conversation. "Look here, mister, I'm a United States marshal. This man's in my custody. There ain't no reward no more. You're too late. Now, back outta my way."

"I'll take my prisoner," Cobb demanded. "I don't care about no damn reward."

For a brief moment, there was a stand-off. Tom, his hands and feet tied, didn't like the way things were shaping up. He tried to slowly back Billy up to allow a little more room between him and the sinister figure holding Pickens's horse by the bridle. Breezy moved his horse in closer to Tom's, forcing him to remain where he was. Tom was between Breezy and Pickens when Pickens made his move.

"Mister, I've had about enough of you," Pickens stated with little more emotion than if he had asked for the time of day. His hand closed around the handle of his frontier model Colt. The barrel was not even halfway clear of his holster when Cobb raised the double-barreled shotgun from beneath his robe and fired at point-blank range. The blast knocked the surprised lawman out of the saddle. He landed in a heap beside the trail.

When the roar of the shotgun ripped the still mountain air, all three horses reared in startled fright. Tom lost a stirrup, but managed to hang on. Breezy Martin's paint bolted, and instead of checking him, Breezy kicked him hard with his heels. His only thought at the moment was to save his own hide. Cobb whirled and fired the other barrel after him. He hit Breezy in the back, but by that time, he was far enough away to escape mortal damage. He kept on going. Without hesitating, Cobb pulled the rifle from Pickens's saddle and sighted down on the deputy. He took his time aiming, confident he had plenty of time to make the shot. When the sights were on him, he squeezed off two shots, both of which caught Breezy between the shoulder blades. Breezy rolled off the paint, his body landing with a thud on the rocky trail.

Tom held back on Billy's reins. He knew it was useless to run. For now, he was staring down the barrel of Pickens's rifle as Cobb brought the weapon to bear on him. His hands were tied, but, if his feet had not been held together by a rope under Billy's belly, he would have lunged at the man, knowing that anything would be better than sitting there waiting for the fatal bullet. As it was, he was helpless. He couldn't even make a run for it like Breezy, for now Cobb had Billy's bridle in one huge hand. Tom braced for his own execution.

"Well now, Mr. Tom Allred . . ." He pronounced the name slowly in a deep, guttural voice, rolling the words across his tongue as if tasting them, savoring the pleasure they obviously brought him. "Mr. Tom Allred . . ." he repeated, his eyes deep and aflame with the vengeance and rage pent up in anticipation of this meeting. When Tom made no reply, he hissed, "You thought I was dead, didn't you?" He reached up and grabbed a handful of Tom's coat, pulling him down until his face was almost in Tom's. "Well, I ain't dead, but I've been to hell. I got you to thank for that. Now I'm gonna let you see what hell is like." He drew a long skinning knife from his belt and cut the rope between Tom's feet. Then he pulled him from Billy's back as easily as if Tom had been a sack of flour.

Tom landed hard, but his instinct for survival took over, and he quickly scrambled to his feet. Cobb anticipated the move and caught him beside the head with a blow from the rifle butt. Tom tried to dodge the huge man standing over him, swinging the rifle like a club, but he was unable to escape the blows. At a distinct disadvantage against this mountain of a man, with his hands still tied together, Tom fought for his life. Rolling and dodging as best he could, he tried to lessen the impact of the beating he was taking. At one point, he succeeded in catching the flailing rifle butt in his hands. Both men paused for a tense moment. During that brief moment, their eyes locked, and Tom knew that he was staring directly into the face of death. The brute was half-crazed with anger. His eyes burned with the intensity of live coals, boring deep into Tom's mind. Then the moment was over, and the struggle for the rifle ensued. It was no contest, for Cobb was a man of enormous strength, and he tore the weapon from Tom's hands and smashed it against the side of his skull. The earth beneath him started spinning, and he knew he was losing consciousness. Still Tom tried to fight, aiming his foot at Cobb's groin. It did some damage, but not enough to prevent the last blow from the rifle butt. Then everything went dark.

Gradually, the veil of darkness that had engulfed him melted away, and Tom became immediately aware of the pain. At least this told him he was still alive. At first, he wasn't sure where he was, but it was only a moment before it all rushed back to his conscious mind, causing him to lunge upward in an effort to get to his feet. He almost cried out with the pain that resulted. His efforts served only to bring pressure on his arms and legs, causing him to lie back on his side. He forced himself to remain calm and take inventory of his condition. When the fog cleared a little more from his brain, he realized tha he was trussed up hand and foot with his arms tied behind his back. There was no slack in the ropes, so every time he struggled against them, a sharp stab of pain resulted. He couldn't be sure, but he suspected that his left arm was broken because of the excruciating bolt of pain that surged through it when he tried to roll over off his side. He was helpless.

Near exhaustion from his efforts, Tom lay there resting. He heard no sound to indicate there was anyone else around. It was dark, but a good-sized fire was burning brightly about fifteen feet from him. As his senses gradually returned to normal, additional aches and pains now pushed their way through to his conscious mind. His face was swollen, and his whole head seemed to throb with each beat of his heart. On the ground where his head had rested, a dark circle of blood was nearly dry. He had to slide forward a few inches to avoid putting his face back down in it. Then, from behind him, he heard Cobb approaching. He knew his plight was hopeless. The only thing Tom had left was his pride and the will to die with dignity. He resolved not to give Cobb any satisfaction for his efforts.

He jerked involuntarily when the cold water hit him, causing him another jolt of pain in his arm, and he grunted with the agony. "Well, you ain't dead yet, are you? That's too bad—too bad for you." Cobb took hold of the rope around Tom's ankles and dragged him over toward the fire. Tom bit his lip hard in an effort not to scream with the pain it caused. "I just wanna tell you somethin', Mr. Dakota. You gon' wish you was dead a hundert times before I finish you off. You left me with a world of hurtin', with a hole in my innards, and my head all tore up. But I promise you, you gon' hurt a lot more than that before I finish with you."

"Kiss my ass, you son of a bitch," He spat at his tormentor. It was painful even to say it, but words were the only weapons Tom had left.

"Well now, I'm sorry to hear you talk like that to me. I was thinkin' on goin' easy on you, maybe just beatin' you to death. Now, since you got so uppity, I think maybe I'll skin you." He took out his long skinning knife and turned it over, back and forth, in front of Tom's face, letting the firelight cast its reflection on the steel blade. "I skinned a man once, a Blackfoot Injun—tried to steal my horse. I was plumb surprised how long it took that Injun to die. Matter of fact, I et part of him, sawed off a piece of his flank, and let him watch while I cooked it over the fire. He didn't like that none. How you think you'd like that?" Finally, Cobb tired of the verbal torment when he failed to get the response from Tom he had hoped for. He reached down and grabbed a fistful of Tom's hair. Pulling his head up hard, he placed the point of his skinning knife against Tom's throat. "Mr. Dakota," he hissed softly in his ear, "your hell is just starting." Tom felt the point break the skin on his neck.

"Not just yet it ain't, you sorry sack of shit!" Came a sudden low growl. At the same time, Cobb's head was yanked back by his own hair, the steel blade of Squint Peterson's knife pressing heavily against his throat.

Cobb released Tom and grabbed Squint's arm, twisting away in an effort to avoid the knife. He broke free and leaped across the campfire, turning to face his attacker. Squint, his knife in hand, moved in a half crouch, stalking. Cobb, also in a crouch, waited and watched as Squint moved to confront him. They stood there for a full minute, measuring each other, the fire between them, two great grizzlies preparing to do combat.

"You're pretty handy when a man's half dead and tied up, ain't you, you ugly son of a bitch. Let's see how you like it with somebody your own size." Squint kept motioning Cobb to come to him while he taunted. •

The two big men circled slowly, keeping the fire between them, each keeping a wary eye locked on the other. Cobb was in no hurry to push the action. It was plain to him that Squint was not to be taken lightly. The look in the man's eye told him fear had never taken seed there. Then a movement from the shadows caused him to start as a tall figure emerged from the darkness. He was naked from the waist up. His hair, dark and long, held a solitary eagle feather. Beaded armbands bore the markings of the Cheyenne nation.

"No, my friend," Squint said softly, "I want this coyote myself. If he takes me, kill the son of a bitch."

Little Wolf hesitated a moment, studying the look in his friend's eyes, and he understood. "It will be as you wish."

"Take care of Tom," Squint added. Then he turned his full attention back to the menacing form across the campfire from him. "Now come on, you murdering sack of shit."

Cobb roared like a wounded grizzly and charged straight through the fire, sending sparks and hot splinters flying. Head bowed, he caught Squint in the stomach, and the two of them went down in a heap. They rolled over and over, each fighting to gain the advantage, slashing at each other when possible, fists flailing, their roars of outrage shattering the still night air. Apart and on their feet again, they circled cautiously, both men gasping for breath. Suddenly,

Cobb roared again and charged. This time, Squint dodged the outstretched knife and came up under Cobb's arm, plunging his knife to the hilt in Cobb's belly. The wounded man doubled up and backed away, Squint's knife still embedded in his midsection. He stared at it in disbelief for only a moment before pulling it out. His heavy coat had limited the depth of the wound and prevented it from proving mortal. With a knife in each hand now, and Squint with none, he charged again. Squint managed to get a wrist in each hand, and the two giants strained against each other in a test of strength that seemed to make the very forest shudder. Finally, Cobb began to slowly weaken as Squint forced his arms farther and farther back until Cobb was forced to cry out in pain and drop to his knees. Squint sent him down on his back with a blow from his right fist and Cobb lay still, beaten.

"Now, you bastard," Squint said, standing over Cobb, his breath coming in short, panting gulps. "Get on your feet." He glanced over at Little Wolf. "I'm gittin' too damn old fer this shit."

Those were his last words. Unnoticed by Squint, as he stood over him, Cobb slowly reached into a pocket inside his coat where he kept a tiny double-barrelled Derringer. Both shots hit Squint under the chin, killing him instantly.

Cobb wasted no time scrambling to his feet, hoping to escape into the night. He had barely cleared the firelight when Little Wolf's arrow struck solidly between his shoulder blades. He stumbled, but did not fall, and kept on running. Little Wolf was instantly on his trail, his long legs eating up the distance between himself and the heavier, clumsier Cobb. Like a great cougar, he was on him before Cobb had run thirty yards. Seeing it was useless to run, Cobb turned and prepared to fight. Little Wolf stopped barely two paces in front of him. Cobb lunged for him, but Little Wolf deftly avoided the charge of the huge man. Like a great cat, the Cheyenne warrior came up beside him, smashing Cobb's knee with his foot. Cobb stumbled and Little Wolf was on his back immediately, one powerful arm around his head, the other around his leg. With his knee firmly planted in Cobb's spine, he closed the powerful vise. A sharp crack echoed when Cobb's back broke, followed by the eerie scream of a Cheyenne war cry.

Chapter XIX

Squint Peterson was dead—a possibility Little Wolf had never considered. He had known death and dying since he was a small boy. It was as much a part of life as being born. Every Arapaho and Cheyenne boy knew this. It had been a possibility that hung over every war party he had led, every battle he had fought. Death waited for every man. But not Squint Peterson. Somehow he had assumed that Squint would always be there, like the mountains and the rivers. It didn't matter that he had aged, that his eyes had faded during the last two years. Didn't the mountains age and erode? Still, they would always be there. Though wind-blown and etched by the storms of time, they stood towering over the plains, the very essence of strength and immortality. There was now a great void in the mountains. Squint had left a shadow too large to be cast by any other man. Little Wolf wept silent tears as he carefully sewed his old friend tightly up in a buckskin burial robe. He would take him back to their valley and bury him on the mountainside, overlooking their ranch. From there he could watch the horses run in the meadow. Squint would like that—he always liked watching the horses run.

But Little Wolf had a more pressing responsibility.

Squint had asked him to take care of Tom. The thought of this task brought forth a mixture of emotions. Although the man was his brother by birth, he was, in fact, a total stranger, and for many years of his life, his enemy.

Little Wolf studied the man's face intently, looking for something that might provide some spark of recognition. He had never really seen Tom Allred's face up close but twice. One time was on the banks of the Little Missouri River when he, Little Wolf, had spared his brother's life. On that day neither man had known they were brothers. And Little Wolf had sworn to kill him if ever they met again. The other occasion was when he had been captured by the soldiers at the Little Big Horn and Tom, with Squint's help, had arranged his escape. That incident, Little Wolf reminded himself, caused Tom's dismissal from the army. He stared hard at the man whose life was now in his hands. It was difficult to read Tom's face because it was so badly swollen and misshapen from the terrible beating at the hands of the bounty hunter. Squint himself would probably have been unable to identify Tom in his present condition.

After making Tom as comfortable as possible, Little Wolf went about seeing to his wounds. Tom had taken a severe beating from Cobb's rifle butt. His arm was broken, so Little Wolf straightened it and bound it. As for the head wounds, he had no way of knowing if Tom's head was cracked or not. He slipped in and out of consciousness several times during that first night. Little Wolf was uncertain whether his brother would live or die. He did not feel strongly about it one way or the other. He would try to tend to his wounds and watch over him to see which way he would go. He was deeply in sorrow, but not for his brother. He mourned for Squint Peterson, the common link between the two brothers. Little Wolf did everything he could for the injured man, then lay back to wait and see if his brother would survive the night.

The next morning, he arose to find his patient peering at him though puffed and swollen eyes. He said nothing at first, returning the gaze and wondering if those eyes were lucid or merely the glazed stare of the dead. Then, as if to answer the question, the split and swollen lips moved slightly.

"Little Wolf?" The voice was labored, but strong.

"I am Little Wolf."

"Squint," he rasped. "I saw Squint . . ."

"Squint's dead," Little Wolf stated without emotion, hiding the sorrow he felt at the loss of his friend.

"Dead! Squint dead?" Tom's eyes closed as he tried to digest it in his mind. "How?" He attempted to rise on one elbow, but was forced to lay back.

"He died saving your hide. That bounty hunter killed him. Now you lay back and rest. You took a helluva beating, but I reckon now you ain't gonna die."

Tom wanted to know everything that had happened, but Little Wolf promised to tell him the whole story after he had rested. He busied himself catching up the horses and loading Squint's body on one of the mounts that Cobb had ridden. He loaded Breezy Martin's body on his horse and the marshal's body on his. Then he dragged Cobb's body over to the rim of a deep gully and dumped it over the side, determined not to waste his time and effort on the treacherous dog. That done, he returned to the campfire and stood for a long time looking down at the injured man. He decided Tom was too sick to sit on a horse so he fashioned a travois using two lodgepole pines and skins from Cobb's packhorse. When he finished, he returned to get Tom.

"We can't stay here. This time of year there ain't much time to leave Squint's body out of the ground. You can ride on the travois until you feel strong enough to sit a horse." He gestured toward the bodies of the two lawmen. "When we get near Bozeman, I'll cut these two loose. Maybe they'll find their way home."

"Where are you taking me?"

Little Wolf shrugged. "To my valley, I reckon, till you get on your feet anyway. Squint says we are brothers. Maybe we are, I don't know. But I reckon I owe you that for saving my neck from the army's rope."

"Maybe you oughtn't," Tom replied. "I'm a wanted man. I might bring the law down on you. Maybe you better just leave me here and get on back to your valley. The army would still like to get their hands on you. You better not take a chance on them finding out you're still alive."

Little Wolf looked at him with a cold eye. "I leave you here, you'll be wolf bait before morning."

"I appreciate what you want to do for me, but I'm telling you, as long as I'm alive, they'll be sending somebody looking for me. No sense bringing them down on your valley."

Little Wolf studied Tom's face while he thought over his words. After a few minutes of silence, he said, "Then I reckon it's best if you was dead."

Tom was startled. He wasn't sure what his brother was telling him. Brother or not, it was Little Wolf looking deep into his eyes. His fears were unfounded, however, and he felt a little sheepish when Little Wolf later shared his plan—a plan not without

risk to them both if unsuccessful, but one worth trying at any rate.

Aaron Crutchfield strode out on the wooden walkway in front of his office to see what the commotion
was about. His eyes were met with a curious sight.
A lone rider was leading a string of horses down
the middle of the muddy street. Directly behind him
another horse pulled a travois with what appeared
to be a man on it. Following the travois were four
more horses, and three of them carried bodies. One
of the horses he recognized as Breezy Martin's paint.
The sun was sinking below the hills, and he had to
cover his eyes against the glare as the somber cara-
van approached him. He did not recognize the
leader, a tall man sitting ramrod straight in the saddle. He looked as wild as any Indian Crutchfield had
ever seen, but he was obviously a white man. At
least he was wearing white man's clothes.

"You the sheriff?" Little Wolf asked.

"I am," Crutchfield acknowledged.

"Well, I reckon I got some bodies for you,"
Crutchfield looked suspicious. Glancing at the
paint, it wasn't hard to figure that one of the bodies
was his deputy, Breezy Martin. The thought that
Breezy was dead didn't cause him any grief, but he
couldn't help but feel the irritation in knowing he had
lost yet another deputy. He looked back at the
stranger, straining hard to remember if he had ever
seen him before. "Who the hell are you?"

"Robert Peterson," Little Wolf quickly replied. He
figured that, if he had to use a fictitious name, he
could do a lot worse than taking on Squint's.

Crutchfield continued to study the stranger.
"Maybe you better start doing a little explaining,
mister."

"Nothing much to explain. I came up on these fellows on the Utah trail. Looked to me like there musta been one helluva gunfight. That fellow on the travois was the only one alive when I found 'em. He said to take the bodies back here. You'd know what to do with 'em. Said he was just in to see you a week ago. He's pretty bad hurt. I'm taking him back home to die, and it looks like I ain't gonna make it before he croaks if I don't get a move on."

"What. . . ?" Crutchfield was confused. "Wait a minute. Who shot who? How did my deputy get shot?"

"I'm coming to that. Your man and that other lawman"—he turned and pointed toward Pickens's horse—"they was jumped by that big bounty hunter there." He indicated Squint's body. "His name was Cobb. Anyway, Cobb shot 'em all before the fellow on the travois got Cobb. When I came along, this fellow was about done in. He said to bring the bodies to you so you'd know what happened."

Crutchfield was not at all satisfied with the explanation he had just heard, but he wasn't quite sure which part of it he disbelieved. He stepped off the board walkway and, walking over to Breezy's horse, pulled a corner of the hide covering away to get a look at the body. He immediately backed up a couple of steps as the odious stench assaulted his nostrils.

"Goddam, man! How long have they been dead?"

Little Wolf scratched his head thoughtfully. "I can't rightly say. They were pretty ripe when I found 'em."

"Goddam! We got to git them in the ground!" He grabbed a young boy who had been listening wide-eyed to the account. "Go fetch Doc Brewster and be quick about it." He only gave Squint's body a glance. "I'd know that murderin' coyote by his size." He stopped for a moment by the travois where Tom lay, covered up in animal hides to disguise the difference in his size and that of Squint Peterson's. He stooped and peered through the small open hood over Tom's head at the swollen face, covered with dried blood and hair. "Huh," he grunted, "looks like somebody busted him up pretty good."

Little Wolf relaxed. His hand, which had casually come to rest on the stock of his rifle while Crutchfield bent over Tom, moved slowly back by his side. "I reckon. Well, like I said, I best get moving if I'm gonna get this poor devil home to his loved ones."

"Wait a minute!" Crutchfield bellowed. "What about the prisoner? Where the hell's Allred?"

Little Wolf was busily untying the lead rope from the horses. "Oh, him, well, I reckon that'd be the fellow laying at the bottom of that gully with the handcuffs on." He casually finished with the rope and got back on his horse.

"What gully? Where?"

"Well, let me see. It'd be about four days back in the mountains. I saw him down there, but there was no way for me to get him out. He was dead anyway, so I just brought in the ones I could get to." He nudged his horse gently with his heels. "Well, good evening to you, Sheriff. I best be getting on."

Crutchfield stood scratching his head for a moment, unsure what his official reaction to this turn of events should be. Little Wolf was almost fifty yards away before the sheriff called out, "What about that wounded man? Don't you want Doc to take a look at him?"

"Waste of time, Sheriff," Little Wolf threw back over his shoulder. "He just wants to go home."

* * *

Little Wolf wasted no time once he and Tom were out of sight of Bozeman. He headed directly west for several miles until they came to a wide stream running heavy with winter's runoff. He followed it south for about a quarter of a mile until he came to some small rapids where rocks bordered both sides of the stream, carving a scar through the low rising hills.

"You think you can ride now?"

"Yeah, I think so, if you can help me get up in the saddle."

Little Wolf halted the horses on a flat outcropping of rocks. He stepped down and helped Tom off the travois. It was all the wounded man could do to keep from toppling over. "Think you can make it?"

"I'll make it," Tom replied emphatically. Supporting himself on his brother's wide shoulder, he struggled to get up on the horse. Once in the saddle, he had to hold onto the saddle horn to stay upright, his head was spinning from the sudden change of position. He had not been lucid enough to even question the probability of the success of Little Wolf's ruse. Now he asked, "What if they ride out and find Cobb's body? They'll know right away it isn't me."

"I doubt if they'll even look for it right away. And I didn't exactly draw them a map to that gully. I don't think it'll be that easy. It wasn't that easy for me to climb down there and put the handcuffs on him. By the time they do find him—if they find him, I doubt there'll be more than bones left anyway."

"I hope you're right." Tom closed his eyes to the pain that was starting to build in his head again, his hands clutching the saddle horn.

Little Wolf watched for a moment to make sure Tom wasn't going to tumble off the horse. Satisfied that he was able to ride, Little Wolf led the horses into the stream. He stopped in the middle and cut the thongs holding the travois and let the poles drift downstream. Leading Tom's horse, he backtracked upstream until he found a place where they could leave the water without leaving tracks. Once out of the stream, he started directly northwest toward his valley in the Bitterroots.

Chapter XX

It had been a little more than a week since Little Wolf had passed through this way, when he and Squint were on their way to help Tom Allred. Yet, in that short time, the lower basins seemed to have plunged headlong into spring. This was a time of season that Little Wolf had always appreciated, a time of year when the earth renewed herself. He had been taught, as all Cheyenne and Arapaho boys were taught, to honor and respect the earth. His father, Spotted Pony, had instilled in his adopted son his own love for the mountains, rivers, and plains that provided the Indian with all his needs. And spring was a time of new beginning.

On this day, however, Little Wolf's mind dwelt on other, more troublesome matters as he guided his horse up from the river bottom toward a high mountain pass. It troubled him a great deal that he had not been able to take Squint's body back to his valley and bury him there. But he felt sure that Squint would have approved of what he did. It was the only thing he could think of to make it look like Tom was dead. As far as Sheriff Crutchfield was concerned, the huge body he quickly put in the ground was that of the bounty hunter, Cobb. And Tom Allred lay dead at the bottom of a gully.

Little Wolf looked back at the injured man barely able to remain upright in the saddle. Little Wolf fretted over the situation. This was no good. Tom was in no condition to continue the journey. He was going to have to stop and let Tom rest in spite of the urgency he felt to return to his valley. Finally, when Tom almost fell off his horse, Little Wolf started looking for a suitable place to make camp and let his brother rest.

Tom opened his eyes. He had been asleep for quite a while, and now, as his eyes adjusted to the bright sunlight that filtered down across his bedroll, he looked around to see what world he had awakened to. During the past several days, he had teetered on the edge of consciousness, drifting back and forth in a dreamlike state, never fully aware of his surroundings or what might be happening. Awake now for the first time without the intense pain and nausea, he strained to remember the events that led him to this place.

He remembered being helped on his horse by Little Wolf, and he remembered his determination to ride. But, once in the saddle, everything seemed to fade from his mind and, for a time, he no longer cared whether he lived or died. Now at least he was encouraged that he was going to recover from the terrible beating he had suffered at the hands of Cobb. He unconsciously lifted his hand to touch the wounds on his head. This simple motion caused him to recoil from the sharp stab of pain that coursed through the length of his arm. He had forgotten about his broken arm. Slowly and carefully, he lowered the injured arm. He examined the splint Little Wolf had fashioned. It was a commendable job—a doctor could not have bound him up any better. This prompted him to wonder where Little Wolf was, for he realized that he was alone by the campfire.

"So, you have decided to return to the world of the living after all."

He had not heard his brother approach, an occurrence that he would soon learn was not unusual, and the sudden sound of his voice startled him. "Yeah, I guess I have at that," Tom answered, "but I don't feel like I'm ready to wrassle a grizzly anytime soon."

"I reckon you'll be ready to eat something now," Little Wolf said. "I snared a rabbit." He held it up to show Tom. "Pretty fat for this time of year, too." He knelt down in front of his brother. "Can you eat? Your jaw still looks kinda stove up. Maybe I better make it into some soup."

"No," Tom was quick to respond, "I think I can chew all right." He put a hand up to his chin and felt it. "Although that crazy son of a bitch loosened a couple of teeth for me."

"Good. I don't know how to make soup anyway." He took out his knife and set about skinning and gutting the rabbit. That done, he fashioned a spit from a willow switch and set the rabbit over the fire to cook.

Neither man spoke for a long while as they seemed occupied with the cooking rabbit. When it was done, Little Wolf pulled it from the flame and tested it. Deciding that it was cooked enough, he took his knife and cut the rabbit into two equal portions, and they ate their supper. When the last of the rabbit was gone and the bones sucked clean, Little Wolf sat back against a tree to contemplate the situation.

The two brothers studied each other for the first time. Both men found the awkwardness hard to ignore, and words were slow in coming. In fact, neither man spoke for some time, their thoughts linked by a mutual compulsion to know the other's mind. To Tom, this encounter was like a dream, this face-to-face confrontation with this most feared and notorious renegade. The man before him, gazing intently into his eyes, did not look to be the savage and cruel Cheyenne leader that the army had claimed. Could it be true? Could this man really be his brother? He studied Little Wolf's face. There was, he had to admit, a slight resemblance in the nose and mouth. But that could also be a coincidence. Little Wolf was the first to break the silence.

"So you are my brother Tom."

"That's what they tell me." Another long pause followed while the two continued to look each other over, then Tom said, "I don't reckon you liked it any more than I did when you found out."

Little Wolf smiled. "No, my brother. I wanted to kill you and hang your scalp on my lance. You and your soldiers killed many of my people."

Tom was quick to counter. "You and your Cheyenne warriors killed right many of my friends. There was blame on both sides."

"Maybe. But the soldiers had no business in this land. It has belonged to the people since the land was here. We did not start this war."

Tom became defensive. "Goddammit! I didn't start it either. I was a soldier. I went where they told me to!" They glared at each other for a moment before his eyes softened and he confessed, "You're right, though, we had no business pushing the Indians onto the reservations. Hell, I saw a lot of things I didn't like, but there wasn't much I could do about it."

The tension of the moment eased, and the smile returned to Little Wolf's face. "Let us forget the fighting. It is behind us." He leaned back as if to take a longer look at Tom. "Now I must see if you were worth saving. Your rescue cost a terrible price. Squint Peterson was the best white man I have ever known. If it were not for him, I'm not sure I would have come. He must have some reason for thinking your hide was worth saving."

Tom started to rankle, but saw the glint of mischief in his brother's eye and realized he was being teased. "Well, I think he figured you needed the guidance of an older brother."

Little Wolf's face was expressionless for a moment. Then he suddenly laughed. "Squint tried to be my older brother ever since we met. Now Squint is gone and you are the cause of it. So you will have to take his place."

Though it was plain that Little Wolf's remark was not meant to lay blame on his brother for Squint's death, Tom found his words to have a sobering effect. "I'd give anything to bring him back," he said softly.

Little Wolf sought to console him. "There is no need to blame yourself for Squint's death. He chose the path he walked. I think he knew that he might not return to the Bitterroots. When I started to help him kill the bounty hunter, he asked me not to interfere. I understood why he did it. Squint was a mighty warrior, but he felt the years coming on him. His eyesight was failing week by week, and I know that he could not tolerate the thought of ending his life sitting around waiting for someone to take care of him. It is best this way. He was proud to end his life dying as a warrior dies. And, my brother, he would be happy to know that his death gave you new life."

Tom studied his brother's face for a long moment. "I appreciate what you're offering, and I might take

you up on it for a while till I get back on my feet.
But I don't want to bring any trouble down on you."

Little Wolf understood what he meant. "If you are
worried that the soldiers will come looking for you,
you worry for nothing. That fat sheriff in Bozeman
will tell them that you are dead, your body lying in
the bottom of a ravine in the mountains. He was so
anxious to get those bodies in the ground, he didn't
take time to look at them real close. The army will
forget about you. We will go back into the Bitterroots
and breed horses. Maybe I will give you an Indian
name. What do you think?"

Tom laughed. "I don't know about that. But I do
know a thing or two about horses."

"Good. Now that you look like you can stay on a
horse again, we'll break camp and go home." He
paused for a moment, and with a twinkle in his eye,
said, "There is someone who waits for you there."

"Dammit! Now what?" Aaron Crutchfield looked
up from his plate of fried eggs over fried potatoes
that he had just started working on. It seemed to him
that the only time anything happened in his town
was when he was trying to eat breakfast.

"There's a whole bunch of soldiers down at the
jail looking for you."

Aaron's chewing stopped for a moment, and he
fixed his young deputy with a cold eye. "What do
they want?"

"They want to know about Tom Allred was what
they said."

"Tom Allred? Goddammit! I'm sick of hearing
about Tom Allred! I sent my report to the army. I've
done told them all I know about it!"

"What you want me to tell 'em?"

"Tell 'em to go to hell!" When his deputy started

to turn around and head for the door, he stopped him. "Tell 'em I'll be down there in a minute, as soon as I finish some business here." He turned his attention back to his breakfast.

"Sheriff Crutchfield? I'm Captain Walsh. Did your deputy tell you I'm looking for information on the fugitive, Thomas Allred?"

"He did."

"According to your correspondence on the matter, you say the body was never recovered. Is that still the case? Have you been able to find the body yet?"

"It ain't a question of finding the body. We found the body, what was left of it anyway, after the wolves and coyotes got done with it. There wasn't much to see. We just throwed some dirt over the bones and left it at the bottom of a ravine."

"Are you sure the body was Allred?"

Crutchfield was losing his patience. "Well, who the hell else would it be? We buried everybody else that was in that little set-to on the Utah trail. Hell, the handcuffs was still on his wrists. I'm satisfied it was Allred."

Captain Walsh studied the sheriff's face for a moment as if evaluating this information. Finally he shrugged and said, "I guess there's been about as much confirmation as we can get." He thanked Crutchfield for his help and ordered his men to mount up. "I'm recommending we close this case," he informed the sheriff as he wheeled his horse and prepared to leave.

Far away from Aaron Crutchfield and Bozeman, in a gentle valley painted green with the lush grass of early summer, a simple Indian ceremony took place. It was performed by an old Nez Perce with a handful of friends, as well as God and the towering mountains, as witnesses. This ancient ritual signified a new beginning for the man and woman standing together to declare their love for each other. It was a simple ceremony, but it was sacred to those who came to celebrate with Tom and Ruby. When it was over, he kissed her softly on the lips, as if she was a precious thing.

"I guess this will have to hold you till we can get a parson to do the real job," he whispered.

She smiled. "I don't need a parson to make me know I'm your wife."

"How do you like your new name, Missus Peterson?"

"I reckon one name's as good as another, as long as the 'Missus' is in front of it." Her smile faded momentarily. "I know how much Squint Peterson meant to you. And, if it's best for us to take on a different name, then I can't think of a better one to use."

He stood there looking at her for a moment before confessing, "I swear, I really love you, Ruby. I just never dreamed we would ever be married."

"Hell, Tom Allred, I knew I was gonna marry you when you first set foot in Ruby's Choice."

Their blissful moment was interrupted by his brother, Robert. "Enough of this silly chatter. Come, brother, we have horses to tend to." His broad smile betrayed the intent of his remark.

"Do not tease, Little Wolf," Rain Song scolded.

Tom laughed. "To hell with those horses. I'm on my honeymoon."

❏ Black Eagle   0-451-19491-8/$5.99

When old-timer scout Jason Coles ended the rampage of renegade Cheyenne Stone Hand, he quit tracking outlaws for the army for good. Settling down with his wife and newborn baby, Coles plans to spend the rest of his days raising horses on his ranch . But that dream is savagely torn from him as his ranch is burned to the ground, and his family is abducted by the bloodthirsty Cheyenne Little Claw, out to avenge the death of Stone Hand. With the lives of his family at stake, Coles must once again strap on his revolvers to hunt a merciless killer!

Find out how the saga began with
❏ Stone Hand   0-451-19489-6/$5.99

CHARLES G. WEST